Immortal's Spring

Molly Ringle

central
avenue
publishing

2016

This is a work of fiction. Names, characters, places and incidents either are the
product of the author's imagination or are used fictitiously and any resemblance to
actual persons, living or dead, business establishments, events or locales is entirely
coincidental.

Published by Central Avenue Publishing, an imprint of Central Avenue Marketing Ltd.
www.centralavenuepublishing.com

First Printing
Published in Canada
Printed in United States of America

1. FICTION/Fairy Tales, Folk Tales, Legends & Mythology

Library and Archives Canada Cataloguing in Publication

Ringle, Molly, author
     Immortal's spring / Molly Ringle.

(The chrysomelia stories)
Issued in print and electronic formats.
ISBN 978-1-77168-040-0 (paperback).--ISBN 978-1-77168-041-7 (epub).--
ISBN 978-1-77168-049-3 (mobipocket)

     I. Title.

PS3618.I435I45 2016   813'.6   C2015-907434-7
                                                 C2015-907435-5

IMMORTAL'S SPRING

CHAPTER ONE

WHOA," SOPHIE DARROW'S TWELVE-YEAR-OLD BROTHER, Liam, said as they entered the giant cave of glowing souls. "You weren't making it up."

"Nope. Can't make something like this up." Sophie led him off the raft, up the bank, and into the fields. She trembled, knowing she'd see their mom and dad soon, but at least she wasn't crying. For now. She turned to the nearest group of souls and said in the Underworld's tongue, "Can you please bring us Terry and Isabel Darrow, who arrived here last night? We're their children, Sophie and Liam." Her voice shook but didn't break.

Liam turned an astounded look on her when she spoke that language. Except for the names, all its words would be unintelligible to him. But she'd serve him a pomegranate soon enough and he'd start remembering it.

Sophie's best friend, Tabitha, stood beside them. The Darrow family's one surviving dog, their boxer, Rosie, sat next to Liam. Their parents would probably bring the soul of Pumpkin too—their other dog, who had died in the fire along with them. Sophie's heart almost beat out of her ribs. Too much emotion to contain. But she had to keep it together, for Liam's sake if nothing else.

Poor Liam. Rough as Sophie's night had been, his had been even worse in some ways. For the entire night he had believed he would never see his parents again. Sophie hadn't been able to tell him otherwise, couldn't really explain about the Underworld until bringing him into the spirit realm this morning. Even in the ride across the planet, in Adrian's bus drawn by supersonic ghost horses, Liam didn't quite seem to believe Sophie and the rest when they assured him where they were going and who they'd see.

Sophie glanced over her shoulder. Adrian stood by the river with Niko, Freya, Zoe, and Adrian's dog, Kiri. They were talking to some souls; Sophie recognized Adrian's mum and Rhea among them.

Adrian glanced anxiously at Sophie. Sickness punched into her gut, and she looked away. The screaming, clawing, multi-layered guilt inside her, all tied up with the mere sight or thought of Adrian, wasn't something she could process at the moment. It would have to wait. Right now she needed to see her parents.

The souls had whispered the request outward. The crowd parted and two translucent figures walked toward them, a small ghost dog trotting at their heels.

Their mom and dad gazed serenely at Sophie and Liam as they approached.

"Sweeties, you're both here, thank goodness," Isabel said.

"I am so glad to see you two," Terry said.

At that, Liam fell to his knees, wracked with sobs, and buried his face in his hands.

"Mom, Dad." Sophie's voice still shook. "Forgive me, please. This is all because of me, because I got involved with—this." She flopped her hand miserably at the unearthly fields.

"There is nothing to forgive." Isabel used her most Mom-like voice, firm but loving.

"You and Adrian are good kids," Terry said. "We knew it before and we know it clearer than ever now."

"But—" Sophie began.

"If you need me to say it," her dad added, "then yes, we forgive you. Of course."

Sophie looked down at the grass in anguish. Naturally they forgave her. Souls were always forgiving. Sophie's conviction of her own guilt, however, remained as anchored as a mountain. Her gaze drifted to Pumpkin and Rosie, who were enjoying their strange reunion. Both dogs wagged their tails and poked their noses together, looking intrigued at how they couldn't smell or touch one another. She tried not to start crying; tried to think this was actually good: her parents had one dog on their side of the life-death boundary, and she and Liam had one on the other. All balanced. Sure. Perfectly fine.

"But what happened?" her mother asked. "We haven't been able to find out down here."

Last night. The whole story… "Well." Sophie swallowed.

Tabitha cleared her throat and stepped forward. "Hey, guys. Let's see if I can sum up."

Tab took over. She told them of the attack by the cult Thanatos, followed by the criminals' temporary kidnapping of Sophie and failed attempt to kill Adrian, and finally Niko and Zoe rescuing Sophie and Adrian, and Niko killing Betty Quentin, the cult's leader.

As Tab spoke, and Liam sobbed at Sophie's feet, Sophie's gaze rose to her parents. She would never feel those arms around her again. She would never again rest her cheek on the rough flannel shirts her dad favored. She would never smell her mother's lavender perfume as her mom engulfed her in a welcome-home hug. There was no home to return to.

Sophie's throat closed against speech and her eyes filled with tears.

When she couldn't answer the next question turned her way, silence fell. Then her mother said, "You kids should rest. You need it. We'll be here, don't worry."

"We won't be going anywhere," her dad assured. "Not for years and years. You rest, kiddos."

Sophie nodded and helped Liam up, and they stumbled off to the main bedchamber.

Zoe was there, spreading fresh sheets over a camping mattress against the main bedchamber's wall. "This one's for you, Liam," she said. "Adrian says you can have the bed, Soph. He'll…sleep elsewhere."

Liam conked out, exhausted. Sophie got into bed and drifted in and out of an uneasy doze most of the night—or rather, day. They were nine time zones off from their usual, in Greece now instead of the Pacific Northwest. Sometimes she let her eyes slip open, and gazed at the battery-powered blue nightlight glittering against the gems in the cave walls.

She wasn't sure which "elsewhere" Adrian was sleeping in. Another part of the cave, probably. He'd barely spoken to her or anyone else throughout the journey, and hadn't touched her after her request that he stop doing so, back in Washington.

She did want to rest. She couldn't handle anything—funerals, relationships, revenge, family, friends, acceptance, moving on—until this horror had abated, and she had spent a long while recuperating. But how long would that be, before she could handle life again?

Years and years, her father's voice echoed in her head. *Years and years.*

AFTER TABITHA ESCORTED AWAY THE TEARFUL SOPHIE AND Liam, Adrian Watts approached the souls of Isabel and Terry Darrow. He felt sick with misery.

"I'm so sorry," he said. "More sorry than I'll ever be able to say. If I were you two, I would hate me right now."

But even Terry, who had excelled at glaring at Adrian while he was alive, wore a sympathetic expression.

"We don't hate you," Terry said. "I know this outcome was

the last thing you wanted, and you were doing your damnedest to prevent it. We just didn't get out of there fast enough."

"You know how it works down here," Isabel said. "We all become a lot better at understanding. Just, please, help our kids through this. I already know you're going to."

To that, Adrian could only nod and shuffle away.

The fields would do for a bed tonight. He curled up on his side under the drooping branches of a willow, nothing beneath him but the pale grass. Kiri lay beside him, chin on her forepaws. The cave air was cool and dank, but at least the little white flowers sprouting near his face smelled sweet. It wasn't as cold as the nights he'd spent camping on Mary's Peak in September, when he'd been circling Sophie like a shark. Before going in for the kill. Which was essentially what he'd done to her life.

He slumped into a weary sleep. His mind shut off the past-life memories and tormented him instead with a dream in which he begged Sophie to forgive him, and she snarled insults at him and stalked away.

When he awoke with a shudder, he found Nikolaos near him, sitting against the tree.

"At least we can trace them now," Niko remarked, as if they had been in the middle of a conversation.

Adrian creaked himself up to a sitting position. "Uh. Thanatos? Well. One of them."

"Two." Niko gazed at a willow switch he held, dragging it against his opposite palm.

"Two? I could only sense the woman. The one who was Ares."

"I can sense the boy, too."

Adrian blinked in confusion. "You didn't tell me."

Niko shrugged. "I only realized last night when I saw him in person."

"Who was he?" Adrian asked.

"Just one of the many people I connected with in the old days."

Only immortals could track someone with their special sense, and they could only do so if a bodily-fluid connection was made while the sensing party was immortal. Sex was the most common way such links were created, but a small exchange of blood did the trick too, as did having someone be your biological child. So this young man was probably someone Niko had been with in his days as Hermes, long ago, or one of Hermes' children, of whom there might have been more than Adrian knew about.

"Anyone I knew?" Adrian asked.

"I doubt it."

"An immortal?"

"No."

"Well. All right. Two we can grab and hold hostage. Or simply kill." Adrian clenched his hands in the grass. "I'm leaning toward 'simply kill'."

"Not yet." Niko brushed the willow switch around his knee.

"Then at least we learn their names and report their where-abouts to the police. Identify them as the ones who blew up Sophie's house."

"When Quentin was locked up, Thanatos just got her out again. They'd likely do the same for those two."

"But we can track those two. We can get them caught over and over, as many times as it takes."

"Yes, we could, but *think*, Adrian. They're our windows onto the cult. We should look in upon them a while, figure out what Thanatos is going to do, how they work. That way, we can stop them, perhaps for good. Let's watch and learn."

CHAPTER TWO

*L*ANDON OSBORNE DUMPED HIS BAG ON THE MOTEL BED, HIS limbs shaking. He made sure the door's deadbolt was locked and its security chain fastened. As if that would help. He turned on the lamp at the bedside table, for it was the middle of the night and the room would be pitch black without it. But he wondered, with the same sickening dread that had chased him all day and night, whether he should turn it off and hide in darkness.

Would that keep the immortals from finding him? Would anything? The immortal man—the one who had almost certainly killed Landon's grandmother last night—had said he would find them. But he could have been bluffing, only trying to scare them. Maybe.

He slumped to his knees on the carpet beside the bed, resting his dizzy head on the bedspread. It smelled of stale cigarettes, like the rest of the room. When you checked in under a false name, paying with whatever cash you had, you couldn't choose the finest accommodations.

He did need to rest. As the leader of Thanatos now, he had a difficult road ahead, perhaps one every bit as deadly as his grandmother's had been. And though he longed to slide under the bedspread and sleep—even with the likely nightmares—he had a task to accomplish first.

He raised his head. Tension throbbed from the base of his

skull to the bridge of his nose. He opened his laptop computer, and while it booted up he dug out the notebook his grandmother had given him. It was small, with worn gray cloth binding. Her precise, antiquated handwriting filled half the pages, in ballpoint ink of blue and black. The sight sent a pang into his heart. He longed, for about the hundredth time, to race back to the site of the cabin and look for her, because what if she was still alive and needed help?

But chances were a hundred to one the man had killed her. And since he'd probably done so in their other realm, Landon would never find her. He pulled off his glasses and pressed finger and thumb to his aching, closed eyelids. Then he opened his eyes, slipped his glasses back on, and logged in to the email account written in the notebook.

He addressed the email to the ten recipients she had written down, all supposedly safe accounts for such a message. Still, he was careful not to include specifics of location, and began with the established SOS phrase she had taught him. It meant "horror and fear" in ancient Greek, which fit his current mindset all too well.

Daimos kai Phobos. My name is Landon Osborne. Betty Quentin has mentioned me to you. She was my grandmother. I say "was" because last night during our attempted job, the opposing faction captured her. I am almost certain they've taken her to their other home and that we'll never see her again.

This places me, by her wishes, as the new head of operations. But I will need as much help as you all can give me.

My coworker Krystal was injured last night and is being cared for by one of our team. We will need your guidance in sheltering us and discussing our next steps. Our job failed to achieve its target, or at least I don't know yet if it succeeded. But I do know collateral damage was sustained in the family of the central young woman being recruited by the others. The opposing faction will definitely wish to retaliate, and Krystal and I need your protection urgently.

Anyone who can help, please respond.

He sent off the message, changed his sweat-soaked shirt, and flopped onto the bed. While his mind whirled in a cyclone of fear, he prayed for safety, for just enough strength to face the next day. And the next. And the next.

ADRIAN SCRUTINIZED THE SOUL OF BETTY QUENTIN IN HER solitary cell of rock deep under the Earth. Her pale eyes stared at the blue-edged flame burning in the floor of her cell. The Underworld had woven an especially thick willow-and-ivy vine to confine her, wrapped at least three times around her middle. That told him the Fates intended to keep her a long time, and that she'd had a hand in killing and harming even more people than he already knew about. He'd interrogate her about those later, when he could bear to take it in. For now Adrian kept his arms folded, gripping his elbows to keep himself from lashing out and tearing down the rocks around her, burying her soul under a heap of suffocating stone. Little good that would do.

"What will Thanatos do next?" he asked her.

"Landon and Krystal will gather the troops, tell them what happened. Form a plan." Her voice had the same clarity as in life, but now with hollowness behind it. She lifted her gaze to his. Sadness accentuated the age lines around her eyes. "They won't give up. I fear it'll be fatal for him."

"Yes, I suspect it will. We may not find every last one of them, but we'll find him. Easily." Adrian had never before been in the habit of threatening old women with the murder of their grandsons, but he possessed little mercy after what Thanatos had done to Sophie's family—and to himself, Rhea, Sanjay, and others.

Quentin lowered her face. The firelit stone walls shone

through her translucent body, only the vine rope solid and opaque. "Poor boy. I shouldn't have brought him into it."

"My father. Will the group go after him?" She would have to tell the truth, at least. Souls always did.

"We've considered it. But you seemed not to care about each other anymore, so we chose someone you did care about."

Sophie. And Goddess everlasting, hadn't she and her loved ones paid the price. He shut his eyes a moment, then opened them. "Who are the likeliest next victims? Who will your people go after?"

"I expect they'll try again with Tabitha Lofgren. And they'll probably try to find out who the man was who killed me. He must have been one of you." She glanced at him, faint curiosity rising in her face for a moment.

He said nothing. Even though she couldn't communicate with her Thanatos associates anymore, he felt a profound disinclination to tell her any truths about his friends and family. "What about my father?" he asked again.

"They'll keep investigating him. It's likely they'll try something if they can't find a better hostage."

He exhaled and glanced away, tightening his grip on his elbows. "He's innocent. So were Sophie's parents. You can see now, can't you, how evil you all are?"

"The group perceives you as a dangerous threat. Even now I'm not sure they're wrong."

Adrian jerked his gaze back to her. "But you must see it now. Don't you regret it?" Quivering in rage, he took a step closer. "I want to hear you say you regret it."

"Regret isn't a strong enough word for what I feel down here. Were you ever one of these souls?"

"Not down here. Not this bad."

"Yet surely you feel regret too, now."

Though she spoke with the bland depression of every other soul in Tartaros, rather than with the malice she had shown in life, the words penetrated with a sting. "At least I'm alive," he said, and turned and left.

CHAPTER THREE

DIONYSOS AND HERMES BOTH SLEPT IN THE UNDERWORLD near Hekate, or sat awake outside her room, for the first several nights after her parents and grandmother were killed.

Dionysos had lost his parents too, a few years ago during the plague. "Your trauma's so much worse than mine," he told her that first night. "But I do know your grief, and will do anything I can to help you through it, and to make things right."

Then as she was walking dispiritedly toward her bed, Hermes stepped in front of her and held her shoulders. "They are not gone," he said. "No one is ever gone. You're blessed, because you know this better than most. I loved them too, and you know I grieve." Indeed, his green eyes shimmered as tears filled them, and at his touch she sensed the heartache emanating from him. "But we will not despair. Agreed?"

She smiled despite the lump in her throat, and nodded.

But now, three nights later, she had lost another cornerstone of her life. Her magic was gone. She had brought it on herself, and didn't even have the strength to tell her friends yet.

All of them were silent and shaken upon returning from the massacre, where they had released wild spirit-world carnivores upon a band of Thanatos members. They'd left only carnage behind, and the message inked in blood upon a few tree trunks nearby: *These were murderers. The Goddess has taken her justice.*

The message might scare some of the mortal world into behaving. Then again, it might also incite hatred and spur a new rush of membership into Thanatos. Was there anything the immortals could do to prevent that, though? They had tried the diplomatic route. They had healed people, defended coastlines against invaders, thrown festivals full of ribaldry and enlightenment. The killer cult had attacked Hekate and her friends anyway, and murdered Persephone, Hades, and Demeter, along with several others.

So the immortals had retaliated, and now the specter of murder shadowed them all. Hekate saw it in the avoidant faces of those who stayed in the Underworld with her that night: Hermes, Dionysos, Aphrodite, and Rhea. And she felt it in the blankness that met her fingers and mind when she reached out to the world, the rocks and water and trees that used to sparkle and sing with magic for her.

She plodded to her bed in the small cavern just off her parents' larger chamber. Their possessions still sat about where Persephone and Hades had left them. Hekate didn't allow anyone to move them. In the previous three days, she had entered the chamber and touched things—her mother's faded red robe lined with rabbit fur, her father's green rope belt, the wool blankets of their bed, their combs and the leather strings they used to tie back their hair. The residual energy of their living selves had shone forth as she rested her fingertips on each item, so strong and real it made tears stream down her cheeks, but comforted her heart as well.

Now that comfort would be gone. Their possessions would seem to her the sad, empty relics they seemed to everyone else.

Aphrodite and Rhea had made up beds on the floor in a different room of the cave, and had stayed for the past few nights. They had run errands or provided help as Hekate needed. But tonight they retreated in silence, surely disturbed by the bloody revenge.

Though Dionysos had been sleeping on the floor of Hekate's room on previous nights, she now stretched her hand in silent invitation to him. His gray eyes solemn, he followed her to her bed, and they curled up together. They hadn't touched intimately since the one encounter at the deadly Dionysia those few nights ago, and wouldn't tonight either. But human warmth was one of the few consolations left to her, so she took it. With her back curved against his chest, and his arm latched over her, she tried to relax enough to sleep. Hermes took up the spot on the floor he had occupied the past few nights, and pulled a blanket over himself.

Dionysos eventually fell asleep, his breathing steady. Hekate still couldn't. She opened her eyes. Beside Kerberos lay a leashed ghost dog, whom she had brought in so his glow could serve as a flameless light during the night. The faint green shimmer illuminated Hermes' profile as he lay on his back, arms folded behind his head, gazing at the stalactites on the ceiling.

Hekate shifted, pushing down a fold of her blanket. Hermes' gaze moved to her, dark and complicit, bereft of the merriment that usually cavorted there. Her desolation became unbearable. She slipped away from Dionysos and dropped her bare feet to the cold stone. Hermes scooted over to make room for her on his mattress of folded wool. She sat on its edge and drew her legs up beneath her long tunic. Hermes' body warmed the small of her back.

"Show me something," he whispered. "I need some happy magic tonight, love."

She lowered her forehead to her knees. "I can't. It's gone."

"What do you mean, gone?"

"The magic left me," she whispered into the cloth that covered her legs. "It's my punishment."

He drew in a breath. His hand slid onto her back, smoothing the tangles of her long hair. "You should have let us go there tonight without you."

"How would you have? My magic called the beasts to us. Then it left me after I used it for murder."

"It will come back. I'm sure it will. No one's ever punished forever, not even in Tartaros."

"It might come back someday." She kept her head upon her knees. "And someday my parents will be reborn, and someday we might make them immortal again. Someday life will be happy once more. It's a long way ahead, though. How do I get through all those years until 'someday'?"

Hermes pulled her hand away from its clutch across her shins, and kissed it. "With us. We'll all get through together, love."

She sniffled, and lifted her face. "Am I still your 'love' when I can't do my tricks anymore?"

"Always."

Chapter Four

Sophie paced along the beach, the smooth gray and white rocks shifting under her feet. Liam darted around near the surf, and Zoe and Kiri wandered nearby, serving as their protection against spirit-world animals.

They had attended their parents' funeral a week ago—a strange experience, having to play the part of shocked, grieving children when in truth they were still hanging out with their folks and talking with them every day. She and Liam had let the police's protective escorts stand around them like a wall, and had kept their eyes and voices down during the service, letting everyone think they were too damaged to interact.

She'd felt like she was lying to the whole extended family and all her parents' devoted friends, torturing them needlessly, in fact. A few days later she talked to Liam and they decided to make it up to at least one relative, their grandmother, their dad's mom. So Grammy was down in the cave right now, on a two-day visit to see her deceased son and daughter-in-law, along with her husband, Sophie and Liam's grandfather, who had died over a year ago. Zoe had fetched her here at Sophie and Liam's request. Sophie couldn't bear to let Grammy live the rest of her years without ever speaking to her son again, and letting Grammy in on the secrets helped with some of her guilt. But plenty more guilt still howled around in her mind like a hurricane.

.After all, hell, she'd even gotten her dogs hurt. Sophie glanced at the boxer Rosie, who hobbled around on her bandaged leg, sniffing logs and seaweed. Zoe had been giving Rosie daily doses of healing magic with her supernaturally talented hands, and said the dog was well on her way to recovering from her broken leg. Bones took longer to heal, even with the help of magic, than a flesh wound did, like the one Sophie had incurred from Krystal's bullet.

Sophie touched her stiff shoulder, where a bandage still covered the stitches. But it was a lighter bandage now, and the muscle seemed to be limbering up and giving her fewer neckaches than she'd suffered the first week. Zoe had, of course, been speeding Sophie's recovery along too, and when Sophie flew back to Washington for her check-up yesterday, they'd been impressed at how quickly the wound was healing.

Good to know magical people, Sophie supposed. Except for how it also was the entire reason she got shot in the first place, and got her parents and Pumpkin killed.

But she chose this. She could have turned down Adrian's outstretched hand back in fall, and she hadn't. So now, to figure out how to heal the rest of her life, beyond just her shoulder. As to that, she didn't have any ideas yet.

The police and doctors had begged, practically forced, Sophie and Liam to accept psychiatric counseling. After such a devastating experience, people freaked out if you didn't have a counselor. So Sophie and Liam each visited the assigned therapist for half an hour a week, meetings they fit in around the other police and medical check-ins, and they also took regularly scheduled phone calls from her a couple of other times a week. It didn't help much, since Sophie and Liam couldn't tell her much of the truth.

Sophie did morosely ask the therapist if she had PTSD, post-traumatic stress disorder. Or just PTS if you were going to be modern about it; some people felt taking "disorder" off the name made it less of a stigma. Sophie had already Googled it, certain she had it.

But the therapist said it was too early to call it that. At the moment Sophie just had "trauma," which was a completely normal reaction to such an ordeal. If her mood and coping ability didn't improve gradually over the next few weeks or months, then maybe it would start to be called PTSD.

So that was her future: everlasting PTSD. She felt convinced of it. Liam suffered from trauma too, but less so than Sophie. His mood *was* improving lately. Even though it'd been less than two weeks since their parents died, he'd been able to have fun once in a while during the last couple of days, which was still not something Sophie could manage. It seemed to make him feel better that he could talk to Mom and Dad, and it should have made her feel better too. Instead she continued to have panic attacks and nightmares—or at least, she'd had nightmares until Zoe had noticed the issue, and had laid a nightly spell on her to put her sleeping brain at peace. She'd done the same for Liam, who had awoken shrieking a couple of times.

Sophie had shut off her past-life memory-dreams, because they were all tied up in her problems too. Therefore not much was left for her agitated mind to do but scurry around and around in frightening rumination.

The therapist told Sophie to make a list of triggers, things that set off her panic and flashbacks. Sophie didn't have to show the list to her or anyone else; it was an exercise for herself alone. So now, on Sophie's phone, in a note-keeping app, she had typed in a list:

visiting the house
fire
explosions
the people who took me
Adrian

Naturally it would still upset her to see the ruins of their house, or to be near fire, or her actual attackers. (One of them was now dead, but even the thought of visiting Quentin's soul made Sophie's throat close up.)

But that last item—that really made her feel like crap.

Still, if the therapist was right, you could take baby steps toward facing each trigger, build your tolerance back up, and one day cross each item off your list.

"Trauma can be, and regularly is, treated," the woman told her. "You do not have to live in fear forever."

Unless maybe you had Thanatos after you. Then wasn't fear sort of the smart thing to feel?

She watched Liam, who flirted with the breakers, darting at them when they retreated and skittering back when they advanced, his bare feet splashing in and out of the foam. He had scrunched up his skinny black jeans to his knees, but the Mediterranean had sloshed high and soaked them. At least playing on the beach had to be healthier for him than spending yet another stretch of hours down in the Underworld with the souls of their dead parents. Still, she longed to return to them, and felt itchy and anxious every minute she spent above ground.

It was the day before Christmas, and even here on the southwest coast of Greece it got cold. The wind had brought the temperature down to refrigerator levels, and the sea was chilly too. Though she wore her ski coat, Sophie shivered as she paced. She couldn't imagine why Liam would enjoy wading on such a day.

"Be careful," she shouted after an especially large wave thundered around his legs and sent driftwood spinning like chopsticks. "There are sea monsters in this realm. I have it on good authority."

"Cool!" he shouted back, and turned his attention to the waves in search of one.

Of course, Liam was the reincarnation of Poseidon. That probably explained his fondness for the sea.

He must have been thinking about that himself. After chucking a stick and watching it tumble under the next breaker, he ambled up to her, wobbling on the sliding rocks. A trail of wet footprints darkened the stones behind him.

"When am I going to remember the Poseidon part?" he asked.

She handed him his coat and frowned as he sat down and used it to dry his legs off. "Depends. Are you scooting the memories back like we told you?"

"Yeah. Well, I'm trying."

"Then how far back are you?"

"I don't know. Last one was, um…" He retrieved his socks from inside his shoes. "I lived on some island. With palm trees. If you mean, like, what year was it, I have no idea."

"You say that for practically every life you've remembered so far. 'Some island, no idea what year.'"

"I lived on a lot of islands."

"I guess your soul likes to be born near water," she said. "Or move to it if you weren't born near it. Anyway, you only ate the pomegranate a week ago. So it could still be a couple more days before you get to the immortals."

He tugged on his black sneakers and tied their teal laces. "Are we doing anything for Christmas?" He didn't look up as he asked it, and his voice had become guarded.

The question triggered a swoop of sickly dizziness inside her. Her mind conjured an image of their Christmas tree and the gifts under it burning up in a roaring inferno. She hadn't even seen that happen—the destruction of the tree and gifts specifically—but having seen the house collapse in flames from the outside gave her plenty of ability to imagine it.

"We'll…try to get something good for dinner," she said. "Send someone out for food, maybe. I don't think we'll do much in the way of presents, other than bringing Grammy here. That's the main present we can give her."

"It's a good one, though."

Zoe trudged up to them, Kiri at her side. "Ready to go back down?" she asked.

"Yeah," Sophie said.

Liam hopped to his feet.

They climbed over rocks and threaded between boulders on their ascent of the hill. Souls flowed past in the sunlight, looking like the streaks of iridescent color on soap bubbles. Halfway up the slope, the souls joined into a glimmering torrent that poured down into the cave's mouth.

A figure in black rose from behind a boulder where he'd been sitting. Since meeting him in September, the sight of Adrian approaching had regularly thrown Sophie into a blend of alarm and attraction. She had learned to balance the feelings better for a while there. Attraction had even won. But imbalance had now become the definition of her life, and when he walked toward her, her heart thudded, sickening chills raced through her, and she couldn't meet his gaze for more than a second.

Considering he had been sleeping on a mattress in a different part of the cave for the past week and a half, and had barely touched her and only spoken to her to ask softly if she needed anything once or twice a day, he apparently understood. But she felt guilty that her body went into such a reaction, and wished the sight of him *didn't* do this to her.

If wishes were horses, beggars would ride, as her dad used to say. No, he still would say it, wouldn't he? Seeing her dead parents on a regular basis did make life strange and complicated—another piece of her imbalance.

"They're having a nice visit down there," Adrian said.

"Good," Zoe said. "We're headed back down."

Sophie looked down at Rosie and stroked the bristly patch of fur growing back where the dog had been burned.

"I want to take the ladder." Liam sprinted forward.

"Slow down," Sophie called.

"Woot!" Liam hooked a safety harness around his waist, then grabbed the tops of the rope ladder and swung himself into the hole.

"Goddess almighty," Zoe muttered. "I'll go with him." She raced after Liam. "Wait up! Jeez, mate, careful."

Since a couple of mortals had moved into the Underworld for the time being, and couldn't safely handle spirit horses, Adrian and Zoe had rigged up a rope ladder that dropped into the entrance cavern to allow Sophie and Liam to get in and out when they liked. Liam loved it, but a hundred-foot climb or descent on a rope ladder was not Sophie's idea of fun, even with the harnesses to protect against falls. Today Zoe had brought her up on a horse while Liam climbed the ladder.

But now Zoe was taking the ladder down, so Sophie had to decide: face the grapple on swaying ropes, or accept a lift in Adrian's arms?

He did have a spirit horse saddled and ready. Probably he'd been out for a ride. Sophie followed him to the cave mouth where the souls flowed in. She watched the rope ladder twitch as Liam and Zoe descended it. After a minute Liam's voice echoed upward, calling something. Zoe called back, "Almost down. I'm not as fast on this as you."

Her brother and Zoe and Tabitha managed to be cheerful, even if they were faking it. Sophie couldn't even fake it. She was faring the worst by far of everyone.

Maybe she only needed to try harder. Baby steps.

She looked at Adrian. "Can I ride down with you?"

In his glance she caught a flash of hope before he smoothed his face into impassivity again. "Sure." He untied the horse's reins, and clicked his tongue to the dogs. "Here, girls."

He had lately built a small open cage, a roofless box of metal bars. It was all wrapped about with cables that met in a carabiner, which he clipped to the horse tack. Kiri trotted over and hopped into the box. Sophie gathered up Rosie's stiff wriggling legs, and fit her into the box next to Kiri.

"Dogs all set?" Adrian asked.

"Yes."

Adrian stepped aside to let Sophie mount the horse, which she did easily enough, even on an intangible horse: foot in the stirrup, hands gripping the saddle, and a quick swing up. She had ridden the neighbor's horses in Carnation lots of times.

Back when she had a life in Carnation. Back when her parents were alive.

Panic spread in her stomach.

Adrian climbed on behind her and took the reins. His arms touched her on both sides, caging her in, though he didn't actually embrace her. She clung to the saddle's pads and buckles while the horse rose into the air. To keep the panic at bay, Sophie watched the rope go taut as it lifted the dogs' metal carrier off the ground. They dangled just below Sophie's and Adrian's feet, safe in their box, untouched by the swimming ghost legs of the horse.

Adrian gave the reins some slack, and the horse succumbed to the Underworld's pull. They plummeted into the cave. Sophie closed her eyes.

It took only a few seconds, then they landed, the dog carrier settling first and the horse on its spirit feet afterward. Sophie slid off and took a deep breath of the cave air. Its wet rock smell and the sound of the babbling river calmed her a bit. They had never changed in thousands of years, and likely wouldn't for thousands more.

In that moment of reassurance, she pushed forward with her attempt at baby steps. *Face this trigger. Face your lover.* When Adrian turned after helping the dogs out of their box, she stepped up and slipped her arms around his neck. She set her forehead against his shoulder and breathed in, though his scent threw her deeper into anxiety instead of comfort.

He embraced her, hands tentative against her back. Then his arms closed tighter around her. One hand slid up into her hair, and he turned his face to the side of her head and inhaled. Though he didn't speak, he managed to make merely that breath express both anguish and relief. After all, she hadn't let him hold her like this since…before.

She lifted her chin and kissed him. Given all they'd done in the past, this seemed like it should only count as a baby step too. Adrian's mouth barely moved in response, as if he were being careful not to break her.

But despite his gentleness, she tasted acrid smoke on his lips, a phantom scent filled in by her mind. In a flash of memory, he leaped at her and knocked her down while her house exploded. Her parents' bodies lay on the winter grass before her while flames roared in the wreckage of their house, and the horrible red-haired woman electrocuted her over and over, and Adrian lay beside a different fire with a bullet hole in his forehead and blood down his scalp.

Sophie tore loose and spun away, sure she was about to throw up. She crashed to her knees and hung her head, hands splayed on the stone floor. She took careful breaths.

No sound came from behind her for several seconds. Then one of the dogs whined, and a collar tag jingled as the dog padded closer. Rosie. Kiri didn't wear a collar. Rosie nosed Sophie's ear, then sat beside her and rested her chin on Sophie's hunched back. The comforting contact eased Sophie back to the point where at least she felt she wouldn't vomit right now. With a sigh, she sat back on her knees, shaking. Rosie slid her front legs down and rested her chin on Sophie's thigh instead.

The bright blue-white of the cave mouth pierced Sophie's eyes in the gloom. The incoming souls flickered against the stalactites and the river. Just eleven days ago, her parents had been among them, two of the hundreds who entered every minute.

"You don't have to pretend everything's normal." Adrian's voice was husky, unsteady. "It isn't. I know that. Please take your time."

"I'm pathetic." She blinked at the brightness above. "With your mom you had it so much worse. You couldn't come see her. You didn't know about this place. She was just gone to you, and you thought you'd never see her again. I shouldn't complain, when I have this."

Anger swept into his tone. "Of course you can complain. Those bastards attacked you and your home and destroyed everything they could touch. You've been violated, horribly. My mum wasn't the victim of murder like that. Her death was natural, or at least an accident. It was horrible and sad, yes, and I…" His voice became gravelly, and he turned quiet a few seconds before continuing. "I would have done anything to keep you from going through that. I tried."

Her knees hurt against the stone. She stayed put. "I know."

All this horror had been brought on because of her association with him. She should have just said no to him, back in September. Everyone would still be alive if she had.

"Blame me if you like," he said. "I should never have approached you, with people like that on my tail. But don't ever blame yourself. Please."

Not an option. Guilt rode her constantly.

The colors changed upon a stalactite as the souls passed it. She envied them. If a painless method existed to end her life without grieving Liam or anyone else, she would take it. Oh, to acquire the serenity of the dead, and to abandon the aches and queasiness and vulnerability of this physical body.

Because becoming immortal wouldn't fix things either. Adrian was thoroughly wretched. And these days Zoe and even Nikolaos wandered around looking haunted and damaged a lot of the time, too. Tab seemed optimistic enough, but Tab was good at acting; it could have been a ruse. There was no escape from pain but death. And even death was only a temporary reprieve, since no one stayed in the fields forever. They just kept getting reborn, undergoing the torture of life again and again. What was the point of it all?

"Tell me what I can do," Adrian said. "Anything."

She rested her hand on Rosie's head and stroked the rumpled skin behind the dog's ears. "Keep trying to fix the world."

"I'd rather fix you."

She slid her fingers back and forth beneath Rosie's collar. "I don't know how to do that." After all, she'd tried some of those baby steps just now. Epic fail.

"Are you ready to come see everyone?" Adrian asked quietly.

"In a minute."

"I'll wait by the raft."

He and Kiri departed, their footsteps a whisper on the stone.

CHAPTER FIVE

HEKATE SAT ON THE CLIFF ABOVE THE UNDERWORLD. THE RIS-
ing moon hovered resplendent above the sea. The third
full moon since her parents' death, and still she could not pull
a sliver of magic from it. But even remote and untouchable,
it soothed her the way it did all humans, with its beauty, its
light, its reliably cycling nature.

Dionysos approached, climbing the rocks to her. She
sensed him before she heard him. At least she still had that
power. She remained equal to the other immortals, far above
the powers of mortals. It was horribly ungrateful of her to feel
so desolate.

His new wildcat cub danced up to her. Captured from the
spirit realm like his first cat had been, this one was all black
with a golden underbelly. She was still only half-grown, all
skinny legs, long tail, and big paws. She knocked her fuzzy
head against Hekate's knees in affection. Hekate scratched
her fondly behind the ears.

Dionysos had begun to move on, unlike Hekate. He'd at
least acquired a new pet to care for after Thanatos had killed
the first one. Hekate hadn't done much except brood around
the Underworld.

Dionysos' leg touched her back, warming a length of her
windblown body through her wool robes. The fur-lined edge
of his cloak flapped against her arm in the breeze. He sat be-

side her, draping the cloak around her. The cub hopped into his lap.

Hekate burrowed into his warmth, the brightest and most soothing power in her life these past three months. Winter still chilled her heart, in spite of the spring bulbs now blooming. But she had recovered in small ways at least: she had dismantled her parents' bed a month after they died, packed away most of their possessions in a trunk, and turned their large bedchamber into her sitting room. She had also by now invited Dionysos to rejoin her as a lover. When he held and stroked her, she believed, for a few relaxed moments each day, that life and happiness would return again. Dying-and-rising gods were inspiring that way.

"Full moon," she said. "You should be at a festival."

"They go on whether I'm there or not. I don't need to preside."

"Don't you miss them?"

"A little. I'll return one of these months."

At the last Dionysia they had attended, everything had fallen into bloody pieces. Going to another would be difficult, but surely a necessary step for conquering her sadness and fears. Someday.

She pulled her knees up under the fur cloak and chose a different topic. "I wonder where Zeus and Hera will end up."

"I wonder too. Aphrodite will be able to track him, at least. None of us can track Hera."

Hekate nodded. The souls of Zeus and Hera had departed the Underworld that morning. They hadn't waited to say farewell in person to any of their living immortal friends, though they left well-wishes via the other souls, such as Hades and Persephone.

"They felt it was time to move on," Persephone told her daughter when Hekate awoke today. "They didn't want to make a fuss or have anyone try to stop them."

So they were gone, out into the living world to be reborn.

Hermes had immediately dashed to Aphrodite's island to ask her to trace Zeus, but she was unable to sense him yet. Perhaps the Goddess hadn't yet assigned his soul to a new unborn child, or else it took some time before the soul of the child was strong enough for other immortals to sense.

"I wonder how long before we'll know if he's immortal again," Dionysos said.

"I wonder."

"Your parents will never leave like that," he assured. "They would talk to you first, make sure you were all right with it."

She hadn't been thinking of that sobering possibility this particular moment, but it had certainly haunted her much of the day. "I know they wouldn't."

"They'll wait a long while yet. They'll want to know what happens to Zeus and Hera too. Or Zeus, at least, since we can't know where Hera is."

She nodded. But even in the best case scenario, where her parents were reborn immortal once again, or at least were kept safe as mortals until they could be fed the orange, they would almost certainly be born without their memories, and definitely to new parents who would love them. How could Hekate step in and claim someone else's children as her family, and take them back to the Underworld to reinstate them in their former lives? How could she break apart other families that way? She could wait till the children were grown, perhaps, and about to go their own ways as everyone must, but that would mean waiting twelve to eighteen years, watching from a distance. All without her parents' souls knowing who she was.

So on the day they did decide to fly free from the Underworld and be born anew, then she would know grief. It would be their second death, and their true death to her.

She shrank into a tighter ball beneath Dionysos' cloak. Even with the knowledge of reincarnation to console her, her best case scenario felt like a sea of sadness that would one day drown her.

"DUDE!" TABITHA LEAPED IN FRONT OF ADRIAN IN THE FIELDS. "Freddie Mercury is down here. I found him and talked to him!"

Adrian smiled, though the expression felt foreign on his face now. "Course he is. Lots of people are."

"I am only just now realizing how potentially awesome this place is. I want to talk to John Lennon! And June and Johnny Cash! And—oh my God, do you think Marilyn Monroe's still here?"

"Haven't thought to look for her. Feel free." He looked past her at the group sitting beneath a grove of silver-leafed trees: Liam and Sophie and their grandmother, along with the souls of Terry and Isabel and Terry's father. Zoe played with Kiri nearby, staying in range in case the family needed anything.

Tab tossed her smooth blonde hair over her shoulder as she turned to look at the family too. "They all seem to be doing good. Well, except Sophie, maybe." She shot Adrian a troubled look. "I do think she'll come around. Seriously. It's just…it's tough, what she went through."

"Don't let her blame herself, all right?" he said. "I've told her that, but if her friends say it too, maybe it'll sink in."

"You say that like you're not one of her friends."

"I'm not sure she sees me as one anymore." Before Tab could get out more than an, "Ah, come on," he stepped away and followed the path.

He wanted to help. He ached to cradle Sophie in his arms and let her cry on his shirt for however many hours it took before she felt better. But she wouldn't let him. Of course she did cry—he saw it in her puffy eyelids, saw her from a distance wiping her eyes when she talked to her parents' souls, and heard the choked sniffles sometimes from the bathtub or the bedchamber, when he crept near enough outside the rooms to listen, because he couldn't bear *not* to check on her. But from Adrian she wouldn't, or couldn't, accept even the smallest touch now. Evidently when she tried, it made her physically sick.

His friends should have let Thanatos kill him.

From a distance he studied the family he had torn apart. Sophie sat in the deepest of the tree's shadows, quiet but composed. Grammy looked beatifically happy, her lined face all smiles. Liam piped up with another excited comment to his parents about past lives—they were letting Grammy over-hear all that, which hardly mattered anymore; she was clearly going to have to be in on the secrets.

Adrian turned away. The Darrows were getting along fine without him. Would be getting along far better if they'd never met him.

He walked the path that wound toward the pomegranate orchard. Kiri shot into view, running past and then circling back.

Zoe fell into step beside him too. "Everyone asks how *they* are," she said, tilting her head in the direction of the Darrows. "But how are you?"

He cut a glance toward her, then reached his arm out, palm down. "You tell me."

She enclosed his wrist in her hands. He felt nothing but her cool touch, but after a moment she hissed in a breath as if burned. "Ah, mate."

He yanked his hand away.

She grabbed it back. "Hold still."

He felt a sensation of calm; nothing as dramatic as happiness, but a lessening of anguish. He pulled in his breath, realizing he'd been tight in the chest for he didn't know how long.

Zoe let go of his hand. "There. If you're going to let me read that kind of pain, you have to let me treat it, too."

"Thanks."

"Not that it'll last. Immortal bodies throw off spells as fast as we throw off injury. But try to hang onto it, all right?"

He nodded to appease her. But she was right; within a minute the anguish had begun to creep back. He kept walking and tried not to let it show.

"Let's find Niko," he said quietly.

They followed their tracking sense to Niko, and found him wandering between columns and stalagmites near the back of the cave, in a section of the Underworld without the usual grasses and flowers. It looked more like a proper cave back here, all rock formations in bizarre shapes, as if the wax from giant candles had dripped and solidified.

Niko wore his dark red fleece and warm hat, and black jeans and sneakers. Lately he'd been more subdued than usual in his choice of wardrobe. He acknowledged their arrival with a glance at Adrian and a flicker of a smile at Zoe, then continued tracing his fingers along a column and peering up into the cave's dark ceiling.

"Look, it's no good," Adrian said. "Someone has to go back to the battle, and it might as well be me."

"Ade," Zoe said. "She's just suffering. She does love you."

"Loves me so much she nearly loses her lunch when she tries to kiss me, yeah. What she needs is to be rid of the sight of me." He folded his arms, digging his fingers into his elbows.

His friends only gazed disconsolately at the rock formations. Niko didn't even take the opportunity to tease Adrian like he ordinarily would.

"Someone does need to apply themselves to spying on Thanatos," Niko said. "More than just the occasional look-in I'm giving them." Nikolaos had been following Krystal and Landon—Quentin had supplied their names—and stealing opportunities while they slept to open their computers or go through the messages on their phones.

Landon was mostly staying in motels, moving around a

lot, and Krystal was recuperating from her gunshot wound in a house in southeastern Washington that, they presumed, was owned by another member of Thanatos, or at least someone sympathetic to the cause who would hide her from the law and wouldn't press her to go to a hospital. From the messages, Niko had a few names, or at least aliases, of other members, but definite information on the cult's plans was still lacking. The cult members knew better than to be too specific in writing; they used vague wording and code phrases that Adrian and his friends couldn't always work out.

"I want to crush them. Krystal and Landon." Adrian pronounced the names with bitter enunciation. "We've let them lurk about long enough. I'm going to have them thrown in jail, and if they get out, I will kill them. Personally."

"It's interesting," Niko said, "having you be farther on the wrong side of the law than me for a change."

"You threw Quentin off a horse from a hundred meters up! Why won't you let me do the same to her hired thugs?"

Niko turned his face away, the muscles in his cheek hardening.

"Ade," Zoe beseeched.

"You wouldn't like it, killing anyone," Niko said, his gaze upon the dark spaces between columns. "Not even those people. I'd rather I hadn't set that precedent."

"Besides, we've been over it," Zoe added. "The longer we watch them, the more we learn about what they're up to. If we swoop in on them, they'll know we've been spying. And if we take out Landon and Krystal—whether by killing them or by having them arrested or by grabbing them and bringing them here for questioning—then we lose our two best leads into Thanatos. We can't track anyone else so easily, even when we have names and mobile numbers."

"So, what, we wait until they attack another innocent family?" Adrian said.

Niko glanced at him. "I've seen no signs of an upcoming attack. I would tell you if I had."

"Would you? You seem content to tell us things only when it pleases you."

Niko's eyes grew colder.

Zoe closed her hand around Adrian's arm, hard. "That's enough. Bloody hell, wouldn't Thanatos love this? Fighting amongst ourselves? Stop it already."

Adrian said nothing, but flattened his lips in semi-apology at Niko.

Niko accepted it with a lift of his chin. "At least they're doing the same. Squabbling with each other over what to do next. Meanwhile, Landon's going mad with fear."

"Does he know you're spying on him?" Adrian asked. "Or do you mean he's only fretting about being caught?"

"Oh…" Niko swiped a water drop off a column. "I'd say he knows."

CHAPTER SIX

*L*ANDON POURED THE BOURBON INTO THE PLASTIC MOTEL CUP and chugged it.

"Merry Christmas," he said out loud to whomever might be listening, though he was alone in the motel room. Or so it appeared. "Wait till I'm passed out before you kill me, all right? Thanks."

Talking to nobody. Great. He was losing his mind. Ongoing terror could do that to you, it seemed.

At first he thought it was his imagination that he was being stalked. If the immortals could follow him that easily, they'd simply kill him, or seize him as a hostage, right? But when he awoke some mornings, he could swear his phone or computer was a few inches off from where he had left it, and that the power level was a bit lower than it should be. And when he went to check the recently accessed files in a fit of paranoia, he found the history wiped clean—which he hadn't done, at least not that he remembered. Maybe the computer did that automatically sometimes? Side effect of some harmless update?

He slept with his grandmother's little gray notebook tucked under his pillow, so at least no one should easily be able to get that. But if anyone actually was sneaking around his motel room, he wasn't going to be able to sleep anymore anyway.

Lately he had been hiding out in a motel in Boise, a city he'd never been in before, so no one should look for him there. Theoretically. The terse coded emails and equally terse phone calls Landon had been getting from the Thanatos members around the globe hadn't exactly been helping. Most didn't like the idea of being subject to a new leader, younger than themselves, whom they'd never met. They tended to disagree on what steps should be taken next to pursue the unnaturals. And they didn't care for the uncertainty of what had befallen Betty Quentin. One even hinted that Landon might have done away with her himself to gain control of the group.

"I would never want to be in control!" Landon shouted.

"Well, of course, you could resign if that's how you feel," the man had said smoothly. His name was Erick Tracy. He was a British guy who lived in Australia now, and who was, to judge from their few conversations so far, basically an asshole. "In any case," Tracy had added during their phone call, "I suspect you'll feel more chipper after you've heard my ideas at the meeting."

Tracy was taking the lead in organizing the upcoming meeting and therefore was acting like the group's leader, even though he wasn't. But new ideas, super, might as well hear them.

From what Landon's grandmother had told him, and what Google turned up too, Erick Tracy was an academic who taught a mix of subjects: criminal justice, atmospheric sciences, and the overlapping territory of science and law. His students loved him, to judge from the numerous teaching awards listed on his professional contact pages. He also traveled a lot and had been involved in student work/study-abroad programs between various countries.

"And the ladies have to look out around him," Quentin had remarked.

Landon believed that. In the few online photos he had seen, Tracy was a handsome man with a sexy-librarian-adventurer thing going on. He was in his fifties, but appeared to be one of those guys who could make graying hair, glasses, and tweed jackets look hot. And in three of the five photos he had his arm around young, pretty women, probably his adoring students. Ick.

Tracy was the one who had flown over to New Zealand last month to look for Adrian Watts—and had completely failed, Landon would like to note. At least Landon had come a few feet away from throwing Adrian into a fire. Failing at that was neither something he was proud of nor ashamed of. He couldn't help shuddering at the idea of killing someone with his own hands, even someone who was partly a monster. But at least he'd been on the right trail.

As to whether Adrian was in fact dead, no one knew. That made Landon nervous. They hadn't ascertained what happened to Adrian after that night. If these people were honestly as hard to kill as the Decrees warned, well, Adrian might have survived and now he'd be furious, which was a scary thought. Wasn't any better if he was dead, though. Then his immortal friends would be furious. Landon was on their hit list no matter what. Thanatos was his only hope of safety.

What with the holidays, they'd been unable to schedule the council meeting until two days after Christmas. Christmas was today, not that Landon was doing anything for it. Indeed, he'd never known a lonelier, more awful Christmas, and that was saying something.

Landon's father had died of a heart attack three years ago, which of course had been traumatizing even though Landon had never been close to him. He hadn't been much closer to his mother. She and Landon hadn't talked in months. Possibly she didn't even know he had left Massachusetts. He had changed his phone number without telling her, because chances were excellent the police would be looking for him back home. The immortals had probably found out who he was and would be trying to cause legal trouble for him. An anonymous tip would do it, same kind of thing he and his grandmother had placed to mess with Adrian.

So yes, the menace from the immortals hadn't diminished at all; in fact, it kept piling up, like a thunderhead. His grandmother had made Thanatos sound so glorious, a noble adventure in scholarship and international intrigue. Instead it was turning out more like being the victim in a horror movie.

Two nights ago Landon had left a note on top of his computer: *Is my grandmother alive or dead?* He'd written it in red ink and laid the pen across the note, with a large space left below for an answer.

I'm being paranoid, he thought before retiring to his motel bed. It was hours before he could fall asleep.

But when he woke up and dashed across to his computer, like a little kid looking for evidence of a visit from some evil Santa, he reeled back instantly upon seeing the note.

The pen lay beside the computer now, and *DEAD* was printed neatly across the lower half of the page, with *Have a nice day* written in smaller letters below it.

He'd been so terrified he couldn't eat. He'd moved to a different motel, and phoned Jim Farnell, the nearest Thanatos representative, the guy in southeastern Washington who was housing Krystal. Landon spilled the story to him: the stalking, the note. "You've got to help me," he begged.

Jim was a retired Army man, and knew some younger sniper types who would ask no questions if assigned a surveillance-and-possibly-lethal-assault job. They sounded like Krystal that way, Landon thought. Indeed, the young man with the reddish-blond crew cut who showed up a couple of hours later at his motel did remind Landon a bit of Krystal. Especially when he assembled his weapons with a fond gleam in his eyes—tranquilizer gun, stun gun, and thick handgun. The idea was to knock the immortal intruder out with those, then transport him elsewhere to incinerate him.

Landon fell asleep while the sniper stayed up all night in

a hiding place under the sheet-draped luggage rack in the room. But no one showed up.

The sniper went home to sleep for the day, and returned for one more night's vigilance. Still no immortals turned up. Jim Farnell let the sniper go home for Christmas, and told Landon to calm down and wait for the Thanatos meeting. "It's only one more night, son," Jim said over the phone. "You'll be fine. You've probably been sleepwalking, is my guess. That would explain the note."

"It wasn't my handwriting!"

"Writing in your sleep, though, it'd look different. Understandable. You've been under a lot of stress. Think about it: if these fiends could get you that easily, wouldn't they have just ended you by now?"

Such was a Thanatos member's way of being reassuring, Landon supposed.

He sloshed another inch or two of bourbon into the plastic cup, swigged it, and fell on his back on the motel bed. The ceiling swirled dreamily. "Just kill me in my sleep, 'kay?" he murmured. "Don't do stuff to scare me. Just don't anymore."

CHAPTER SEVEN

ADRIAN WAS DETERMINED TO PROVIDE SOPHIE WITH A GOOD Christmas before he left, or at least as decent a Christmas as he could give her under the circumstances. Her grandmother was here, which helped. But since Sophie wasn't comfortable around Adrian, learning what else she wanted meant going through intermediaries. He'd asked Tabitha, who reported back that Sophie seemed only concerned about making Liam happy. Liam missed his video games—he spent a lot of free hours borrowing everyone else's phones and playing whatever game apps they had on them—so Adrian sent out Niko and Zoe to obtain electronics. Food pleased Liam too, as it did for most rapidly growing twelve-year-olds. So Freya and Tab took on the task of planning and bringing down a Christmas feast for the group, sourced from Greek towns nearby.

Thus on Christmas morning, Sophie, Liam, and their grandmother came out of the bedchamber to find their immortal hosts laying out plates of bacon, eggs, fresh fruit, pastries, and hot chocolate in the fields. The souls of Terry, Isabel, Rhea, Sophie's Grandpop, and other friends lingered near, smiling. Liam pounced on the bacon. Grammy kissed Niko's cheek when he brought her a cup of chocolate. Sophie finally smiled too—a weak smile compared to the blissful grins Adrian had once been privileged enough to receive, but it gave him hope. She sat on the grass with the rest, and ate some eggs and fruit. She kept her gaze lowered while the others chatted around her. Adrian was quiet too, across the circle from her, pulling apart a mandarin orange on his plastic plate.

They exchanged gifts after breakfast. He and the other immortals had insisted they needed nothing. Nonetheless, Zoe weaseled over to Adrian and thrust a squishy paper-wrapped bundle into his hands. He unwrapped it to find two T-shirts and two long-sleeved button-downs, all new and in a variety of subdued dark colors.

"Your shirts are all getting quite worn out and impossible," she said. "Plus it's so exciting being able to pick out colors for people!" After all, she'd been born blind, and hadn't been able to see until eating the fruit of immortality a couple of months ago.

Adrian hugged her. "Cheers, Z. They're great. And um, here." He took a tiny box from the paper bag he'd brought along, and handed it to her.

She opened it and lifted out the silver ear cuff. "It's gorgeous! Ooh, it's got a moon."

"Moon and a sun and those wavy lines that looked like water—I don't know, it made me think of you. Since you were complaining that becoming immortal made your earring holes heal up, and you can only wear that type now…"

Zoe kissed him on the cheek. "I love it. Here, I'm putting it on."

A few paces away, Liam was on his knees opening a large box and hauling out its contents: a game system, monitor, and meters of cables.

"And," Niko was explaining to him, "I've finally fetched a generator for the Underworld the way I did for Ade's trailer, so you can run the thing as soon as we hook up the wiring."

Liam kept up a stream of excited comments as he pawed through the game boxes. Tab and Grammy sat near him, grinning, and Sophie watched with a soft smile. She absently stroked the sleeve of the black cashmere sweater she wore, a present Tab had just given her. Adrian tightened his fingers on the paper bag, which still held his gift for Sophie. Would he dare give it to her?

Then, to his surprise, she approached. She glanced into his eyes for a second, then dropped her gaze. "I have something for you," she said. "It's over here, by the orchard."

"Oh. Great." He tried to sound friendly and relaxed.

He followed her to the orchard, away from the chattering group—quite aware that several of their friends watched them walk off together, with a mix of curiosity, hope, and pity in their eyes. She tapped the flashlight app on her phone and lit their way with it as the glow of the souls dwindled behind them. Adrian added the beam of his key-ring light. He said nothing as they walked. What could he say? *Enjoying your Christmas in the land of the dead? Fun and different, right?*

Between the pomegranate orchard and the river lay the large expanse where Persephone's gardens had once grown. It had been overtaken by plants and trees that, as far as Adrian could recall, had always lived in the Underworld, along with some garden plants gone feral—willows, ashes, ivies, wild-flowers, herbs, and others, all with leaves in shades of gray, white, or black, with occasional bursts of color in the flowers.

But the flashlights' beams landed upon one knee-high tree sporting slender shiny green leaves. Sophie stopped beside it. Small red flowers peeked from the foliage. The earth around its trunk was freshly turned over and tamped down, and showed a dark circle where the tree had been watered.

"It's this," Sophie said.

Adrian crouched by the tree and stroked a leaf between thumb and finger. "It's pretty. Looks familiar; what is it?"

"It's a titoki tree. I had this idea you might miss home when you're down here, so I asked Zoe what plants were in your garden in Wellington. She said she remembered a titoki tree, because her house had one too. So I had her find one for me at a nursery. I thought, since it's native to New Zealand, there's probably never been one planted down here, so... maybe it'll do something cool, magic-wise. I don't know. At least you could have it to remind you of home."

She sounded so somber. Adrian's throat swelled and he blinked against tears. "It's perfect," he said. "I love it. Thank you." And he couldn't even kiss or hug her in gratitude. Not with yesterday's reaction. "I'd...been meaning to try new plants down here, the way we used to," he added, "but hadn't got around to it. Really, it's such a good idea. Thanks."

Her lips stretched in an expression that was almost a smile. "Good." She reached down to pick a dry stem off the little tree.

The gift *was* perfect, and so very Persephone. It boosted his hopes that she might yet recover and take joy in the Under-world—and in him.

Then again, she could easily have thought of this gift and arranged it with Zoe a couple of weeks ago. Before.

Letting himself hope was self-destructive. Action only, for a while yet. He rose and took out the one small box that remained in the paper bag. He handed it to her, though re-luctance almost pulled his arm back. Ugh, jewelry, what had he been thinking? So cold and inorganic compared to her gift; such a typical symbol of men trying to buy and possess women. Not at all the message he intended, but she might take it that way.

As she took the box, he said, "Don't open it now. You can wait till later, after I'm gone."

Her eyes lifted to him, guarded. "Gone?"

"Well, I should visit my dad, for starters."

"Oh. Yeah, of course you should."

He folded up the paper bag till it was just a hard little square between his hands. "After that, well, someone has to apply themselves to seeing what Thanatos is up to, so I thought I'd track them down, find out what I can. Stop them if possible. I'd still come back here sometimes, but it might be a while. It could be days or weeks that you…wouldn't see me. I'm not sure yet how it'll go."

He paused, but she stayed silent.

"I just thought, maybe it'd help if I gave you some space," he went on. "Some time. Since I know you'll want to be down here…and, probably it's best if I'm out trying to do something about them."

Sophie swung her flashlight beam slowly across the titoki tree. "You *should* fix the world. Stop them so it's safe for us. If you can do that…" She let her arm fall still at her side. The beam of light became a stationary circle by her feet. "I don't know what I want, for the most part. But I do want that. I want them stopped."

THAT NIGHT, ADRIAN PACKED UP HIS BUS, HUGGED EVERYONE who had gathered in the entrance chamber to see him off, and promised to be in touch. Hugged everyone except Sophie, that is. Seemed he wasn't about to touch her again. She longed to take the initiative and step up and hug him herself, but she felt anchored to the floor. The whole parting scene sent storms of uneasiness fluttering up and down her, deep in her belly and out to her fingertips, especially when he tried to give her a reassuring goodbye smile while misery swam in his dark eyes.

Then he snapped the whip and was gone. The remaining group started migrating from the entrance chamber toward the fields, talking about having Christmas-night dessert and wine. "No wine for you, Liam," Tabitha said with a laugh.

Zoe suggested card games before bed.

"Join us, Sophie?" Niko ruffled an Uno pack in one hand. "I promise not to cheat. This time."

"I'll be there in a minute," she said.

The rest of them continued on to the fields. With a flashlight, Sophie walked alone through the tunnel to the bed-chamber. She sat on the edge of the mattress, Adrian's gift in her lap, and switched on the camping lantern that rested on a wooden crate by the bed, so that she had a light on each side of her.

She untied the purple ribbon and opened the hinged jew-elry box. Every muscle stilled for a breathless moment, then she swallowed and let her fingers fall to brush the necklace. Her ancient memory recognized it at once, though this piece was new and only an approximate copy of the one Perse-phone had worn.

Five small purple amethysts, cut into ovals, formed the petals of a single violet flower framed by tiny gold leaves. The pendant hung from a slim black leather cord, gold wire coiled tight around the sides of the clasp in back.

As Sophie lifted the necklace out, a note fell from the top of the box where it had been wedged. Sophie draped the necklace across her leg and unfolded the note.

The first thing that struck her was that she'd never seen Adrian's handwriting before, a fact both sad and strange. They'd only corresponded in texts or blog comments. The second thought was that his handwriting suited him: low and casual, with bolder straight up-and-down lines on some of the verticals, and an impression of honesty and sweetness throughout.

She smoothed out the page.

Dear Sophie,

This is a replica of course, and not a very accurate one since I was relying on memory and then trying to describe it to the jeweler. But the gold and amethysts are from the Underworld, so at least that part is the same. I considered having the crown remade but a necklace is more like something a person could actually wear in this day and age.

Whether you wish to wear it or not, and whether or not you ever want to see me again, I want you to know a few things.

You're welcome to the Underworld and everything and everyone in it, anytime. It's yours as much as mine.

You don't owe me anything.

I'll always love you and welcome you.

I just want you to be happy and I want to help you. That's why I left. You're right, we have to fix the world. Though it may be a lost cause, I'm going to try. For you, your family, our friends, all the innocent people. For Persephone and Hades.

I'll be in touch. Please stay safe and don't give up hope.

Merry Christmas,

Love,

Adrian

She slid the paper farther up her knees so the tears dripping off her nose wouldn't land on it and smear the ink. Why was she even crying? Only that everything made her cry these days, for starters. And because he was so sweet, and because even though she loved him as much as ever on the inside, shock had damaged her on the outside and she couldn't reciprocate his affection the way he deserved. It hurt him, and it hurt her too.

Now he was off to fight Thanatos, which yes, someone had to do. But they might catch and kill him next, and he'd drift down here as a ghost, and then his death, too, would be her fault.

CHAPTER EIGHT

ERICK TRACY FLICKED HIS GAZE ACROSS THE GROUP. A SORRY assemblage for saving mankind, but they would have to do. Perhaps in his hands they would succeed.

He was fifty-five, not the oldest member of Thanatos, but one of the longest initiated, and almost certainly the best educated. He'd been brought into the group at age twenty-one at Oxford by the elderly chaplain of his college, who recognized the proper mix of interests in Tracy: ancient religions and the modern occult, and the zeal to do the right thing against those who would throw the world into chaos.

Now Tracy's day had come. Those chaos bringers were, without a doubt, walking the Earth again.

Only six members of Thanatos in total had been able to attend in person today, but the rest of the central council attended online in tech-shielded video calls. Half the group was female, half male, with citizenships, ethnicities, and religions from all around the globe. Ages ranged from the young Landon and Krystal to the white-bearded Swami in India, who was calling in via video today.

Tracy let his gaze rest on Krystal, the red-haired girl with crutches leaning against her chair and perpetual bitchiness in her eyes, then on Landon, who looked about to fall apart in a frazzle of nerves. Honestly, no wonder they had botched the elimination of Adrian Watts. The girl should be confined strictly to weaponry, and the boy shouldn't be anywhere near the leadership of such an important organization. Quentin had grown a bit soft in her aging mind, it would seem.

Everyone exchanged polite greetings. The screens and tablets had been set up to include the video callers in the circle. The group sat around the dining room table in the house where Krystal was recuperating, in the small city of Richland in southeastern Washington.

Tracy straightened the cuffs of his tweed suit, then leaned forward in the chair and steepled his fingers above the tabletop. "So. First off, Adrian Watts, our primary target, the only one we can identify with certainty and by name: no news there, I'm afraid. We've still no idea if he's alive or dead."

"He's dead," Krystal said. "I shot him in the head, point-blank. No one's *that* immortal."

"Unfortunately these people may be," Tracy said. "Our Decrees suggest they survive such things."

"They don't survive fire or explosives," Landon said tentatively. "But…"

"But we know Adrian Watts survived, and healed quickly from, a gunshot wound in February," Tracy said. "It's likely to be no different this time, even with a head wound. Especially since they've all gone into hiding: Sophie Darrow, her brother Liam, Tabitha Lofgren. Probably Adrian is with them, sheltering them. They're likely watching and waiting, and planning. So a new plan is what we need as well."

"They're following me," Landon said. "I'm sure of it. Please, can't someone stick with me and trap at least one of them and get rid of them? I'm…I can't sleep, I'm going crazy, I—"

"Yes, we'll deal with your problem," Tracy cut in. "We might have no success with it, but at least it can be a diversion while we try for the brass ring."

"Diversion?" Landon protested.

"What brass ring?" a woman asked from one of the computer screens. Her name was Joaquina and she had worked in the governments of three South American countries so far.

"The real problem," Tracy said, "is that our enemies can escape to their other home all too easily, yes? Where they're doing who knows what. Making more of their kind. Building an arsenal. Brewing biological weapons of supernatural origin. We simply have no idea, and we're powerless as long as they have their 'other realm' in which to go on doing mischief."

"And?" Krystal said. "What the hell are we supposed to do, other than kill them when they do show up?"

"What if we could get into the other realm?" Tracy said.

Everyone stared at him in astonishment.

"We can't," one of the men said — an influential businessman from China. "The one who converted, Sanjay, he made it quite clear. Only immortals can get across."

"All our Decrees and records say the same thing," Joaquina agreed.

"Our Decrees and records are incomplete," Tracy said. "They're ancient and fragmented, as is to be expected. But they do mention allies of the immortals. Cults dedicated to them, and *to their secrets.*"

"Yes, they have allies, we know that," said Swami, Sanjay's former guru, from another computer screen. "We are already targeting them as well, are we not?"

"We are," Tracy said. "But I've long suspected that those secrets which the allies learned might include a way to enter the other realm. Even for regular humans." He let that sink in, then added, "Our own records, of course, don't tell of such a method. The allies have kept it under wraps. But were it possible to get into their realm, we could eliminate the problem at its root, once and for all."

"The tree," Landon said.

"Yes. The fruit of immortality, in the land of the dead. All sources agree that's where the evil comes from. Find that and destroy it, along with the enemy, caught in their own lair, and we will finally have triumphed."

"And this way of getting in, you think you can find it?" Yuliya said, her words accented. She was in her late thirties, and had recently moved to the US from Russia. Tracy hadn't met her till today, but he liked her voluptuous curves and planned to pursue them in his leisure time.

"I think I have found it." Tracy gave Yuliya a lingering smile before continuing. "Those allies of the immortals, they've been around as long as Thanatos has. Doing almost nothing, perhaps, other than telling sad stories about days long past. They started out as the Eleusinian Mysteries, and have evolved under other names, in various regions. But they, too, have kept their records and secrets preserved. For many years I've looked for such groups, such records, and at last I've been successful at…" He coughed to shade over the distasteful details. "Infiltrating a particularly valuable collection."

They gathered the meaning of the cough.

"Who did you have to kill?" Joaquina asked dryly.

Tracy didn't answer. No one expected he would. In such matters, the fewer people who knew specifics, the better. "The important thing is I've obtained the instructions. How mortals get into the spirit realm. How, and where."

The group looked enthralled. Even Landon dropped his haggard expression and adopted one of hope.

"Where?" Swami echoed.

"*Where*, it turns out, is a very important question." Tracy clicked open the hand-drawn map he had scanned into his tablet, and turned the screen to display it to his comrades. "Each of these marks represents an ancient sacred site. They're all over Europe, more than a hundred of them. Tourists visit them every day. But at any of them, if you have the right materials and the right method, you can enter the other realm."

"Nonsense," Swami said after the collective stunned pause. "We would have heard of this."

"Not necessarily," Tracy said. "The secret's been closely guarded. In most places, I daresay, it's even been forgotten. The group whose records I obtained…they were quite protective of the information. Which suggests to me that it's true."

Landon stared at the map. "Wait. Is one of those sites…the actual Underworld?"

Tracy lifted his chin, pleased that Landon had caught on. "I think the odds are fairly high. Wouldn't it be regarded as a sacred site, after all? So. What do we know of the so-called Underworld? The detailed account from the late Sanjay told us a good deal, and his information corresponded with many of our ancient records."

"We know it's a cave in Greece," Swami said.

"Near the sea," Landon added.

"Indeed." Tracy clicked to the next graphic: a detail of the same map, this time showing only Greece and vicinity, with orange circles placed around five of the sites. "Sacred sites that are caves in Greece, along the coast." He smiled at his team. "Who's up for an expedition?"

CHAPTER NINE

ZOE CONNOLLY LEANED CLOSE TO HER LAPTOP COMPUTER AND squinted to make out the lines of text on the screen in the bright sun. Its cord trailed off her lap and plugged into a briefcase-sized solar-powered charger.

A generator hummed on the hillside a few meters away, sending electricity down to power Liam's video games along with some lights and even a refrigerator. They were getting quite high-tech in the Underworld lately. Still, Zoe preferred to use natural sources, such as her solar charger, as far as she could. Supplemented with supernatural in her case, a talent reawakened with her immortality. But in truth, even as a blind mortal she'd often been told by others that her ability to identify things by sound, smell, or general "feel" bordered on uncanny.

She used to attribute it to necessity, the reliance on other senses that any blind person had to resort to. But lately, in reviewing all her past lives, she realized she often had accessed the world's energies with a native fluency that some would have called witchcraft (and some did, in occasional harrowing episodes over her lifetimes). However, the powers had never surged through her as strongly as they did with her two immortal bodies: as Hekate and now as newly-immortal Zoe.

She glanced at the battery level on the laptop and found

it sinking. The solar charger collected energy slowly, and seldom kept up with Zoe's computer usage. She turned her palm upright in the sun and drew in energy until her hand felt almost on fire. Then with her supercharged hand she touched the shell of her laptop delicately, right over its battery. The screen glowed brighter. The battery icon filled to black in a nanosecond. Satisfied, Zoe shook out her hand and blew on it. It would hurt for a minute from that intense sunburn, but, nice thing about immortality, the damage wouldn't last.

She sensed Tabitha swooping in. She squinted up into the blue winter sky, and in a few seconds the ghost horse soared into view, Tab's long blonde hair streaming like a flag above it. Tab landed the spirit animal on the hillside and hopped off.

Pulling the horse by its ivy-willow reins, Tab walked to Zoe. She was wearing those gorgeous leather boots Zoe adored. Her cheeks were rosy, and in her oversized sunglasses, fingerless black gloves, and thigh-length multi-zippered leather coat, she looked like some steampunk adventurer just descended from her aeronautic vehicle.

So hot. Quite unfair.

"Got yourself properly dropped out of college?" Zoe asked.

"Yep." Tab eased down beside her. "For now." She sounded wistful.

"Sucks," Zoe said. "After taking all that trouble to get into it."

"Whatevs. I wasn't doing so awesome in classes anyway." Tab pulled off a glove and flexed her fingers. "What about you? All dropped out of life in Wellington?"

"Yeah. My parents know what's up, of course. But I quit my job, and the story for them and everyone else is I'm having depression issues and needed to go abroad for special treatment." Zoe grimaced at the computer screen full of the curriculum vitae of Thanatos members. "Not exactly untrue."

Tab wrapped the horse's reins around her boot, then

planted her foot against the rock to hold it there. She gazed out across the hills and shores, eyes unreadable behind her sunglasses. "I'm sorry I was a jerk to you. I like you so much, and I...I screwed it up."

The knot in Zoe's chest finally began to relax. For weeks now she had carried around so many unpleasant feelings, mainly fear because of Thanatos, but also resentment and hurt because Tab, her first real hook-up in this lifetime, had treated her casually, like a one-night stand. Now that Tabitha apologized for it, sounding small and contrite, Zoe realized hearing the words was all she had truly wanted.

So instead of unloading some lofty speech onto Tab as she had sometimes envisioned, she ended up saying, "It's all right. I like you too, loads. But it's not like we had an agreement. I just...feel better knowing you. You cheer me up."

"Yes!" Tab sounded more her warm, gushing self again. "I mean, look, I'm the last person who thinks we ought to base everything we do on our past lives. But still, you and me, all those past lives—we had tons of fun, and you totally made me happy when we hung out. But can you think of one time we had an actual successful love thing going on? Hekate and Dionysos is probably the closest, and even that..." Tab tilted her head at Zoe. "I haven't gotten that far yet, but it kind of feels like it fizzled."

"I've not quite got that far either, but I have the same impression." Zoe smiled wryly. "I think some lives I didn't even know you. Other times we had a fling, or we were friends. There's some nice memories, but, jeez, it's nothing like Adrian and Sophie. They've got one epic love story after another, life after life, starring the two of them and no one else."

"I kind of envy that," Tab said.

"Doesn't everyone. Still, even if we're just friends..." Zoe slid her fingers under Tab's bare hand, the one from which she'd removed the glove. At the touch of skin, she felt sweetness and gentle desire emanating from Tab, which intensified as Tab closed her grip around Zoe's hand.

"There's things friends can do." Tab's voice had lowered. "Especially if they're going to live a long time, and might want to be...flexible."

Zoe swallowed, leaning toward Tab. "Mm-hm."

Their lips met, the kiss delicate as it formed around the obstacles—the laptop balanced on Zoe's thighs, the sunglasses Tab still wore, the uneven rocks they sat upon. Tab slid her gloved hand into Zoe's short hair and held her closer, and her lips became more ardent. Zoe scooted over till their legs touched, managing to do so without overturning the computer or breaking the kiss.

A flicker of interference crossed her mental screens.

Tabitha felt it too, and sighed against Zoe's lips. "Niko."

"Figures." Zoe nibbled Tab's lower lip, a lingering touch that stretched into several seconds.

By the time Nikolaos landed his spirit horse in front of them, they were only just pulling apart. He stayed on the saddle, watching with keen interest. "No, please. Continue. Why do you think I immortalized you two together, if not to watch things like this?"

"Gross," Zoe informed him, though she grinned.

"Old perv." Tab chucked a rock at him, which sailed through his horse's ethereal body and bounced down the hillside.

He slid off the saddle and strolled to them, reins in his hand. "What's new, loves?"

"Well..." Zoe recollected what she'd been doing before the distracting last few minutes, and nodded at her computer screen. "My parents sent a few more bits of information. They pulled some hacker tricks to track down who owns those mobile phones and email addresses, and found out what they could about these people."

"Not that it helps, though, right?" Tab said. "We can't call the cops on them for being in a secret club. Especially when we found out by totally illegal spying."

"There's that," Niko said. "Also we can't tell where exactly they are right now, or what they're doing. Any luck breaking into the email accounts?"

"For some. I'm feeling my way into how to do cyber-magic, which, needless to say, isn't something I ever learned in Hekate's day. But..." Zoe twisted her lips in frustration. "They're all being too cagey. None of the messages say anything that strikes me as terribly useful. What about you? Been to look in on Landon and Krystal?"

"Yes." Niko pushed back his fleece hat and scratched his forehead. "They're still hiding, recuperating. Seem to have met more Thanatos members recently. Landon's messages suggest some conversations that were lately had, and plans lately made. They're evasive as to details, as you say." Niko whipped the end of his reins against his leg. "If only I'd been around on that day, whenever it was."

"Now Adrian's over there, though, right?" Tab said.

"Not yet," Zoe answered. "He's in New Zealand first. Then he'll go to wherever Krystal is."

"So what should *we* do in the meantime?" Tab asked.

"We take care of Sophie and Liam," Zoe said.

"But how?"

"I don't know exactly," Zoe confessed. "But I was thinking." She glanced up again at Niko. "You've done me good, both of you. Not just these last couple months, but when I was Hekate. It was mostly you two who got me feeling alive again after my parents died." Zoe looked down the slope into the gray-green valley of olives and oaks. "It was an awful place to be. And that's exactly the place Sophie's in now. We've got to help her recover."

"If you've got any ideas, I'll do 'em," Tab said. "That girl is made of awesome. No one knows it better than me." Tab pulled off the sunglasses and peered at Zoe and Niko. "So how'd we do it in the old days? How'd Hekate get fixed?"

Zoe lifted her face again in question to Niko, since she herself hadn't reached those memories yet, while he had lived with them a couple of years longer.

He was already gazing at her, green eyes narrowed in the sun. "Long story. But if you want the useful parallel, then it's this: we're a bit thin on the ground now, same as we were then. There's only so much the handful of us can do. We need help."

"But we can't make new immortals yet," Zoe said. "The tree isn't ready. I'd make it grow faster with magic, but that might screw up how the fruit works; I just don't know."

"Not other immortals, necessarily," Niko said. "Allies."

"How can we be sure who to trust?" Zoe asked.

He nodded, his gaze climbing the hillside. "Isn't that the eternal human question?"

Chapter Ten

EKATE HAD WEEDED AND PRUNED THE UNDERWORLD'S GAR-
dens and orchards. Persephone had instructed her how
to care for each plant, and they had exchanged ideas about
new plants to try. Dionysos returned to the living world to
preside over a festival, and came back a few days later to report it had gone better than expected.

"We do still have allies, lots of them," he assured Hekate,
along with the souls of Hades, Persephone, and Demeter,
who stood with her. "Yes, Thanatos is still going strong too—
I heard stories about vicious speeches and new recruits. But
the good people are with us, and they're the majority."

Hermes reported the same when he dropped in for his
visits, which he did every few days. He had gone back out
into the world about a month after Hekate's parents' death,
because confining Hermes to one place was as impossible as
keeping water cupped forever in your hands. But he always
did return, reliable as rain (if as erratically scheduled), and
brought Hekate gifts each time: food, potted plants, an interesting animal she could study before releasing it back into
the wild, or linen and wool for clothes. "Next time," he kept
chiding her, "you'll go out into the world and get these things
yourself."

It was her father who finally tipped her courage into resolve.

One day in summer, she went into the fields and found Hades surrounded by a small crowd of souls. He appeared to be talking to them like a teacher, addressing each in turn and soliciting their responses. Persephone wandered nearby, listening to him, running her intangible hand through the branches of a willow.

"Ah, Hekate," Hades said. "Good, you're here. I've collected a group of souls who need justice. They're from areas we know how to get to, and places we've usually been able to speak the language."

Hekate smiled. "You know, Father, most people retire from their life's work after they've died."

"Only because most people can't do their life's work in the Underworld. But I can. I've done the seeking and sorting, at least. You'll have to do the errands into the living world, or send someone to. I'm sure Hermes or Dionysos would help."

Hekate glanced over the assembled souls. They watched her with hope in their benign faces. A middle-aged man, an elderly woman, three young men of various sizes and coloring, four women ranging from teens to thirties, and a boy and a girl not yet ten years old. All murdered, for that was who her father weeded out of the crowds. All with grieving families who wanted their murderers found and brought to justice. Hekate could see it done, if she only would.

You see, she told herself, *you are not alone in your grief. People's family members are murdered every day. You have hidden down here long enough.*

She met her mother's gaze, then her father's. Both of their faces radiated trust, pride, and encouragement.

Hekate swallowed, her mouth dry. But her voice carried clear enough. "Let me fetch a tablet. I'll write down the details."

That afternoon, Hekate walked to the entrance chamber, leading her black spirit horse, a stallion she had allowed to roam free in the fields these past months, since she hadn't been using him. He could have vanished to be reborn, for animals did that as well as humans, but he had remained. In fact, he still approached her nearly every day when she entered the fields, as if checking whether he was needed. Finally today she could reward his loyalty and take him out again.

She saddled him, and put on a light cloak over her gown. Even in the summer the winds would be chilly at those speeds, and she might be out long after sundown. In a sack over her shoulder she carried the wax tablet with the names and towns etched upon it. She planned to visit the nearest two towns today; that would be enough to occupy the afternoon and evening.

She mounted the horse, snapped the reins, and commanded, "Up!"

He soared out of the cave. The sunlight blinded her and warmed her. She twitched the reins northward, and the horse obeyed. Her vision adjusted to the daylight, and she caught her breath at the beauty of the land beneath her.

The air smelled of warm saltwater and wild herbs. The sea gleamed clear blue in its depths and crashed in white foam at the shore. The forest rolled out across the land, dipping into valleys where the trees turned brilliant green at river shores, and climbing halfway up mountains before giving way to crags and cliffs. A flock of red and white spirit-world birds, easily a thousand of them, wheeled together above the trees and soared out to sea. Chirps, roars, and screeches arose from the beasts hidden under the trees.

Oh world, you've never stopped being magnificent, and I've neglected you.

But as she followed the landmarks to the location of the first village, and lowered the horse to touch the ground at the crossover spot, fear stole back into her heart. This was farther from the Underworld than she'd been since her parents' death, but it was still the spirit realm. The living world, that realm ruled by the most dangerous blood-spilling creature of all—humans—could she cross its boundary again and re-enter that maelstrom?

Heart pounding, she tied up her horse and stepped to the switch-over spot her fellow immortals had set up for this village, a tall bundle of sticks set up in pyramid shape, their ends planted wide in the earth, their tips tied together with strips of blue cloth. She closed her hand around one of the fluttering strips, and breathed deeply. But her fear continued to mount, rising all the way into panic.

She stood immobile and sick, eyes closed, wondering if she would have to return to the Underworld in defeat.

Someone's essence intruded on her terror-hazed mind. Hermes. She opened her eyes and turned in his direction, her hand still clutching the cloth strip.

He landed his brown spirit horse a few paces from her. His red cloak swirled in the warm wind. "Good afternoon." He studied her a moment, then dismounted and led his horse to her.

"You followed me?" Her voice felt faint.

"I was roaming about and sensed you this direction. Quite far from where you usually are lately. Thought I'd investigate."

"I'm on an errand. For the souls. The way my parents used to." But she stood motionless, surely looking an anxious mess.

The bright sun lit up the green of his eyes. "Has something happened? Are you all right?"

"Nothing. Only..." She let go of the cloth strip and dropped her hand to her side, where she clutched a fold of her skirt instead. "I'm not sure I can go back to that realm."

He clicked his tongue. "Is that all? Gracious, I thought someone had tried to murder you again, the way you looked. Here, wait a moment." He tied up his horse next to her stallion, then walked up and interlaced his fingers with hers. His hand felt so warm that she knew her own must be clammy.

"Look at me," he said.

She did. Her heart still palpitated, but the presence of a friend took the sickening edge off her panic—his warm hand, familiar green eyes, youthful shaven face, and ever-mischievous half-smile.

"You can do this," he said.

She nodded, just once and jerkily, but an agreement nonetheless.

"I'm coming with you," he went on. "But only for my own peace of mind. I want to make sure no one tries any nastiness on you again. You *could* do this alone, we both know that."

Her mouth relaxed into a sheepish smile. She fully doubted she could do this alone. "Please come," she said.

"Shall we? Three, two, one."

They switched realms. The forested wilderness transformed into a green and gold field of barley. They stood on a dirt path between the rows, their feet atop a small heap of grains and flowers.

"Ah." Hermes lifted his sandal and looked down at the crushed red poppies. "We're standing upon our offerings."

Hekate breathed in the warm air, which smelled of barley grass and the smoke of a distant cook-fire. Men and women worked far off in a neighboring field, singing a cheerful, chant-like song as they picked vegetables. She let out her breath. The knot of panic melted to a small kernel. The living world: it had charmed her when she was younger, and now she remembered why.

Hermes let go of her hand and removed one of his gold-threaded sandals to shake grain out of it. He replaced it on his foot. "Ready?" he asked.

She nodded and stepped down from the heap of offerings.

"Hurray," he remarked, and flung a handful of red poppy petals into the air above her.

She smiled and shook them off her head. Then she turned toward the village and set off down the path, Hermes at her side.

CHAPTER ELEVEN

ADRIAN'S DAD LET HIM GET THROUGH THE WHOLE PICNIC DINner, eaten outdoors in the summery spirit realm of New Zealand, before he brought up Sophie. Adrian had told him about the disaster not long after it had happened, in a broken and jumbled phone call. Adrian hadn't told him the whole of it since then—how their relationship had pretty much come unraveled as a result. They didn't get to talk much, given the caution they had to use so Thanatos wouldn't target his dad, nor use his dad to find Adrian.

Still, his dad and Sophie had met once, and had got along well. Adrian knew his dad must be concerned about her.

After the dessert of packaged chocolate biscuits, his dad crumpled up the wrapper and tucked it into their grocery bag, and finally said, "Your poor girl."

He sounded so sympathetic, so understatedly grieved, that Adrian already felt tears sting his tired eyes in response.

"It's all my fault."

"No. Oh Adrian, don't think that."

"She doesn't…" Adrian scowled at the crumbs scattered on his lap, and pulled in a breath to steady his voice. "She can't bear to be around me right now. I don't blame her. If I hadn't got involved with her, none of it would have happened. She hasn't said it that way, but of course it's true. Everyone sees it."

"You wouldn't wish such a thing on anyone. Everyone knows that, too. You didn't know this would happen."

"I should have, though. I knew the kind of people that were after me. I'm..." Adrian shook his head and shut up before indulging in some rant in which he called himself a monster, a criminal, a curse. Even if he was all those things.

"You have the right to be happy," his dad said. "Same as anyone. The right to be with people you love."

"Unless they don't want to be with me."

Kiri bounded over, returning from a romp in the meadow. Adrian turned to her and began picking seeds out of her fur.

"Give her time," his father said. "It's still so horribly fresh for her. I think she'd rather have you near, even if she isn't herself right now. I do speak as someone who's known what it's like."

Adrian glanced in guilt at his dad, who had lost not only his own parents in recent years, but his wife when Adrian was just eight. They'd hardly ever talked about that. About Adrian's mum when she was alive, yes, but not about their grief in losing her.

"It felt like it took ages for us to get over it," Adrian said. "Years."

"Some part of you never gets over it. But the worst is over sooner than you think. A matter of months, I'd say. People are resilient, though it never feels that way at first."

"Well, in any case, she's got friends and family with her, and I can't just be there all the time. I've got to be out here doing something about Thanatos. What exactly, I don't know, but something."

"That worries me more than anything you've said. Isn't there some—some army or detective force you can set to this task instead of doing it yourself?"

"Not so far. I think we have to form our own armies and forces." Adrian flicked the last seed out of Kiri's fur, and sent his dad a hopeful glance. "Once the next fruits are ripe, you'll become immortal too, right? Come on, do. We'll save you a slice."

He had asked before, and his dad had chuckled and turned him down. But this time Adrian's voice wavered with anxious sincerity. He couldn't bear the thought of watching his dad age and eventually die—or be slaughtered by Thanatos.

But his dad shook his head. "That way's not for me. Don't you think I want to be with your mum someday in those nice calm fields? Then starting over again eventually...yes, I think we'd both like that."

Adrian bowed his head in acceptance, but the last hopeful part of his heart seemed to break at the answer. Of course his dad would be among the minority who actually didn't want immortality.

Someday everyone would leave him. Everyone.

Sophie had taken Liam out of school for the coming semester, so he was free to grieve and recover until at least September. As for herself, Oregon State University had a bereavement leave option for students who had lost someone close, and Sophie definitely qualified. It gave her a quarter off—basically three months, till around the beginning of spring—before she had to decide whether or not she would take up classes again.

She discussed the quandary with Tab and Zoe, as they all sat beside a pool of the underground river. It was the same pool Hades, Persephone, and Hekate used to bathe in. It still looked much the same as it had three or four thousand years ago. Rocks like these were slow to change, evidently, even with constant water running through them.

"Would I be safe going back?" Sophie speculated. "Because I kind of don't think so. Even with all the police protection."

"I know the feeling." Chin on her hand, Tab glumly

watched the river. "If I go back to being Tab On The Internet Who Interviews Famous People And Goes To Parties, which I would totally love to do, then some Thanatos asshole is just going to car-bomb me again." She sighed. "Tomorrow's New Year's Eve, and I have at least three awesome party invitations, and I can't go to any of them."

"Life is hard," Zoe said dryly. She lay on Sophie's other side, belly down, chin on her folded arms. "I wish I could protect you all with magic. Some spell that honestly is bombproof and bulletproof. But the only spells that strong are temporary, more of an emergency measure. They fall apart in a minute or two, after getting you out of a tough spot. So, yeah, I'm useless."

"You're not useless," Sophie said.

"My protection failed you." Zoe sounded quietly heartbroken.

Though Sophie's panic leaped up again at the reminder of that night, she insisted, "No. I mean, I don't know, maybe without your spell, we'd *all* be dead—me, Adrian, Liam..." This was getting too scary. Her voice didn't want to work anymore.

"Still. Not exactly a win." Zoe kept her eyelashes lowered.

"Girl, you rocked it," Tab told her. "You made Sophie throw Quentin across a field, and shoot Krystal. That was awesome. I mean, I wasn't even there, but I am sure it was awesome."

Sophie said nothing. She had fully dropped back into her nauseating fear. She watched the slow black swirl of the river, listened to it gurgle around the rocks. Told herself to breathe.

"Sorry," Tab said a second later. "I'm a douche. Nothing was awesome about that night—of course it wasn't. Sorry, I'm really sorry."

Sophie nodded to reassure her, but her throat still felt too clenched up to speak.

Zoe reached out and curled her hand around Sophie's

ankle. A few breaths, and Sophie's panic began to subside. The clammy chill receded from her hands and feet, replaced by everyday warmth. Her stomach stopped fluttering, and she breathed deep again.

She glanced shyly at Zoe. "Magic?"

Zoe pulled her hand back, folding it beneath her other arm. "Yeah."

"Better. Thanks."

"Only treats the symptoms, though. The cause...that takes time."

"It's too early for you to worry about what exactly you're going to do with your life," Tab told Sophie. "You just need to start feeling better. Fix your trauma."

"Jeez, Tab, blunt much?" Zoe said.

But Sophie nodded, unoffended. She looked at that list on her phone every day, and wished she could check off just one damn thing from it. So far, no go.

"Adrian texted me this morning," she said, "basically just saying hi, and that he was going to the US now. But even that, just seeing his name...I freak out. Everything freaks me out."

Zoe lowered her arm over the rocks and dipped one finger in the water. "Me too. So I can imagine it's even worse for you."

"Is it 'cause you don't know whether you want him back?" Tab asked Sophie.

"Again, blunt," Zoe accused.

"I'm not saying you *have* to decide," Tab added. "I totally think you should feel better first before making the big life choices."

Sophie rearranged her legs in their criss-cross. "Kind of. But I also worry it won't be him sending the message; that some Thanatos jerk has captured him and is texting me to say they're about to kill him, or...I don't know. I imagine all kinds of scary things. As to the relationship..." She swallowed and continued, "I just want to be able to talk to him without feeling all weird."

Tabitha nodded. "You associate him with what happened. He's your trauma trigger—or one of them anyway. So, I bet if you get over your trauma you'll be golden."

"But how do I do that?" Sophie asked. "Other than having Zoe give me a magic boost every so often."

"Which I'll do," Zoe said. "But it isn't a long term solution. Time mainly, I'd say. That's the cure."

A minor commotion from the tunnels diverted Sophie's attention. Liam bounded in from the bedchamber, swinging a flashlight. Rosie trotted up behind him, panting. Liam's clothes were rumpled and his dark wavy hair stood in an unruly cloud, its dyed-green streak corkscrewing up and outward. He had evidently just woken up. He'd been up half of last night playing his new video games with Niko, and had slept in. But now he looked alert and re-energized.

"Hey," Sophie greeted.

"Hey, man," Tabitha said. "You're so late for breakfast it's pretty much going to be dinner."

"Dude," Liam said. He looked at each of the women in quick succession, his gaze ending upon Sophie. "I got to the Poseidon stuff."

CHAPTER TWELVE

For Liam, these past-life memories were seriously weird. Like, he could remember being an old guy, five hundred years ago or something, and having all these deep thoughts an old guy would have. And they'd make sense at the time, while Liam was dreaming or spacing out and living those memories. Then he'd come back to himself and think, *How'd that get into my head? I couldn't have come up with that.*

Which was how he knew the memories were real. Of course, they had to be, since the Underworld and the immortals and the spirit horses and the whole other realm were real. He felt like he'd been dropped into the fantasy world of his video games, which was totally cool with him.

The reason they were living here for now, though…that sucked. No, "sucked" didn't cover it. Sucked *ass*. It was a nightmare.

His parents were dead. He and Sophie were orphans. Maybe it would be cool to be an orphan if your parents had been jerks, or if you'd never known them, and after they died you inherited a castle or something. But Liam loved his parents. They'd been dorks sometimes, but they were all right. They had loved him and taken care of him even when *he* was being a dork. And some freaking evil cult had torched their house to the ground and killed them. They were trying to kill

Adrian, but the bastards didn't even care who else they got in the attempt.

This would have shut down Liam's brain completely, he figured, except that he still got to see them. They weren't actually gone. So...he kind of got to put off his grief. After the shock of realizing he'd still get to talk to them for years and years to come, he managed to chill a little.

Their therapist told him to make a list, just for his own eyes, of positive things in life he might look forward to, even if they'd be a long time in the future.

Liam's list so far was:

go surfing in Hawaii

go parasailing

get a monkey or a forest dragon or a sugar glider or other awesome new pet

see Landon and Krystal and anyone who helped them dead or jailed for life

Yeah, he wanted revenge. In a big way. No one was ever going to talk him out of that, even though the therapist kept telling him to let go of "hostility" and let the police take care of punishment.

But with all this supernatural stuff to explore, past lives plus the good chance of becoming immortal himself—hell yeah, immortal!—well, Liam figured he could survive. Someday he might even use his immortal strength to deal out his revenge personally. That was the kind of idea that kept you going.

But his sister was unhappy. He could see that. She had to be the grownup in the family now, which had to stress her out. And there was some kind of weirdness between her and Adrian, because she felt guilty or Adrian felt guilty or they both did, and Liam couldn't do anything about that.

Sophie kept telling him it was important to get to the life

long ago in which he had been Poseidon. His dad said the same, because now his dad, being a soul, could remember all his past lives without any of the confusion of sorting it out that living people had to go through. His mom and dad just *knew* everything now, or at least everything they had known in any past life.

And what his dad said was that he—Dad—had been this woman, the immortal Demeter, Persephone's mom, in the era when Liam had been Poseidon.

"And you ought to be warned about this, Liam," his dad said in the Underworld a couple of days ago, after taking Liam aside so they could talk privately. "Demeter and Poseidon, they had a…well, 'relationship' is too grand a word. It didn't last. But they hooked up for a short time, as you kids might say."

Liam's tongue had frozen in his mouth. His horror must have shown on his face.

"Yeah," his dad went on. "I'd feel that way too, if I were still alive. But I wanted to assure you, it was *just* that one life. And it didn't last long in that one. Didn't work out. A non-issue basically. Listen, souls get into all kinds of configurations with each other. Ask anyone down here—or your immortal friends. In any case, those Greek days were a long, long time ago. Every other life since, when we've known each other at all, you and I have only been friends. Or family when we're lucky. Like in this life."

He sounded so encouraging, so *not* totally embarrassed, that Liam tried to act mature too. He nodded. "Okay. Right. Cool."

"Would you feel better if we never talked about this again?" his dad asked.

Liam nodded immediately, and escaped to the game-room cave off the bedchamber for a long session of electronic pirate-ship combat.

So yeah, he did want to get to the Poseidon life, but that one detail, even if it was a non-issue, kind of put him off.

Also, getting to that life was taking him longer than the few days Sophie had guessed at because he kept getting distracted by the lives in between. There was *so much sex* in them. He needed to screech to a halt and observe. So he ended up losing a few days in learning about all the women he'd done interesting things to in past lives. (He'd pretty much always been a guy, and always interested in women, though there'd been the occasional exceptions, which were weird, though also interesting.)

Once he had accepted that sex in real life—at least in his soul's past—could be all kinds of things, including far more awesome or a lot more boring than it looked in internet porn, Liam finally sped his memories up again to travel backward in time.

And last night, after a marathon of pirate battles played against Niko, Liam passed out on his bed and fell straight into ancient Greece.

When he sensed he was in a new lifetime, one he hadn't seen yet, he flipped to the start the way he'd learned to do. Everything made a lot more sense that way, like reading a book from the beginning instead of trying to page backward from the last chapter.

You didn't usually remember anything from birth or the first couple of years. Then the memories started coming in, patchy at first but getting stronger with age.

With Poseidon the first thing he remembered was, of course, the sea.

CHAPTER THIRTEEN

POSEIDON PLOWED INTO THE SEA ON HIS SMALL LEGS WHEN he couldn't have been more than three years old, on his home island of Skyros. His mother shrieked in terror. She and his uncle ran toward him as the waves knocked him down and the undertow pulled him out. But little Poseidon wasn't afraid, not even when the current flipped him upside-down underwater, and swimming creatures bumped against his arms and legs.

His mother hauled him out. Poseidon coughed the salt-water onto the sand, then beamed at his worried uncle, and looked wistfully at the brilliant blue sea while his mother harangued him to never, ever walk into it again. It was not a promise he kept.

His father had died at sea when Poseidon was a baby, and now he lived with his mother, uncle, and little sister. As Poseidon grew up he learned he was very strong. Stronger than anyone on the island, even when he was only ten. He never got sick. When rocks or barnacles scratched him, the cuts always healed so quickly that no one could believe it. Poseidon figured it was the healing quality of seawater, but he had to admit it didn't do that for everyone.

Once when he was thirteen, and helping launch a newly-built boat, it slipped off its ramp and crashed onto his leg and broke his bones. *That* hurt like ten hells. His family and neighbors thought he'd be crippled, or at least that the bones would take months to heal. He had a dark night of thinking he'd never swim or run again. He begged the gods to heal him, promising he'd take extra care of his mother and little sister, would fish for them every day and bring in as much as he could. The gods must have heard him, for in the morning his leg was fine.

This time everyone's amazement turned to fear. It really must be the touch of the gods, they said.

"Then why aren't you happy?" he asked his mother.

"Because it probably means the gods have some grand plan for you, and I don't want them to take you. I want you to stay here with us."

He assured her that staying on Skyros was all he planned to do. But his curiosity about the greater world, or at least the greater sea, grew along with the rest of him. Poseidon swam tirelessly and handled boats like an expert, even as a child. He understood the water. The curl of a wave, the force of a current, the strength of a surge, the pull of a tide; he saw or felt them easily, and navigated his boat or turned his body accordingly, and always avoided being smashed against rocks or menaced by sea creatures.

It even felt like he could influence the water, as if it was listening to him when he was near—but that was impossible, surely. Unless there was a god of the waters who invisibly cooperated with him? Perhaps that was the divine touch everyone spoke of. If so, he judged it a blessing. Despite going out in a boat nearly every day from childhood onward, the vessels he was in almost never overturned; he'd been in far fewer sea accidents than most islanders. And when the boats did overturn, he always easily caught hold of all his shipmates in the water and brought them to safety. Sometimes it felt as if he sent out an urgent wish for the current to shove a sinking friend back up to the surface—and, curiously, the water obeyed.

The island's position in the middle of the Aegean Sea put them in the path of occasional raiders from Anatolia. Usually these violent men arrived on just two or three ships at a time, and the soldiers of Skyros could fight them off, killing those they could and sending the rest sailing away.

But one cloudy autumn day, as a storm approached, the worst possibility materialized. A fleet of nineteen Anatolian ships appeared on the horizon, arrowing straight for Skyros. Poseidon and his fellow islanders ran to the shore, but they all knew they couldn't defeat a force like this. The Anatolians would sink any boats they launched or deflect any arrows they shot, then they'd sweep onto shore, rape or kill or kidnap everyone, and steal everything of worth.

So with every bit of his desperate mind, Poseidon embraced the sea, the large patch of it that still lay between them and the raiders. He pulled in the turbulence of the storm, and pushed with all his will.

The sea dipped as if it were sinking, then rose again in a huge wave that rolled toward the Anatolian ships, growing until it was higher than their masts. The sailors scrambled to be ready, but there was nothing they could do against such a wave. It scooped up one ship, then two, three, and four more under its curl before it finally crested and crashed. The ships caught up in the wave were plunged deep below. The ensuing cataract of white water turned the surface into a roiling mess, and swirled and smashed the remaining boats against each other until almost every one was swamped or broken.

The Skyros citizens cheered in victory—except Poseidon, staring stunned at what he had called forth. The Anatolians pulled their remaining men into the two most seaworthy boats, turned tail, and rowed away amid a sea of wreckage.

The people of Skyros chanted grateful prayers, and chattered about the strange wave.

"I've heard such things can arise at sea during a storm," one of the men said.

"My father's seen such a wave, yes," another man said. "Swallowed up three ships before his eyes."

"But waves usually go toward shore, not away from it," the first man said.

All eyes turned to Poseidon. He gave a sheepish shrug, and turned toward home before anyone could ask further questions.

Poseidon was thankful not to have to throw the sea against anyone for a long while after that. Enemies stayed away, perhaps hearing of the treacherous waters around Skyros, and he was able to return to his calm existence of sailing, fishing, and swimming.

In warm weather, swimming was his favorite. As he grew up, his strength increased, and soon he could easily swim all day. When his mother spent a few days away, visiting family in other villages or taking pigs or linen to markets, Poseidon sometimes took very long swims indeed.

He started by swimming to the tiny island of Skyropoula, just off Skyros, which would have been a challenging swim for any ordinary person. But it was too easy for him, so he continued on, swimming past the little island, southwest all the way to the nearest point of mainland Greece. He knew how to get there from his many voyages by ship, accompanying merchants. From the bearing of passing ships in the distance, along with the position of the sun and the sense that the sea itself gave him, he felt as confident as if he were walking a well-marked road, instead of swimming alone in a sloshing, deep expanse of chilly salt water. The fins of dolphins, whales, sharks, and other great fish slid into view above the surface near him from time to time, but he felt no fear. The creatures wouldn't hurt him. Being in harmony with them was part of his water-sense.

Euboia, the Greek land he finally reached on such swims, was technically an island, but it was so huge and nestled so close to the mainland that it was practically a part of it. Every time he approached Euboia, swimming in among the boats that came and went from its harbors, the people on the ships shouted to him and tried to rescue him. A man overboard! Surely he needed saving. But he laughed and shouted back that he was fine, only swimming, and waved off any help.

Of course, word did get back to Skyros that he was behaving in this eccentric way. That, along with his other uncanny attributes, damaged his eligibility as a potential husband. He had a string of sweethearts, but their families always wound up disapproving of him, and it was just as well, as he didn't love any of the women long enough to wish to spend his life with them. After his mother fretted a while, she gave up and let him live his bachelor existence, and turned her attention to his younger sister, who soon did marry and began producing grandchildren for her.

Poseidon's appearance and strength lingered at around that of a man in his twenties even after he entered his forties and beyond. It became a problem. People who had known him his whole life now looked uneasy when they met him, and kept studying him as if trying to discover the mark of some demon. He got tired of it, and took up residence alone farther down the coast, though he still served in the island's navy in order to protect his village.

Long-distance swimming remained one of his greatest joys. He set out on a swim to Euboia on an idyllic summer day when he was fifty-five. The water flowed like cool crystal around him, shimmering in all shades of blue from palest turquoise in the shallows to cobalt in the depths. The sun flashed white fire on the surface. Boaters near the mainland once again tried to rescue him as he swam in, and he declined. He rode the surf in to the rocky point. His feet met the bottom, and he waded onto shore. A steep hill rose up from the beach. A small temple, painted white, stood halfway up the slope among the pines.

Poseidon waded into the tide pools. He squeezed water

out of the linen loincloth he wore, and tilted his head to tap the water out of his ears.

"Where did you swim from?"

The question was demanding, and spoken by some female. He turned.

She sat on a rock in the shade of a boulder, her legs in the water of the deepest tide pool. Her skirts, a grayer shade of the green-blue of the water, were tucked up around her thighs to keep them from getting wet. She was probably in her late teens, and he would have hesitated to call her "pretty," given the unevenness of her nose, the thickness of her dark eyebrows, and the skinniness of her body. But her hair was beautiful, a sleek, loose fall of the darkest brown that glinted reddish around the crown of her head. And her eyes were arresting, some light color he couldn't make out from where he stood, with a graceful curve to their upper lids.

"Skyros," he answered, and waded closer to her.

She snorted. "No you didn't."

"I did. I'm a strong swimmer." He stepped into the next tide pool over from hers. Blue-gray with a hint of green, that was the color of her eyes. Like the sea in the shallows.

"You can't swim from Skyros. No one's *that* strong a swimmer."

"I am. Besides, can't you tell I'm from Skyros by my accent?"

She circled one bare leg in the water. "I suppose. But you could have hopped from a boat just off the point and swum the rest of the way."

"You think I'm lying?" He pretended to be insulted.

"Men lie all the time."

Now he snorted. He was likely three times her age; what did she know of such things?

He jingled the pouch he had tied to his waist, containing minor pieces of bronzework—rings and chains that could be bartered for food or goods. "I'm off to buy lunch. Then I'll come back here and swim away, and you can watch until I disappear over the horizon."

She flicked water at him with her toes. "Very well."

"Very well," he returned, and strolled off barefoot toward the village that lay over the hill.

"AMPHITRITE," LIAM SAID, INTO THE CONTEMPLATIVE QUIET that fell after he explained his dream. "That's who the girl was. I just know somehow."

Sophie felt a rush of poignancy, an echo of the feeling she had first experienced when Adrian brought her to the realization that they had shared love in the life before this one, and the life before that one, and the one before that…

She smiled at her dazed little brother. "Pretty cool, dude."

"I married her, right?"

"Yup," Tab said.

Eagerness rose in his face. "Who is she now?"

The three women glanced at each other and shrugged.

"Haven't looked her up yet," Zoe said. "But we can do."

"I bet Niko has." Tab pulled out her phone. "Ah, crap. Cave. No reception. Hang on, I'll run up to the surface and text him."

Liam sat still, gazing at the river as Tab jogged out. Though he was still his twelve-year-old self, skinny and out of proportion, with his muscles not having filled out over his fast-growing bones, he had a new depth of maturity in his dark eyes.

"When did I marry Amphitrite?" he asked. "How did it turn out for us? Did Thanatos kill us right away, or did we live a long time, or what?"

Sophie glanced again at Zoe, who had her brow furrowed as if trying to recall something she rarely thought about.

"Well, I know you guys were married a long time," Sophie said. "Longer than us; Hades and Persephone. What happened to you…I haven't gotten there yet, honestly." She shifted on the rocky riverbank, and tucked one ankle under the other. "I've kind of shut off the memories lately. I'm being a wuss. I haven't gotten much past Persephone and Hades dying. Right now, I just can't."

"I've not either." Zoe sat up straighter and rolled her shoulders back. "But we should. We need to know how it went. How we all moved forward. Even though it means how we all eventually died."

The three of them chewed on that in silence a few seconds.

"Maybe we can get the sum-up from one of the others, so it isn't a shock," Sophie said. "Niko or Adrian or Freya. They've had the memories longer; they already know."

"I've had sort of a sum-up from Adrian," Zoe said. "But he's had to piece some of it together secondhand, or from what we said to each other down here between other lives. Because he wasn't personally there for some of it—some of my life, I mean. Hekate's. Because…Hades and Persephone, they chose to be reborn."

A chill ran through Sophie—her usual reaction lately to anything startling—but it was followed by a rising warmth, a glow of…could it be hope? "Oh," she said. "Then I really should look at what happened, shouldn't I."

"He did say it was rather sweet, that next life," Zoe said. "For the both of you. No life is perfect, but from what he said, it's one you don't have to be afraid of."

Sophie breathed inward, cherishing the glimmer of hope as it spread through her body. Life did go on. It always would. "Well then," she said, lamely. "Okay."

Liam jumped to his feet. "I'm going to go tell Mom and Dad about the Poseidon stuff."

Good sign: Liam was excited enough that he was willing to discuss Poseidon with their dad again, even after the horrifying revelation that they'd been involved in a very Greek-mythology kind of way. Sophie rose. "Wait up. I'll come too."

Chapter Fourteen

*M*ESSING WITH MARS & PETAL. OUR POLICY? B/C I REALLY *want to mess with them*, Adrian texted Niko. Mars was their code name for Krystal; Petal for Landon.

It was New Year's Eve and he had just left New Zealand and arrived in spirit-realm North America, near the house in eastern Washington where Krystal was staying. She was the only one he could sense among Thanatos, though if he caught any other members by chance he'd happily mess with them too. Dawn had begun to lighten the clear sky, and an icy wind tore across the rolling brown land and worked its fingers into his coat. Kiri, lying across his feet on the floor of the bus, looked up at him with patiently suffering eyes.

"Sorry," he told her. "I know. New Zealand was comfier." He pulled out an extra blanket from under the seat and spread it over her.

A text buzzed in from Niko. *I admit I've messed w/ them a little. Good to keep them nervous, I reckon.*

Like what? Adrian responded. *Sending some msg? I was thinking of that.*

I went with a message, yes. But then you have to stay away a few days afterward as they'll be looking for you.

What msg did you send? Adrian asked. *You didn't tell us.*

Nothing much. Just something to scare Petal. Suppose you could do the same to Mars.

Yes. I plan to.

Adrian tucked away his phone and got up. Best do this now, before everyone here started waking up, and before he lost hold of the fury-driven courage blazing in him.

Kiri rose too, and shook off the blanket with reluctance. She gazed at him, awaiting instruction.

"No, lie down," he told her. "You stay."

It was quite possible he'd get shot at, and he didn't want Kiri to get hit. Even though she was immortal, there was no need to put her through the pain. He hadn't liked it one bit the time a Thanatos goon had shot her in the head, even though she'd quickly recovered.

She slid back down to her resting position. He draped the blanket over her. "Good girl."

He moved to the back of the bus and opened a metal storage box welded to the floor. From it he took the pieces of body armor he had lately bought, a grim Christmas present to himself. He put on the helmet and vest, which were thick and heavy enough to make him feel like a cop on riot duty. Or an astronaut. But they should also be enough to keep a bullet from taking him out too easily again. This was merely a mischief errand, definitely not worth risking his life or rendering him a hostage.

He buttoned up his coat over the vest and lowered the clear shield of the helmet. He walked through the frozen scrub until reaching the spot where Krystal's presence resonated. That obnoxious chord of Ares' personality now sang louder than he liked, the only familiar soul around for a long stretch.

She was above him, likely a second-story room. He considered for a moment, then jogged back to the bus and unstrapped the stepladder he had packed into the cargo space. He carried it back to the house's location, set it up, and climbed it.

Her presence glimmered in the mortal realm a half-meter or so to his right.

Taking his chances, he switched realms.

The ladder vanished and he fell—fortunately only a tiny distance. He ended up sprawled on hands and knees on a carpeted floor, in a quiet bedroom that felt luxuriously warm after the outdoor air. He crouched low, glancing around. He saw no one in the room except Krystal asleep in bed. Her red hair splashed across the pillow, and she snored softly. It was six a.m. The house was silent; the other inhabitants were probably still sleeping too.

Adrian rose and tiptoed to the mirror over the dresser. He had brought a dry-erase marker, but when his gaze fell on a tube of lipstick on the dresser's cluttered surface, he reckoned it was more intimidating to use that instead.

With his gloved hand he uncapped the lipstick and scrawled on the mirror in the largest letters that would fit:

MURDERER
THE UNDERWORLD
WILL CLAIM YOU
SOON

He put down the lipstick, took out his phone, and snapped a photo of his message.

CLICK. For some reason, the volume was way up on his phone, and the snapshot sound was like an alarm clock in the silence. He froze, watching Krystal in the mirror.

Her snores halted. She shifted, her eyes still closed. Then they opened, and faster than he could have thought possible in an injured person who had just woken up, she whipped a gun out from under her pillow and pointed it at him.

He hit the floor. The shot, ear-splittingly loud, blew a hole in the wall beside the mirror.

Time to go.

He switched realms and plummeted through frigid air into a prickly bush. He rolled out of it, dusted himself off, and sat on the frozen ground, watching the bright sunrise and waiting out the adrenaline rush until it subsided.

He allowed himself a smile as he imagined the chaos surely erupting in that house right now. But his smile faded as he reflected how pathetic it was that delivering a ghoulish message to someone he hated was the most fun he'd had lately.

"REALLY, KRYSTAL." ERICK TRACY FROWNED AT HER. "YOU could have killed poor Jim, you know."

She was back in bed after her shooting spree, sitting up and glaring at Tracy, Landon, and Jim Farnell, the worried homeowner and host. "There was a fucking intruder!" she said. "One of *them*! Check the security cameras!"

"We did," Jim said. "They don't cover the inside of your room, you know that. They show there was no one in the hall, or outside the house."

"Well, he found a way in," Krystal said. "Straight from the other dimension or whatever. Hello! It's possible."

"Look," Tracy said. "I can't prove they aren't coming after the pair of you. But I also can't prove they are."

"He wrote a goddamn message." Krystal swept her arm toward the mirror.

"Krystal, you're on painkillers. Strong ones." Tracy picked up the bottle of oxycodone from the dresser's top and rattled the pills. "You *could* have written it, acting under those, half asleep."

She gritted her teeth. "It. Was. Not. Me. I saw him!"

Landon touched one of the bullet holes in the wall. There were three near the mirror, and another in the floor. He knelt to look at it, then looked up at Tracy like a puppy seeking assurance from its mother. "They've messed with me too. This same kind of thing. I think they're finding ways to get to the two of us. Because we…because of Sophie's family."

Tracy sighed. "Again, it sounds as if we cannot prove such a thing. But, all right, if they've figured out where we are, then let's move house. It's going to cause further delay in our plans for Europe, but I see you're going to be causing delay over and over if we *don't* move."

"Thank you," Landon said.

"Fine," Krystal snapped.

Tracy looked about at the bullet holes, shook his head, and walked out of the room. He had arrangements to make, now mundane domestic ones as well as the grander ones for their expedition. Landon, though still the titular head of operations, had allowed Tracy to take charge of their European mission, since Tracy had been the one to get hold of the enemy documents. In order to make such arrangements, Tracy also needed access to the financial accounts controlled by Thanatos, and Landon had given up the electronic passwords for those too after only the weakest hesitation.

Tracy was fast becoming the most important person in the organization, if he wasn't already. But it meant he had more than enough to do, even with the help of the others. For example, they needed to locate pilots within the organization to fly them to Europe, so they wouldn't have to go through the highly trackable commercial airline system. Once they got to Europe they needed places to stay, personnel, supplies, and weapons. And they had to make sure all these arrangements were made with as little trace as possible. He suspected their emails and texts were occasionally being read—though how, he wasn't sure—so when communicating electronically, they all used codes, along with in-person meetings and calls from different phones whenever possible.

Then there was the sorcerer. Tenebra. Tracy had never met her, only heard of her. But if he could get her on their side, they stood a much better chance of obliterating the unnaturals. However, even locating her and being granted a meeting with her was proving a challenge of epic-quest proportions.

Meanwhile his team was going mental. What a headache. At least he now had Yuliya and her willing sensuality to relax him at night.

To be honest, yes, Tracy did suspect the immortals had found out who Landon and Krystal were, and that they might have been dropping in on those two from time to time to meddle with their peace of mind. Tracy would do the same if he were them. But that only made Thanatos' mission more imperative.

And if the immortals kept tracking down Krystal and Landon over and over, no matter where they were moved — well, Tracy wouldn't rock the boat by telling them so, but in that case Thanatos was much better off cutting its ties with the both of them. He could achieve the glory of conquering the immortals quite well without them.

CHAPTER FIFTEEN

ISTENING TO LIAM TELL HIS STORIES OF THE YOUNG LIFE OF Poseidon did boost Sophie's mood a little. He seemed more determined than ever to become immortal. But then, that had never been in question for him. Of course he'd leap at the chance. He was twelve; who wouldn't at that age?

So if he was going to eat the orange when it ripened — in probably just a couple of months now — she had to think hard about whether she would eat it too. On the one hand, invincibility and getting to join her friends and brother for as long as they were allowed to live. On the other, becoming a more central target to Thanatos than ever. Because maybe if she stayed mortal and renounced all ties to the immortals, they would consent to leave her alone. Didn't seem likely, but maybe.

It also didn't seem likely that becoming immortal would make her happy, though. So. No easy answers yet.

It was New Year's Eve. Adrian had just texted her along with Zoe, Niko, Freya, Liam, and Tab. *Got into Mars' room* was his message accompanying the photo of the lipstick scrawl.

As ever, her stomach clenched at the sight of his name, and even more so at the photo. It was partly the danger of his being in Krystal's room, and of inciting the woman with such a gesture. But what also disturbed her was the vicious long-ing for vengeance that arose inside her. She almost wanted to answer, *Why didn't you strangle her while you were there? That's what I really want.*

Except she didn't really want that. Well, sometimes she did. Then her sanity caught her from thinking such things. Over and over; that was how her day generally went.

While she thought about how to answer, the others responded.

My, aren't we dramatic, Niko texted.

Sweet!! Liam texted.

Nice, Zoe answered. *"Claim," really Ade?*

I know, Adrian texted back. *But I thought it was more Hades-ish or something.*

Is that fuchsia lipstick? Tab texted. *Ugh, that would look awful with her hair.*

Srsly, Freya agreed.

Finally Sophie responded, to him and the rest of the group: *Thanks. I hope it rattles them.*

Don't know if it'll help, Adrian answered in a minute. *But had to try something.*

Should set them scurrying to fuss abt their house security instead of focusing on latest nefarious plan, Niko answered. *So, good.*

They let the thread end there. At nightfall, Tab strolled up to Sophie, who was visiting her parents' souls. "Hey, girl," Tab greeted. "We were thinking of switching over and staying local, seeing how they celebrate in Greece."

Beyond her, near the river, stood Liam and Zoe. They both waved in encouragement.

"I don't know, I just figured I'd stay..." Sophie glanced at her parents.

But they motioned her off. "You should go," her mom said. "I would if I could."

She said it matter-of-factly, but the thought was so poignant that tears stung Sophie's eyes, and she was on the verge of planting her feet in the cave soil and refusing to budge.

Then her dad added, "Heck yeah. You and Liam go have fun, then come back and tell us what you saw."

When they put it like that, she couldn't argue, especially with Tab, Liam, and Zoe beckoning to her eagerly. So she followed her friends and brother out, though all the while she was thinking how it was her first New Year's since her parents died. Then soon it would be her dad's first birthday (in early February) since they died, then her first Valentine's Day since they died, then her own first birthday (March 21) since they died...how long would this accounting go on? The first full year? Longer?

Niko was out somewhere, as was Freya. They left the dog Rosie in the Underworld, since she seemed content to hang around with Mom and Dad and Pumpkin's souls, and anyway it was awkward to bring her on a spirit horse. Sophie climbed onto a horse behind Tab, and Liam onto one behind Zoe, and they darted up into the chilly, starry night.

They switched over outside a Greek village in the living world, a little seaside town relatively unfrequented by tourists, where consequently few residents spoke English, and native customs stayed strongly in force. Adrian, Zoe, and the other immortals ventured here occasionally to buy food or supplies. So Zoe knew her way, and led the others down to the square in the middle of the village.

Lights framed the awnings of taverns, and were strung across the narrow streets from roof to roof or balcony to balcony. Music rang everywhere too, most of it live: singers, acoustic guitars, accordions, and what sounded like a clarinet. Kids ran around with sparklers—at which Sophie relapsed into worry. Not only was fire on her list of triggers, but what if a kid got burned? Or accidentally set something on fire? At the idea of one of these sweet little white-painted houses going up in flames, she went cold with anxiety.

But then she caught sight of Liam grinning as some cute teenaged Greek girl raced up and pushed a slice of cake into his hands on a paper napkin. The girl handed out slices all around, and tried a few languages on them before guessing correctly, "English?"

"Yes!" they all chorused.

"Happy New Year," Zoe added.

"Happy New Year," the girl echoed, in a heavy accent that reminded Sophie of Niko's fake accent that first day she had met him. Then the girl spoke in a burst of lovely Greek syllables, which presumably meant the same thing in Greek.

By the time they had all tried, failed, tried again, and finally succeeded at pronouncing the Greek "Happy New Year," Sophie was smiling again.

The girl raced off down the street to hand out more cake. Sophie and her friends nibbled their slices. It turned out to be like pound cake, dense and lightly sweet. It had coconut sprinkled on top, which Sophie chewed with pleasure. She probably hadn't eaten coconut in months. *My first taste of coconut since they died*, she thought, but at least the thought was wry this time.

They found a spot to sit on the hood of an old red car parked near the square. An elderly man insisted with hand-waving gestures that they sit upon it, as the curbs and sidewalk chairs and balconies were already filled with people.

The countdown in Greek began at midnight, then everyone burst into cheers and embraces. Sophie smiled, accepting a high-five from a young local man who danced past with his friends. Tab smacked a kiss onto Sophie's cheek and Liam's, and Sophie returned it, though her thoughts traveled with sadness to Adrian. If she hadn't been such a mess and driven him away, he would be getting his proper New Year's kiss from her. Maybe sometime within this new year, she could repay him with sincere passion. Was that her wish? Should she even make a wish? Were there gods out there yet, above these puny immortals, who would take wishes and twist them cruelly the way they always did in myths and fairy tales?

The explosion blew her out of her brooding. It was right overhead, no higher than the buildings, and showered sparks down almost into their hair. Some people shrieked, and most cheered, but Sophie couldn't breathe. Panic clamped around her like a suffocating hand. *Just a firework, just a firework*, she thought, looking around in alarm, but her heart wouldn't slow down; the cold nausea wouldn't subside. Another sizzle of flame hissed nearby, and another and another, and three new shells exploded above: blue, purple, white. Someone set off a string of firecrackers down the street. It sounded like machine gun fire. A boom thundered from the hillside—one of those mini-dynamites some people liked to set off, probably, but what if it wasn't? Goddess, what had she been thinking, stepping into the living world? This would be a perfect occasion to shoot or bomb someone without anyone realizing what was going on until too late.

Beside her, Liam was looking around uneasily too. Her flight instinct kicked in. Sophie twisted and slid off the hood of the car, pulling him with her. She set off running, shoving through the crowd, knocking people aside.

"What, what is it, what's happening?" Liam begged. But he ran with her. He had as much reason to freak out as she did.

"I don't know—it's too much—we just have to…" She raced out of the square, along the street they had arrived from, and up the slope, back into the darkness of the hillside.

Tabitha and Zoe, however, being immortals, got in front of them in short order and stopped them. They barely even looked out of breath, though Sophie felt about to faint between the effects of running uphill and being in a full panic attack.

"Whoa, girl. Hey." Tabitha drew her in and hugged her. "Where you think you're going, huh?"

Sophie trembled against Tab's soft, warm steadiness. "Switch us, please, can you switch us?"

"Sure, no prob." The world wobbled. The sounds of singing and fireworks evaporated into quiet. The sea sighed, over and over, down at the base of the cliffs.

Beside them, Zoe had embraced Liam and switched him into the spirit realm too.

After a few deep breaths, Sophie pulled away from Tab and slumped down onto a rock. "I'm sorry," she said, gazing at the dark shapes of the scrub. "The explosions…"

"Totally understandable," Zoe said. "Ugh, I should've realized. Bad night to come out in the world."

"It was my idea," Tab said. "I am such a moron. I'm sorry, you guys. Are you okay?"

Liam laughed shakily. "Hey, I'm cool. I just thought Sophie saw some Thanatos dude in the crowd or something."

"The fireworks didn't get to you?" Zoe asked him anxiously.

"Well," he admitted, "a little. I guess."

Tab sat beside Sophie, sharing the rock, and rubbed Sophie's shoulders. "You are going to conquer this, babe. I know you are."

Sophie managed a smile. As the others remarked about how the cake was pretty good, and tried to repeat how to say "Happy New Year" in Greek, Sophie gazed at the moonlight scattered over the Mediterranean.

Secretly, and to her surprise, she found herself comforted by her freak-out. It clearly wasn't just Adrian who set off that reaction in her. It was other things like fire or explosions too. He was just one feature of what happened, not the whole of her problem. In fact, quite likely, he was part of what would make her life whole again. She just had a lot of healing to do first.

And she had to pray Thanatos didn't obliterate him before her healing was done.

NIKOLAOS STROLLED UP TO LIAM IN THE FIELDS ON NEW Year's Day. Liam had braided together a rope of Underworld willow and ivy, and though it was uneven and ugly, it totally worked: it glommed onto the souls of the spirit dogs who liked hanging around Rosie. He was entertaining himself now by hitching four of them together and trying to get them to run like a dog-sled team, pulling him on his skateboard.

"Now that's innovation," Niko remarked.

Liam hopped off the skateboard and tugged the dogs to a stop. "They aren't that good a team yet. And it's hella bumpy trying to roll on this stuff." He thumped his sneaker sole against the grass-covered rock of the Underworld.

Niko approached and picked up Liam's skateboard to examine it. Raindrops glittered on his fleece coat and snow-boarder hat. "This the board you saved from home?"

"Yeah. Most of the stuff in the garage wasn't...too burnt." Liam dropped his gaze to the willow rope, and picked a leaf off it.

"Good. I wonder that Adrian hasn't tried pulling his bus with spirit dogs instead of horses. Maybe because it would make Kiri jealous."

"Plus Hades' chariot is supposed to have black horses. Not dogs."

"True. Adrian's a stickler for tradition in some cases. Speaking of the old days..." Niko set down the skateboard and took his phone out. "Our girls tell me you've got to the Amphitrite memories."

"The start of them anyhow."

"And you're curious who she is now. Well." Niko turned his phone's screen to Liam.

Liam peered at the photo. Excitement bloomed in his chest. An Asian girl, older than him but not way older, sat on a bus or a train or something. She was reading her phone screen. She was Japanese maybe—she wore one of those school uniforms with navy jacket, plaid skirt that stopped above the knee, and dark socks. She had long straight black hair with shaggy bangs, and what looked like a really cute face, though it was hard to tell in a smallish photo from the side like this.

Liam's head felt a bit floaty. He looked up at Niko. "Who is she?"

"So far I don't know. I can't speak or read Japanese, other than *konnichiwa* and *arigato*, which rather complicates this particular stalking adventure. But I tracked her and got near her, at least." Niko nodded to the picture. "Boarded a train with her, and managed to snap this picture. This was in Yokosuka, on Tokyo Bay." Niko smiled. "She lives by the sea. Appropriately."

"How old is she, you think?"

"High school is my guess. Sixteen maybe? I'm sure a little more stalking and we could find out, along with her name and such. But for now I thought you'd like to see this."

Liam couldn't take his eyes off her. "That's awesome." Then a sort of hilarious despair crossed his mood, and he grimaced up at Niko. "Sixteen? Dude, she'd never even look at me."

Niko clapped his hand on Liam's shoulder. "Well, what do you think the immortality fruit does to a boy? Makes him a man. She'll look then. And by then, you'll be able to sense her yourself. You can go and say *konnichiwa*."

Liam studied the girl again. "*Konnichiwa*," he echoed. He looked eagerly at Niko. "Send me this pic, okay?"

CHAPTER SIXTEEN

STEPPING BACK INTO THE LIVING WORLD SOON SHOOK HEK-ate's courage further, for Thanatos struck again. Worse yet, they targeted two of the gentlest immortals, Hestia and Hephaestus. The cult swarmed into a feast at a clifftop temple where the two were being honored, slayed dozens of mortals, and managed to kill Hestia before the locals drove them off. Meanwhile Hephaestus only survived by throwing himself off the cliff. He switched realms and spent the night in agony on the rocks while his broken legs healed themselves.

Once again the immortals dealt swift and lethal vengeance, but this time without Hekate's magical assistance. The cold strength of hands and weapons sufficed, after Hermes and Artemis tracked down the cult members who had fled the scene. Hekate, in fact, didn't even come along. She spent three days in the Underworld, trembling in revived trauma, help-lessly watching Hestia's soul drift around with the souls of her parents and grandmother.

Then she asked herself if this was helping the world, and knew she must return to her justice missions. Which she did, though fear accompanied her like a fist in her chest for the next month.

In as many islands, towns, and countries as she could reli-ably reach, in places where she could communicate with the people, she brought word from the murdered to their surviving friends.

She wished she could help people in more of the world. As her parents had found before her from talking to the dead, the world was far larger than anyone realized. Like them, she tried to sketch a map to work out where all these different lands lay, based on what the souls could tell her. But she had to give up. No one knew the geography of the whole world. All she could conclude was that, yes, there were lands beyond every ocean, and no, she did not have the courage to fly all the way across and investigate them. Even if she did, she couldn't deliver justice there, since she didn't speak those languages. The souls could have taught them to her, but that would take intensive months of study for each language, nowhere near as easy as the instinctual ability that the pomegranate memories gave her for the languages she'd spoken in past lives.

She did heal people sometimes, too. Her mother and grandmother had taught her several methods and plants to assist in all kinds of ailments, plus she had the stamina to stay long at a bedside and prop up or carry patients if need be. So on her journeys to other villages, she often asked around when her justice errands were finished to see if anyone needed a temporary nurse or midwife, and gave the exhausted family a night off. Soothing and sponging and encouraging these suffering people, she felt soothed herself. At least this was a service to humanity that did nothing but good. And it showed mortals that these mysterious messengers from the Underworld were not out to hurt them; quite the contrary.

She still heard hostile whispers in most places she visited. Sometimes Thanatos was behind the sentiments—its name was shouted at her in defiance. The story of the murderers counter-murdered by mysterious beasts—her own handiwork—had traveled far indeed, and become even more fearsome in the retelling. Even in places Thanatos hadn't penetrated yet, people naturally mistrusted an outsider with uncanny knowledge from the dead. Hekate kept tranquil, pursued her errands, and more often than not, won the citizens over.

What she really wished for was some more established way to spread the truth about herself and the other immortals. Her mind mulled it over, and kept coming back to the priests and priestesses who were already friendly with them—but then what? More festivals? More temples? She wasn't sure.

Spending more time far afield did mean seeing Dionysos less. It soon became their custom to meet only twice a month, once at the new moon and once just after the full, when he had finished presiding over the Dionysia. He showed up reliably in the Underworld at those times, and she stayed home those nights to await him.

In the days between, other immortals often accompanied her on her outings to ensure she was safe. Sometimes it was Rhea, Artemis, or Apollo, but most often it was Hermes.

"I love to travel anyway," he said one day as they walked toward a city in Kypros. "Might as well throw some killers to the executioners while I'm at it."

Though he spoke lightly, he studied the far mountains with a steely set to his eyes. It was now almost a year since her parents had been killed, and though the intensity of her grief had diminished, the sadness had never left her, nor had the fury against their enemies. Her friends felt much the same, evidently. But her mind still recoiled, just as her magic had done, at the thought of the blood she had shed in retaliation.

"I haven't forgiven myself yet for the massacre," Hekate confessed. She dropped her gaze to her sandals on the dusty path. "I don't even like catching people for these executioners, even though it's justice. I do it so they don't hurt anyone else, and so the victims' families can know what happened and find peace. But I don't enjoy it."

"Love, you showed great restraint. If other people had the power to direct wild animals against their enemies, the world would have become a slaughterhouse long ago. The rest of us, your accomplices…well, perhaps sometimes deep in the night we don't forgive ourselves either. Yet if we had another chance we wouldn't have done it differently. Bastards deserved what they got."

She smiled. "Is it wrong to say I'm glad you're all in it with me?"

Hermes slung his arm around her. "We'd follow you into hell. In fact, we do. Regularly."

"I DON'T KNOW ANYTHING ANYMORE, DAD." SOPHIE PRESSED the heels of her hands against the rock she sat upon. "What I'm supposed to do, what our future's supposed to look like—mine and Liam's. We can't walk away from all this entirely, because, well, you guys are here now."

Terry was seated beside her on the bench-like cave formation at a bend in the river. The black water gurgled past in front of them. "Sweetie, we'd be delighted if you both got back into school, and took on the world again. Don't worry about us. You know we're fine here."

"Maybe *you're* fine, but it makes me feel better to see you, so I have to keep ties with this realm. Still, all this immortal stuff—" She waved her hand up the river. "I mean, look at it. It's all death and violence these days. I want to stop Thanatos—who wouldn't?—but I can't get on board with that mood. I wanted a life of, like, gardens. Fruits, vegetables, flowers."

"I hear you. But you know, gardens are pretty important down here too. These folks wouldn't *be* immortal if it weren't for those fruits."

"Yeah. And that was one of my plans, at first. Get Persephone's gardens back into shape, use the plants to help people somehow. But now it doesn't seem important compared to what everyone else is doing."

"Course it's important. Gardens are always going to be

important. People need to eat. Maybe if you called it a 'victory garden.'"

Sophie smiled. "Keep calm and grow magic pomegranates?"

"Exactly. Bringing a little bit of spring into the Underworld, putting some life back into death—isn't that Persephone's whole thing?"

"Well, you can look at the myth that way. In reality it was..." She shrugged, since her dad, being Demeter's soul, knew already. Still, her mind completed the thought. Persephone marrying Hades, in the actual past, hadn't been about life mating with death, or seasons being invented by emotional gods. It was a love story, a man and a woman. Simple as that.

Now even that timeless love was all out of whack.

"I think this realm needs you and your gardens," Terry said. "And so does the living world. That's what I think."

The orchard needs you, Persephone. Adrian's soul had said it to hers, last time they were dead, down here between lives.

"Both realms?" she said. "That's a lot to balance. I'm sucking at balance lately."

"You'll find it again. You'll stop wobbling one of these days. Believe me, honey."

CHAPTER SEVENTEEN

DETECTIVE KINNAMAN WAS AT LEAST AS OLD AS LIAM'S DAD, and pudgy with gray thinning hair. Liam hadn't known him before all this. They'd brought in cops from other parts of the state for this case, because apparently no one could solve it. They never would, of course, unless they figured out about immortals and the spirit realm, and Liam got how that would be too much of a mind-blower to share with them. Still, he felt kind of sorry for the cops. They didn't have the important clues and they were trying really hard to help.

Detective Kinnaman frowned at his computer screen, clicked a bunch of times, then looked over the top of his glasses with sympathy at Sophie and Liam. They sat in front of his desk in the police station in Carnation. The office door was closed to help make Liam and Sophie feel safe, though what made Liam feel a lot safer was knowing their immortal buds Tab and Zoe were waiting for them in the lobby like a couple of expert bodyguards.

"I don't know what to make of it," Kinnaman confessed. He turned to Sophie. "We have all these pre-existing tips about Betty Quentin being involved in the attacks on you before the house explosion, and you say you suspect she was in on this too. That makes sense to me."

Sophie nodded. They weren't telling the cops about how Quentin, Krystal, and Landon had abducted Sophie briefly while the house burned down. They also couldn't tell the cops that Quentin was dead, killed in the other realm, so they might as well not bother looking for her. There was no way to explain all that without talking about immortality and gods, which would get them locked up in some kind of psychiatric hospital. So Liam kept his mouth shut, though luckily he was only twelve and the cop barely ever asked him anything except whether he was doing okay.

"The only trace we can find of who fired the rocket," Kinnaman went on, "is footprints in the field. But our team swears they belong to a *young* woman, not an elderly woman like Quentin. And they're not yours, Sophie; we already confirmed that."

Sophie nodded again. They also weren't telling about Krystal and Landon, even though they knew their names, because Team Immortal wanted to keep tracking Thanatos themselves and watching what they were up to. It was seriously frustrating. Liam wanted to get the fuckers caught and put on Death Row. But Adrian and the others, even though they felt the same way, also said they would alert the police to stop Thanatos if they were about to hurt anyone. Just not yet.

Liam had strong suspicions none of them knew what the hell they were doing. Lately he wondered if anyone on Earth knew what they were doing. After all, if the police didn't know and the immortals from the Underworld didn't know, then who did?

"Nothing useful's been found in the remains of the house," Kinnaman continued. "No one among your family's friends or neighbors has thought of any leads. We've looked and looked, but we can't find anyone in your past, or your parents' past, who'd be this much of an enemy, who'd go this far to hurt you guys." He lifted the cover of a file folder with the tips of his fingers, then let it fall and dropped his hand on top of it. "Look, I'm begging you: have you thought of anything?

Any leads? I mean, these people can't just be allowed to walk free. I'm sure you agree."

"Oh, I'm with you." Sophie spoke with quiet decisiveness. "All these attacks were insane. And random—out of nowhere. I still hardly believe it's happened. But I'm searching too, trying to get help from everyone I know."

"You're staying safe?" Kinnaman's forehead crinkled up. "I really wish you'd let us put more security on you."

"We're safe for now. I think we're safest this way, by not telling many people where we are."

"As long as we can easily reach you. You're keeping your cell on, right?"

"Right," she said.

"And doing your check-ins with your doctors?"

She nodded.

Kinnaman heaved a sigh. "Jeez, kids, I'm sorry. I wish I had more to tell you. This case is incredibly frustrating."

Sophie drew her bag up onto her lap. "Is that all for today? We were going to visit the house again. It might help us remember something. Or at least..." Her words trailed off.

Kinnaman nodded, rising as she stood. "Of course. We've got a couple guys over there right now. I'll give them a call, let them know you're coming."

Kinnaman shook hands with her, then with Liam. Then he tousled Liam's hair, like Liam was six or something.

"Thanks," Liam mumbled to him on their way out.

"You take care, guys," Kinnaman said.

Liam and Sophie didn't speak or make eye contact as they walked down the corridor, rejoined Tab and Zoe, and left the Carnation police station. His sister finally glanced at him as they crossed the street.

"They're going to catch us," Liam accused. "They'll figure out we're hiding something."

"They probably already have." Sophie sounded like she didn't really care. "They'll never guess what."

"That's the trouble, really." Zoe sounded bummed. "It might be nice to tell more people about immortals and have them believe us. We could use the bloody help."

"For reals," Tab said.

They walked out of the town's small business center and along the path beside the highway. Zoe and Tab stayed on the outer sides of Sophie and Liam, as if ready to jump any attackers.

"Why are we walking?" Liam complained. He liked riding those spirit horses, and in any case, it took fifteen whole minutes to walk from town to their house. Or rather, to where their house used to be.

"It's a nice day and we can use the exercise," Sophie told him, in a firm voice that sounded a lot like their mom's.

Liam scowled at the highway. "It's cold. And windy."

Which it was, but they ignored him, and honestly it wasn't too bad for January. The sky was clear blue, and the sun felt almost warm in those seconds when the cold wind calmed down and stopped slicing through your clothes.

As they drew nearer to the remains of their house, the wind carried whiffs of burned wood to his nose. Even after almost a month, with daily rain washing over it, you could still smell it. Liam wondered how long the stench would last. Till they cleared away all the burned timbers and plowed up all the scorched grass?

Like Kinnaman had said, there were uniformed people with latex gloves standing around. One picked around in the debris, and two others stood aside and talked. As Liam and Sophie and their friends approached, the police moved aside the crime scene tape and waved them in.

"Just stay in this area here." The middle-aged woman gestured to the garden and shed area. "There's spots in the house where you could fall through to the basement."

Sophie was gazing silently at the pile of ruins.

"That's fine," Tab answered for her. "We just wanted to visit a little."

Sophie glanced at the woman and murmured, "Thanks," then walked off alone toward the trampled, dormant herb garden. Zoe trailed her.

Liam approached the house's borders and pushed his foot against the concrete steps that used to go up to the kitchen. Now they went nowhere. But they still sat here like they might be useful to someone someday. Poor steps, he thought. You're only going to get busted up and thrown out like all this other shit.

He turned to check on Sophie. She was crouching near the fence, and for a moment he worried she was sick or weak. But Zoe leaned on the fence near her, and seemed relaxed, so Liam relaxed too. He wandered over.

"It seems early," Sophie was saying, "but I guess January is actually when they start to come up."

"When what comes up?" Liam asked.

Sophie pointed to the green tips poking up among the dead leaves. "Flowers. These are crocuses, these are snowdrops, and these are bluebells. Remember? They always came up on this side of the garden."

"Tough little flowers," Zoe said. "They're good at coming back."

"Yeah." Sophie cleared the leaf litter around them. She looked up at Liam. The sun hit her hazel eyes, lighting up a purpose and clarity in them that he hadn't seen in a long time. "Can you check the shed and see if there's a trowel? I want to take some of these with us."

"What for?" he asked.

"To grow in the Underworld."

CHAPTER EIGHTEEN

THE LOW SETTING SUN STREAMED FROM BEHIND HEKATE. Her shadow and Dionysos', joined at the hands, stretched long in front of them. It was still early spring, and the evening wind blew cold.

Dionysos stopped and smiled at her. He wore his purple robes for the opening of the festival, decorated with fur, flowers, and vines. He held his cloth mask in his other hand. "Ready?"

She nodded, though she shivered with nerves.

They slipped on their masks. She had redecorated her old cloth one so that now in addition to the flakes of colored stone, it bore small gems from the Underworld. Hephaestus had cut them for her, and had also designed her a new necklace that she wore tonight, strung with gemstones in all hues, like a rainbow.

Her mother and father used to wear the Underworld's jewels as a sign of pride in their domain. She would do the same. Not just tonight but every day.

When Persephone and Hades had seen her off for the festival today, they had admired Hephaestus' new work and complimented her appearance in it. And of course they had urged her to be careful. But they hadn't seemed particularly concerned. No need to be: this Dionysia was hosted by the city of Athens, where Athena and her legendary wisdom were held in high regard. Crime and Thanatos did crop up here too, of course, but there was almost no place where the immortals were more respected. Besides, Dionysos had a strict rule now of keeping armed guards at every festival—some at the outskirts, watching for intruders, and some patrolling within the grounds. In addition, he no longer slept in the living realm. Very few immortals did anymore.

Thus they were not about to fall into the same trap that had snapped shut around Hekate before, the one that had led to the self-sacrifice of her mother, father, and grandmother. Nevertheless, with the memory of her last Dionysia shadowing her, Hekate trembled as they switched realms. Drums played nearby, musicians entertaining the crowd before the festival.

Dionysos slipped his arm around her. They walked toward the crowd. "This is an especially friendly city. We'll be fine."

"I know." Her voice felt tight.

They reached the crowd's edge. Everyone wore robes and masks, purple being the predominant color. No one gave Hekate and Dionysos a second glance—except Athena, whose tall, masked figure strolled toward them from the midst of the revelers.

"You made it!" Athena drew Hekate in for a hug, and beamed at Dionysos. Olive leaves twined around Athena's gold crown; only small gleams of metal showed through. "I'll take good care of her tonight," Athena said. "Until you're free to fetch her."

Dionysos bowed. "Thank you, my lady." He turned to face Hekate. "I need to get set up. You'll be all right?"

"Yes." With Athena beside her, and the armed guards about, Hekate did feel safe, or at least just safe enough.

"See you soon." He darted into the crowd to join the priests and priestesses.

The procession began. Athena kept Hekate at ease by chatting with her while they walked. Hekate took the opportunity to bring up the idea of spreading the truth about the Underworld.

"I like it," Athena said after pondering it, "but it's going to be hard to keep the story from getting bent into inaccuracy every time we turn our backs." She shook her head. "Goddess above, how Greeks love to make up stories. Nonetheless, I'll think about how we could handle such a thing. Special training for priestesses and priests who already run the festivals or shrines—yes, something like that could work."

"And mortals do understand magic, more than I usually give them credit for," Hekate said. "I did myself when I was mortal, and I don't think it was just because I grew up in the Underworld."

Athena smiled at her. "Though surely that helped."

They reached the site of the festivities, partway up a hill that overlooked the city, and the crowd hushed as the orator began his narration. With his speech about death reaching its fingers into every life, fear swept over Hekate. The memory of her last Dionysia and its aftermath reared up in lurid color, and she began shaking and sweating. Only Athena, beside her, seemed to guess she wasn't merely acting the part like most of the crowd. Athena took her hand firmly, and didn't let go for the remainder of the speech.

But then, Hekate thought, as she forced in one breath after another, was anyone here truly pretending? Everyone knew grief. Everyone knew fear. That was why these festivals worked so well.

Her breath came easier. She did belong. She wasn't so different from the light-born mortals after all, Underworld's daughter though she was.

"Summon him, my friends!" the orator was saying. "Summon back our lord of the spring!"

The chant of "Dionysos!" began and rose in volume until the shouts and drums echoed off the rock walls and across the valley.

Flames burst into sight: the unmasked Dionysos made his appearance beside the orator, illuminating the dusk with torches in both hands.

Cheers swept through the crowd, as if winter had indeed this moment turned to spring. People lit torches from the ones Dionysos held, spreading the flame about. The light brightened. The music flipped to a gleeful frolic, and people began dancing.

Hekate squeezed Athena's hand gratefully, and let go.

She ended up dancing too, and accepted wine, and laughed at the theatrics. Athena, along with Pan and three of the Muses who were in attendance, came to talk to her from time to time, as if checking on her, but she was contented and saw them relax in satisfaction as they realized it.

Soon Dionysos swooped in upon her in his latest costume, all goatskin and flaxen tassels. "Hello," he said. "You look happier than expected."

"I feel happier than expected." She pulled him down by the ears of his mask and kissed him.

"Then I'm so glad I share your bed tonight," he purred.

Their night was indeed sweet, and full of heated urgency. And afterward she easily relaxed and slept, since they were staying in a room in the spirit world, in the palace Athena had lately built there.

Hekate continued enjoying the next evening's portion of the festival, and even had to suppress laughter during the sacred marriage. The noblewoman was about forty years old and took lewd delight in her role. She grabbed at Dionysos' chest, crotch, and rear over and over through the ceremony, and he kept deftly and comically dodging her hands, or catching them and moving them aside, then wagging his finger at her as if telling his "bride" she must wait till they were married.

When the time came for him to sweep her up and carry her off into the darkness, he did so with the skill of a practiced actor. But Hekate suspected he would escape any sexual intimacy with her, and would soon bring her back to rejoin the crowd.

Meanwhile the dancing commenced. Hekate remained at the edge of the throng, swaying in time to the drums, her back against a clump of trees.

Hermes' presence stole up beside her. She smiled without turning, and didn't even look when he slid his arm around her waist and said in her ear, "What a fetching young woman. I must fondle her."

"Hello, Hermes."

"Hush, my darling. We are all masked tonight. No names." He drew her forward and began dancing with her.

"You're not even *trying* to disguise your voice. And I can sense who you are, stupid."

"Oh, come now. I'm many terrible things, but never stupid."

She conceded with a shrug, and spun in the dance in harmony with him.

His mask covered the top half of his face, a fitted piece of leather that sparkled with scattered gold leaf. Mistletoe wreathed his head. "It makes me happy to see you at another of these," he said.

"I thought it time to come back."

"I agree. Hey, Aphrodite gave me a new perfume. I tried putting it on my mask. Smell it and tell me what you think."

Hekate leaned her face close and inhaled. She was about to tell him she could hardly smell anything when he took advantage of her proximity and kissed her on the mouth.

She planted her hand on his face and shoved him, though her annoyance was mixed with laughter, and she didn't bother trying to escape from his arms.

He was grinning. "Such a simple trick, and you fell for it. Now who's stupid?"

"Goddess. I knew you liked to steal, but I didn't know it included kisses."

"Well..." He stroked her back, as if soothing an irritated cat. "I hated to think that the last time we kissed was that terrible night. Now it isn't. One less dreadful thing to associate with that event."

She resettled her arms around his neck. "I suppose kissing you isn't *so* dreadful. And I might as well hang onto you as a partner. Otherwise someone even more repulsive might try to dance with me."

"You and your honeyed words." He bent her back over his arm in the dance, then let her straighten up again. "How about this. If the stolen kiss bothers you, do anything you like to me in return." His eyes gleamed with mischief from behind the golden mask. "Anything."

She smirked, and was about to remark that if she had her old powers back, he would regret that suggestion. But her gaze fell upon Dionysos then, who had returned, and was several paces away in the midst of the dancers. The sacred bride—the local noblewoman—was wrapped around him like a climbing vine. She twisted her way downward, kissing his bare chest and navel, and he had his arms spread and was grinning down at her, acting his part as the god of debauchery receiving his worship.

Then the bride twirled to another partner, and another woman stepped in to take her place. Aphrodite.

Uneasiness built in Hekate's chest. The goddess of love wore a lightweight pale green gown that left one shoulder bare and afforded glimpses of her thigh and the edges of her breasts. Her black hair was pinned up in a loose knot of braids, starred with white hyacinths. She was fleshly and gossamer, earthy and ethereal, everything a man could want.

She and Dionysos slipped both arms around each other, and tempered their dance steps to a more subdued form. Through their jeweled masks, their eyes were locked upon one another. Dionysos still smiled, but he had become quieter, and seemingly more serious.

Hekate drew a breath, willing the air to crush the jealousy rising in her.

Her will succeeded: the unhappiness soon faded to resignation. Aphrodite and Dionysos had a long history together. They would always mean something to one another, but he didn't want to go back to her. He'd said so, and Hekate believed it. Besides, Hekate had told him he was welcome to cavort with Aphrodite, or anyone else at these festivals. Indeed, wasn't Hekate supposed to do the same if she liked?

Hermes glanced back at Dionysos too, then examined Hekate with careful eyes. She smiled dryly for him. If she did have her powers back, she would know what he was feeling through the touch of his skin. Pity? Amusement? Something else? He said nothing to give her any clue. He only kept dancing with her, observing each step and twirl with correctness. He seemed to be awaiting her word, or her actions.

Actions. Indeed. A new possible activity for tonight occurred to her, thrilling her to her toes with its boldness.

He'd already stolen a kiss tonight and invited her to retaliate. So she drew her face close and stole one back.

Hermes paused only a moment, his feet finally faltering in the dance, then he slid into reciprocation, his mouth and arms caressing her.

"My my," he said. "What's this for?"

"I might as well do the same as the rest of the revelers." She brushed another kiss onto his mouth.

"Oh?" He indulged it, sliding his lips softly back and forth on hers. They had become hot despite the chilly air. "We aren't showing up Aphrodite? Not that I'd mind."

"Not at all. I'm allowed. So is he."

"Mm. Well, in that case…"

They both dismissed words, and sank into a hungrier, wetter kiss. The jewels and gold on their masks clinked against each other, which made them grin. To avoid colliding with other dancers they staggered, linked together, back to the clump of trees. Hekate drew him around to the opposite side, within the dark curve of tree trunks, hidden from view. She spun Hermes, placed his back against the largest trunk, and leaned against him, savoring the feel of someone else's body, someone who wasn't her lover. Yet.

To a woman who, in this lifetime, had only been intimate with one man, gaining a new lover was a heady thought. She melted closer against him, getting to know his contours. She felt them with strange clarity, considering he'd been wearing a thick wool cloak all around him. She slid one hand down his front in curiosity, glancing down, and laughed: with his characteristic dexterity, he had slipped his cloak out of the way so his chest was now bare and only a thin linen tunic covered him below the waist. All without her noticing, and without interrupting their kisses.

He nuzzled her jaw and neck. "Now where's that snake you once threatened me with if I ever tried to kiss you?"

"I was twelve. You remember that?"

"Of course. You said you'd keep it in your clothes. I'm searching. Nothing so far."

She yelped, for he had gotten his hand inside her clothes without her knowing quite how. He stroked her lower back, skin on skin. His nimble fingers brushed down to the curve of her rear.

"I'm beginning to see how you can steal anything off anyone." She was becoming short of breath.

He pulled her tighter against his hard body. "I can. Though some things I would never steal. They're only enjoyable when freely given."

Her heart pounded as fast as the drums. She meant to throw back a piece of banter, but her hand treacherously distracted her by exploring the heat of his chest. Then he distracted her further by quick, light demonstrations of where he could slip his fingers unexpectedly—places ranging from semi-innocent to fully obscene. She was laughing and gasping at the same time. One of his tickling touches buckled her knees, and he fell with her to the ground. They sprawled together across their cloaks on the chilly hard roots and turf, in the darkness behind the trees, wrapped up in a horizontal dance of caresses, laughter, and wine-flavored kisses.

Approaching. Someone approaching, someone she knew. Dionysos, and Aphrodite. Hermes lifted his head, surely sensing them too.

Hekate teetered between shame at where her hand almost was, and impatience to get it there and see what it was like. But then, if Dionysos was looking for her, maybe it was a better idea to stop now. In fact, why was she doing this, exactly? To prove some point about non-exclusivity, which wasn't necessary? She needed to stop and think a moment...

"Hekate?"

Dionysos wasn't just looking for her. He was looking *at* her. Backlit by the festival torches, he peeked through a gap between tree trunks, Aphrodite looking over his shoulder.

Hekate scrambled away from Hermes, who calmly whisked his cloak back over himself.

"Hello, friend," Hermes answered, still lounging on the ground. "How are the pair of you?"

"Fine." Dionysos sounded amused, if puzzled. "And the pair of you?"

"Fine. Hello." Hekate leaped to her feet, her face so heated with shame that she felt it must be incandescent. She stepped to the space in the tree trunks and smiled as innocently as she could.

Dionysos only laughed. He glanced at the sprawling, mussed-up Hermes and then back to her. He reached through and straightened her mask. "You're allowed to, you know. It's all right."

Behind him, Aphrodite wore a serene, triumphant smile

below her mask. For some reason it enraged Hekate. "No, we should go," Hekate said. "I'm tired. Are you ready to go?"

"No need to be rude to Hermes," Dionysos said.

"It's all right." Hermes rose and shook the leaf litter off his cloak with a snap of fabric. "I told her she could do anything she liked to me."

Without any clear idea of what had just happened, Hekate had no answer at hand. Especially with Aphrodite as audience to the scene. Hekate's gaze flew from one man to the other. They were both difficult to read, what with the nocturnal darkness and the masks. "Thank you," she said. "I—I've had a good time, but I'm ready to go for the night. If you're ready. If—if it's all right."

"Of course," Dionysos said. "Anything you want."

Hermes walked with Hekate back around the trees to rejoin the party on the other side. He stepped up next to Aphrodite, who draped her arm around his waist. "Goodnight," Hermes said cordially, to both Hekate and Dionysos, as a person would to a married couple.

He hadn't even given her one last secret grope as they came out from the trees. Hekate almost felt offended—or perhaps comforted?

Hermes and Aphrodite walked away together, arms around one another, with every appearance of being about to indulge in their long-standing friends-with-intimacy arrangement. And did *that* make Hekate feel relieved, or jealous? Tonight was turning out very confusing. How did people do these things so casually at these festivals?

She and Dionysos switched realms and returned again to their room in Athena's palace.

They said nothing until they had built a fire in the hearth, removed their masks, and were undressing for bed.

Then Dionysos spoke. "Hermes. Really?"

"He was convenient. And I can trust him."

Dionysos smirked.

"What?" Hekate said.

"Nothing. It's only, Hermes being trustworthy. That isn't something I hear often."

"He won't try to kill me. Let's put it that way."

"No, I know what you mean." He poured wine into a silver cup, and drank some. "But I suppose there's also..." He tilted the cup from side to side, watching the wine slosh around. "Well, I don't know for sure, but I suspect he slept with one or both of your parents. A long time ago, before they had you."

Hekate snorted. "So? Back when you were Aphrodite's teenaged lover, you and my mother fondled each other for 'educational purposes.'"

"Hardly at all."

"Still, I manage to live with it. Mind you, I do try not to think of it. Ever."

"A different lifetime." He drank more of his wine. "I've since been reborn, thanks to you." He lifted the cup to her in tribute.

"When people are going to live extra-long lives, they may simply have to be forgiven the extra-high number of lovers they might accumulate in that time."

"Fair enough. And nearly everyone living is one of Hermes' lovers, so there's nothing unusual in that."

"Indeed," she answered, trying to sound as mild as he did. But dismay slinked around her, coating her with its residue. How sordidly she'd behaved, how truly unremarkable she must have seemed to Hermes, who ran through lovers like most people ran through food.

The Dionysia and its dirty details usually did become memories its revelers tried to forget or disregard for the rest of the year. Having acquired such an experience, perhaps now Hekate was truly one of the people. She smiled in wry acceptance, and borrowed Dionysos' wine cup to take a swig.

CHAPTER NINETEEN

SOPHIE CURLED UP ON HER SIDE IN THE LARGE, EMPTY BED IN the Underworld. The blankets took a while every night to warm up when you didn't have a bedmate. Their dog Rosie usually slept at Liam's feet, across the room on his mattress, so he got the benefit of dog warmth while Sophie got the supposed benefit of the nicer bed. Usually it was no nicer at all; just chilly and lonely.

Tonight, though, she held her phone in her cupped hands, her cheek on the pillow, and gazed at the photos she'd taken of her transplanted spring bulbs. She had safely flown the crocus, bluebell, and snowdrop sprouts across the Atlantic, and given them a new home in the sunless but magic-rich soil of the Underworld. She found her parents in the fields and brought them over to look. They were delighted, and praised her for such a sweet idea—bringing their own flowers here to grow.

Thanks to those little green spikes, this was the first time she had visited the site of their house and not lapsed into a panic attack. The four times they'd been there up till now, she had trembled and felt nauseated, and fled as soon as possible. But today, with new life and garden dirt in her hands, she'd been able to gaze upon the ruins with sorrow but composure.

She whisked away the flower-bulb photos for a minute and called up the list of triggers. She highlighted "visiting the house" and selected "strikethrough" in the font options. A horizontal line slashed through the text.

There. One down at last. A victory.

Satisfied, she brought up the photos again. She had taken only twelve bulbs, leaving several back in their garden in Carnation to continue growing and spreading. Down here she had planted them at the foot of Adrian's titoki tree, where perhaps they'd open in colors they'd never worn before, and of course they might develop magical properties. Always a good chance of that in the Underworld.

Sophie considered texting one of the photos to Adrian, but hesitated. He might wonder what message she was trying to send, and honestly she wasn't sure what the message might be, other than, *Here's something I'm trying, to claw my way back up from this pit of trauma.* And how would that be any use to him?

So she sent nothing. Still, the photos held her attention a long while, and finally calmed her into turning off the phone and shutting her eyes.

She rested her hand on the empty half of the bed where Adrian had lain beside her so often in happier days. Maybe when those flowers bloomed, she'd be ready to invite him back into the bed.

The thought surprised her, but she kept her eyes shut, still sleepy. She spread her fingers on the cool sheet, and sent a message to him through the Goddess, or the Fates, or the mysterious magnetic currents that drew them to one another life after life; whatever was out there that might connect them. *Please be careful. Please stay alive. Don't despair. I'm trying to come back to life for you.*

There was another method to try. The memories were there, waiting for her to resume them. Life did go on—had gone on—for Persephone's soul. Maybe, then, rather than knocking Sophie further askew, opening up those memories would restore her balance.

Sophie turned the latch in the heavy door she had mentally installed lately between her mind and the ancient lives. She pulled the door open, and felt the vastness of time and life on its other side surrounding her like a rush of cool air.

For quite a while in Persephone's afterlife there was nothing but wandering the fields as a soul with Hades, and being visited by their living daughter, Hekate and others. Sophie twitched in pain at stepping back into that mindset—a parent lately dead, like her own mother and father, complete with a grieving daughter. But she pushed the memories forward faster, scanning them, and to her relief and surprise, the grief dwindled. It lost its original rawness, in any case. For Hekate it gradually tempered to acceptance, and a return to the living world, with stronger-than-ever resolve to spread the truth about the immortals and fight Thanatos. For Persephone and Hades, their muted sadness soon became pride in their daughter, and gratitude that their powerful friends lived on and sought to avenge them.

And if Persephone fretted a little about Hekate's ongoing relationship with Dionysos, who surely wasn't the best match for her even though he was a good man—well, worries like that were far easier to take than worries about Thanatos.

Did this mean she should caution Zoe and Tab against getting together as a couple?, Sophie wondered drowsily. Or did it not really matter who hooked up with whom in old times versus modern days? After all, now that she got to this part, she was identifying more with Hekate, the daughter whose parents had been killed, than she was with her own soul. Strange…life was strange.

Sophie fell asleep, her hand still spread upon the empty half of the bed.

NIKOLAOS PLUNKED DOWN NEXT TO ZOE, WHO WAS ONCE again hunched over her computer on the mountainside in the winter sun. She glanced at him, then back at the screen. Following those memories further along in Hekate's life had led her onto some quite awkward ones, hadn't it? Pashing with Hermes at the Dionysia! Again! This time in actual crazy lust, not merely as a trick to snare Dionysos. And his sneaky fingers down her top and around her bum and right up in—oh, she couldn't even bear to think of it.

"Are you blushing?" Niko asked.

She scrolled through the email on her screen. "Am I?"

"Did I interrupt you in porn-surfing?"

"Oh yeah, naturally."

He nudged her. "Or…please tell me you've reached certain memories."

She pressed her lips together, and continued scrutinizing the email. "Don't know what you're talking about."

"You can't pretend I'm not a good kisser. I've asked you between lives, when you couldn't lie, and you said I was. Besides, I was trained by Aphrodite, so of *course* I was excellent."

The shameless boast made Zoe laugh. "Fine, but whatever, there's not that much to discuss, right? A minute or two of pashing. So what."

"Riiiight," he said, so deadpan that Zoe knew there must be even more of such kinkiness in Hekate's future.

Jeez. Fantastic.

She cleared her throat and tried a slight topic shift. "No, I was more thinking about, you know, all this awkwardness with Tab."

"Oh? Looked like it was going slick enough for you two the other day."

"Yeah nah, I don't know." She squinted at him. "Were you really trying to match us up this life, introducing us and immortalizing us together the way you did?"

"Thought it worth a try. The two of you both being lesbians and of about the same age. I do want you to be happy, you know."

"Cheers, but lately I'm thinking she and I are not the full love connection."

"Still, having some friends with benefits around for eternity never hurts."

Zoe smirked. "Guess you'd know about that."

"Wouldn't I just." Niko stretched his arms up into the blue sky. "Speaking of which, I actually dropped by to tell you I'm on my way back to America to meet up with Adrian."

She stared at him. "Who was not one of your lovers. Please tell me he wasn't."

"I don't mean him. We'll be dropping in on Landon."

"Ah. So he *was* one of your lovers. We supposed he must be, since you can track him, but you haven't said. Who was he, then?"

"Just a guy. No one you ever met, I don't think."

"Bit of a crazy coincidence, though, isn't it? Or I suppose it's the Fates, or our magnetism to each other, or whatever we're to call it."

"Indeed. Something out there keeps forging a way for us all to cross paths again." He glanced at her. "Have you spent any time in Tartaros chatting with Quentin?"

Zoe shuddered. "Yeeks, no. Why would I?"

"Well, I have. And it's interesting: apparently the rest of you never thought to ask her who *she* was in ancient times."

"She was someone we knew?"

"She…" He picked casually at his teeth. "…was Hera."

Zoe jolted, almost tipping her computer off her lap. She shut it to keep it from harm. "No fucking way."

"Yes fucking way. And doesn't it sort of make sense? Hera, along with Zeus, actually did a fair amount back then to undermine our cause, although that wasn't their intent. Also makes sense that Quentin would be strangely driven by an obsession with immortals, and seek glory in something to do with us."

"So Landon, her grandson in this life. Who was he back then?"

"In the old days I occasionally went down to talk to Zeus and Hera when they were dead, in the Underworld. I'd bring them news they asked for. One thing Hera wanted to know was how her family was doing—great-great-grandchildren and such. She'd mostly lost touch with them, but she wanted to know what they were up to."

Zoe began to understand. "Landon's soul was one of them."

"Hera's great-great-I-forget-how-many-greats-grandson."

"What was his name? Where did he live?"

"Hera was originally from Crete, like Zeus and Hades, and her descendants still lived there." Niko spent a moment cleaning his fingernail before answering the first question. "His name was Krokos."

"So you went to find them for Hera, and…"

Niko's lips curved up a moment as she let the sentence hang unfinished. "He was obviously interested in me and in need of affection. So I provided a little."

"One of your many loves."

"'Love,' well…" Niko gazed toward the sea. "Wouldn't say that. Mostly I pitied him."

She felt an unexpected twinge of pity too for Landon's ancient soul—along with fondness toward Niko for being unusually open with her. "But he loved you?"

"If he keeps on his current path, he'll end up here in our domain quite soon and we can ask him." He hopped to his feet.

She guessed this rare confessional hour was over. "So now you and Ade are off to torment him."

"Hmm, I sense reproach. The boy's fallen under a bad influence, I'm sure you'd agree. But I think he might be malleable. Perhaps we can convince him to help us." His sinister emphasis on the word "convince" made Zoe uneasy.

"Make sure you two don't turn as bad as them," she said.

"I won't let Ade do the dirty work. As for me—well, love, isn't it already too late?" He smiled, but his eyes had reverted to the haunted look they'd carried too often lately.

"No, it isn't. Niko…"

"We'll let you know how it goes." He lifted his chin in farewell, and walked off.

CHAPTER TWENTY

A LOT WAS HAPPENING IN POSEIDON'S LIFE. LIKE, A *LOT*. LIAM zoomed through it, eager to get the whole picture like Niko and Adrian and the others had.

Poseidon finally figured out he wasn't merely slow to age but actually immortal. That became pretty clear when a man jumped him on a road on the mainland one night, trying to rob him. Poseidon threw him off, but the man lunged at him again, and sliced his blade into Poseidon's chest, all the way through to his back. In agony, Poseidon crashed to the ground. The thief knelt and swiftly began untying the bag of bronze and jewels from Poseidon's belt.

In what he thought was his dying burst of strength, Poseidon yanked the sword out of his body and stabbed the man with it. The thief fell twitching and gasping, and soon went still, blood trickling from his mouth into the dust.

Poseidon sat dizzily, his hand over the wound in his chest. Blood pulsed out with each heartbeat. Surely he was about to die.

But the bleeding stopped, and his strength crept back. He wiped off the blood and stared in astonishment at his chest in the moonlight. The wound was closing up, sealing itself. He sat straighter. His dizziness was receding. His breathing, his heartbeat, his strength—all were quickly approaching normal.

He sat very still, barely even thinking about how a criminal lay freshly dead next to him and he'd have to report it to the nearest town.

Instead he thought about one of his last conversations with his mother, who had died recently after a long illness.

"You never get ill," she had said. "You don't age. When you're hurt you heal instantly, or at least overnight."

"Mother…"

"And your strength, and your water miracles—listen, I've heard of such people."

"I'm just me. I don't know why this happens, but it's good, isn't it?"

She shook her head, closing her eyes in her feverish weakness. "You can't stay. Not much longer. You've seen how people have started behaving around you. Before long everyone will shun you."

"But where am I supposed to go?"

"Ask around. Not here—on the mainland. Ask about others like you, where to find them. But be careful. Don't let people know about you. Not until you find the others."

For the last few months he'd been recovering from the grief of losing her, and had been helping his sister and nieces and nephews feel more settled. He hadn't given much thought to finding others like himself, and rather doubted they existed. But now…

He didn't return to Skyros this time. Instead he spent a couple of days visiting the nearest two cities, and did some asking around, in which he tried to sound merely like a curious traveler in search of tales. Eventually he tracked down the stories his mother had heard. A priestess who lived in Crete was said to know actual immortals. Poseidon would have thought it just a fanciful invention, except that the accounts matched his own experience eerily: those immortals were people born like the rest of humanity, but they never aged, never got sick, healed amazingly fast, and wielded unheard-of strength. None of the stories mentioned these people controlling water the way he could, but the rest was enough to convince him. There weren't many of such people, it would seem. One story said just two, another claimed maybe five or six but no more than that.

Where did these beings live?, Poseidon asked.

A palace on a mountaintop, some said.

No, their own island, farther south, said another.

No, they were itinerant, someone else claimed; moving about and performing miracles—defeating armies single-handed, and so forth.

The only thing everyone agreed on was the woman in Crete, the high priestess of Knossos. She was the one who had befriended them all.

At the shore at Euboia the next afternoon, Poseidon joined the crew of a large ship on its way to Crete. They wouldn't sail till morning, so he walked alone a while on the shore, in a turmoil of confusion. About to undertake a journey to a priestess to ask about immortality, he felt far more out of his depth than he ever did while swimming alone in the middle of the sea. He clambered over a rocky headland and down the other side to a spot that suddenly looked familiar. Lambent tide pools reflected the last glow of light in the sky. The rocky headland sheltered the beach from the wind, creating a calmer haven here.

It was the place he had seen the young woman on that swim. And here she was again.

As before, she sat by a tide pool, but this time her legs weren't in it. Her back was to Poseidon and she held her hand cupped over the surface of the water, looking down at it, as if watching reflections.

He tried to reach her before she noticed him, but one rock scraped against another under his foot, and she turned.

Maybe it was the twilight, but she already looked prettier than the first time he'd seen her, last year. Her eyes seemed to have an extra velvety darkness of lashes around them, and her hair was twisted and pinned in a way that especially became her, with pieces of it coming loose beside one ear.

"You," she said.

"Been looking for me?" He sounded cockier than he meant to, then made it worse by putting a swagger in his step as he walked toward her.

She looked away in disdain. "I guess Skyros is as boring as they say, if you keep coming over here to bother me instead."

Still, she didn't sound truly scornful, so he sat down next to her. "This time I'm going farther. To Crete."

She looked at him again, and her eyebrows twisted up in disbelief. "Swimming?"

"No, on a ship." He looked out to sea. "It's…all very strange."

She swung her hand over the tide pool's surface a while. He saw the motion in the corner of his eye, and heard the ripple in the water. "So you really swam all the way back to Skyros last time?" she asked.

She had been waiting here, as he suggested, when he'd returned to swim home that day. She had told him with annoyance, "You'll probably drown, you know," but then she'd climbed higher on the rocky slope to watch him as he swam away. Every time he'd looked back, she'd still been there, a little white spot on the rocks, until he couldn't see her anymore.

"I did," he said. "Were you worried?"

She snorted as if to tell him not to flatter himself. The water rippled again as she moved her hand. "The sea must like you."

He looked at her. She kept her gaze turned down to the tide pool. "It seems to," he said. "I don't know why. But I feel like it'll never hurt me, which is not something I can say about other people."

She returned his thoughtful gaze a moment. Then she

tilted her chin toward the tide pool, where her hand still trailed, and asked, "Can you do this with water?"

He looked at the pool, and blinked in astonishment. The surface still rippled in response to the movement of her hand, but she wasn't actually touching it. Her fingers and palm hovered just above the water—and the water pulled in little waves toward her, as if she was causing an invisible tide.

He cast a long, searching look at this woman. Could she be like him, with all the same powers? Could he persuade her to join him in going to Crete, if so? He suddenly had a thousand questions for her and his tongue knotted up, lost as to where to start.

Meanwhile she looked at him with fiercer and more fearful defensiveness. Showing him this skill was clearly risky for her. If others learned of it, she'd be labeled a witch, an unnatural, just as he was.

Rather than answer in words, he clasped her wrist and drew her hand back from the water. As her touch grew distant from it, the ripples died and the pool went still. Poseidon then opened his own palm toward the pool. He didn't even need to do that; he'd always been able to work his influence with thought alone. But the gesture would make it clear that he was the acting power behind what happened next.

A bucket's worth of the water surged up out of the tidepool in a great slosh, and splashed down, half of it washing into the next pool over, the rest scattering in drops on the rock between.

The woman gasped, then stared at him.

He shrugged self-consciously.

She looked him up and down. "The water does like you."

"My name's Poseidon. What's yours?"

Her uncanny eyes returned to his. "Amphitrite."

They talked until the sun's light had vanished entirely from the horizon, and stars came out to dominate the sky. He learned she was nineteen, and didn't have the same powers as he did. Her water affinity only extended as far as the modest influence she had just demonstrated, along with a general feeling of safety in or around water. Though healthier than most people, she did get sick sometimes, and her wounds didn't heal unnaturally fast. Unlike Poseidon, she had no reason to think she might be immortal. He told her everything about his strange experiences, down to this latest idea of finding the Knossos priestess to learn what he was.

"Then that's obviously where you should go," Amphitrite said. "After that, you have to come back and tell me what she said, because I'll be dying of curiosity."

"You'll be pining away without me?" he teased—or meant to tease, but hopefulness emerged in his voice.

"You wish." She ducked her head, and her hand found his, between them. "Even if I was," she added, "I'm a concubine, so it doesn't really matter."

The pang to his heart told him he'd be doing more than a little pining himself. "You are?"

"Have been since I was fifteen. He needs heirs, and his wife is slow to conceive, so I have babies for him and they raise them. Three so far. Two girls and a boy."

"It sounds like you hate him. Is he awful? Should I kill him for you?"

She smirked. "He's rich, so at least I'm comfortable. When he doesn't beat me, that is."

Poseidon opened his mouth to rage against this boor, but Amphitrite continued in a matter-of-fact way, "Anyway, he's getting old, so with any luck he'll die one of these years. Then at least I can become a servant in the household of one of my children, when they grow up and marry."

Poseidon grimaced at the starlight dancing on the sea. He'd rarely realized how lucky he was to have been born male, and to have had a mother who hadn't pushed him into marriage. Instead she had only urged him off the island, to find out how to stay safe and live his unusual life best. But what good was his unusual life if he didn't help those he liked?

"You could run away," he told Amphitrite. "Come with me. To Crete."

"I can't, stupid."

"Why not?"

"I barely know you. This is where I live. You're crazy."

"Well, then how about this: I'll come back as soon as I can and find you, and if you want to run away later—whether you think I'm crazy or not—then I'll help you."

"Very well," she said. "But I'll *always* think you're crazy." Nonetheless, she kept her hand on top of his.

CHAPTER TWENTY-ONE

EKATE THREW HERSELF INTO THE WORK OF ESTABLISHING centers of learning for the allies of the immortals. The first was in Athens, under the protection and encouragement of Athena, and was presided over by some of the priests and priestesses who had proven loyal in the Dionysia and similar festivals. Athena herself, with occasional help from Hekate or other immortals, oversaw the first several months of instruction. Knowledge seekers of nearly all ages came to learn the truths that only the immortals could give, the foremost truths being the existence of the spirit realm and the Underworld, and that the immortals did not cause plagues or wars, and wished only health and prosperity upon mortals. As for the tree of immortality and other Underworld powers, those were kept secret for now, though Hekate and her friends did of course consider their longest-running and most companionable supporters as candidates for immortality. But the fruit's powers, they agreed, were too contentious to speak freely of, even in trusted circles.

Thanatos did grow vocally irate at the word of this new temple. However, within Athens, a well-guarded city where immortals were popular, the enemy had almost no luck infiltrating and causing actual damage. So the Athens Temple flourished, its membership numbers growing every month.

After so long living with grief and fear—and minor shame

about certain Dionysia moments, even though Hermes treated her the same as ever when she saw him lately—Hekate finally began to find life inspiring again. She worked hard, what with errands for murdered souls, taking care of the sick, delivering babies, and assisting at the Athens Temple, but she felt happy.

Dionysos remarked upon it last visit, curling her hair around his finger fondly. "You're so alive again. You're unstoppable. It's wonderful."

"If I had my magic back, then I'd be unstoppable," she answered. Still, she now felt as contented by the good work she was doing as she had ever felt when exploring her powers.

But her magic would have allowed her to do even more good. She sometimes thought so, wistfully, when gazing upon a rising moon, or wandering the seashore on a summer night, sand warm under her bare feet, mysterious luminescence sparkling within the waves. Ah, to feel those powers again, and to direct them toward those who could benefit: the students, the suffering patients, the ailing crops or livestock.

With the success of the Athens Temple, the immortals decided after another year to establish similar centers elsewhere. The Athens priestesses insisted upon Eleusis, a town not far from Athens, on a gulf coast. "It's a sacred site," they told Hekate and Athena. "It has a beauty and a magic. Everyone feels it. You'll see."

When Hekate arrived at the Great Goddess' sanctuary in Eleusis, and knelt to dip her fingers in the placid water of its spring, she did feel a hum of something almost like the energies she used to feel. The Eleusis sanctuary was every bit as lovely and tranquil as promised. The hillside overlooked the shining sea. Olive trees and tumbled gray-white boulders lined the roads that led past the town's houses and up to the temple. Several large stone slabs had been dragged here and set up on end in a circle around the well, and a roof of timbers and stone tiles had been laid across them, with a hole left in the center—where, Hekate assumed, the moon sometimes shone in and touched the water that welled up in the spring.

The head priestess and her assistants greeted Hekate, and proved themselves even more charming than their surroundings. They already so keenly understood the workings of natural powers that Hekate laughed and wondered aloud if there was anything left to teach them. But there was, of course, since most mortals could only catch glimpses or hints of the spirit realm, and knew little about its details. The group at Eleusis begged her to stay all day and talk to them. By evening, Hekate already felt ready to defend this town against Thanatos with all the ardor of a soldier.

Which was exactly what she had to do a few months later.

Thanatos heard of the new alliance between the Eleusis sanctuary and the immortals. A group arrived from another city, six men and women who preached their hate on the streets and shouted threats against the temple of "unnaturals." Eleusis' priestess answered with calm defiance, telling the itinerant preachers to go home to their own towns. The threats mounted. Eleusis' answer was the same. But the priestess, along with the worried Hekate, Apollo, and Artemis, arranged for armed guards during the times when students came to the sanctuary. Eleusis had walls encircling the town, like most cities, but it was a small town with nowhere near the fighting power of Athens. Nonetheless, the guards' presence worked for a while; Thanatos grumbled but retreated.

Then on a spring afternoon, when the darkness was falling early behind thick clouds, the enemy returned. Hekate happened to be there that day, sitting under the sanctuary roof with twenty students and six priestesses, priests, and attendants. Everyone was wrapped in wool cloaks, for the wind had been blowing cold all day, and now was picking up and threatening rain. But the students all wore bright expressions as they soaked up Hekate's explanations and peppered her with questions.

A lively debate about the punishment of souls in Tartaros was interrupted by the clang of swords and a barrage of shouts. The tumult came from below, near the town walls. One of the sanctuary's armed guards ran down the road to find out what was happening, and soon raced back up. "Thanatos," he said. "They've gotten over the wall."

Everyone scrambled to their feet. "Home, all of you!" Hekate commanded. But only a few obeyed. Most refused to leave, insisting upon defending the sanctuary, and she had no time to convince them. The enemy surged up the road—more than thirty this time. The sanctuary's ten armed guards now looked frighteningly inadequate. But they rushed forward and engaged Thanatos in a cacophony of clashing blades, while Hekate and the rest picked up every knife, axe, or stone they could find.

Holding a double-bladed axe intended more for ceremony than battle, Hekate stood front and center in the row of terrified people ready to defend their temple. Neither she nor any of the rest were soldiers. They only used knives or axes for preparing food or cutting firewood. And now these brilliant, sweet-tempered students were about to die because she was here—because she had brought the word of the immortals to the living realm.

Five of the guards had fallen, while at least twenty Thanatos soldiers remained. The remaining five Eleusis guards edged back, drawing closer together to protect the students, but Hekate could see they would soon be overpowered and then the real massacre would begin. Cold sweat drenched her. Every memory of her own kidnapping and torture, and the sacrifice of her parents and grandmother, crashed over her in a horrible wave.

The terror would have defeated her except that with it came righteous fury. Thanatos had already destroyed so much. They would not, *would not*, hurt anyone else tonight.

A flicker of lightning illuminated the clouds over the sea.

Hekate lifted her axe and, without thinking, called upon the immense power of the incoming storm.

The power obeyed.

Almost as strong as if lightning had struck her, she felt the magic surge up from the Earth, through her feet and legs and body and into her raised arms. With a roar of triumph, she pointed the axe at the Thanatos army.

All their weapons, swords and spears and knives, flew up, tumbled through the air, and landed at the feet of the sanctuary students.

"Her power is back!" The head priestess seized one of the fallen knives.

With a chorus of cheers, the students grabbed the rest of the weapons and brandished them at Thanatos. As if in answer, lightning forked across the sky, and thunder shook the ground.

Hekate saw the fear in the eyes of the now-disarmed Thanatos soldiers. At the feeling of her magic running up and down her, dancing all over and through her, she could do nothing for a moment but laugh, half-maniacally.

"Get them!" shouted the Thanatos army's leader, and he lunged forward to try to wrestle the knife away from a slender woman.

But she and her fellow students fought back—and now they held all the weapons. Some from Thanatos turned and ran. Others stayed to fight, but they were losing ground, being forced back down the road away from the sanctuary.

Lightning flashed again, closer. It was only the natural path of the storm, not Hekate's doing, but since it was near, she could harness its power.

She dropped the axe and seized the hands of the priestess and priest who stood at either side of her. At her will, the power rushed to her eyes. A glow glared there and nearly obscured her vision with its brilliance. But its light reflected on the faces of the enemy, and she saw the terror in their gaping eyes and mouths. A glance to either side showed her trick was working, simple but effective: the eyes of the priest and priestess glowed like captured lightning, a white light blindingly bright in the darkness.

The students gasped and stared too. The fighting dwindled to almost nothing.

"You have brought forth the wrath of the Earth itself." Hekate deepened her voice. She kept the glow pouring from her eyes and her companions'. "Leave now and never act against the immortals or your fellow humans again, or the Goddess will drag you to the flames beneath the Earth."

Lightning forked over the hill and thunder rumbled— again not Hekate's doing, but conveniently timed.

The students and guards jabbed blades at the shrinking-back Thanatos soldiers.

After glances at each other, the remaining members of Thanatos turned and raced away. The guards and students chased after them, shouting in victory.

Hekate dropped the hands of her companions, and let the glow vanish from their eyes. The three of them stood swaying and blinking a moment. Hekate was surprised, when her vision recovered, to find the priestess and priest dropping to their knees at her sides and kissing her hands fervently.

She tugged her hands away. "Oh, get up! I'm no queen. Come, let's make sure they're gone, and heal these poor men."

The tumult continued a while longer. The enemy soldiers were chased far out of town, sent along with rocks thrown after them and the hearty curses of everyone in Eleusis. Of the fallen guards, miraculously none were killed, and though some of the wounds were serious, Hekate now had the power to speed along their healing with her bare hands, and felt confident each would recover.

Then, of course, she had to be lauded and hugged a thousand times by the citizens. A special impromptu ceremony of gratitude at the sanctuary had to be held. During it she noticed a palpable tingling of power, which she had felt during the fighting too, and which she now realized didn't come from herself. These mortal temple folk did indeed wield magic, deliberate and controlled. Their abilities didn't match hers, of course; as she'd known when she was mortal herself, having an immortal body and an upbringing in the Underworld combined to form a sort of magical perfection that made her the ideal conduit. All she had to do, in many cases, was reach for energies and use them. Mortal practitioners needed years of meditation and practice, and then had to rely on spoken spells and physical objects to help focus the magic, and they probably had to stand on these sacred spots in order to sense results. Still, she felt and knew it now: these people, and others like them all over the world, were using the same powers she did, and they had worked out how to do it on their own. She had underestimated the folk of the mortal world, and tonight she was glad in her humility. She clasped the hands of each person who had taken part, thanked them and assured them they had successfully channeled the Earth's powers, and watched each stand up straighter in pride.

The lightning storm passed, leaving a cool and steady rainfall in its wake. Finally Hekate was able to walk off and be alone a while.

She followed the road to the sea, her feet bare, each raindrop, pebble, and leaf a tangible blessing. She climbed over the driftwood at the shore, gathered up her skirts, and waded into the surf. Luminescent waves crashed around her knees in a flood of magic. The air smelled of freshly-washed earth and salty sea. Tears of joy ran down her cheeks, mingling with the rain. She lifted her face to the sky with eyes closed.

The presence of someone drawing near became a new note in the blissful song. She opened her eyes.

Though it was dark and he was only a shadowy shape walking toward her, she knew Hermes by his signature sense.

"Is it true?" he called.

She laughed. It took only a mild effort to draw the tiny lights in the warm sea up into her garments and turn them into a shining line of blue pinpoints strung in the air between her hands.

Hermes waded into the sea and laughed. "It came back to you. Ah, love, is this the happiest day of your life?"

She held up her palms, playing with the strings of lights. "It might truly be."

An incoming wave washed around their knees, dragging their cloaks about on the water's surface. "And am I ruining it by being here?" But she still heard mirth in his voice.

In answer she let the lights disappear, and grasped the powers of air. She pushed a concentrated gust like a hand against his lower back, shoving him toward her. He made a sound of surprise, which he turned into a murmur of interest, and moved forward, only stumbling in the knee-deep water for a moment. She caught his hands.

His thumbs stroked her palms. "Do you know what I think?" he said. "The Fates were never punishing you. You were punishing yourself. Tonight you finally earned your own forgiveness, that's all."

She was too joyful to be disturbed by the suggestion. "Perhaps. Whatever the reason, I couldn't be happier." She looked down at his hands, realizing she could once again sense his emotions—or anyone's, if she touched their skin. "Such love. Desire. Are you just back from seeing a lover?"

He smirked, as if she were being quite obtuse. "Perhaps I'm with one now?"

Then he dropped to his knees, and kissed her belly through the chilly wet fabric, and her bare thighs where she'd pulled her skirts out of the sea. Kneeling like that, he was almost chest-deep in the water, but it slowed him down none. She gasped and planted her feet wider for balance in the back-and-forth rushing currents, giddy with surprise both at his movements and at her own reaction of sudden desire. His thief's hand slipped between her legs, caressing.

You did these things with people at the Dionysia, yes, and there it mattered not at all. But this wasn't the Dionysia. Tonight it was only the two of them, in the dark sea. The lust and love emanating from Hermes' flesh where he touched her blazed like an invisible fire. She hadn't sensed a lover's feelings with magical enhancement since the one first night with Dionysos—a night that also had begun with Hermes' kisses, now that she thought about it.

Her mind filled with strange new questions about how long and how seriously he had wanted her, and her freshly found magic couldn't tell her all the answers. But the desire issuing from his skin chased out her breath with its strength.

His touches and kisses grew more determined, more rhythmic. A sound escaped her throat, the need surging to a concentrated ache low in her belly. The sea's next wave swept inward and knocked them a few staggering steps toward shore. Hermes managed to stay on his knees and not fall underwater; he clung to her legs and laughed.

She laughed too. "Come on." She tugged him toward shore.

He sloshed to his feet and hooked his arm around her waist. Rivulets of seawater ran down her legs. Together they tottered up the slope and picked a spot on the beach to tumble down. Hekate landed on her back on a patch of sand, Hermes atop her, a dark silhouette and a heavy weight of warm flesh and cold wet cloth.

Her skirts fell up nearly to her waist, and she wrapped her unencumbered legs around him, savoring the feel of his body through the thin soaked cloth. He echoed the throaty sound she had made, lower and more determined, and rocked against her as he captured her mouth with his.

Oh sweet fertile Goddess, could she do this? Right here and now? Haul up her gown and take Hermes on the beach, in the living realm just outside Eleusis, with hardly any preamble or discussion? What would he think of her, what would it change about their friendship, shouldn't she slow down? Or did this count as a perfectly valid celebration of her triumph tonight?

Once again the decision was made by an interruption of familiar friends approaching. Hermes sighed and informed her, "Oh yes. I was to tell you, Dionysos and Athena are on their way."

"Oh." She tempered her voice to a reasonable tone, as if discussing gardening with a mere acquaintance, though he remained on top of her and they kept straining subtly against each other. "You were all together when you heard, then?"

"Yes, in Athens." He sounded casual too, though at least one certain part of him seemed to throb in its contact with her. "A rider came from Eleusis with news of the attack, and told us of the return of your powers. Athena and Dionysos went to Eleusis first, to make sure everyone was safe."

"But you came to *me* first." She tightened her legs around him, although Dionysos and Athena must have left the town now; they were coming closer to the beach.

"Couldn't help myself." He breathed the words, and pressed against her for another long moment before dragging himself up with reluctance.

She stood too, shivering in her wet clothes. Was he again going to pretend they were just playing? Is that all they'd been doing? Did love and desire flare up and burn out that quickly for him?

Before she could speak any of those questions aloud, a torch appeared down the road, emerging from behind the town wall. Dionysos called, "Hekate!"

"Hello," Hekate called back.

Athena and Dionysos hurried down. Hekate had to tell them the account of the battle all over again, and demonstrate that her powers were back. The sheer joy returned to her as she talked of it, and she laughed and embraced her friends with unfeigned happiness. To herself she marveled that she could have been so strangely distracted by Hermes and erotic matters even for a short time.

But whenever she glanced at Hermes, his face now illuminated by torchlight, the look in his eyes triggered a flash of excitement within her. Ordinarily it was well-nigh impossible to know what Hermes was thinking. But tonight, in those glances, she was certain of at least one thing he wanted.

"Have you told your parents?" Dionysos asked.

The reminder jerked her back to the present. "Not yet. I should."

"Let's go now," Athena said. "I'd love to be there when they hear."

Hekate couldn't refuse when her friends were so delighted. She began walking along the road with them.

Hermes stepped apart from the group and asked, "Shall I spread the word to the rest about your magic? They'll appreciate some good news."

She nodded, mainly because she couldn't see a way to insist he stay near her—and what would that accomplish right now, anyway? "Thank you," she said.

"I'll visit you in the Underworld before long," he answered. His gaze flicked down her body. "See how things are down there."

She pressed her lips together to keep from laughing in shock at the secret, brazen double meaning. She nodded in response.

He bowed to the three of them and dashed off.

CHAPTER TWENTY-TWO

*L*ANDON WAS ABOUT TO GET A TRIP TO EUROPE, JUST LIKE HE always wanted. And gosh, he didn't even need a passport and didn't have to spend a penny in airfare. Kind of handy, operating illegally.

He poured himself a glass of bourbon in the rented Tahoe vacation house where Erick Tracy had relocated their temporary headquarters. From Washington they had moved for a week to an apartment in Roseburg, Oregon, and now they had moved again just to be cautious. This place was a condo on the Nevada side of the lake, done up like a ski chalet: suffocatingly thick comforters, fake animal-hide lampshades, wall paneling that was probably supposed to resemble natural timbers but looked more like plywood. At the lake's high elevation, January snow blanketed everything. Landon had seen lots of skis and snowboards strapped to roof racks on their furtive drive here last night.

He stared out the kitchen window. Above the pines, the sky was darkening to twilight. A clump of snow fell off the eaves and dropped past the window. From the forecast and the look of the clouds, more snow was on the way.

He gulped the bourbon down. Maybe Greece would be warmer. If they were even going to Greece. Erick Tracy was still being a micromanaging ass and "working out" where they had to go first. There was some sorcerer lurking somewhere in Europe that he was trying to arrange a meeting with, to lure her onto their team. Sounded creepy. Landon was about ready to hand the full management over to the jerk and just drop out of Thanatos.

Then do what? Turn state's evidence against them, enter the Witness Protection Program, and hope his former allies never tracked him down to kill him? Even if Landon did drop out of Thanatos, the immortals would still hold a grudge for his part in the death of Sophie's parents.

At those thoughts, his chest and stomach knotted up until he felt like he was having a heart attack. Unlikely at his age, he supposed, but a panic attack, sure, that made sense.

He poured one more slosh of bourbon and drank it. *Please don't let them find me. Please let them lose my trail.* He prayed it a hundred times a day. But then, he had little faith in prayers.

A clunk and shuffle behind him signaled Krystal's approach on her crutches. He didn't turn.

She leaned a crutch against the kitchen counter and slid an arm around him. Her cheek pressed his back, warm through his shirt. The smell of her perfume swamped his nose, like the blast of scent inside hair salons. "Hey," she said. "Everyone else is out. Now's your chance to help me with my bath."

Krystal trying to sound sultry merely turned his stomach. He'd tried so hard to like her, just as he'd tried hard in the past with other girls, but it wasn't working. And that was going to be trouble, because he had indeed led her on, and Krystal wasn't the kind of woman you wanted to piss off.

Jesus. At this rate *everyone* was going to want to kill him.

He laughed nervously. "Yeah, I'm…a little too stressed out. Sorry."

"There are things I could do to relax you. Come on, you've got to want more than just those little kisses."

Those little kisses, their only remotely intimate contact so far, had been effort enough for him. He edged away, catching her arm and guiding it to the counter so she wouldn't fall.

"It's just...I'm creeped out about this witch woman Tracy wants to find. I mean, what do we know about her? Are her powers for real?"

Please let that change of subject work, he added to his collection of useless prayers.

Krystal shrugged, one corner of her mouth twisting down. "You know how much research he does. He's good at digging this stuff up. He says Tenebra's the one to get, the most powerful practicer in the world."

"Practitioner," he murmured into his bourbon glass.

"Whatever. Look, the evil freaks do dark magic, so we need someone on *our* side doing dark magic. Don't know about you, but I sure as hell can't do that kind of thing."

"No, me neither." He rotated his glass, gazing down into it. "So I guess, when he finds out where she is, we have to go there first and get her. Convince her."

"Tracy'll manage all that. Stop worrying." She shifted closer, and stroked the inside of his arm. "How about something to put you in a better mood?"

His body wanted to shudder. He turned it into a shivery smile instead, and thumped his glass down on the counter. "You're sweet. But I...feel cooped up in here. Let me go for a walk, and maybe when I get back..."

She stared at him with unflinching eyes. "Tracy and Yuliya will be back soon."

Yuliya was the Russian woman recently moved to America, one of the central council of Thanatos. She had joined them for the duration of this European endeavor, and was already banging Tracy, as far as Landon could tell.

"I know, but—let me go out for a bit, okay?" he begged. "I'm going crazy in here."

Her suspicious gaze stayed on him the whole ten or fifteen seconds it took him to dart to the door, yank on his snow boots and coat, and dive outside.

In the twilight, he gulped down the thin, icy air. His boots crunched in the snow as he followed the path between condos. Tall pines creaked overhead. When he glanced up at them, feathery falling snowflakes brushed his cheeks and lips.

Maybe he could just run away. From them all—immortals, Thanatos, Krystal, the whole world. If he kept walking, he could reach the highway and hitchhike out of the mountains, down to Las Vegas where it was always warm and you could purchase things like fake ID's and a whole new life, or so rumor had it.

Someone trotted down, whistling, from the steps of another condo as Landon passed. Landon glanced at the man, glanced away, then looked again with a shock of terror.

The stranger with the merry smile leaped over and got his arm impossibly quick around Landon's throat. With his gloved hand covering Landon's mouth, he tugged him behind a hedge. Landon fought and kicked, but the stranger didn't budge. Then the world swooped bizarrely and the hedge disappeared. The stranger flung Landon to the ground. "Hello, cupcake. Miss me?"

The condos were gone, as were the cars and the whole parking lot. Huge trees stood around them in the falling snow—different trees, massive and gnarled. The wind whispered, and some animal he couldn't identify howled in the distance.

The spirit realm.

"Oh, Christ." Landon scrabbled for the revolver that should have been in his coat pocket, but it was gone too.

"Looking for this?" The stranger tossed the gun from one hand to the other, then pointed it casually at Landon. "Sorry, they should have warned you. I'm an expert thief."

"You left me that note?" Landon's voice shook.

"Thanatos is pathetic, it would seem. Allowing me to pluck away one head of operations after another, so easily."

"Then you did kill my grandmother."

The stranger's smile hardened into something more bitter. "Of course."

Landon fell back in the snow. His gaze staggered among the exotic treetops. "Fine. You got me. Kill me fast, all right?"

"Oh, so dramatic," the stranger chided.

New footsteps crunched nearer in the snow.

Landon sat up. His heart palpitated as he recognized Adrian Watts, alive and well.

"Hello, Landon," Adrian said.

"Oh my God," Landon whispered.

Here before him stood the same young man he'd almost thrown into a fire a few weeks ago, who at the time had been unconscious with a bullet hole through his skull. No one could recover like that, not unless they were indeed immortal. It was fucking terrifying.

"Didn't expect to see me again after your girlfriend shot me in the head?" Adrian's New Zealand accent had a gentle lilt at odds with the menace in his eyes.

Landon's mouth was dry. "She's not my girlfriend," he heard himself answering, of all the stupid things.

Adrian glanced at the stranger, who laughed. "Indeed, Adrian," the stranger said. "Is your gaydar broken or something?"

Landon tried not to wince. Wonderful—humiliation on top of imminent death. He was fooling no one. They might as well kill him now.

"Oh," Adrian said. "Is that how it is."

"Certainly," the other said. "Besides, come on. Krystal? Would *you*?"

"Well, *I* wouldn't." Adrian studied Landon. "But who knows what he likes."

"I have a few guesses." The stranger knelt in front of Landon, not even bothering to point the revolver at him anymore; it dangled from his hand. Landon could have snatched at it, but he guessed that would be a disastrous idea. Adrian was probably concealing a weapon in those coat pockets, and taking on two immortals by yourself—in the other realm, no less—was a hopeless proposition.

"What are you going to do to me?" Landon asked.

"We're a bit curious what Thanatos plans to do next," the stranger said. "You're in a position to tell us—head of operations and all that. Congratulations on your promotion, by the way."

Landon glanced from the stranger to Adrian and back again, waiting to see if they had more to say before he committed to any answer.

"You tell us some specifics," the stranger continued, "and we let you go. For now. But you'll keep giving us updates, and if it turns out your information is false, or you're trying to trap us, we fetch you back here." The stranger's gaze scanned the darkening sky. "And next time, you won't leave."

Except maybe there *was* a way to leave this realm, Landon thought, his heart hammering. If Tracy was right, there were places where even mortals could switch back and forth, if they had certain artifacts—which Tracy said he did. Their team hadn't tested it yet, but getting left here might not be hopeless, as long as the immortals didn't actually kill him.

But then, of course they'd kill him, if he didn't cooperate. He had to get out of this, had to at least make a show of playing along.

"So what is it you want, Landon?" Adrian Watts asked. "What's more important to you? Eradicating immortals, because of what's written on a few ancient scraps of parchment? Or going on living: is that more important to you?"

Good question, actually. Landon's life was looking less and less desirable these days. But humans were funny. They always hung on so tightly to life.

He swallowed, trying to moisten his parched tongue. "There's a new idea. This guy in our group came up with it." Landon hesitated as both young men stared at him in silence, then he plunged ahead. "He thinks maybe we can get into this realm. And...get you guys that way."

Adrian snorted in derision, but the stranger sent Adrian a pensive glance, then asked Landon, "How's he going to do that?"

"There are temples, he says. Or things like temples. Special places set up a long time ago. Ancient stone circles and shrines and things. All over Europe, not just Greece." Might as well not mention getting directly into the Underworld, if he could avoid it.

Now Adrian's smile faded, and he looked at the stranger, who kept gazing at Landon. "Go on," the stranger said.

"There were people who worshipped the immortals, all those years," Landon said. "They used to be the Eless...El-yoo...I can never pronounce it."

The other men were quiet a moment, then Adrian said, "Eleusinian Mysteries."

"Right. That. And other names too. Some of them kept their cults alive all these centuries, and...they had some special artifact that, if you brought it to these temples, you could get into the other realm."

"He has this artifact?" the stranger asked.

"He says he does. But we haven't tried it yet. We don't know of anywhere in the Americas where it would work. Only those sites in Europe."

Adrian glared at Landon. "So the plan is to sneak in and attack us? Take us by surprise?"

Landon hesitated. He saw no need to spill the details about destroying the tree of immortality. Nor the bit about the sorcerer. If they did let him go tonight, maybe Tracy and the others would cut him some slack for holding that stuff back, and find some way—any way—to use this encounter against the immortals. As long as they didn't kill Landon for this slip-up themselves. God, was he in trouble.

"Well," he answered, "that's the usual objective, yeah."

"Like little hobbits journeying into Mordor," the stranger remarked.

Adrian frowned at him. "That makes us Sauron, mate."

The stranger gave a carefree twist of his lips, then regarded Landon. "Where in Europe? Where are you going to try this?"

Landon averted his eyes. "I don't know. We haven't chosen yet. I mean, it depends whether this even works. We have a lot to figure out."

"What about living targets?" Adrian asked. "Who are you going after, other than me? Who are you going to threaten as hostages this time?" His voice shook a bit on that sentence, as if his fury couldn't be contained.

Landon bowed his head. It still sickened him, thinking about how they'd killed Sophie's parents. And how Krystal didn't feel a crumb of remorse over it. "We're...still looking for Tabitha Lofgren. To see if she's one of you." He sent them a swift glance, but they kept their expressions fixed, and didn't let anything slip about whether Tabitha was in fact immortal.

"Anyone else?" the stranger asked.

Landon glanced at Adrian. "You're the only one we know about for sure, so...it's kind of routine to look for people you might care about."

"Such as Sophie," Adrian said, in almost a growl.

Landon looked down again and nodded. His hands, still half-lifted in surrender at his sides, were going numb in the freezing air. "We haven't found much on her yet. She's hiding or something."

Adrian crouched to look closer at Landon. Landon sent him one timid glance, found Adrian's dark eyes burning in rage, and looked down again. "You're an accessory to two counts of murder," Adrian said, "along with arson and possibly more. We could turn you in to the authorities in a heartbeat. Your life is effectively over. And believe me when I say the afterlife won't be kind to you either, the way things stand. But if you turn against your evil friends now, and help us stop them, then just *maybe* you won't have to spend so long in hell."

Landon tried not to tremble visibly, but his lifted hands were starting to betray him and do so. "Because you control the afterlife?" he said in a temporary attempt at defiance. "And you reward your worshippers?"

"Not at all, mate," Adrian said. "Because the afterlife controls itself. And it knows right from wrong. Do you?"

Landon had no answer to that. He gazed at Adrian's black boots in the snow. Prolonged fear—and bourbon—were making his head pound.

"I'm putting a number on your phone," the stranger said.

Landon looked up to find that he had pickpocketed his phone off him too at some point, and was now typing into it.

"This is where you text us with updates," the stranger went on. "Twice daily, nine a.m. and nine p.m., or else you're back here in a flash."

"What if there's nothing to tell?" Landon protested.

"You'll come up with something, I'm sure." The stranger handed him the phone. After hesitating a second, Landon took it. "And don't bother trying any fancy tracking techniques on that number," the man added. "You'll learn nothing. It's just a throwaway phone we got for this purpose."

"And you may think you can run and hide after we let you go today," Adrian added, "but you can't. We have ways of finding you."

"Magic ways?" Landon wasn't even being sarcastic anymore. From where he sat now, he couldn't really go claiming magic didn't exist.

"Something like that." The stranger slipped Landon's revolver into his coat pocket. Landon clearly wasn't getting that back today, or probably ever. "Let's drop you off, then," the stranger said. "Send your first update tomorrow morning at nine. Or else." He gave Landon a broad, charming grin.

CHAPTER TWENTY-THREE

ERICK TRACY CLENCHED HIS HANDS INTO FISTS IN THE POCK-
ets of his suit jacket as Landon babbled his tale. It was
all he could do to keep from slapping the boy. All right, maybe it wasn't Landon's fault that the unnaturals had shown up
against all odds, seized him, and threatened him, but Tracy
couldn't help feeling it *must* have been Landon's fault somehow.

Krystal and Yuliya stared as Landon, seated on the sofa,
pale and shaking, spilled the details and showed them the
new number on his phone. Krystal looked disgusted. She'd
surely begin to regret her crush on Landon any second now—
which was just as well, given the boy was obviously gay. And
closeted too, another choice Tracy couldn't abide.

"All right," Tracy said when Landon finished. He forced
a calming smile. "All right. This is an opportunity, if we look
at it correctly. Let's see what we've learned that we can use
against them." He steepled his fingers and paced back and
forth in the condo's living room. "Adrian did survive. Important to know. Also, they're unaware what we're up to, and
they need information. Good."

"You *told* them what we were up to," Krystal said to
Landon. "Not good."

"They were going to kill me!" Landon protested.

Krystal rolled her eyes.

Yuliya flattened her mouth, looking resigned and sympathetic, then seemed to switch into mother mode: she sat beside Landon and folded her hands soothingly around his elbow.

"But," Tracy went on, "they do have some way to find us. Or at least, you." He glanced at Landon, then at Krystal. "And possibly you, given how Adrian Watts appeared and disappeared directly in your room."

Both of the young ones widened their eyes.

"Do you think it's like that sensing thing in the Decrees?" Landon said. "Sanjay reported it too. And we know Adrian could sense Sophie. He followed her to the house in the mountains that night."

"But why the hell could they sense *us*?" Krystal said.

"We don't know how it works, in all its details," Tracy pointed out.

"Wait a sec." Landon looked even paler. "If they can track me, or Krystal, anytime? Holy shit, no. We can't…there isn't… wait, there was the oak thing! They can't sense through oak. Remember, that worked? With Sophie, and the van?"

"And what do you propose to do?" Tracy asked. "Wear a suit of oak armor everywhere you go?"

"I'm considering it," Landon countered.

"Let 'em come to me." Krystal jutted her chin higher. "I hope they do. I want this fight."

Tracy pressed his fingertips to his forehead a moment. Idiots; such a pair of idiots. "Look. We don't know yet if they can track you at all. They might simply have managed to follow us when we drove here. It's true, we took precautions, but someone determined enough could have done it, even without magic. It doesn't change our plan."

"But what do I do tomorrow?" Landon whined. "When it's time to send them a message?"

"Send them one," Tracy said. "Something false and misleading that will waste their time, I would suggest."

"No! If it's false they'll kidnap me again and this time I'm dead!"

The sooner the better, Tracy managed not to say, though in his annoyance he was tempted to. "Fine, then something simply useless, such as 'Everyone slept in today, no new plans.'"

"I can't always give messages like that, though."

"You won't always." Tracy walked to the window and moved the closed curtain aside a centimeter to peer out into the darkness. "Eventually we'll use this as a way to close the trap around them."

"Calm down," Yuliya told Landon gently. "They are obviously weaker than we think, or they would have taken you or killed you."

"I don't know," Landon said. "See..."

Tracy tuned out Landon's monologue of angst. He let the curtain drop into place, and took out his phone to gaze again upon the email that had finally arrived. All day he'd been looking at the message like one admires a new piece of art one has bought.

Through labyrinthine networking efforts, he had acquired an email address for Tenebra, the sorcerer. His first cordial message had gone ignored. But in his second he included a virtual dossier on the proposed expedition: no exact names, dates, or locations, but an outline of what Thanatos was after and how they might step into the Underworld itself, the source of the terrible power, to achieve their ends. And, of course, he promised that Tenebra would be amply compensated, in money or maybe in witchcraft-worthy souvenirs from the other realm, or both if she wished. Tracy would be happy to discuss.

It took a few days, but to that message she—or at least someone—responded. *Let's meet. Tell me when you are in Vratsa.*

Tracy closed the message, his confidence brimming again. Vratsa. Bulgaria, then. That's where they would land first. After that, they had a few Greek caves to explore.

"Thanks, all, for coming to our little emergency meeting," Niko greeted.

"I'm glad to see you both still alive after meddling with Thanatos," Rhea said. The soul of the dark-skinned, wise-eyed woman smiled at Adrian from where she sat, two places away, between Zoe and Freya.

Adrian smiled back in gratitude. But as Niko began explaining everything they'd learned from Landon, Adrian's eyes kept pulling toward Sophie, across the circle from him. He hadn't seen her in person for over two weeks. She still looked pale. Or was that just the cave's darkness and the greenish light of the souls? Her parents sat on either side of her in the grass, their glow bathing both her and Liam.

Along with all the living immortals and their allies, their deceased friends—Rhea and Sanjay, Terry and Isabel, Adrian's mum, Sophie's grandfather—had gathered here too. As a group they needed to analyze what Thanatos was doing, then plan their own next move. It would be nice if Adrian's mind could focus on that, rather than filling itself with longing for Sophie.

At that moment her gaze moved to him. It was like your crush catching you staring in high school. Adrenaline flashed through him, and he looked down at his fingers, which dangled over his folded legs. He swatted at a clump of blue clover flowers, feeling like a complete twit.

Niko finished relating their meeting with Landon.

"He's sent his first text." Niko held up the "throwaway" phone to display the message. It was now the morning after they'd grabbed Landon. What with time zone differences, they'd had to wait till now before they could get to the Underworld and assemble everyone during waking hours. "All he says," Niko went on, "is 'Everyone's still asleep. Supposed to talk to European contacts later. May have more tonight.' I'm going to assume he's already lying, but for now we'll leave him unpunished. It was more important to come and consult the rest of you."

"These European sites," Rhea said. "They still work, then?"

Zoe, Tab, Sophie, and Liam looked at her in confusion. Yesterday Adrian would have too. He had barely given any thought to the ancient sacred spots.

"I've no idea," Niko said. "I always assumed they couldn't possibly. Thought the secret had died out long ago, and likely the power along with it."

Zoe turned to him with bewilderment all over her features. "Do you mind telling the rest of us what you're talking about?"

"You wouldn't have got to those memories yet, Zoe," Niko said. "But you will soon."

Adrian must have said that same thing a dozen times to Sophie. A faint smile tugged at his mouth, and he lifted his gaze to her. To his amazement, she returned the glance with the same tiny smile of recognition. Then the moment and the smile slipped away, and she turned to listen to Niko, who was continuing:

"Turns out if you roam round Europe—and I assume the rest of the world—you'll find spots where something's just right about the energies, or the magic, or—well, Hekate could have explained it. Zoe perhaps will. But what it means is, with a little training, the right plants, and a special artifact made of Underworld-sourced gold, mortals can cross into the spirit realm at those spots if they wish."

Everyone stayed silent. Adrian shivered. Like Niko, he had dismissed the possibility of anyone using those sites any-more, and had put them out of his mind. But if Thanatos had caught wind of them, they had no choice but to investigate.

"They're like portals?" Sophie asked.

"Exactly," Niko said.

"Wait, now," Tab said to him. "How come you remember this and Zoe doesn't?"

"I've lived with the memories longer than she has," he said.

"And did *you* remember this?" Zoe accused Adrian. "You never talked about it."

"I sort of remember," Adrian said. "Hades was dead before those sites were discovered and set up. By then I was in my next lifetime. And, well, I knew a certain amount about the immortals, and those sacred spots, but mostly I was tending to my own ordinary life. Then afterward, between lives…well, I didn't think it mattered, because I don't remember hearing of any great influx of mortals stepping into our realm."

"That's because there wasn't a great influx," Freya said. "They seldom ventured past the sacred spots even if they did cross over. They only switched realms for special ceremonies, or emergencies. And they were instructed not to speak of the 'mysteries,' as they were called. Those were only for the initiated."

"Would those be the Eleusinian Mysteries?" Sophie asked.

Freya nodded. "Among others."

"The Eleusinians were the first," Rhea said. "In honor of Demeter, Persephone, Hades, and their bloodline. Others came later." She smiled at Tab. "Some were called 'Bacchic' Mysteries, after Bacchus—another name for Dionysos."

Tab raised her fists in the air. "Go me."

"But if Landon's right," Adrian said, "they have one of these artifacts—some bit of Underworld gold. And they've dug up the secret on where the sites are and how to get through."

"Hang on." Zoe's eyes were wide. "Is *this* one of the sacred sites? The Underworld?"

Niko looked grave. He nodded, as did Rhea and Freya.

Sophie looked instantly at Adrian, her eyes wide with panic.

Adrian spoke as steadily as he could, though his limbs had begun tingling with terror. Why hadn't he thought of that in the past several hours? Why hadn't Niko said something, the bastard?

"Well. Yeah. As you know, in the living realm this place is a cave system, a tourist attraction. People take boats in on the river, to view the formations. It's why we don't switch realms inside here; we'd likely end up in the middle of a tour group. But in ancient times these caves were regarded as a sacred site, on the living side. There were offerings, rituals. People often spoke of it as the entrance to the Underworld, though most of them couldn't have actually known..." His voice trailed off as fear closed down his vocal cords.

"But Thanatos doesn't know this is it," Zoe said anxiously. "They don't know we're here. Right?"

Niko and Adrian exchanged a glance.

"Landon didn't say," Niko answered. "My impression is they aren't sure."

"But if they can get into this realm," Rhea said, "they could find out pretty easily. All you have to do is follow the souls. Or ask one."

"If I were them, that's what I'd do," Terry said. "Figure out which site is the Underworld, then go there, appear right in the middle of it, and do some damage."

Everyone went silent again. Adrian, his mouth dry with fear, looked across at Sophie. She was definitely pale now, her gaze resting unfocused on the flowers. He ached to crawl across the circle and wrap his arms around her to soothe her. And to be soothed. Here it was, barely a month since her parents had been killed, and it was all starting up again.

"But they could be completely bullshitting, right?" Tab said. "They might not be able to switch realms at all."

"True," Niko said. "We have no evidence they've actually

done it. But we'd better test that ourselves, with some mortals of our own." He looked over at the Darrow siblings. "Sophie, Liam? Care to be guinea pigs?"

Sophie drew in a breath, met Niko's gaze, and nodded. Liam, mute and worried, nodded too.

"As for me," Zoe said, "I'm going to start setting up the strongest bloody protective wards I possibly can around this cave."

CHAPTER TWENTY-FOUR

SOPHIE WALKED IN THE MIDST OF THE GROUP OF SOULS AND living folk, across the fields toward the back of the cave. Fear still made her tremble, but deep down and against all probability, Sophie found she was the tiniest bit excited about the prospect of switching realms all by herself.

Niko had ventured off alone, but now returned and thrust a couple of silver-gray leaves at her and at Liam. "You'll need these."

Sophie examined hers. "What are they?"

"Strawberry tree," he said. "Magic plant of choice for this endeavor."

"Andrakhnos," Zoe murmured, using the tree's Greek name, sounding as if she was just now remembering it.

"Does it have to be a strawberry tree from the Underworld?" Sophie asked.

"Didn't in the old days," Niko said. "But that's another thing we'll have to test."

"Let's try back here," Adrian said. He'd been leading the group, and now stopped by the back wall, not far from the entrance to Tartaros. "If I recall, this part of the cave is off limits to the public in the living world."

"I'll check," Niko said. He vanished, then reappeared a few seconds later. "Yep. Complete darkness. Quite out of the way."

"Would anywhere around here work for this trick?" Sophie asked.

"I'd expect so," Zoe said. "The hot spot is pretty much the whole cave system. The magic energies of the place—I mean, they're all over down here." She squinted around, looking worried, even though she had already spent hours dashing about and setting up magical protective walls of some sort, which should resist attempts at entry by the uninvited. Or at least would alert her if anyone did somehow get through, or such was Sophie's understanding.

"You'll also need this." Niko took a lumpy rock from his pocket and handed it to Sophie. It was shot through with veins that sparkled in the flashlight beams. "Underworld gold. It's all I could find at the moment."

"Oh. I've got that covered." She handed Niko back the rock, then took the amethyst necklace out from under her sweater. She slid her thumb under the violet-shaped pendant, and timidly met Adrian's eyes. "This has Underworld gold. Right?"

Adrian looked vulnerable all of a sudden, his black eyebrows relaxing from their scowl, his flashlight swinging forgotten at his side. He seemed transfixed by the sight of the necklace on her. She felt the heat flood back up into her face. After Christmas she'd sent him a brief text to acknowledge the gift: just *Thank you for the necklace. It's beautiful. And thanks for being patient.* She hadn't known yet how to address the fraught contents of his letter, nor had she told him she was actually wearing the necklace every day. Since it had been under her sweater, he likely hadn't seen it till now.

He blinked a couple of times, then glanced into her eyes and nodded.

"Then you're ready," Rhea said.

"You remember how it goes, switching realms?" Tab asked.

Sophie nodded. "From the memories. I remember the feeling, even though I can't do it."

"Or can you?" Freya said. "Let's try."

They all drew back a step from Sophie, as if she required space.

"I'll wait for you on the other side so you'll have company there," Tab said. "Good luck, chica." She gave Sophie a finger-gun point, then vanished.

Sophie looked at her parents, who stood proudly watching her. Then she met her brother's nervous, excited gaze, and smiled to reassure him. She didn't quite look at Adrian again—too flustering. She wrapped her left hand around the necklace, encasing the amethyst-and-gold pendant. In her right she clutched the fresh leaves.

She closed her eyes and concentrated. She felt fear again, but this fear was less about life-threatening doom. It was more the fear of failing, of disappointing her friends by not being as deeply in touch with magic as certain mortals thousands of years ago were.

Souls murmured in the distance, their voices like wind. The river's tributaries flowed and chattered. Sophie stood still, eyes shut. Remembering how she had learned from Hades to switch realms long, long ago, she envisioned the boundary between the worlds as a ridge, and imagined herself striding up toward it on a trail, reaching the level where the other side of the mountain came into view, moving on up and stepping over the top—

The world wobbled as if a great hand had shaken the globe. The voices went silent, though the water kept trickling. Sophie opened her eyes to find herself in pitch darkness except for one halo of light from the flashlight Tab held.

It was just her and Tab, standing alone in the living-world cave. Tab squealed, bounced up and down, and hugged Sophie.

Sophie's whole body tingled with wonder.

She had switched realms. All by herself.

As he watched Sophie fade away, then glimmer back into sight a minute later, Adrian felt the strangest thing: not terror, as he rightly should, but pride. Pride in her, for managing to do it.

Actually, everyone else seemed halfway-positive about it too. Murmurs and gasps sounded all around at her disappearance. Liam was especially excited. The second Sophie returned, he dove forward shrilling, "Me next!", and everyone gamely set him up to try it. Liam seized Niko's gold-veined rock, held it in a clutch with the leaves, and soon flickered away over the spirit-realm boundary too. The same collective gasp of wonder and congratulation swept through the group.

"I want to do it again!" Liam said the second he got back. So he did, jumping realms back and forth, while the rest stood around discussing the implications.

To Adrian's surprise, Sophie turned and walked straight over to him while the others talked.

"Well done," Adrian greeted.

"Thanks." She stopped in front of him, and smiled at the ground. "I know this means trouble. But, like…" She lifted her lashes to glance at him. "I'm kind of stoked. I feel so *powerful*."

Tenderness sent cracks through the ice around his heart. She had come to him, was confiding in him, was sharing and enjoying the magic of his strange lifestyle again. At least a little. "You are powerful," he said. "Always have been. Starting with peach-juggling powers, and getting stronger every year."

She laughed, sounding charmed at his reference to their online correspondence before they'd met. At the sweet sound, more of the ice melted away.

"Still," she said, "we don't know much about this. Like,

could Liam and I only switch realms because we have past-life memories from immortals who knew how to do it? If so, then no one in Thanatos should be able to. They haven't eaten the pomegranate."

The chill stole back over Adrian as he recalled their complicated new raft of problems. "Yeah, but supposedly some mortals learned how in the old days, and presumably they taught each other and wrote down how to do it. So it's possible Thanatos got hold of those instructions, along with stealing one of the gold bits."

"True. Well, we can try it with other mortals who haven't eaten the pomegranate. See if they can do it."

He nodded. "Zoe's parents. They'd be up for it."

"Right."

Adrian and Sophie both fell silent. The group had already discussed that idea; Zoe was going to fetch one or both of her parents tomorrow to try it.

Sophie's hand fluttered up to grasp the necklace. "Hey, good thing you gave me this. Came in handy."

Adrian gave a shaky laugh. "You've no idea the goosebumps it gave me, seeing you wear that down here. Bit of a time warp."

She let go of the pendant and· reached out to brush her fingertips along the scruff on his jaw. The motion was brief and awkward, and she let her hand fall away a second later, but she seemed to stay composed. "I do have an idea. Seeing you with a beard down here does the same to me."

Self-conscious, he rubbed his chin. "Oh. Yeah. Haven't got round to shaving for, um, couple of weeks."

"It's all right. Looks kind of nice." She strayed back a step.

"Sophie," Niko called.

She looked back, seeming relieved to have a reason to turn away.

But she'd spoken kindly to him. She had touched his face

and hadn't seemed to be outright sickened by it. That was reason enough to stay alive.

Niko and Zoe walked over.

"We ought to move you and Liam out of here," Niko told her.

Sophie's gaze darted to the souls of her parents, who were talking to Liam. "No, I—I don't want to leave them."

"No one can hurt your parents anymore," Zoe said. "But you two, if mortals can switch realms in spots like this…"

"But your wards should help," Sophie said.

"My magic is *not* failproof." Poor Zoe sounded desolate. "You all must see that by now."

Niko slid his arm around her shoulders and kissed her on the temple. She didn't even push him away, Adrian noted. Interesting.

Adrian addressed Sophie. "I agree. I'll rest a lot easier if you two are away from one of these hot spots."

"Not too far away," she pleaded.

"Just a couple miles should suffice," Niko said. "We can find you a nice hillside with a view around here. You could still come to the cave and visit your folks every day."

"What, like camping outside?" she asked.

"Say I fetched the Airstream," Adrian said. "And another similar caravan, so Liam can have space of his own. We could set you up, with…" He glanced around the group. "Two of us staying with you whenever you're there, and bringing you here and elsewhere as needed." He dropped his gaze. Not him, of course. Not overnight with her. Not these days.

Terry had wandered over to linger beside Sophie, and had caught this suggestion. Sophie turned anxious eyes to him, but he nodded firmly. "I want you two out of harm's way, kid. And you know…" Terry looked in speculation at Niko and Adrian. "Those ropes you harness the horses with. Could you keep us tied up that way too, somewhere outside the Underworld?"

Adrian's eyes widened. He cleared his throat. "Well. I kind of don't believe in tying up human souls with my own hands, but...I guess if they wanted me to, then yeah."

"Souls *can* be brought out of the Underworld," Zoe said. She was frowning abstractly at the cave wall, as if remembering. "Only to other places in the spirit realm, mind. But I did it once or twice as Hekate, on the rare occasion someone asked to try it. They just always feel a pull to come back here. Most never have the wish to leave, except to be reborn."

"Well, I have the wish in this case," Terry said. "That way you could bring us along. The vines would keep the Underworld from pulling us back, just in case our free will doesn't do the trick."

Sophie looked as astounded, almost scandalized, as Adrian felt. Persephone, too, would never have dreamt of interfering with the cave's natural order of how it handled human souls. "Really, you'd want that?" she said.

"We'd get to see the sky again. Could stay outside all night. Bad weather, well heck, that wouldn't bother us. Sure, let's try it."

Sophie finally looked at Adrian, and cracked a smile. "Would the poor Airstream survive getting towed over here by the horses at those speeds?"

He scratched at his beard and blew out a breath. "One way to find out."

CHAPTER TWENTY-FIVE

I T WAS DIRECTLY AFTER ADRIAN FLEW AWAY, BACK TO NORTH America to prepare the Airstream and check in on Thanatos, that Sophie remembered a happy bit of Persephone's afterlife. *Finally*, she thought, *some good news.*

Hekate, with Dionysos and Athena in tow, burst into the fields one day in an overflow of joy. Her magical powers were back. Persephone felt as much delight as a dead soul possibly could. Her daughter looked whole again for the first time since Persephone and Hades had died. Life was truly continuing.

As if she needed more proof, the next day Hekate came to her with an interesting question indeed, which suggested her thoughts were traveling some new directions.

"Mother," Hekate said, after drawing Persephone aside to talk in private. "It isn't important, I just wondered. Well... Hermes is a good friend to me of course, and I've heard rumors that he...he'll have romances with anyone..."

Persephone laughed. "That's a diplomatic way to put it."

"Then did you and he ever—?" She cringed.

"No, never." Persephone was amused. "Just friendly kisses. Though I'm sure he would have taken more, if I had offered."

"I'm sure. Then with Father, did he? I know he'll go either way. Hermes, I mean. I'm not sure about Father."

"No. Hermes certainly tried a few times, but Hades wasn't interested."

Hekate smiled. "Thank you. It really doesn't matter; I just wanted to know more about the old days. How you all were back then. Who I can trust."

"Oh, I'm sure you can trust Hermes, at least in the ways that count. He loves you, you know."

Hekate looked at her, astounded. "Hermes does?"

"I suppose we never told you. But when you'd been kidnapped, and he was dashing out with Kerberos to find you, he seemed so heartbroken. It occurred to me to ask him if he loved you. And he said, 'More than you'll ever know.'"

Hekate's lips parted, but she said nothing. A flush infused her face, a soft beauty kindling in her dark eyes, as if the revelation had taken her breath away.

"As you say," Persephone added, "he loves many people, often quite temporarily, and in any case it's unwise to believe half of what he says. But I did feel in that instance that he spoke honestly."

"Thank you," Hekate echoed, and wandered away looking stunned.

Sophie pulled apart a pomegranate from the orchard so she and her friends could have some fresh produce for lunch alongside their peanut butter sandwiches. While recalling the memory, she had absentmindedly set out plates under a willow tree. Now she looked across the field at Zoe, who chatted with Liam, Freya, and Tab. A few steps off, Niko talked with Sanjay's soul, but kept stealing glances at Zoe. In fact, Zoe sent him a few random glances too, and looked a bit flustered and preoccupied.

Maybe his kiss on Zoe's temple earlier wasn't just platonic, then.

Sophie smiled, and dealt a handful of pomegranate seeds onto each plate. Okay, the relationship statuses around here had officially gotten way too complicated to keep track of.

HEKATE PACED ALONGSIDE THE UNDERGROUND RIVER. SHE touched stalagmites and plants along the way, relishing the magic effervescing within them. At least half her mind considered what she might now be able to do, with her magic back, to help people, for truly the possibilities were immense.

But it annoyed her how the other half of her mind kept asking, *And what about having sex with Hermes? Should we do that, when he comes down here in search of it, which he's likely to do any moment?*

It had been two nights ago now, the return of her magic followed by the unexpected tangle with Hermes. Dionysos had spent the first night here, and of course she'd celebrated with him in amorous fashion. It would have felt wrong not to. At the same time it felt a little bit duplicitous, when he didn't know she had almost celebrated, and might yet celebrate, in the same way with Hermes. Then again, he likely wouldn't throw any jealous fits if she did. So she hadn't brought it up, and besides, there were more important topics to discuss.

Yesterday had been filled with visitors, her fellow immortals coming down to congratulate her and talk about the uses she might put her magic to. Hermes had been among them, but he hadn't lingered long. From the number of immortals already down in the cave, he likely deduced they wouldn't get a moment alone all day, and he had kissed Hekate's cheek casually and told her he'd come again the next day. Her heart had galloped at the promise.

Dionysos had left this morning after spending one more night. He had festivals to arrange, temple priests to talk to, especially now with the exciting plan of incorporating Hekate's magic into his activities somehow. Hekate was alone at last, her mind constantly swerving back to that phrase her mother had dropped upon her this morning: *More than you'll ever know.*

Suddenly Hermes' presence was near, likely breaking past the forest of oaks that surrounded the cave on the surface. She gulped down a swift breath, then turned and walked back toward the entrance chamber. She pushed her hair back from her face and smoothed her midnight-blue gown.

It was silly to be nervous. Immortal friends sought pleasure in each other all the time. She hadn't been in the habit yet, beyond Dionysos, but she had to get used to it. Hermes was a good place to start, really, since he bedded everyone. It would mean nothing. No reason to be jittery.

Unless he loved her more than anyone knew. Oh, Goddess. Could she intuit the truth with someone like Hermes? Even when she read emotions through touch, she couldn't always be sure where they came from or how long they'd last.

She turned a bend in the river and there he was: a figure in red cloak and cap, hopping up the bank after crossing on the raft. He pulled off his cap and strolled toward her. By some sleight-of-hand trick, he made a plant appear in his hand, a small shrub with little bell-shaped white blossoms, its root ball tied up in sackcloth.

"And how's the magical lady today?" He handed her the plant.

"Quite well, thank you." She took it and sniffed the flowers. "Lovely. Andrakhnos, isn't it?"

"Yes. Makes little red fruits. They taste bland, but perhaps if it grows down here they'll at least have some uncanny property."

"Always likely." She met his eyes and found them, as expected, a fathomless green sea of unknowable mysteries and undeniable interest. She swallowed, her face hot, and she lost the ability to go on pretending plants were interesting at the moment.

His mouth twitched at the corners. He held out his bare arm. "Oh, go on. Drink in today's crop of lust."

She set her cold fingertips on his forearm. Not only lust but love, the same mix as before, unique to him, surged straight to her heart, feeling like the first golden beam of sunlight at dawn.

His red cape fell around her as he drew her body against his and began kissing her neck, in no hurry at all, as if he were a vine that naturally grew to curl around her. She melted against him, closing her eyes. One hand still clutched the andrakhnos plant, but she spread the other upon his chest, over his swiftly beating heart, where the desire shone brightest. Well, not quite. A little lower down and currently poking her in the belly, that was where it'd be brightest.

"Tell me," he said. "When you feel such wants in others, do they spread to you?"

"Not with everyone." Her words rippled with a laugh.

"Ah, good. You have standards." He was still kissing her throat, her shoulders. "But right now?"

"I admit it enhances things at the moment."

"You do seem to like my touch. A little better every time." His palm coasted across her breasts, giving each a teasing squeeze. She shivered with pleasure. "You even seemed to enjoy my touch once without your magic. That night when you returned to the Dionysia."

"And you seemed to desire me that night even though I had no magic."

"You," he suckled her earlobe for a moment, "always have magic."

He smelled bewitching, like fresh sea air and fragrant spices along with the indescribable scent of his own skin. She was about ready to drop the plant and haul him down to the grass right here. And this was really not the location for it.

She blinked, focusing over his shoulder at the souls who drifted by and glanced at them. She wriggled out of his grasp and caught her breath. "That's good enough for a greeting between friends. Otherwise it'll be all over the Underworld soon."

"So?" He propped his hands on his hips, amused.

"There's—I don't know if—I haven't talked about it with…"

"You and Dionysos aren't exclusive," he reminded her. "You've both said so."

"Still, I don't think he expects—well, and if we do, what then?"

"What then?" Hermes lifted his eyebrows slightly, as if what happened *after* a wild sexual liaison couldn't possibly matter.

Honestly. Men.

"Is this just friends helping each other out?" she accused. It annoyed her how much she wanted this liaison despite all its sordidness. "I assume it must be."

"A little more than that. Aren't we a fairly good match, you and I, in our strange way?"

"Oh, as if you're going to become my new partner. You aren't the type to stick around. Even if you want me, even if you *love* me, you're still you."

A flicker of vulnerability changed his eyes, then he adjusted his expression to mild amusement. "Well. Luckily I didn't *expect* any sweet sentiments from you."

She exhaled, and steadied the plant between her hands. "I'm sorry. I don't mean to be hurtful. But I'm…having trouble understanding what you want."

The amusement spread on his face, lifting his lips and eyebrows.

"I mean, I know what you want," she amended. "But I don't know what you want to be in regards to me."

"People often have trouble fitting me into categories. I advise everyone not to try." He advanced on her, smooth as a shadow. "But I seldom object to the category of 'lover.'" He caressed her face with his fingertips and then with a kiss on her lips.

The warmth of his mouth almost toppled the last of her defenses. "Well," she breathed, her nose brushing his. "I suppose I understand sufficiently, if that's all."

"Good." He slipped his hand between the folds of her tunic so his palm cupped her breast. "I'll be happy to explain in further detail what I want from you, if you like."

She swallowed, and tried to slow her breathing. "Not here. Come on."

She strode past him to the river. She set the andrakhnos plant on the ground near the dock, for later planting, and led him onto the raft. They crossed the river and climbed the opposite bank. She led him through the tunnel, neither of them speaking. In the entrance chamber she picked up a folded wool blanket from a stack against the wall, and took it to her spirit horse. Hermes smiled smugly as he glanced at the blanket, but obeyed when she jerked her chin toward his horse. They mounted on their separate horses and flew out of the cave, though not far: Hekate descended into the thick oak forest outside the Underworld and landed in a clearing. Hermes settled beside her.

She hopped down. Acorn shells broke under her sandals. Her hands trembled as she tied her horse to a branch.

Not in the Underworld, not this first time. For one thing, it would feel inappropriate somehow—her parents' former home, and the bed where she had lately hosted Dionysos. For another, more immortals might come seeking her today, and she didn't wish to be interrupted if she was going to do this. The surrounding oak trees out here would block them from being tracked.

Last night's rain had blown away. Spring sunlight warmed the trees and brought up a sweet fresh smell from the ground. Spirit-world animals shrieked and chattered out in the forest.

In the clearing, the sun lit up gold threads in Hermes' shaggy brown curls. He took her hand and drew her closer.

"Do you love me?" she asked.

He kept gazing into her eyes. "Of course I do."

"But don't you say that to lots of people in order to get their clothes off?"

"Of course I do," he repeated, and his white teeth flashed in a grin. Then he touched his forehead to hers, barely having to lean down for it, for she was almost his height. "But in your case it's true."

"And surely you say *that* to lots of people." But she nuzzled his nose, and all she could think about was the feel of his lips, his hands, his body…

"I'm sorry; was this a seduction or a trial?" He took the folded blanket off her arm and stepped back into the shadows of the forest, pulling her along.

He spread the blanket over the mosses and ground-creeping plants at the feet of the massive oaks. Hekate's heartbeat pounded in her ears. Hermes unhooked his cloak and spread that out on top of the blanket. He toed off his sandals onto the moss, leaving him wearing just his tunic, pinned over one shoulder. He stretched out on his back on the blankets, arms behind his head, gazing up at the treetops as if enjoying a picnic alone. Then he looked at her and reached out his hand. "Are we done bantering?"

She took his hand.

IF HE'D ACTED SMUG OR COCKY, AS HEKATE DREADED, SHE likely would never have done it again. But instead he touched her unhurriedly, reverently, and at his touch she received such a rush of delighted, vulnerable love from him that she relaxed her guard. Straddled on top of him, she closed her eyes and let herself enjoy.

But Hermes sat up carefully, his body still locked with hers, and said, "Open your eyes."

She did. They breathed swiftly, close enough to exchange the same air, and she gazed in wonder at the living green of his irises.

He seemed equally fascinated with hers. "Eyes like nightfall," he said. "Magical eyes. You haven't even been trying to bewitch me, have you, but you've done it all the same."

Somewhere around there, Hekate's casual desire for a friend, which she suspected would be as ephemeral as a cut flower, put down roots and began blossoming into something larger.

Those roots deepened afterward when she lay in his embrace and felt the tenderness radiating from him. It was real, at least for now. Maybe it was real with every lover he visited, and maybe it would be gone in a month. But its existence today was enough.

"You'll come back tomorrow?" she asked.

He chuckled, deep in his throat. "Try to stop me."

CHAPTER TWENTY-SIX

SOPHIE THRUST THE SHOVEL'S POINT DEEPER INTO THE PALE rocky soil, in the beam of a camping lantern. Sweating, she paused to wiggle the trunk of the little pomegranate tree, but its roots still held tight under the earth.

"Jeez," she told it. "Didn't expect you to put up such a fight."

The tree was only about three feet tall, one of the many that had sprouted up from fallen seeds around the orchard.

She leaned on the shovel and rested a minute, then set to work again, throwing all her weight downward to make the shovel's blade bite deep.

Finally she got the blade beneath the tree's root ball and levered the whole thing out of the ground. She plunked it into a large plastic plant pot, and filled it in with dirt.

"There." She blew out a satisfied breath. "One pomegranate tree ready to move."

She hadn't slept well after that revelation about Thanatos possibly being about to dive straight into the Underworld. True, she and Liam usually stayed in the sleeping quarters across the river, not among the trees and souls where invaders would be likeliest to look, but it was still scary. And she worried about the trees and the other plants, too. This was the Underworld's sacred garden patch, damn it. Persephone's pride and joy. Sophie knew Thanatos' ways, how they liked to throw explosives around. This sprawling black-leaved pomegranate orchard had been growing nicely and reseeding itself on its own for millennia, sure, but she was betting it couldn't stand up to getting firebombed.

So yesterday she had asked Tab to take her to a market in one of the larger Greek cities nearby, and she'd bought dozens of plant pots of various sizes, along with shovels and trowels and gardening gloves.

Most of the trees were too big to move without a backhoe. And she didn't dare disturb the roots of the developing chrysomelia tree, nor the newly planted titoki and spring bulbs. But these plants had to live in the Underworld in order to retain their magic, and she could at least move some of them to somewhere else in the cave. Just in case.

ZOE FELT LIKE SHE'D BEEN BLUSHING ALL DAY. THOSE MEMOries about Hermes—holy good goddamn.

Starting with that day in the oak forest and continuing, like, every day, or two or three times a day for at least the next month (likely longer; she hadn't moved farther along than that yet), Hekate and Hermes were in full-on smoking-hot affair mode. Zoe's freshly revived memories fed the sensations to her in high definition. Racing hearts, heavy breathing, rhythmic slapping together of sweaty skin, constant excitement and distraction and longing, the whole deal.

If it was just fun sex between friends, maybe she could've laughed off the recollection. But Hekate hadn't quite succeeded at feeling that way, and that threw Zoe's balance off too.

Hekate couldn't exactly say she loved Hermes at that point, but she found herself irrationally jealous of his other lovers—even ones in the past whom he never saw anymore. As for whether there were current ones, she couldn't bring herself to ask. Shooting truth magic into him to get answers would have been a most disrespectful way to treat a lover, and anyway, she told herself she didn't mind as long as he still kept her as one of his lovers. But sometimes she did mind.

Dionysos was easy to understand once you got to know him; he gamely told all to his friends, as candid as the tipsy people at his festivals. Hermes was a different creature altogether, not exactly opaque but composed of so many ever-shifting layers that you could never see all of them at once. She now understood how such mystery could be enticing. She craved him, enjoyed him, kept receiving him in the Underworld or meeting him elsewhere, and all the while itched to peel away those many layers and learn the ordinary things about him. Who did he see, really? Who did he love, honestly? He said he kept several houses here and there around the Mediterranean, each of which he stayed in as was convenient to his roaming, but did any of them feel like home to him? Would he ever settle down somewhere? What did he need and long for?

He gave her seemingly honest answers to the questions she did ask, but he was unpredictable and unreliable at heart. He excelled at telling half-truths and making them seem whole, or at dodging topics he didn't want to discuss, even when she saw no reason for him to avoid them. He played with you because that was what he did, and you simply had to let him, and not allow it to drive you mad.

Only in those erotic tangles did she lay hold of his vulnerable and true self, or so it felt. In his climactic broken breaths and shudders each time, he lost his grip on control for the space of a few blissful moments just like any other human. Hekate had her arms and legs around him when it happened, and soaked up the love and longing that bled from his skin into hers.

But then he'd grin and pop up and turn straight back into his elusive everyday self. And her longing would spin out further.

Hekate ventured into the wider world a lot during that

month, exploring with her revived sense of magic, and visiting temples. Hermes often went with her, or "happened" to meet her at the sites, which of course led to more intimate leisure activities afterward. Nonetheless, even with such distractions, it was then that Hekate started noticing how the sacred sites were often placed exactly at spots where magic thrummed most vibrantly.

She brought it up with priestesses or priests, and they usually nodded and said the site had been chosen because it "felt" sacred, or because here the Goddess could be sensed more strongly, or similar reasons. They couldn't explain it more fully than that, and at the time she didn't even consider the possibility of mortals switching realms at those sites. Still, the placement of the temples lit up Hekate's mind with questions about magical abilities among mortals. She spilled her overflowing thoughts into Hermes' ears, and he drank them up and responded with insights of his own.

See, it wasn't all sex; they did still have intelligent conversations. His mind, the quickest and most complex of anyone's she knew, only made him more dangerously alluring.

All in all it meant they spent a lot of time together. And Dionysos—well, he was sure to notice one of these days.

Huge angst. Total messiness. All taken together, Zoe couldn't look Niko in the eye today. And he totally knew why.

At the moment they were all outdoors, on the promised hillside with a view a couple of kilometers from the Underworld. Adrian had safely landed the Airstream here, after strapping down everything movable inside it for the flight, and now Niko and Adrian were fussing with the generator to hook it back up. Sophie and Liam, with Tab and Freya and the dogs, were strolling around the two caravans, for Niko and Freya had fetched another from somewhere in Greece for Liam. It was a camper trailer of some kind from the 1970s, white with light blue stripes around it. Liam evidently loved it, judging from the grand plans he was chattering about. They hadn't yet tied vines to Isabel and Terry to bring them here, but planned to after they'd got the caravans set up.

Zoe had been clearing sticks and rocks from around the site to make it easier to stroll about. She paused now and let her gaze rest a moment on Niko while he was occupied in fixing the generator. But, as if sensing her, he glanced over, caught her eye, and winked.

Ugh. Cheeky bastard. She spun around and seized up another armful of sticks.

Sophie came around the corner of the Airstream, her hand tracing its shiny surface. "You look deep in thought," Sophie said.

Zoe chucked the heap of sticks out into the shrubs. "Memories. Where have yours got to?"

"You've gotten your magic back. Hekate, I mean. Hades and I are still souls, but…" Sophie stuffed her hands into her coat pockets and squinted out at the wild valley. "I have the feeling we leave soon to get reborn."

"Sad. It shouldn't be, but it is. It will be for Hekate."

Sophie glanced at her. "So that's not what your memories were about?"

"Ah, no. Um. The magic coming back, yes. Also…" Zoe grimaced. "The whole thing with Hermes. Wow."

"Ohhh." It sounded like a missing puzzle piece had fallen into place for Sophie. She glanced back toward Niko. "So it's true. We heard gossip in the Underworld, but never saw anything for sure."

"It's weird, you know? Because—he's Niko. And I'm not straight, but it all feels real. And wrong, yet not wrong. I don't know. Sorry. Ancient history, literally."

Sophie nudged her elbow in a way that reminded Zoe, fondly, of Adrian. "Nah, it's sweet. I'm not sure, of course, but I could swear the guy loved you. Maybe even still does."

They both glanced at him again, though Zoe only dared

look for a second. "No one can ever be sure with him. I think that's always the problem."

"Plus now he's a dude and you're not into those."

"Another problem."

Sophie turned to look at Tab and Freya, who giggled and talked together outside Liam's caravan. "Too bad he couldn't have been born into one of their bodies, huh?" Sophie said.

"Seriously. Though with Tab, I don't know. It just doesn't quite work between us. In *any* lifetime."

"How about Freya?"

"Oh, sure, physically she's a ten. It's the personality that destroys it for me." Zoe sent Sophie a bashful glance. "But this may be more than I ought to talk about with my mum."

"It's okay, I'm one of those cool mums."

Something rustled among the bushes several meters away at the edge of the clearing. Zoe caught motion in the corner of her vision, and turned to look, grateful for the diversion. Sophie noticed too, and they both stared into the thick tangle of the spirit-world forest.

"Thought I saw some monkey-thing earlier," Sophie said. "Might've been that."

"Might be all sorts of things. Never know out here. Let me see." Zoe stretched out her life-force senses, scanning the nearby animals. There were always lots more than she expected, even in the living world. Animals did a good job hiding. "Yeah, there's monkey things up higher, bats too, squirrel and rabbit type things...and something dog-like. Pack of jackals? Wolves? Anyway, they're sneaking off now. Probably just curious what we're doing, dropping two trailers in the midst of them."

"As long as nothing too big and hungry shows up." Sophie sounded nervous.

"Don't worry. That's why we scary-scented immortal types are sticking with you out here."

"Ooh. But this gal is cool." Sophie knelt to examine a fat blue bumblebee that had landed on a yellow wildflower.

"Wow, very." Zoe bent to look at the bee too. But a moment later she frowned aside into the forest, trying to work out what had felt so familiar about the dog-like things.

CHAPTER TWENTY-SEVEN

SOPHIE APPROACHED THE AIRSTREAM, GATHERING HER COURage to enter it. The generator hummed, and both trailers stood ready for moving into. She halted as Adrian appeared in the Airstream's open door. He paused too, then jumped to the rocky ground in front of her.

"Nothing broken inside, I don't think," he said. "I must have strapped it all down well enough."

She nodded. "Super."

"Rearrange stuff however you like. Make it comfy." He shoved his hands into the back pockets of his jeans. "I haven't used it for a while, of course, and wasn't planning to, so it's yours as long as you need it."

She nodded again. The Airstream had been sitting neglected in the spirit realm in Oregon for over a month, near the university campus she no longer lived at. For now. She tacked "for now" onto so much of life lately.

"Well then." He squinted over at his team of horses. "Niko and I better get back to the States, keep watch on the bad guys."

Sophie found her voice. "Please be careful. They'll destroy you so fast if they get a chance. Just—please, be extra careful."

His gaze met hers, and for a moment it was like looking at Hades again, with those stormy dark eyes, black windblown curls, and facial hair, here sharing space with her on the forested coastal hills of spirit-world Greece. "I will," he said. "You be careful too. We'll keep in touch."

Then with a blink of his eyelashes as a sort of goodbye, he moved past. She stood there a few seconds, aching at how the wall of trauma still oppressed her, preventing her from embracing him. She even felt anxious about entering the Airstream, because oh Goddess, the memories linked to this little silver trailer. Maybe she should trade with Liam, give him this one…

But Liam was already playing with the windows from inside the other trailer, calling to Zoe through the screen, "I found a good spot for Rosie to sleep!"

Nope. Sophie was stuck with the Airstream.

She womaned up. One foot in front of the other, and repeat. In a moment she was up the steps and inside.

The smell of it knocked her back in time. Emotion swamped her. She stood there breathing it in, letting it happen.

The trailer smelled like Adrian, of course; there was that. But it also smelled like itself, old upholstery and chilly metal window frames and the ghost of all the food cooked over the years in the kitchenette. The smells together made up the experience of her relationship with Adrian. There on that bed, she had curled up with him lots of nights, either terrified about Quentin or steaming up the windows in lust, or alternating between those two. In this tiny bathroom—she stepped forward and peeked inside it—she had gotten ready for classes several mornings after spending the night here. At this kitchen counter she had made squash soup on Halloween, feeling morose because she wasn't home in Carnation.

At least her house in Carnation had still been standing at the time. Should have counted her blessings.

Okay, so count them today.

She walked to the bed at the end of the trailer. One blessing: Adrian had made the bed for her with fresh sheets and blankets. A sweet gesture.

Another: Tab was off to wrap vines around Sophie's parents and bring them here for the night. They'd probably sit outdoors between the two trailers, so they'd be within earshot the whole time Sophie and Liam slept.

Another: this kitchenette, though tiny, was better laid out and equipped than the awkward camp stove, toaster oven, and fridge combo they had in the Underworld lately. She could finally cook better.

Another: well, did she have decent pantry supplies here? She opened a cabinet in the kitchen, and pulled out the plastic storage box that Adrian had packed all the pantry goods into before hauling away the Airstream. She popped off the lid. Yep, flour, sugar, baking soda, cinnamon, and more.

She moved aside the bag of flour and found two pillar candles. She pulled them out, then looked over at the table against the window. There they had sat one cloudy fall afternoon, while Adrian explained how he had become immortal and what Thanatos was. These candles had burned on the table between them, because he had just gotten the Airstream and didn't have the generator yet for electricity. She set the candles on the tabletop again now.

Among the pantry supplies she also found a box of matches. Sophie took it out. Her hands shook; it took five strikes to light the match, and the flame flaring to life almost startled her into dropping it. But she kept her fingers clamped around the match's wooden end and lit both candles, then blew out the match and sat on one of the table's bench seats. She stared at each flame until they no longer made her think of the house burning down. She pictured instead normal, nice candle-related things: Christmas cards, jack-o'-lanterns, birthday cakes. Adrian's eyes glimmering with candlelight while he told her that, yes, the owls Persephone painted on the clay jar were purple, just as Sophie remembered.

Sophie reached out and flicked her fingertip through one

of the flames, fast enough not to burn. She did it to the other candle too, then repeated the trick a few more times.

She got out her phone and struck through "fire" on her trigger list. One foot after the other, and repeat.

Chapter Twenty-Eight

No," Landon said. "No, no, no."

Tracy gazed at him with a calm smile, which Landon wanted to smash his knuckles into. "Then are we simply to do nothing?" Tracy said. "Keep feeding them tips exactly as they request?"

"If I call a meeting with them, and they realize you guys are nearby, watching, and they think even for a second that it's a trap? Then I'm toast. Would you *care* that I was toast?"

"Surely you see the opportunity this has given us. Shouldn't we use it?"

"So you're going to kill whichever one shows up?" Landon asked.

"Hell yeah." Krystal glowered from across the room, her arms folded.

Yuliya gave her an affirming nod.

"If we can manage it," Tracy said. "But even if not, this meeting would be valuable as a test. Just to observe who shows up and what they do."

They'd been arguing all afternoon, and Landon was sick of pacing around the Tahoe condo's living room; sick of Yuliya and Krystal throwing in supportive comments—supporting Tracy, that is. Sick of it all. He leaned against the windowsill and rubbed his face.

It had been almost a week since the immortals had waylaid him. He'd been obediently sending his twice-daily texts, usually with information that was at least half true, so that if they checked on it, they wouldn't discover an outright lie. He'd said stuff like, *We're probably flying over next week, date TBD* (true), and *Albania looks likely* (somewhat true; Bulgaria looked likelier, since that's where this sorcerer supposedly lived), and *4 of us plus a few on Europe side I haven't met* (true about the four, though they were aiming to pick up a couple dozen over there rather than just a few). The immortals never answered, which was unnerving, but Landon still didn't dare skip a text.

Now Tracy wanted him to request an in-person meeting. If Landon refused, surely Tracy would steal his phone some night and text the request himself, pretending to be Landon. Then it'd be Landon who'd get punished if—or rather, when—they discovered the deception.

Similarly, if he called the meeting and the immortals showed up and realized they were about to be attacked, and somehow escaped—which they were excellent at doing—it would be Landon whose doomed ass subsequently got torn apart in the spirit realm.

On the other hand, say this trap worked? One good shot from Krystal's rifle, then one grenade strapped to the unconscious immortal, and Landon's nightmare could be over. Or at least part of it. He didn't want to think about how the rest of the immortals or their allies might retaliate in such an event. God, he was in it deep, no matter what he did.

He lifted his face and took in Krystal's glower, Yuliya's sympathetic but stubborn jaw, Tracy's unruffled tweediness. "Fine. Let's try."

They had already concluded that the only way the immortals would agree to meet him in person was if there was some tangible, important item he could give them. Claiming to have information he wanted to convey in person would be an obvious lie. Since he had already told Adrian and the other guy that they had an artifact for getting into the spirit realm, Landon and his teammates agreed this artifact was the best piece of bait they could offer.

Tracy claimed not to have it with him. Much too valuable, he'd said; it was in a "safe place" until he was ready to fetch it. Landon suspected Tracy was lying and totally did have the thing with him, but it didn't matter much, since they wouldn't be offering the real artifact anyway.

Yuliya donated a broken golden earring to stand in for it. When she pulled off the wire piece, it left a disk with concentric circles and random symbols engraved on it, which did have a sort of ancient look to it. It wouldn't convince them once they saw it, but then, it only needed to absorb their concentration for a few seconds. As long as it took Krystal to aim and pull the trigger.

That evening, fingers icy with fear, he texted to the mystery phone number: *Say I get you this artifact and return it to you. Then I run. Away from this club for good. I'd be out of the fight. Would you leave me alone after that?*

It took over an hour, but an answer finally came. *Potentially. Do you have it?*

Yes. Can you meet me tomorrow at 10 am?

Tomorrow yes. Can't promise the time. We'll text you when ready.

OK. I'm just done w/ it all. That, Landon thought tiredly, was at least mostly true. *Parking lot of St John church on Lincoln Hwy.*

"THINK IT'S A TRAP?" ADRIAN ASKED, AFTER STUDYING THE messages back and forth between Landon and Niko.

Niko had flown to southern Arizona to meet with Adrian. Adrian had been camping out down there in his bus in the spirit realm, among the cacti, because Lake Tahoe in January was too bloody cold when you were sleeping in the back of a bus with no windows.

"Almost certainly," Niko said. "That church closed last year and the building's abandoned. The parking lot would be empty, not many people around to witness anything happening in it. Good place to hit someone with a bullet or Tazer, then drag them into a car and transport them elsewhere to blow them up."

Adrian handed the phone back to Niko. "You don't think there's any chance he really is giving this artifact to us and running out on Thanatos?"

"I could see him being tempted to," Niko said. "But I expect he's too scared. They're his best hope at safety. Or so he thinks."

"So if he really is trying to murder us..." Adrian's heart constricted with dread. Goddess, he hated being obligated to kill anyone.

Niko looked equally unenthused, his tan skin a shade paler than usual, his lips firmly set. "I'll take care of it."

"I'm coming too. If he's bringing backup, so are you."

Adrian expected resistance, a cool brush-off. But Niko only nodded and said, "Let's get Zoe as well. Extra magic on our side won't hurt."

THE IMMORTALS TEXTED AT LUNCHTIME, NOT THAT LANDON had been able to eat a bite today. *At the parking lot. Whenever you're ready.*

Landon, Tracy, Krystal, and Yuliya were waiting in their rented van down the highway a quarter-mile from the locked-up church. Tracy said, "Off we go," and turned the engine on.

They parked on the shoulder of the highway, not in the lot itself. The lot was behind the church, hidden from the road. The former church was a dreary building of blue-painted boards, not much different in structure from the lumberyard office at the next property over. Yuliya got out and assisted Krystal with her crutches. The two women made their way into a stand of trees that ran between the church's lot and the lumberyard. In their brown and camouflage clothes, they soon disappeared. Even leaning on a crutch, Krystal could fire a gun with accuracy, as long as she got a clear shot.

Landon remembered last time, the blood all over Adrian Watts, the bullet wounds, his weight heavy in Landon's hands. The world swayed as Landon climbed out of the car, his pulse tapping so fast and his lungs taking in so little air that his vision showed white sparks at the edges. Oh, God, let it be over fast this time. Let this work; let the immortals give up and leave him alone after today.

Tracy stayed behind the wheel. "When I hear the shot," he reminded Landon, "I'll drive in, and we'll load up our... friend."

They had layers of old blankets spread across the back of the van. To keep bloodstains off the upholstery. Landon suppressed a shudder. He nodded and turned toward the church.

"Be careful," Tracy said behind him. But he sounded impassive, like a teacher seeing off a kid at the school bus.

As he walked, Landon sent panicked glances all around, half certain the immortals would drop on him and kill him without bothering to check if he'd been lying.

But when he turned the corner into the empty parking lot behind the building, there against the wall lounged the tall, lean stranger who had jumped him last week. The guy was alone. He had one knee bent, the sole of his soccer shoe propped on the wall, hands in his fleece coat pockets. He looked perfectly relaxed. When he spotted Landon he lifted his chin in acknowledgement, but didn't move. Landon hoped this made it easier for Krystal to take aim. He glanced at the line of trees past the asphalt, but saw nothing; the women were well hidden.

She wasn't to fire until Landon had handed him the fake artifact. Maybe in less than a minute now.

"And what have you got for me today?" the stranger asked.

Landon held out the earring, wrapped in a scrap of newspaper.

The stranger glanced at it for a second. "Open it and show me."

Landon hesitated, but decided it wouldn't matter much if he did the unwrapping. He pulled off the newspaper and handed the stranger the gold disk. "Here. That's...that's it." As soon as it changed hands, Landon drew back three steps. He had no wish to be in the line of fire.

The stranger examined it. Landon's heart pounded. Any second now. Why wasn't she firing?

The stranger looked at Landon with reproach and pity. "Come on, mate." He tossed the earring to Landon, who reflexively caught it. "Clearly a fake. Can't you do better?"

"I—I honestly thought..." Landon glanced at the trees in increasing panic. Why wasn't Krystal shooting?

"Oh, Landon," the stranger said. "Landon, Landon."

What was happening to Krystal? This was going one hundred percent wrong. He had to escape. Now.

"Look, I tried..." Landon began.

The stranger pushed off from the wall and disappeared.

Landon choked back a gasp. A second later, someone seized him around the middle and yanked him backward.

He yelled in terror. The stranger let go and shoved him so he tumbled across the bumpy forest floor. Which should have been an asphalt parking lot.

Oh, shit.

"Landon," the stranger sighed again, standing above him with hands on his hips. "We told you what would happen."

Gigantic, weird-looking trees towered over the stranger's head and spread out on all sides of them in a massive forest.

Landon's body shook as if it wanted to rattle itself apart. He curled up, closing his eyes. He fished his latest handgun from the pocket of his coat and tossed it blindly toward the stranger's feet. "Do it fast. Please."

More footsteps approached, rustling in the undergrowth, but no one spoke. No one shot him, either. After a prolonged silence, Landon dared to open his eyes.

Now three people were looking down at him with distaste: the stranger, Adrian Watts, and a tall young woman with short hair and a brown ski parka.

The stranger was holding Landon's gun, but kept it pointed at the ground. He exchanged glances with the other two. They were taking long enough that Landon considered scrambling to his feet and running for it. A lion-like roar somewhere in the near distance checked that thought, though.

"Did you kill the two women?" Landon asked them, his voice creaky.

They looked down at him. "No," Adrian said. "Only knocked them out."

"We're nicer than you lot," the woman said. Her accent sounded like Adrian's. Maybe another Kiwi.

"Except that now you have to kill me," Landon said.

The three exchanged dismayed looks again, as if they really hadn't made up their minds about that.

"There is still information to be got from him," the stranger said, with the kind of tone that sounded like he was repeating an argument he'd made before.

"I don't want to be a murderer," Adrian said, in a similarly tired way. "But being a jailer doesn't appeal either."

"I said I'd take care of it," the stranger said.

"I'll help," the woman added. When Adrian glanced at her, she said, "Really. It's—look, it's true about the information."

They all looked at Landon again.

"Well, Landon," the stranger said. "Your choices, then.

One: turn state's evidence—and be committed to a mental hospital for your story, most likely. Two: cooperate with us. Give us information we can use. Consider even turning against your former allies, since they were hardly being good to you, were they? Three..." The stranger lifted the gun in a sort of shrug.

While Landon swallowed and tried to grasp the idea that maybe he didn't have to die today, the woman shoved the stranger's arm down. "Oh, don't give *him* the choice." She glared at Landon. "You get option number two. You're coming with us."

CHAPTER TWENTY-NINE

*L*IAM HAD A LOT GOING ON. THERE WAS OF COURSE SWITCHING realms as a mortal, both in the Underworld and at the other special sites, which was so cool he insisted on doing it at least ten times that first day before the others told him to chill. He also got to move to his new trailer in the wilderness, which was actually a pretty awesome location, looking out over the land where he caught glimpses of spirit-world animals in the trees now and then.

In Liam's memories, Poseidon had a lot going on too.

Poseidon found his way to Knossos in Crete. It was an amazing city, with architecture and murals like Poseidon had never seen. Through careful inquiries to the junior priestesses, he got his request taken in to Rhea, and she had him brought in to meet her.

She was tall and brown-skinned and with hair growing in tight curls, like the people of Egypt, which indeed she said was her original homeland. She carried a speckled brown snake that lazily wound and unwound itself around her arms and shoulders as she spoke to Poseidon. He found it unnerving, as he assumed everyone did, which was probably why she wore it. But he soon forgot the snake and became fascinated with her story. They sat in a cool, shaded stone room of the palace at Knossos, sipping mint-flavored water and eating herbed flat bread as they talked.

Rhea was like him, it turned out, though most people didn't know it. For now she was holding onto her position as high priestess, because she could do a lot of good for her citizens that way, as well as looking out for other immortals. She would someday have to step down and leave the island, before everyone noticed she wasn't aging. However, she estimated she could carry on for many years yet.

As for Poseidon, she instructed him to follow her exact directions to a mountain in the north of Greece, where the other immortals lived, ones she had personally brought together and still corresponded with.

So he was soon off on another sea voyage. After a trek inland to Mount Olympos, he finally met Zeus, Hera, and Demeter. He settled in with them a while, to compare stories and figure out what they were all going to do with these long lives of theirs.

He hadn't forgotten his home island, nor Amphitrite down in Euboia. He found a traveler headed to the nearest docks, and entrusted a letter with him to send on the next boat going to Skyros, telling his sister where he was and promising to visit at some point. He didn't dare try writing to Amphitrite. That might get her in trouble with her husband—or "master" was more the term really—and he didn't know her well enough to be as bold as that.

There was plenty to keep him busy in his new environment. He and his companions compared their uncanny abilities, including a tracking sense of one's lovers, which Poseidon had always noticed. He had assumed it was connected somehow to his water-related abilities, because it felt a bit similar, but when he mentioned those water affinities, everyone looked in total incomprehension at him. So he mumbled that it was nothing, never mind, and didn't bring it up again. Not much use for a sea affinity anyway when you were living on a mountain in the interior.

Besides, Poseidon quickly gathered Zeus and Hera were

keen on helping favored cities win wars, and in a country like Greece, sea power counted for as much as land armies; sometimes more. Poseidon could too easily see himself being coerced into flinging waves at other people's enemies in return for gold and worship, and the idea disgusted him. He let his friends know he was good at boat-building, navigating, fishing, and swimming. But the magical relationship between himself and the sea he hoarded as a secret, and used his powers only when alone, off visiting islands or coasts, if he encountered an opportunity to be useful without his abilities being detected.

He got away after about a year and managed to visit his family on Skyros. It could only be a brief visit; his sister's household didn't want to risk the island figuring out that Poseidon still hadn't aged and likely never would. So he departed after a few days, and went to Euboia.

Finding Amphitrite wasn't simple. Asking around after someone else's concubine didn't do any favors for the woman in question, and indeed could get her beaten by her master despite her innocence, since he was a horrid man from what she'd said. But eventually Poseidon learned from a seller of herbs in the marketplace that, yes, Amphitrite still lived in this city in her master's household, and was now once again with child.

He nodded, feeling more disappointed than he had any right to, and told the herb seller, "Next time she comes by, please tell her that her kinsman Poseidon from Skyros is doing well, and living in the north, and hopes to see her again before long." Claiming himself as kin, though a lie, would give him the social right to leave her such a message. Perhaps the greeting would provide her some cheer.

He returned to Mount Olympos and his circle of charmed friends. They soon found more like themselves: Apollo, Artemis, Athena. Everyone was around his own age or a little older. Only Rhea had substantial years on the rest of them—she was over a century old already, according to anyone's best estimation. They had no idea, and no way to know, whether immortals had always been born on occasion and their group had yet to discover the rest, or whether this was a new phenomenon limited to basically the handful of them.

He eventually had lovers once in a while, mortal and immortal both. Here Liam drew back his close focus, because... okay, yeah, it was like Liam's dad had said. Poseidon and Demeter eventually hooked up. Liam totally sped through those memories, though actually they weren't *quite* as horrible as he expected. But even at the time, the affair felt like a mistake. It was short, less than a month, but Demeter latched onto Poseidon in a way that suggested she was hungry for a settled family. Poseidon knew he couldn't be that husband for her, thus they underwent a lot of conflict.

She'd left behind a family, as nearly all of them did, and for her it had been a serious hardship. She felt bereft without children, a home, domesticity. She kept mentioning to Poseidon her desire to be a wife and mother again. In response he drew back further. They argued, they made up, they got exasperated with each other.

By then the group had acquired Hades, shipped over to them from Crete, as well as others such as Hermes and Aphrodite, familiar souls Liam was now hanging out with again. Events in the memories were unfolding just as Sophie and the rest had told him.

But what the others didn't know so well, and therefore hadn't told him, was how Poseidon couldn't shake the thoughts of Amphitrite. Not only because she was the only other person he knew who had any water magic, but because of *her*. Her eyes. Her defiance. Her hair in the sunlight and the moonlight. Her touch on his hand. Her bare legs in the tide pools. And she seemed like she could use rescuing and therefore he worried about her.

He managed to see her again a few times over the years,

on journeys down the coast. In her twenties she was still a fertile concubine, heavily pregnant when he found her in the marketplace in Euboia. She glowed with health though she claimed to be unbearably tired. They managed to talk a short time, standing close together in the crowd and holding textiles from the nearest stand so it would appear they were discussing the goods. In a rushed undertone he told her he'd found more folk like himself, had been thinking of her, it was so good to see her, and (he dared ask) would she be willing to run away with him? He saw the temptation light up her eyes, but she shook her head. She couldn't, not with this baby on the way and her other children still young, even though they barely cared about her and considered the head wife their mother...

He had to leave her, and went back feeling twice as lonely as before. He came again a year later. This time he approached her master's house, and walked back and forth on the road a while in the guise of a traveler until she finally came out on an errand to the market. He fell in step beside her. She was slim again, though looked tired and harassed. Though happy to see him, her answer was the same: she was too busy with the children, and didn't dare leave. But this time she asked him outright to come again, because she liked his visits. She was itching to hear more about these amazing immortals, she added with a smile.

He kept paying clandestine visits, though long months often stretched between them, as life kept both of them busy in separate regions of Greece. One autumn evening when she was thirty, he found her alone at the same tide pools, at sunset. The beach was one of the few places she managed to get away to on her own. Tonight she admitted she also came here because it made her think of him. Though she said it matter-of-factly, Poseidon's heart swelled in hope.

But still she refused to come away with him. Her master was ailing, and the illness was making him meaner than ever, and more needy of everyone in his household. So she couldn't disappear now; she feared what would become of the children if she left before everything was legally settled for his death. Poseidon vowed to return for her. Then he paused and asked, "That is...do you even want me to keep coming back like this? Am I being annoying?"

Her smile brought out fine lines around her mouth and eyes. They made her more herself; his love for her solidified and became less an airy dream. "Wouldn't I tell you to leave if that's how I felt?" she said. "Do come back." She set her hand atop his. "Please."

He looked into her blue-green eyes, then down at her lips. He knew he shouldn't kiss her, or if he did, he shouldn't do more than that. By now he and his friends knew about the danger mortal women ran if impregnated by immortal men. He had remembered, with a chill of horror, how two of his former sweethearts on Skyros had suffered dangerous miscarriages and almost died. He had even told Amphitrite about it tonight, as part of the discussion of his strange nature.

But she took hold of his tunic, tugged him close, and kissed him. The taste and warmth pulled him down like a whirlpool. From this kind of mutual desire he couldn't escape, and didn't want to.

They moved down the beach to a sea cave, a stretch of sand under a hollowed rock ceiling. At high tide it would be full of churning water, but this was mid-tide and ebbing. They had the smooth sand to themselves, and the shadows hid them. Poseidon refused to enter her, despite her invitation—no sense putting her life in even more danger. But they still caressed one another as lovers, and brought each other to joy, surrounded by the low thunder of the surf and the smell of salt.

"Now I can't go away from you," he said afterward. "Don't tell me to."

She didn't.

He bought a small house near the shore, and hired a servant, whom he sent back to the north to tell his friends he would be staying here a while. He had the servant fetch the better part of his belongings and bring them back. Then he waited for Amphitrite's master to die, and for her children to grow until she felt she could live apart from them. If it took years, if she was middle-aged or elderly by the time she was ready to join him for good, he didn't care. He loved her and would stay near her as long as life allowed. But he didn't tell any of his immortal friends about her, because he was certain they wouldn't understand. They'd try to talk him out of an attachment to a mortal, and he would tolerate no such attitudes.

Her master died the following year, but Amphitrite legally became the slave of his chief wife after that, who wasn't a kind woman. Careful to keep their affair a secret, Poseidon nonetheless managed to observe most of Amphitrite's household at one point or another, and the wife reminded him of Hera, only without any of Hera's generous points. Poseidon and Amphitrite exercised extreme caution in how and where they met. An owner could have a slave flogged nearly to death for any perceived wrong, which certainly included sneaking off to meet a lover without permission.

So he went cold with fear when Amphitrite came to his house one day and told him wretchedly that she was pregnant—and yes, it was his, which he wouldn't have doubted for a moment anyway.

"B-but how?" he stammered. "We've been careful…"

She gave him a bitter smile. "I've heard women say that pulling out doesn't work. It would seem they're right." For they had indeed become more daring in their intimacy, and now faced the cost.

Twice the usual risk, twice the expected fear. Not only would she be found out by her vicious mistress and punished, but the pregnancy itself could kill her even in the best of living conditions. He was immortal and she wasn't.

He held her tight, breathing the familiar scent of her hair while he watched the sea out his window. "All right," he said. "First, your servitude ends now. I don't care if it breaks the law, you're coming away with me before anyone can hurt you or make you work another day when you should have the chance to rest."

She laughed incredulously. "No one's let me rest during any of my pregnancies. It sounds wonderful, but the children—"

"Are older now. And you've said they scarcely notice you, don't even acknowledge you as their mother."

"True, but they aren't horrible like her..."

"We can come back sometimes and see them. But you won't be safe here anymore." Poseidon pulled back to look at her. "Second, we'll get you safely through this pregnancy. I'll talk to Aphrodite. She might know of ways. Third..." He dropped to his knees, kissing her chest on the way and adding a kiss to her swelling belly. "I marry you." He looked up at her, partly in fondness and partly in challenge.

Her eyebrows rose in astonishment, then a smile broke across her face. "I marry you."

He rose and held her a long moment before releasing her. "Fetch your things. We're going tonight."

He helped her sneak out. They escaped the city in Euboia where she'd lived her whole life, and traveled many days until reaching Aphrodite's house. Aphrodite was planning to move to an island of her own, but for now lived in a secluded house in a cool, forested valley. She welcomed them with calm grace, as if men brought their technically stolen pregnant mortal wives to her for advice all the time. Which possibly they did.

After seating her guests on cushions on the floor, and having her servants bring herbal tea, Aphrodite listened to their story. Then she rolled her eyes and leaned across to swat Poseidon on the arm. "You didn't know pulling out doesn't

work? Goddess above, how did you live this long without figuring that out? Well, stop worrying, both of you." She smiled
at Amphitrite. "Sounds as if you've got good luck when it
comes to babies so far."

Amphitrite nodded. "No miscarriages or serious problems
yet. But then, this is the first time I've been pregnant with an
immortal man's child."

Aphrodite waved her hand as if to dismiss the concern.
"It's been managed. There are more healthy children out
there, born of mortal mothers and immortal fathers, than you
might realize."

"Really?" Poseidon frowned. "I've only heard of a few
who survived."

"More than a few," Aphrodite said. "You think you're the
first to come to me with this problem? No, there's a certain
someone who's gone through this *lots* of times."

Poseidon barely had to think about it. "Zeus."

"Naturally he doesn't want Hera to know, so…" Aphrodite drew her fingers across her lips, a casual command to
keep it secret.

"We won't breathe a word," Amphitrite said. "But the
mothers, the children, they were all healthy?"

"Not all. As in any pregnancy, sometimes things go
wrong. But the ones who survived were like you: healthy
and fertile already. And some say local midwives or witches
helped them—taking time every morning to bless the waters
in the womb that the baby rests in, something like that? Sorry
to say that kind of thing is beyond my skill. But I can give
you some herbs that keep the womb in good health, which I
promise won't turn your stomach."

Amphitrite and Poseidon accepted the herbs with thanks,
but at Aphrodite's mention of blessing the waters, they had
exchanged a charged glance.

The couple headed for a neighboring farm, where Aphrodite said they could find lodgings until they found a new

home. As they walked Poseidon said, "The waters. It almost makes sense."

"It makes a great deal of sense," Amphitrite said. "I've always felt I could use my water influence to heal a little faster, and keep my babies healthy when I was pregnant, because after all people are largely water of a sort, and there *is* plenty of water in the womb."

Poseidon slid his hand around her broadening waist. "Then I will be sending all my water influence every waking moment."

CHAPTER THIRTY

LANDON WAS GETTING A TRIP TO EUROPE, ALL RIGHT. ON THE back of a freaking ghost horse at unbelievable speed while he clung for dear life to the stranger sharing the saddle with him. They'd bound Landon to the stranger with bungee cords so he wouldn't fall off, but he was taking no chances; he had the guy's coat gripped tight in both hands, even though they had also tied his wrists together, which made the grip awkward. Landon had never liked heights, nor rides on open-air vehicles like motorcycles, so this was a several-hours-long exercise in terror. It didn't help that he was likely to face torture at the end of it.

The other two immortals flew alongside them, the woman on a separate horse, and Adrian in some kind of junked bus covered with welded metal and vines, pulled by four ghost horses. God of the Underworld, modern style, or so Landon supposed was the idea. Looked outright crazy to him.

Now they were over the Atlantic Ocean and the sun was setting. His hands were numb with cold.

"What's your name? What should I call you?" he asked the back of the man's head.

The guy didn't bother turning. "M'Lord. Your Excellency. Your Illustrious Highness. I'm not picky."

"Nice. Fine."

"Niko," the woman called, drawing her horse up near theirs.

He glared at her. "Or call me that. Yes, Zoe?"

"What? He'll have to call us something. I just wondered if we should phone ahead and have any particular part of the Underworld prepared." She glanced at Landon, then back at Niko.

"No need," Niko said. "I've got it worked out."

Landon swallowed, feeling sicker. Got the torture chamber in hell all set up, sounded like. He'd break. He'd tell everything. He knew he would.

He thought of his grandmother and tried to be brave for her.

"Is this where you took my grandmother?" he asked.

"No." Niko sounded curt. "But you might get to see her if you behave."

Landon lifted his head, intrigued in spite of his fear. "She's there? Even though this isn't where you took her?"

"She's dead, therefore she's in the Underworld, which is where we're going. Is everyone in Thanatos this thick? You really shouldn't go trying to kill people when you're so dreadfully ill-informed about who they are. Hang on tight."

Landon gasped and clenched his hands, as well as latching his legs around Niko's, because they were plunging in a nose-dive toward the ground. "Stop stop stop, no no no, what are you doing, *stop!*"

He held the last word, the vowel turning into a scream. But right when he expected to smash into the ground in a quick death, they swooshed into darkness, slowed in a descent, and thudded to a stop. Solid ground bumped against Landon's feet. He'd never been so grateful simply to feel the ground before. The air felt calm and warm after the frigid, blasting wind.

When he looked around and found himself in a big cave with stalactites and an underground river, that didn't exactly surprise him. That matched the accounts he'd heard. But the glowing stream of human figures pouring like a waterfall into the cave and gliding into a tunnel—well, he'd technically been told about those too, but the sight still made his guts go watery in terror.

"Come." Niko hauled Landon off the horse, spun him toward a path following the river, and pushed him.

Landon hated being underground. He didn't even like basements. But there was really nowhere he could go and no benefit in fighting. Cooperating might even be a good idea, in the long run. So he walked with his captors through the tunnel, stooping as the ceiling lowered.

Then the tunnel let out onto the immense cavern he'd heard about—the Elysian Fields or whatever they might technically be called—and amazement eased his fear a little. He tried to stare in every direction and take it all in, even as Niko, Adrian, and Zoe tugged him down onto a raft on which they crossed the river, then prodded him up the other bank.

If this wasn't the Underworld, if this was some special-effects team's doing, then they deserved every award in Hollywood. It was ghoulish and creepy, but fascinating. Ghosts! So many ghosts. All ages and races, drifting about, their curious hands passing through him, their strange glow serving as the light for the whole unearthly landscape. He looked around for his grandmother or anyone else familiar, but didn't recognize anyone yet.

A small group of normal-looking people—solid, not glowing—hurried into view from over a hill covered with whitish grass. Maybe these were immortals too, or at least living mortals.

One of them, Landon realized, was Sophie Darrow. The recognition made him suck in his breath with a hiss. Fear flashed through him. If anyone on Earth, other than Adrian Watts, had reason to mutilate Landon, it was Sophie.

She apparently recognized him at the same moment. Her

eyes widened, and she stumbled to a stop, her friends jostling around her.

Landon took in the three people with her and realized one was young Liam Darrow, the other survivor from her household. Okay, make that the third person on Earth who'd want to torture Landon.

"What's he doing here?" Sophie said, her voice rusty.

"He's going to tell us everything he can," Adrian said, "or he's going to be sorry."

"In fact," Niko said, "I think he's going to be sorry either way. I think he's *already* sorry."

"He looks pretty sorry," Zoe said dryly.

Landon, shaking, scraped up the courage to look Sophie in the face. He parted his chapped lips, finding he had the absurd wish to apologize to her. But his throat stayed paralyzed. Wouldn't it sound like mockery if he said he was sorry? Or wouldn't the words at least be horribly, nastily inadequate?

"Who is that?" Liam asked. "Is that—oh my God, is that the guy?"

He must have gotten a nod from Adrian or someone, because his young face suddenly contorted into a look of homicidal fury.

Sophie grasped her brother's arm as if to hold him back, though he hadn't lunged forward yet. "Where are you taking him?" Sophie asked.

"I have a spot picked out," Niko said. "You needn't ever see him. Unless of course you're after some dreadfully boring conversation." Niko yanked at Landon's tied wrists again, and led him off down a path between hills.

SOPHIE'S KNEES GAVE OUT. SHE SANK TO THE GROUND AND bent her head over her lap. *Breathe, don't be sick, just breathe.*

She and Liam had left the trailers and had Tab and Freya

bring them down here when Zoe texted ahead that they were returning with "news."

Or a prisoner. Guess that counted as news.

Somewhere in the world, every day, someone faced their family's murderers in court. She wasn't the only one to feel like this. Seeing Landon Osborne face to face was a gruesome shock, but it could be survived.

Someone hugged her, and leathery-chic perfume wafted around her as Tab sat beside her. "It's okay, dude. We captured him. Head of freaking Thanatos, and we got him. Things are going to get better now."

Sophie nodded, and breathed in and out a few times. "Just didn't like seeing him. Never will, I'm thinking."

"I get that."

Sophie lifted her head. Freya walked up, along with Isabel's and Terry's souls. They would have heard one of their killers had been captured. Liam stood farther down the path, alone, watching Landon get marched away by Niko and Zoe. Liam had been braiding together another rope of willow and ivy to attach to spirit dogs for fun, and now he flicked the length of it against the ground as if wanting to whip Landon with it. Adrian walked behind the prisoner, but he slowed and glanced back at Sophie. When her gaze met his, he pivoted and returned to her.

He knelt in front of her. "Sorry. God, I'm sorry, we should have warned you."

She gave a half-shrug, and glanced up at her parents. Being souls, they were always so serene. At times such as now, that quality was comforting.

"Glad you got one," Terry said to Adrian.

"We know where another is," Adrian said, "but we're waiting to see if we can spring a larger trap. Stop the whole organization, not just the ones who were directly involved in…" He swept his gaze across the Darrow family.

"What are you going to do to him?" Sophie asked.

Adrian sank back on his heels. Fallen gray leaves from a nearby ash tree rustled under his weight. "Get information. Try to convince him to help. Ideally without having to…" He lifted his hand, palm up, then let it drop. "I don't want to kill anyone. I don't want to torture anyone. Not even them."

"It was pretty bad-ass what Niko did to Quentin," Tab said. "But still…"

"It's disturbed him," Freya said, standing nearby with her arms folded.

Adrian nodded. "It's clear he doesn't want to do it again. None of us do, except in self-defense. And we *can* get information from Landon, it's just, how much will it actually help?"

Something, Sophie noticed, was starting to push out her sickly fear. Anger. Fury at what Landon and Quentin and Krystal had done to her family, to her life. "I'd say he's earned a little torture. In case you have to resort to that, don't feel too guilty."

Adrian glanced down the path. "Well. Niko's clever, and Zoe's got magic, so possibly we'll get the information some other way."

The prisoner and his captors had disappeared around the bend of the dark path. Liam strode off after them.

"Where are they taking him?" Freya asked.

"I'm not sure exactly." Adrian jumped to his feet. "Niko seems to have a plan. Suppose I'll go see."

The anger tingled in Sophie's limbs, infusing her with strength. She got up. "I'm coming too."

Everyone came: her parents' souls, Liam, Tab, and Freya. They walked a few minutes and came upon Niko ushering Landon into a jail cell of sorts. It stood in the back part of the cave that was mostly columns and stalagmites, where the souls didn't wander much, and where Sophie never went much either, which was why she hadn't noticed it until now. The cell was perhaps ten feet by six, two of its walls the natural rock of the cave, and the other two made of metal bars welded to the columns. Part of the metal section was open as a gate, with two thick bike locks hanging on it. A bucket with an odd lid stood in the corner, which Sophie recognized after a moment as a camp toilet.

Adrian stopped to take in the cage, perplexed. "How long has this been here?"

"Few weeks," Niko said. "Round the time I was bringing down all that material for wiring and plumbing upgrades, I brought this stuff down too. No one noticed when I put it all up, observant lot that you are."

"We did rather have other things going on," Zoe pointed out. "In other parts of the cave."

Sophie marched forward, pushed past Zoe at the cell's open door, and stormed straight to Landon, who cowered on his knees with his hands tied before him. He lifted a cringing face to her. She curled her right hand into a fist, pulled it back, and punched him in the mouth.

It was hard enough to send him reeling sideways onto the ground. She heard a few gasps and hissed breaths around her, but no one said anything.

Landon lay wincing and gasping, his glasses crooked. Blood welled up on his lip and dripped onto the dirty floor.

Liam rushed forward and kicked Landon hard in the stomach. Landon grunted and curled up, gagging.

Sophie caught her brother's arm with her left hand. On her right, her knuckles were throbbing in pain. "We're not thugs, unlike some people. That'll do for now."

Liam was breathing heavily, as if ready to do a lot more beating-up, but he drew back at her touch.

Turning, she expected to see shock or disapproval on her friends' and parents' faces. So it was a pleasing surprise to find them all looking...proud. Yeah, that was definitely pride in her parents' gazes. Her immortal friends gave her nods of approval.

Walking out of the cell, Sophie blew on her bruised, hot knuckles.

"Give me that." Zoe took Sophie's right hand, and with an invisible pulse of magic sent a cool healing sensation through it. She let go. "There, all better, if you want to do it again."

Sophie smiled. She glanced at Adrian. He leaned sideways against the outside of the bars, one hand curled around them above his head, gazing at her with a small smile that suggested admiration.

"Well," Sophie said to him in defense, "I hit you once. And he deserves it way more. So."

"Only fair," he agreed.

"He's got a lot more to undergo before the score's evened," Niko said. "Out we go, friends."

They all trooped out of the cell, leaving Landon alone inside. Niko swung the barred door shut and locked both of the U-shaped bike locks, then pocketed the keys. Landon watched miserably from the floor, licking blood off his lip and still gasping from the belly kick.

"We'll chat later," Niko told him.

"My hands," Landon said. "Can't I at least..."

"Come over here." Niko produced a switchblade knife so smoothly that Sophie couldn't even have said where he'd pulled it from. Landon knocked his shoulder against the ground and heaved himself up, and shuffled over on his knees. Niko swiped the blade between the bars and sliced the rope that bound Landon's hands.

Landon shook out and massaged his cramped fingers.

"Shall we set ghosts to guard you, just to unnerve you?" Niko speculated.

"I'll take a shift on that duty," Terry said. He was staring at Landon with the closest thing to hostility a soul could manage, which was more like coldness.

Pity he wasn't still alive, Sophie thought. Her dad in full anger mode had been a frighteningly righteous dude indeed.

She remembered him sitting with a baseball bat, glaring at Adrian when he'd found them asleep together in her bed.

Her mouth stretched into a smile. Wow. She'd never, ever thought she'd smile at that memory. It had seemed like a nightmare at the time. Now it actually seemed pretty funny.

She stole another glance at Adrian, half hoping he'd be thinking of the same moment. But he was squinting at Landon, probably wondering what on Earth to do with him.

"Thank you, Terry," Niko said. "I wouldn't mind a chance to rest."

Poor Niko did look tired. Even the divine trickster had to sleep.

"Niko," Liam said. "Give me that." He held out his hand for the knife.

Niko lifted an eyebrow but handed the knife over. "Don't shed too much blood yet, mate."

"I won't. Here Dad, hold out your hand."

Terry reached out, looking curious.

Liam uncoiled the willow-and-ivy rope from over his shoulder and wrapped it around the knife's handle, then wound the rest of the length around Terry's immaterial wrist. The blade stuck out across Terry's hand. "There," Liam said. "Can you stab with it?"

Terry made a few punch motions, which indeed looked like they'd stab someone who got close enough. He and Liam beamed at one another.

Adrian stared at the knife. "Liam, you're a genius."

Niko studied the innovation too, as did Sophie and all the rest.

"Huh," she said. "That's pretty brilliant."

Liam sent a crooked grin at Adrian and then at her. "You guys never thought of this? What kind of gods of the dead are you?"

"I kind of like being an armed guard who can't get hurt," Terry said, flourishing the knife.

Landon shrank to the back wall of the cave.

"You look afraid," Freya told him. "As you should. We could form an army of the dead against your side."

"That would be *sweet*," Liam said.

"I will stay too for a while," Freya added, to Niko, "if you'd like to rest."

Niko nodded and walked away from the cage. Terry, Isabel, and Freya stayed behind while Sophie and the rest followed Niko.

"Is it possible, you think?" Adrian asked Zoe as they got out of earshot. "Army of the dead?"

"Well. Yeah," she said. "I'm sure there'd be a limit to how hard they could stab, and how accurate they could be. And probably if their weapon got smacked hard enough, it'd come off and they'd be useless again. But at least they can't get hurt. So."

"That," Adrian said, "could be handy indeed."

"Lot of new things to think about today," Sophie said.

"Therefore I'm sleeping," Niko said. "Cheers." He flapped a hand in farewell and veered off the path and over a hill.

Zoe frowned after him. "I'm just going to make sure he's okay." She turned and followed Niko.

Sophie watched her go, wondering again about relationship complexities. Then Tab stepped between Sophie and Liam and slung an arm around each of them. "Do you know what makes me super proud?" Tab said. "You two. My Darrow peeps. Do you guys realize you faced one of the biggest triggers you've got—one of the actual assholes who attacked you—and you didn't lose your shit? And all without Zoe doing any magic to help you. You realize that? It was all you, dudes."

Sophie glanced at Liam, who looked similarly thoughtful and pleased. "I guess that is pretty cool," Sophie admitted.

"Not only that." Tab whumped Sophie's shoulder. "But you walked right up to him and punched him in the face. And you," she swayed Liam, "booted him in the gut. Seriously. You guys rock! Am I right, Ade?"

"Completely right," Adrian said from behind them.

"Thanks." Sophie slipped her arm around Tab's waist. "You rock too, Tab."

A while later, sitting alone in a grotto where a stream pooled and the Underworld vines formed a pretty screen, she gazed at her phone-app list of triggers and considered crossing off "the people who took me." But then she thought of facing Quentin's soul—or facing Krystal, the truly horrible one who had actually fired the weapons—and her courage wobbled again. She closed the app and played her flashlight beam across a dripping stalactite.

Okay, but punching Landon in the face and then marching away under her own power did count as progress.

Also, smiling at a memory about the night when she and Adrian had been purring naughty things about olive oil to each other? That was progress too.

ZOE FOUND NIKOLAOS INSIDE A CIRCLE OF STRAWBERRY TREES, one of his habitual places to camp out down here. He was lying on his spread-out red sleeping bag, on his side with eyes shut. Zoe paused to rub one of the trees' leaves between her fingers. She wondered if they were the descendants of the same little strawberry tree Hermes had once brought Hekate. Down here, they developed pearly white leaves and deep purple berries instead of the green foliage and red berries of the upper world.

Niko must have sensed her coming, but didn't open his eyes, not even when she came and sat on her knees beside him.

Dark shadows lurked under his eyes. He hadn't shaved in at least two days, and hadn't laughed in...well, longer than anyone liked to see in the merry Hermes. Now he was obliged to be a jailer, and possibly a torturer.

"You okay?" she whispered.

He swung his arm out without opening his eyes. He hooked it around her waist and drew her down beside him. She wriggled in to spoon him. When she settled her hand on top of his, at the base of her ribs, she felt only unhappy turbulence in him, no lustful intentions. Her sympathy deepened, and she nestled closer on the edge of the sleeping bag.

"Would you have forgiven me," he asked, "if I had simply killed him?"

"Yes, Niko."

"And will you forgive me if I don't?"

She drew his hand up and kissed his knuckles. "Of course, you twit."

He hugged her tighter, and said in the Underworld tongue, "I love you, sweet Hekate."

For some reason the declaration in combination with the sadness emanating from him made her feel like crying. She squeezed his hand and sent him a flow of soothing, soporific magic, and stayed there a long time, even after he had finally fallen asleep.

CHAPTER THIRTY-ONE

ERICK TRACY GLANCED INTO THE REARVIEW MIRROR OF THE van as he sped south. Yuliya and Krystal were waking up at last, stirring and groaning on the blankets. Krystal's arm flailed in undoubtedly lethal intent, but she only succeeded in smacking Yuliya and making her grunt.

"It's all right, Krystal," Tracy called from the driver's seat. "No need to shoot anyone at the moment. Besides, they stole your gun, as they are wont to do."

"Fuckers." She sat up, her face white and wincing in the mirror's reflection. "What happened? Where the hell are we going?"

Tracy kept his voice smooth. He'd had two hours now to quell his alarm. "Landon's been taken. The unnaturals knocked you two out—some sort of magical blow to the head, I wager—and made off with him. I've heard nothing of whether he's still alive, but regardless, I've packed all our things and we're moving shop. We'll fly out of L.A."

"What?" Krystal shrieked.

"God, my head." Yuliya lay down again.

"It's interesting they didn't kill the pair of you," Tracy said. "Shows either weakness or fear, either of which would benefit us."

"Also *good* that they didn't kill us," Krystal said. "Hello?"

"Yes, naturally," Tracy said.

"But they have the boy?" Yuliya said. "Oh, poor Landon."

"We can't help him now," Tracy said. "We merely need to move so they can't stop the rest of us so easily. Also, assuming they keep him alive to torture information out of him, we'd best go to some location he doesn't know about, so that whatever he says doesn't harm the rest of us."

"He was an idiot," Krystal said. "He did it all wrong."

"They may offer ransom, or trade," Yuliya said, her Russian accent thickening. "If so, is a shame and I'm sorry for him, but we must not deal with them."

"Agreed," Tracy said.

Krystal didn't say anything, only scowled out the window, rubbing her temples. She wasn't likely to feel any great urge to rescue Landon, and just as well. Odds were good he was dead already. They'd be better off focusing on their main objective of destroying the tree at its otherworldly source.

"So you're the head of Thanatos now?" Krystal finally said.

"Hasn't been settled," Tracy said. "I'm sure everyone would rather we got to safety and moved ahead with our plan first."

Nonetheless, he was confident the organization would choose him. Who else had done so much for the cause lately? He patted the flat shape in his blazer pocket: the little gray notebook Betty Quentin had compiled, which had been among Landon's things in the condo. There wasn't much in it that Tracy didn't already know, but taking possession of the notebook felt like receiving a new official insignia.

"So we're off to Europe," Yuliya said.

"Quite soon." Tracy felt almost cheerful.

Yes, he had tried a possibly foolish move today and it had sacrificed Landon. But that wasn't such a great loss, really, given it advanced Tracy within Thanatos, which was better for everyone. Well, everyone except Landon. But to achieve the conquest of the immortals, he had to use any means available. He was but a mere human, after all.

HEKATE AND HERMES WERE NOT EXACTLY BEING DISCREET about their affair. Several of the souls in the Underworld surely glimpsed kisses (or more) when he visited her there, and they loved to spread news among themselves. In addition, plenty of mortals at the various sacred sites and their associated villages likely noticed the cuddliness of the two immortals when they were together.

So it really didn't surprise her when Dionysos arrived one day in the Underworld looking more solemn than usual, and brought up the subject himself.

"I hear you and Hermes are together a lot," he said after they had exchanged greetings. "Is that...?" He left the question open.

She laced her fingers together in front of her chest, and nodded him toward the river. They walked alongside it and talked.

She was honest: yes, she'd been sleeping with Hermes, and had feelings for him, albeit confused ones. Of course, that needn't have any impact on her regard for Dionysos...

"Regard?" he said with a brief smile. "Not the most exciting word. But...listen, I'll be honest too."

He had met a woman in Crete while investigating the recent Thanatos-fueled turbulence on the island. She was the new head priestess, Ariadne, a staunch supporter of the Great Goddess and the immortals, which put her and her followers in danger from the Thanatos members who had become highly placed in the king's government. Dionysos was of course going to help her resist them and stay safe. But in addition, Dionysos had developed feelings for Ariadne, deep and stirring ones.

"Confused ones too, as you say," he added. "But ones I

think I need to pursue. She's...well, she's like you, in some ways; mystical and in touch with the elements. Not with your powers, of course, but still easily one of the most magically adept mortals I've ever met."

"There are such people," Hekate said. "More than I used to realize. Many end up priestesses, like her."

"She's of the living world, of course, and that's...well, that's where I must spend most of my time. It's where I come from, too."

Therefore Ariadne was a better match for him than Hekate could ever be. She understood those words he didn't say, and she smiled softly. "Most people do. Don't feel bad about it."

"I cherish being able to visit here, though." He gazed at the dark river winding away between stalagmites. "I suppose you and I can still see each other if you'd like." He sounded almost comically reluctant.

"Perhaps it's less complicated if we don't," she said. "We both seem confused enough for now. Maybe in the future..."

He took her hand and kissed it. "We shall always keep the possibility open."

She felt suddenly sad. "I'd still risk my life for you all over again."

"And I for you. We all must for each other nowadays. We have enemies enough."

She accompanied him back to the entrance cavern. Their talk turned to practical subjects for the short walk, but as he untied his horse, they held each other's gazes with apologetic fondness.

"A little calmer than your break-up with Aphrodite," she remarked.

"Decidedly. Thank goodness."

"Maybe because you and I were never such a grand passion. Only good friends."

"Still, good friends can be great fun. You and Hermes know that." He smiled again, but Hekate looked away in uneasiness. "Great fun" did describe her current affair, but so did more complex words like "shame," "longing," and "confusion." Maybe what she had with Hermes was already more the grand passion than her long relationship with Dionysos had ever been. Oh, Goddess.

They said farewell, and he flew away—likely back to Crete to see Ariadne. Strange that Hekate would know less, going forward, of what he was doing. Or would she really? Likely she had never known as much as she thought she did. They had already fallen into the habit of spending so much time apart.

When Hermes arrived at nightfall, and she told him she was free now, he echoed those thoughts: "But you already were, weren't you? Not so much has changed."

"I suppose not."

He pulled her closer. "You seem a bit down. What would make you happy? I enjoy those little touches of magic you use sometimes. Maybe you have ideas you've been too shy to try out? I'm up for it, whatever it is."

It made her laugh, which helped.

As a matter of fact, she did have some ideas, for which he was indeed game. Those helped too.

Just a couple of months later, as if life felt the need to change for her all at once, her parents approached in the fields and told her they wanted to be reborn into the world.

Tears pooled into her eyes. She tried to swallow them back. "But—but Zeus' soul, he wasn't reborn immortal." They had found out that much by now. Hermes had tracked him, flying farther east than any of them had ever journeyed, and finally located Zeus, now a little boy living in a mountain village. It took a few more visits of observation before he could bring back the verdict that the boy did get sick or injured sometimes. He was not immortal.

Hera's soul, for all they knew, had met the same conditions. They couldn't trace her. The only one who could have tracked her was Zeus, and he could only have done so if he were once again immortal. Demeter had left to be reborn a year ago, and though she had ended up not far away, in Egypt, she too had been born a mortal baby.

"We know," Persephone said. "But we want to live again nonetheless."

"Most people down here," Hades added, "are waiting for their loved ones to arrive, to speak with them again. But we're blessed. We already have our living daughter and our friends coming to see us all the time. We've exchanged all the final words we need to for this lifetime."

"But I need you," Hekate said. A tear escaped each eye and trickled hot down her cheeks.

"Ah, but sweetheart," Persephone said, "you'll be able to track us. You'll see us again."

"You'll belong to someone else. You won't know me."

"It's pulling us," Hades told her gently. "The living world. It's like the Underworld pulling newly dead souls to itself. Life, eventually, pulls everyone back too. And dear girl, you don't need us, not really. You're so full of power and strength. You're the true jewel of the Underworld."

"But…" Hekate wiped the tears off her face, though more were flowing to replace them. "Can't you let the others come down to say goodbye to you? Hermes, Rhea, everyone?"

They consented. So the next day, a cluster of loving friends, living immortals and souls both, gathered at the end of the river where it flowed into its last tunnel before escaping as a sunlit waterfall outside. Hades and Persephone smiled in buoyant anticipation of their new adventure, and spoke farewells to each of their friends in turn.

Hekate didn't hear most of their words. The river rushed loud over the rocks, and her ears rang in grief and disbelief.

They came to her last.

"You know we'll see each other again," Hades said, "so please don't be sad, my darling. But come find us. See how we're doing. See if there's anything your magic can do for us." He smiled.

Hekate nodded, too choked up to speak.

"I only wish I could hug you again," Persephone told her. "Oh, Hekate, be happy. Promise?"

Hekate shrugged with a despairing smile, then finally nodded.

Her parents' souls drifted out over the river. The living world was pulling them. There was no coming back now. They called goodbyes, as did everyone around her. She lifted her hand in farewell, and gazed upon her mother and father until they swept out of sight into the tunnel, with the other departing souls.

She tottered into the fields, which looked darker and gloomier than ever. Her immortal companions touched her arms and back, and murmured soothing words to her. She nodded absently in response. Eventually everyone took the hint and left her alone. With Kerberos at her side, she walked through the white fields and gray groves, over hills and paths, until grief caught up with her and toppled her knees. She huddled under a black cypress and hugged Kerberos, letting her tears drip into his fur.

Hermes came to her; she sensed him without lifting her head. His hand came to rest upon her back.

"It's stupid of me." She sniffled. "They already died five years ago."

"Nonsense. Of course it's sad. I feel it too, see?" He took her hand so their skin touched, and indeed a gentle sadness flowed from him—though seemingly without the pain she was experiencing. Naturally it would be different for her, their daughter.

"I just need time to get used to it," she said. "I don't think I'll be very good company tonight. Sorry. You don't have to stay, if…you know."

His brows drew together. "You think I'd leave just because

you don't want sex? What on earth have you heard about me? Oh, all right, there may be something to that rumor. But I can make exceptions for you." He settled into the grass, pulled her onto his lap, and wrapped his arms around her. Kerberos lay beside them and licked their knees lazily.

She rested her head on Hermes' chest. Gradually her pain eased down to something more like his gentle sadness. "I do love you, you know."

She had never said it before. She had worried it would scare him off, or perhaps that he wouldn't believe her. But today it felt right and honest.

He kissed the top of her head. "I know," he said. "And as you must be able to sense, I do love you."

He also hadn't said it, aside from acknowledging it that first day of their affair when she had asked.

She smiled now, her face tucked low where he couldn't see. "Well. I won't expect your personality to change or anything. For you to stop being a liar and a thief and all that."

"Appreciated. But you know, it's funny. When it comes to you, I have this strange desire to give you everything and steal nothing."

She wriggled into a more comfortable fit on his lap. "Even tell the truth?"

"Sometimes even that."

"Now I feel powerful indeed."

"You should, you vixen."

CHAPTER THIRTY-TWO

SOPHIE'S EYES SPRANG OPEN. IT WAS STILL DARK OUTSIDE. THE orange nightlight in the Airstream's bathroom cast a soft light on the curved ceiling of the trailer. Tab snored from her sleeping bag on the floor. Outside chirped the perpetual nighttime orchestra of spirit-world insects and forest animals. The wind sighed, and Terry's voice rumbled something low, answered by Isabel's. They had been enjoying staying outside all night between the trailers, tied to their vines.

Sophie held perfectly still to avoid disturbing the dream-memory she had just inhabited. She breathed deep and closed her eyes again. Persephone's soul—her own soul—had flown into its new body, a memory that brought with it a flood of fresh air. She had skipped over this life before in her rush to uncover Persephone's, but now she pulled it toward her like an unopened book and lifted its front cover. Even before she could recall anything specific about who or where she was, she sensed the joy of a new beginning. Slipping into the skin of the young life felt like the first day after winter when spring finally arrives and the warm air smells of green leaves and blossoms.

So where was she, and who?

Sophie scooted the memories ahead to get past those hazy years of infancy and toddlerhood. There was a warm beach. A brilliant blue sea. Delicious grapes and olives and fish.

Heavy sacred stones perched upon one another. A language somewhat similar to the proto-ancient Greek of Persephone's lifetime. The Mediterranean again, then. Her soul hadn't flown far, as if desiring to stay close to her friends and family. Surely all souls carried such desires, but maybe in the case of Persephone and Hades, the Underworld granted their wishes a little more.

"Galateia," her mother was calling to her five-year-old self, as she romped through a field of sky-blue flowers. "Galateia, time to eat, come back!"

Galateia. Sophie lay still, smiling, basking in the long-ago sun.

She dozed again and let her memories unspool several years. Galateia lived in a village near the sea. She had brothers, older and younger, and over-worked parents—farmers and shepherds, like everyone, or at least everyone who wasn't a fisherman. She'd begun to get the idea that she lived on Sicily, although they called it something else back then; and so far no one who flitted through her life struck Sophie as being Adrian's soul.

Sophie awoke to find the rising sun lighting up the window blinds. She stepped over Tab to get into the bathroom, then layered a sweatshirt over her long-underwear PJs, picked up her phone, and slipped out the trailer's door.

She said good morning to her parents, and sat on the metal steps. After admiring the yellows and pinks of the sunrise for a minute, she texted Adrian.

My name is Galateia. And you are?

She gazed at the blue sea in the direction she estimated Sicily to be, through the rippling transparency of the souls streaming toward the Underworld. She breathed in the immaculately fresh, cold air, and thought how gorgeous it was around here, and how she ought to get up early more often to appreciate the morning light.

His answer buzzed back in a minute or two: *Akis. Very very glad to meet you indeed.*

"HEY." ZOE CAUGHT UP TO TABITHA AS THEIR SMALL GROUP tromped toward another ancient sacred site, this one in Turkey.

Tab flicked her blonde hair out of her face and smiled. "Hey, chica. What's up?"

Zoe stuffed her hands into her coat pockets. "I got to the breakup the other day. Dionysos and Hekate. Just, I don't know, I felt like I should say 'sorry it didn't work out' or something."

"What for? It's okay. These things happen. Anyway, we already guessed it, right?" Tab glanced down at the city in the valley, a mass of brick-red roofs and off-white walls. "I remembered it the other day too." She threw Zoe a wicked grin. "So that's why you and Niko are being so weird around each other."

"Lord." Zoe pressed a palm against her cheek, as if she could force down the blush that way. "The winks, the naughty looks…"

"Wow. Sounds like he's got quite the special interest in you. Well, that's messy, isn't it."

I love you, sweet Hekate. Special interest indeed. "Quite," Zoe said. "So um, have you heard of the term 'biromantic'?"

"No, but I'm guessing it's like bisexual. Only with just romance, not sex?"

"Basically. I was doing some Googling, because, well. I mean, I still don't think I'm anything but gay in terms of sexual orientation. But with these memories and stuff, these feelings…maybe I'm biromantic? I don't know. I feel like I'm letting down the queer community by saying that."

"Don't feel like that. Anything goes, man. Whatever turns your crank. Biromantic. Huh." Tab gazed ahead, where Sophie, Liam, and Freya were walking. "I don't know if I have that. Which is weird, because I do have plenty of memories of messing around with all kinds of people."

"But falling in love?"

"Hmm, yeah, there it was almost always women. So I'm, what, fem-romantic?"

"'Gynoromantic' was I believe what Wikipedia told me."

"Whereas with you, okay, you feel romantically toward women, but also toward…Niko?" Tab's voice hit higher pitch on the name, as if it hardly seemed believable. Zoe shared the disbelief, actually.

She spread one hand helplessly in the air. "Kind of? It's the memories. Or I thought it was, but lately I'm sympathetic toward him, with all he's doing for us, and…it's confusing."

"You know he's not just a guy but an *old* guy. Like, sixty or seventy or something."

"And a criminal. Yes. It's…yeah, this is all mental. Believe me, I know."

"Just promise me you two aren't going to run off to Vegas and get hitched on a whim. That never ends well."

"Can't see either of us consenting to that." She glanced at Tab. "So. Ariadne, speaking of memories. That seems promising. I mean, that relationship made it all the way into mythology."

Tab glanced toward the city again. The cold wind spread her long hair around her face. "Yeah, it did. I haven't unpacked all that yet, but…feels like there's kind of a lot there."

"I can barely remember anything about her myself, yet. I suppose—hey, can you track her?"

Tab nodded, though still didn't look at Zoe. "North of here somewhere. Long ways off, hard to say where. If I get time one of these days, I may go check that out."

Zoe smiled softly. A remnant of jealousy whispered to life in her heart, then quietly died. In its place grew the gracious wish that Tab should be happy and loved. "Yeah. You should."

AN HOUR LATER, BACK IN THE UNDERWORLD, ZOE TRACKED down Niko and found him weaving a willow-and-ivy rope in the orchard. Its top end was tied to a pomegranate branch overhead while he braided the vines together. She thumped herself down against the tree's trunk with a sigh. "Five for five."

"Both Sophie and Liam could switch realms?" he asked.

"At every single one of the sites so far. And my parents could do it at the two sites I tried with them, after just a little practice. Goddess, we're screwed."

"But only if people know what to reach for, and have the right leaves and the Underworld gold. Not much of that out there, I'd wager. To my recollection, we only ended up handing out twelve of the golden tickets. I expect most of them are either lost or in museums now. If Tracy has managed to find one, that's fairly amazing."

"True. But still possible." She rubbed her eyes. "Argh, what kills me is it's *my* fault."

"Yours? I don't quite see that, Miss Drama Queen."

"When I was Hekate, I was the one who identified all these sites and encouraged the mortals to use them. And what good did it do? We all died out anyway—except Rhea—and all it's done is leave Thanatos heaps of nice glorious entrance gates."

"But only twelve potential keys to open them with. Since you're the one who can do the magic, perhaps you can think of a way to seal the gates."

"They're natural intersections of power. I can't do much about that. It's like trying to make the moon rise elsewhere. The most I could do is put up a block to stop or confuse people for a few hours, but it'd wear off, as spells do."

"Well, let's just hope Thanatos keeps up their trend of be-

ing so incredibly inept that they fail. That, at least, is likely."
He kept braiding, his hands swift.

He still looked weary and bitter. She considered telling
him her "biromantic" theory to perk him up, but foresaw
only ironic teasing as the result. Best not.

Still, there were different ways to go at the subject and mo-
mentarily cheer him. She got up and sauntered closer. "For
instance, as to spells wearing off…"

He paused in his rope-braiding to look at her.

She gathered and released a burst of magic within, aimed
only at herself. Its warmth spread through her, and softened
Niko in her eyes into someone that lured her body closer to
his. Placing a palm against his cheek, she settled a kiss on his
lips. He responded with delicacy — at first. Then his arm was
around her waist and he was dipping her horizontal to the
ground like they were in some old movie.

"Mmm." He broke the several-second-long kiss, still holding her in the absurd position. "Knew you couldn't resist the
memories forever."

Her desire was already receding, but at least laughter replaced it.

She writhed free and fell to her hands and knees, then
stood and dusted off her jeans. "I don't know whether to
be impressed or annoyed that you neglected to ever tell me
about the *years and years* of sex."

He studied her, tip of his tongue still tasting his lips. "I enjoy leaving little surprises for people. So that had something
to do with a spell, just now?"

"Yeah, I can give myself aphrodisiac magic and make
anyone attractive. But it wears off super-fast because of our
powers."

"Couldn't you dose yourself over and over? For, say, however long it takes?"

She snorted. "Lovely. No, come on. That's — for one thing,
that takes a lot of concentration. I couldn't do that and…*that*

at the same time. It'd be like trying to tap-dance and cook a meal simultaneously. For another, doing it under a spell doesn't count. You wouldn't want it that way, would you?"

"Hmm. Then are you saying you couldn't transform me into a woman either?"

"I might be able to, but your body would throw it off in minutes. And it would likely hurt throughout. Think of all the organs being changed."

He rolled his fingers against the dangling rope, still studying her. "We'll find a way around this, you and I. One of these centuries."

"Stranger things have happened." She knocked her elbow against his, and started to walk away.

"Zoe," he said, and she stopped to look back. "Adrian's capitulated on the pomegranate. Your vote?"

She sighed. "I suppose I do too, then. If you aren't going to kill them, convert them. Or something like that."

"All right. Oh, and you have magic to make someone tell the truth, yes?"

"Yeah, but it's the kind of thing I should only do with their permission, or to save lives, or else it might rebound on me. But I guess if used on Landon it could count as saving lives."

"If it does rebound, what happens? *You* have to tell the truth for a while? Is that so different from how you already are?"

"Oh, Goddess." She smiled wryly. "I suppose we'll find out."

Chapter Thirty-Three

*L*ANDON HAD BEEN A PRISONER FOR THREE DAYS, BY HIS ROUGH count of when they brought meals and what they said to each other about daily activities. They rarely said anything to him so far, as if he were an animal they had to take care of. Psychological tactic, probably. Make him feel less human; break him down. It was starting to work, though his main reason for feeling afraid was the possibility that they might yet do something far worse to him than ignoring him.

He'd gripped the bars of his cage, stared at the barred ceiling, and knew with fair certainty he couldn't break out. His only chance would be making a dash for it when they unlocked the gate to switch his camp toilet or bring him food, which they did a couple of times a day. But they'd raise the alarm instantly if he busted out like that, and he'd get tackled, probably beaten up, and maybe outright killed before he could find and destroy the tree of immortality—whichever it might be.

Even if he had leisure to wander around freely and examine every tree, it could take days to decide which was the right one. Just on his march to the cage, Landon had glimpsed hundreds of trees, which was probably only a fraction of the total number of trees down here, and all he knew about the magic one was that it was some kind of fruit tree. Then even if he found it, how was he supposed to destroy it? He didn't have an axe or a flamethrower or even a box of matches. Maybe these immortals could rip up a tree with their bare hands, roots and all, but Landon sure couldn't.

It was probably pointless to contemplate how to destroy the tree anyway, since surely he was marked for death now, and Thanatos' grand objective shouldn't matter to him anymore. But he kept desperately picturing some miracle in which he did kill the tree and escape, and became a hero to Thanatos, and thereafter was protected by them for the rest of his life in some secret apartment in Paris as repayment for the service he'd done the world. He at least hoped Tracy and Krystal and the rest might succeed in their invasion, rescue him, and hide him somewhere more comfortable than this cell. Tracy was surely making new plans now, and it was perhaps a blessing that Landon didn't know what they were. That way he couldn't betray his team, and maybe his team would yet save him.

The knife-wielding ghost guarding him today was Sophie's mother Isabel. Even though she'd been one of the victims of the worst crime he'd ever collaborated in, Landon liked her best of his guards, because she didn't glare at him or insult him. She just stood quiet and alert, like a security guard.

Now Nikolaos and Zoe walked into view between the stalagmites. Landon's skin went clammy. Did the torture begin today?

"Thanks, Isabel," Niko said. "You can go."

"Fetch us if you need us." She held out the knife toward him.

With a tug Niko yanked the knife off her immaterial hand. The bindings fell away, some scraps falling to the ground. Landon had seen it done several times now, and still didn't quite understand how it worked, this tying things to ghosts. Isabel drifted away down the dark path.

Landon stayed where he was, sitting against the back wall. Niko unlocked the door. "We're going for a walk today.

Exercise, so I'm told, is one of your rights as a prisoner." He walked over swinging a bungee cord, pulled Landon up by the arm, spun him, and lashed his wrists together behind his back.

"We're actually observing the Geneva Conventions?" Landon asked.

"We know *your* side never does." Zoe stood at the cage door with arms folded. "But yeah, we do, more or less."

Which meant no torture, Landon thought as they brought him out onto the path. Or at least, *more or less* no torture. How comforting.

Niko walked ahead. Zoe pushed Landon's coat sleeve up so she could grip his wrist directly, as if he might try to escape by wriggling out of his shirt. Not likely. His legs were stiff from lack of use, and he was tired all over.

But during the walk through the fields, he limbered up a bit, enough to start feeling halfway human again. Even Zoe's tight grip felt almost reassuring, like it was helping hold him upright.

"So, Osborne, is it?" she said.

"Yeah."

"That's your real name?"

"Yes. I don't have an alias, though I'm sure some of them do."

"That one running the show." Niko glanced back. "Tweed-suit man. Tracy? Is that an alias?"

"I'm not sure. I only know him as Erick Tracy. How'd you get his name?"

"Your emails. Your cell. Remember how I got into those?" Niko shot him a smile that Landon might have called flirtatious under other circumstances.

Landon didn't smile back. They kept walking across the fields.

"Who's in the greatest danger right now, among us?" Zoe asked. "Who are they targeting soonest?"

"Adrian is definitely enemy number one," Landon said. "Has been for a while."

"So, his family or friends in Wellington?" she asked. "Are they likely to become hostages?"

"We've talked about it. I don't know if they're going to change plans now that I'm not there. But the hostage thing hasn't been working out very well with the last few attempts, so, last I heard, the main focus was on getting us into this other realm. Destroying the tree." Oh well, he hadn't meant to say that, but they would have worked it out eventually.

Niko and Zoe exchanged a look. "Which tree might that be, Petal?" Niko asked.

"Petal?" Landon said.

Zoe gave his wrist a pinch. "Answer him."

He flexed his fingers. "The tree of immortality. The one we learned about from Sanjay. Also, it's in our Decrees. It's got to be down here somewhere."

"Lot of trees down here," Niko said. "Any idea which one you're looking for?"

"Not really, except that it's a fruit tree of some kind. Sanjay wasn't specific. Our best guess is apple. 'Golden apple' is what our translation has."

They brought him to the river and down onto the raft, and crossed to the other side.

"So the plan," Niko said, scrambling up the other bank, "is to burst into this realm at some sacred site, get in here, and destroy this supposed tree, along with the lot of us. Is that right?"

"Yes," Landon said. Zoe, still hanging onto his wrist, pushed him up the slope.

"And do they know where this cave is?" she asked.

"Maybe. We have it narrowed down to a few possibilities. I'm not sure where we are here, geographically, but I guess this could be one of them."

They led him through the tunnel until they stood in the

chamber where he had arrived. Sunlight, blessed sunlight and blue sky, shone through the cave mouth high above. Landon's eyes drank it in.

"So are they aiming to figure out which site is the Underworld," Niko said, "and switch realms directly inside it?"

He kept his gaze on the tiny piece of sky. "Yeah. Ideally."

The others were silent a few seconds.

"Do you think they really know how to switch realms?" Zoe asked.

"They haven't tried it, as far as I know. But Tracy seems confident about this technique he got hold of."

"By stealing it from some modern-day Eleusinian Mysteries group?" she said.

"Yeah. I...I think he even killed someone for it."

Niko and Zoe exchanged another glance.

After a moment Niko turned to him. "Did you want to go up? Get some fresh air?"

"Uh. Maybe." Landon still had to entertain the possibility that they'd do something terribly painful to him up there. Though why they wouldn't just do it down here, he couldn't figure.

"If so," Niko said, "your choices are the ladder or one of the horses."

Landon eyed the rope ladder, which looked like a wisp of dental floss against the giant height of the cave. He shivered. "I guess the horse."

A minute or two later, after a scary but short flight upward, he was let down to the solid ground in the sun. He sat upon a rock and gazed at the sea. At least he got this visit to the Mediterranean, which was every bit as blue as advertised. Even with ghosts streaming past overhead, it was beautiful.

Zoe still held onto his arm. "Did you enjoy it?" she asked. "Being involved in killing all those people?"

"No. I've never enjoyed the killing part. It's just what has to be done. Or seemed like it did."

"Krystal, now," Niko said, seated at Landon's other side, "she seems to enjoy it."

"Yeah," Landon said. "I'm pretty sure she does."

"Is she coming on this other-realm adventure?" Niko asked.

"Probably. I guess Tracy's in charge now. Whatever he decides."

"How long do you think it'll be?" Zoe asked. "Before they fly over and start trying to break in?"

"We were talking about late January," Landon said. "Could be any day, I guess. Again, though, Tracy might change plans. Make things happen sooner, because of my getting kidnapped, or maybe put things off. I don't know."

"Silly question, but," Niko said, "do you suppose they'd call off their hostilities, or make any sort of deal, in exchange for your safe return? No, never mind. Of course they wouldn't."

"I agree. They wouldn't." Landon spoke with only a trace of bitterness. The sight of the blue sea did put a certain tranquility into one's mind.

"Do you even want to rejoin them?" Zoe asked. "You don't seem to like them much."

"I want to be free again," Landon said. "And they're some of the only people who would protect me anymore. But other than that, no, I don't really miss them."

They all sat in silence a while. Finally Niko said, "Well. It's lunchtime. Down we go."

They brought him back to his cell, picking up one of the ghosts along the way to be a guard—Terry this time. Only once Landon was behind bars did Zoe let go of him. She untied his hands and stepped out. Niko brought a plastic plate with a peanut butter sandwich, a carrot, and a juice bottle on it, and set it on the floor for Landon. As they locked the door, and as Landon bit into his sandwich, a sense of outrage slid into him. It felt suspiciously like waking up from a dream.

"Hey. Did you guys drug me?" he demanded.

"In a sense," Zoe admitted. "Used magic on you to make you tell the truth. Except, bloody hell, you don't know much about the plan, do you."

Niko hooked his arm into Zoe's. "Come along, darling. Tell me some more truths over here, farther away."

"Ugh, I don't like this!" she said. "I totally do feel like telling you things. All kinds of true things that I don't really need to say."

"Yeah? Have you been looking at any porn lately?"

"You know, I actually kind of was, the other day."

"Definitely do tell me more," Niko said, and that, thankfully, was where they fell out of earshot.

Landon exhaled in anger through his nose, and drank some of the tart cranberry juice. At least he hadn't told them about the sorcerer—probably only because they hadn't asked a question that led to her.

"They have no right," he informed Terry, "using magic like that."

"Uh-huh." Terry watched Landon set the bottle down. "They can be sneaky that way."

Chapter Thirty-Four

*L*ANDON AWOKE, CRAMPED AND SORE AS USUAL. SLEEPING ON the ground, even on the layer of blankets they'd allowed him, had transformed him into a mass of aching joints. He'd just been having some strange-ass dreams. Unlike your usual dreams that dissipated after you woke up, these stayed solidly clear as he blinked at the bars above him. He dreamed he'd been a Russian guy in the mid-20th-century, working a minor government job, and unhappy about it. He even spoke Russian in the dream. Huh. Must have spent too much time around Yuliya.

Wait. He could still speak Russian. Now. He couldn't do *that* before.

He bolted upright.

Tabitha Lofgren was his guard at the moment. She sat against a stalagmite outside the cell, iPod earphones in, leather-booted toe tapping to her music, Landon's gun in one hand. She played with three ghost cats, whipping a shoelace along the ground like a snake and making them leap at it.

Though he felt nervous addressing Tabitha, since she was one of the people he'd tried to kill, or at least had helped arrange the car-bomb attempt, he blurted out, "Did you guys do some sort of language magic on me?"

She popped one earphone out. "Huh?"

"Language magic. Did you guys do something like that to me?"

She dangled the rope higher, watching the spirit cats jump for it. "Well, let's see. You had some of that juice, yeah?"

He groaned as an affirmative. Of course it had occurred to him that they might poison or drug him, but he had to eat. What choice did he have? Even if he died, he'd still be here. That said, it was fucking annoying to have your mind messed with.

"Geneva Conventions, my ass," he said.

"You're in for an interesting ride, bud."

He walked forward and grabbed the bars. "What'll it do to me? What's happening?"

"Niko said he wanted to have 'the talk' with you." She quirked her fingers in air quotes around the words. "He'll be by later." Tabitha plugged her earphone back in. Discussion evidently over.

Landon shouting questions at her only resulted in her sticking her tongue out at him. And, eventually, pointing his gun at him. He backed off.

Finally Nikolaos appeared, carrying two blue buckets with steam rising from them. Tab leaped up, waved at Landon and then flipped him off, and walked away.

Niko unlocked the U-bolts and opened the door. "You get to take a sponge bath and do your laundry." He shoved both buckets in with his foot, and dropped a heap of clothes bundled in a towel onto the floor. "Stuff you can wear while yours are drying."

Landon did absolutely reek from not bathing for however many days. A bucket of hot water and a heap of clean clothes looked like slices of heaven. He pulled off his down vest and started unbuttoning his shirt, then hesitated at the third button and met Niko's eyes.

Niko leaned against the door to shut it from the inside, and lounged there with arms folded, watching Landon with his usual calm smirk. Fine, so he was going to be a gross prison-guard perv and watch while Landon got naked and sponged himself off. Landon didn't even care.

He finished undressing. Naked and barefoot on the cold ground, he carried his clothes to one of the buckets and shoved them in. Suds and warm water sloshed onto the ground. Landon prodded the clothes down to the bottom, then left them to soak and turned to the other bucket, which had a car-wash-style large sponge in it.

The first squeeze of hot sudsy water down his chest was indeed bliss. He sighed in relief as he sponged off the back of his neck, his underarms, his groin, his feet, and his hair. Throughout, he felt Niko's scrutiny. Landon burned with resentment, determined to last as long as he could, and not give Niko the satisfaction of asking about the weird new language abilities.

"It's midday, if you're curious," Niko said. "Impossible to tell what time of day it is when you're down here, I know."

"Doesn't really matter for my purposes anyway," Landon said.

Niko laughed, and Landon looked up in irritation, crouching nude beside the bucket.

"What?"

"I said that in the Underworld language," Niko said. "And you answered in the same. See?" He switched languages, and this time Landon noticed. *"Aren't you learning all sorts of new things down here."*

Landon pulled in a long breath through his nose. He chucked the sponge back into the bucket. "Son of a bitch," he said, in English.

"Here's what's going on," Niko began, also reverting to English.

He explained while Landon finished his sponge bath.

Pomegranate juice. Past lives. Languages. Dreams. The

importance of skimming backward to get to the ancient Greek lives that had caused this whole mess in the first place.

Landon, feeling sick, picked up the towel and wrapped it around his shivering body. He dried off without speaking a word and put on the clothes: a long-sleeved gray T-shirt ratty at the cuffs, and a pair of jeans with holes in the knees, a little loose at the waist and short at the ankles. Castoffs of Adrian's, maybe. For the moment he went without underwear or socks, since Niko hadn't brought him any. He just zipped the jeans over his naked junk and stuffed his bare feet into his snow boots.

Then he stalked over to Niko, fully intending to punch him, even if it got him killed. Anger, fear, and frustration pounded inside him, a tsunami flooding his every shore.

But Niko watched him with pretty green eyes, not even unfolding his arms as Landon stormed up and stopped two inches from him. Landon hovered there, shaking with fury.

"I suppose you'd kill me if I hit you," Landon said, his teeth clenched.

"Waste of life. And largely pointless. Because guess where you'd end up if I did." Niko sounded undisturbed, conversational.

Landon paced away and prowled the cage.

Waste of life. Something Thanatos didn't care much about, though they probably should. In some ways, Landon conceded, Thanatos would do well to take a few pages from the gods.

"If all this knowledge is real, why would you give it to me?" Landon asked. "Wouldn't you want to hide it from my side?"

Niko still lounged against the bars, like he was at a dull party, but now his eyes sharpened their focus upon Landon. "No. I want to get the truth through your thick skulls. It's proving bloody hard to do. If I could catch you all and bring you down here and stuff pomegranates down every one of your gullets, I would. It'd fix ninety-nine percent of our problems."

Landon continued to pace, processing this. So they were recruiting, as suspected. Trying to sway him and others into believing their worldview.

Granted, their worldview was looking damn convincing from right here. In a cell, in the Underworld, guarded by ghosts, with magic pomegranates for lunch.

"What if it doesn't convince me?" Landon said, just to be belligerent. "What if I still don't believe it?"

At last Niko looked weary. "If this doesn't convince you, then I give up on you."

Though he said it as casually as he said everything else, Landon felt a chill go spiderwebbing through him. Those words sounded like a death sentence.

Erick Tracy lingered in the wind at the ruins of Perperikon, and let the tour group wander past him. He slipped his hand into his pocket and drew out the ancient inscribed gold leaf and the handful of strawberry tree leaves he had found and picked after wandering for an hour in the nearest town. Perperikon was one of the sacred sites on the map he'd stolen. It lay in present-day Bulgaria, in a region that used to be Thrace in classical days. Thrace had bordered ancient Greece, and apparently the Greek gods had spread their unholy word here too.

Tracy had come alone for this first attempt at entering the spirit realm. He had a hunch Krystal was the one among them being magically tracked, if any of them were. So he told her and Yuliya to stay put in their vacation rental flat in Vratsa, and took a train down here on his own. So far, no suspicious stalkers had shown up on the periphery of his vision; he had no reason to think he'd been followed. But entering the other realm, if it worked, might set off some kind of alarm for them—he didn't know. Magic worked all kinds of ways, his research had indicated. So his heart did pound as he prepared for this attempt, which might be the last thing he ever did.

Still, even the risk was thrilling, as always.

He walked behind a jumbled stone wall in the ancient ruins, and stood hidden from the other tourists. He held the fresh leaves and the Underworld gold and closed his eyes. He focused on the hard edges of the gold, and imagined its origin, deep in the Earth, among strange spirits and dangerous plants, across a boundary he now sought and reached for. The document he'd stolen with the map gave the instructions: imagine the spirit realm is on the other side of a steep hilltop, and climb toward it. Focus on your steps. Feel the magical energies around you, for they will boost you over the top and onto the other side.

The ground rippled, changing under his feet. He opened his eyes and reached for the wall to steady himself, but his hand met a tree instead. The wall was gone, as were all the ruins. He blinked and looked all around. The wind whistled; animals chirped and roared from every direction. A squirrel-like creature with striped gray and white fur and a forked tail leaped up the tree trunk, squawked at him, and scampered high up into the branches. That surely was no living-world creature.

The spirit realm. He had done it.

He laughed aloud. He climbed on top of a boulder to look around. Yes: the town and roads had all absolutely vanished, overtaken by a wilderness of trees and rocks. As he scanned the skies, a faint greenish glowing figure streaked past beneath the winter clouds. A spirit?

"Good Lord," he said. "It's real."

He hadn't even realized he'd doubted it until now. It was terrifying and beautiful, this other world. He coveted it all of a sudden. Oh, indeed, he would keep this gold leaf forever and come to this realm whenever he liked, and make what use of it he wished—the possibilities were immense. But first he must unseat and destroy those young punks who had snuck in before him, and were handing out immortality far too freely.

Yes. There was much to be done, and much to explore, but also too much danger for him to do it alone. Those spirit-world animals, he had heard, included several gigantic carnivorous ones. And who knew what the spirits or other magical forces might do to him?

So, to see if he could switch back.

He climbed down, and repeated the operation: eyes closed, hands clutching artifacts, mind taking him back over that ridge and…

The Earth jolted again. Smooth rock formed under his shoes. Voices bloomed nearby: the tourists talking in another part of the ruins. He opened his eyes to find the living world all back in place.

And no immortal had pounced upon him. Indeed, there'd been no sign they had any idea of what he had just done.

He beamed, took a long and happy breath in and out, and strolled back around the wall with his hand trailing the ancient stones.

He was the new official head of Thanatos—it had been determined by unanimous council vote just before they'd flown to Europe. And their further research into the Greek sites had narrowed the likely Underworld locations down to just two. Now he knew they could, in all likelihood, get in. If one sacred site worked, why shouldn't the rest?

All in all, great things were taking place for Erick Tracy.

"What was Adrian like before? I mean, before he found out he was Hades?" The query darted out of Sophie's mouth on an impulse, surprising even herself. Sure, it had been on her mind, the question of whether she and Adrian would love each other *without* all these epic memories. It was important to ponder that kind of thing. Still, she hadn't exactly intended to ask Zoe out loud.

The two of them were standing in the Underworld, awaiting an answer to a request they had sent out among the souls, seeking information about modern Eleusinian Mysteries groups. They might learn something that would disturb them, but Sophie was finding that the asking and taking action felt better than the hiding in quiet corners she'd been doing.

Now her mouth was producing even more asking, it seemed, and on more romantic topics.

Surprise gleamed in Zoe's gray eyes. "Haven't you two ever talked of that?"

"Some. But what was he like to you?"

Zoe smiled. She kicked her hiking boot's heel against a lumpy rock formation. "Well, he was nerdy. At least about some things. He was only average at math, so not nerdy in that sense, but he could be a fireball in class discussions in social studies. Got all passionate about ethical causes and animal rights and things. Also about various comic books and bands and television shows. Those you've probably talked about."

"Yeah. We share tastes there." Sophie found she was smiling, recalling their fandom comment threads on her blog. It seemed like ages ago, but it had only been last year.

"Somewhere on my hard drive I've got bits of stuff he wrote in high school. Essays about things, and write-ups he did for me to describe the visual side of graphic novels or movies, because I couldn't see back then." Zoe chuckled. "He made them quite funny at times. Like: 'She's wearing a dress that looks like those crocheted things my Nana drapes on the back of her armchairs.' I'll send them to you if you like."

"Yes." Sophie cleared her throat to make her voice less timid. "I'd like that. Thanks."

Zoe's attention sharpened as she gazed into the crowd. "Here we go."

An open path was forming in the masses, making way for one soul who walked toward Zoe and Sophie. He was short, around fifty years old, with a thick bristle of graying hair, and smile lines etched into his pale skin.

"You were seeking someone recently murdered, involved in the modern worship of the Lord and Lady," he said in the Underworld tongue. "I believe that was me."

"We are sorry for your unjust death." Sophie resorted instinctively to the answer Persephone used to give. "We'll do our best to bring about justice for you."

He nodded in gratitude.

"What's your name?" Zoe asked. "And when were you killed?"

"Ciaran O'Slatraigh," he said. "I was killed on the thirteenth of December, in Dublin."

"An Irishman." Zoe switched to English, smiling. "Would you prefer English, then? We're a Kiwi and a Yank, so we can accommodate that."

"That'd be lovely. Cheers." His brogue rippled into evidence as he switched languages too.

"I'm Sophie, and this is Zoe. Then do you think you were killed because of your involvement in this group?"

"I'm sure of it. We're a small coven, a select set who's kept certain traditions and secrets safe for, well, thousands of years as far as we know. The central secret was how to step into the spirit realm." Ciaran nodded to their glowing surroundings.

A shiver ran up Sophie's body. "You've done it, then? Switched realms? People have been able to, all this time?"

"Indeed they have. We don't do it much, mind. Only on special ceremonial occasions, and only with the company of a select trained priest or priestess of our coven. And we stayed at the sacred sites, never went far. Wandering off in this realm was generally regarded as a dangerous and ill-conceived idea." He chuckled.

"It would have been," Zoe said with a smile, "but only because of the wild animals. The spirits wouldn't have hurt you."

"No, I see that now," he agreed.

"Then you had a piece of Underworld gold," Sophie said.

"Used to, yes. The gold leaf, kept safe through antiquity. Well, some man, who I now am sure gave us a false name, began studying with us, at our little library archive we keep at Trinity College. We trusted him at first, though not too far of course. No one got all the secrets until they'd been with us for many years, though we were happy to provide study material for those who were curious, up to a point. But he began getting too keen, nosing about in the records without permission. One night I came and found him in the vaults. He'd broken in. He'd found the gold leaf and the copy of the old scrolls that gave instructions for traveling over."

A cold hand closed around Sophie's heart in anticipation of what came next. Zoe's face tensed too.

Ciaran looked down at the ground. "I tried to stop him. He killed me on the spot. Shot me with a gun I hadn't seen him carrying, and ran out."

Zoe and Sophie allowed a few seconds of silence.

"We think we know who he is," Zoe said, "and believe me, we're quite keen to catch him ourselves."

"But he does have this gold leaf, then," Sophie said. "And it really does get people into this realm."

"It does. I've traveled over myself." Ciaran gave them a wistful smile. "The absolute best moments of my life. Pure magic."

Sophie smiled back, pushing down the sadness within. "I know the feeling. Your secret mystery club sounds pretty awesome. Wish we'd known you were around sooner."

"Well, then, we wouldn't be very secret if you knew, would we?"

"Good point. Do you think there are more groups like yours? Who have the gold and the method, and can cross over?"

"There are certainly other covens who know of this realm, and who speak reverently of Persephone and Hades and Hekate and all of you." He cast a respectful glance from one woman to the other. "But the actual crossing-over, that's rare. We suspected there wasn't much of this gold about, so we protected it as best we could. We didn't do a good enough job, sorry to say."

"It's not your fault," Zoe said. "The people who killed you, they're called Thanatos, and they're utterly ruthless and have been around as long as your covens and Mysteries have. It's us they're after, really; us they want to destroy. It's everyone's bad luck they finally managed to steal your secrets."

"One other question, since your group was so good at magic," Sophie added. "Do you think anyone out there could…use it for the wrong purposes? I mean—" She glanced at Zoe. "Zoe's always assured us it rebounds on people if they try. But we seem to keep learning the picture's more compli-cated than we thought, so…"

"Oh, that's always been going on, unfortunately," Zoe answered for him. "And more so as you get further along toward modern times."

"That's what I've heard as well," Ciaran said.

Sophie grimaced in dismay. "What? But how?"

Zoe shifted her stance, resting a foot on the base of the lumpy rock. "I've been thinking back on it, on all the lifetimes where I got involved with witchcraft, in covens and temples and things. *I* never tried the evil stuff, nor did the others I as-sociated with, but we heard about such people. With enough folk amassing enough magical knowledge over the centuries, they're bound to find loopholes. Things that let them do what they want, even if it hurts others."

"But—at least in the afterlife—"

"Tartaros gets them, oh yes, and how. But either they don't know that or don't care, because they're getting away with it in the short term."

"We heard of such folk too," Ciaran added. "Not many, I'm thankful to say, but an occasional lone practitioner out there, pulling some twisted sacrifice that buys them time against the inevitable backlash, and lets them do harm until then."

Sophie let her back sag against the rock. "The world sucks. Bad people getting away with their crap for way too long, all over the place. Tartaros needs to step in sooner."

"Mm," Zoe agreed. "Or maybe that's what immortals are meant to be for. If we're 'meant' for anything."

"Yeah. I've thought that." A corner of Sophie's damaged heart warmed, and her gaze slipped to the red and white wildflowers spangling the grass. "Like what Adrian does. Catching murderers where he can."

"He's the man. In his quiet emo way." They both looked to Ciaran again, and Zoe added, "Thank you so much, Ciaran. Rest assured we're looking for your bastard murderer, and we'll call on you again to let you know how it goes."

He bowed. "A pleasure merely to meet the pair of you. It's I who am at your service, as ever."

CHAPTER THIRTY-FIVE

TRACY WALKED DOWN THE FOREST PATH OUTSIDE VRATSA, Bulgaria, alone as he had promised. If he didn't return in an hour, Krystal and Yuliya and their local Thanatos contact were supposed to come look for him, or for what remained of him. But Tracy wasn't afraid, not even with the rumors of Tenebra's fearsome power. He had more than enough to offer her.

The frigid air invigorated his lungs. His thick Scottish wool cap and coat kept him warm. A light snowfall yesterday had dusted everything with white: path, bare trees, boulders and surrounding crags. A few wide-winged dark birds circled high above in the gray sky. Such a bleak and magical landscape. He wouldn't have been surprised to hear wolves howling, or to see Tenebra emerge from a hut that scuttled about on chicken legs. It was that kind of European forest.

"Erick Tracy."

He came up short, catching a breath as he blinked at the woman.

She surely hadn't been there a second before, standing right in front of him in the middle of the path. She lifted one thin eyebrow. "I was wearing a spell so you wouldn't notice me until I wished you to."

Her English was accented with something he guessed was

Eastern European, though he couldn't place the exact country.

He recovered from his surprise with a gracious smile. "I've heard such magic is your specialty. I see that's no exaggeration."

"*One* of my specialties." She wore all gray: long skirt, winter boots, puffy coat, beret. Her shoulder-length hair was gray too, with threads of white and black. She was of middle height, middle age, average weight, unremarkable appearance—but if you examined those close-set pale eyes and that mouth with its habitual downward turn, you caught glimpses of coldness, hardness. Some people might have called her countenance "chilling." But for all Tracy knew, this was part of a glamour too; a disguise showing her as she wanted to appear.

"You've read the information I sent you," Tracy said. "We have an update."

"Oh?"

"I took the gold token to one of the sites on our map, near here, as a test run yesterday." He held her glinting eyes an extra second before continuing. "It works. We can enter the spirit realm."

"Ah…" The interested syllable reminded him oddly of the wind creaking the door of an abandoned house. "There is much power to be found in that realm, I am certain. Especially the Underworld itself."

"Which is where we'll go directly, or will aim to. We have it narrowed down to just a couple of sites in Greece. I most definitely would like someone of your abilities to come along."

"The golden apple," she said. "This is an immortality fruit, I take it?"

"Yes." He hadn't put it in writing with that exactitude, but anyone with enough mystical training would understand the hints he'd dropped in his email.

"And these unnaturally strong bringers of chaos, they have eaten of it."

"Yes. Which is why we must destroy it, and them."

"My price…" She lifted one crooked forefinger. "Is that I eat the fruit before the tree is destroyed."

He had suspected she would propose such a thing. No powerful loner sorcerer worth her salt could resist a boon like that. Still, he hesitated. "Our mission of course is that no one should be immortal. Not even on our side. Believe me, I understand the temptation, but—"

"That is my price." Her tone had become ominous. "Grant it and you will have only one immortal in the world to worry about, and I plan to keep to myself as much as possible. I would only wish to be left to my devices, to enjoy myself forever. And I would be on the side of your organization forever, too."

Tracy nibbled the edge of his lower lip, nodding. "That does have its appeal."

"In addition, I can help hide your team and this golden artifact from the dangerous others, while we are searching for the Underworld."

"Yes," he admitted. "I was hoping you could. We could use that."

"Another of my specialties that might interest you…" Tenebra glanced up, muttered something, and beckoned to the sky.

One of the large birds circled lower, and finally landed on the ground a few meters away and folded its wings. It was a buzzard, or something similar, and it watched Tenebra alertly.

She cast her hand toward it, and hissed, "*Sormajhaturm*."

The bird convulsed, then collapsed in the snow. Tracy walked slowly to it and touched the toe of his shoe to its limp body. Dead.

He looked at her. "Are you certain you could do such a

thing to our unnaturals? They've proven quite hard to destroy."

"The spell rips the soul from the body." She stood as straight and casual as ever. "I do not see how anyone could live after that."

"I'm interested to try it and find out." He squinted at her. "Forgive me, but I'm curious. In my mystical studies, I was given to understand that magic such as this rebounds upon a practitioner. Threefold, some say. How do you escape that?"

She held up her left hand and spread it open. Her first finger was missing. "Long ago I found another spell that allows one to make a sacrifice as an advance payment. So far, it has worked. There has been no rebound."

Tracy blinked. "I see. You are a dedicated woman indeed."

Tenebra lowered her hand. "Some say the spell exacts further payment after death," she said dismissively. "But I see no proof of such matters."

Given they were about to enter the Underworld, where possibly such punishments were in fact exacted upon departed souls, Tracy wondered if she might change her beliefs before long. However, if she meant to become immortal, then indeed, that payment could be put off quite a long while. And regardless, it would be her problem, not his.

"Well, then," he said. "If you're willing to employ the skills at your disposal toward our ends, I accept your terms. Mind you, I think we should keep this special condition confidential, between ourselves. The rest of our group—well, they might not approve. Ideologically, you understand."

"That is fine." The avarice burned brighter in her eyes. "Then I look forward to working with you."

CHAPTER THIRTY-SIX

*L*ANDON HAD NOTHING TO DO BUT THINK. THEY LEFT HIM alone most of every day, and his guards didn't usually talk to him. The memories pressed in on all sides, and with nothing to lose, he dropped his resistance and let them in. He entertained each lifetime a short while, then moved it along and stepped farther into the past—not so much because Niko had told him to, but because he was grudgingly curious.

It didn't take long for him to start to believe. He understood he'd been in the Underworld lots of times before, and so had everyone else. He accepted that the immortals were legendary down here, known by all the souls as part of the history of the Underworld even during the long span when the "gods" were just mortals like the rest of humanity. He also grasped the disturbing trend that nearly all of the immortals were considered a force for good in the world. And the few that weren't, well, they were really only viewed as nuisances, not sources of true evil. True evil came from people like murderers. People who behaved like Thanatos members, to look at it one way.

And he knew that, on occasion, he'd led a harmful enough life that he'd been confined to the caves of punishment. Not for long; the vine latching him to the wall had been skinny, and had disintegrated and fallen away to free him after a few years at most. But somehow the memory of being there was the scariest of all the disturbing things he could remember.

He was huddled up, hugging his knees, contemplating that place, when Niko arrived, balancing a tray of food on top of his head.

Landon looked at him as he unlocked the door. "Is my grandmother in the caves underneath?" He'd wanted to ask about her again, but hadn't dared for fear that asking would somehow make things worse for him—or for her, even. Now, under the morbid sway of these thoughts, he had to know.

Niko paused, then swung the door open and swept the tray down to the ground. "But of course."

"Then...you don't..." He stopped. No, the immortals didn't control those caves, couldn't free anyone down there even if they wanted to. Landon got that now, or at least his memories insisted it was true.

Niko rotated the keys around his finger. "If you're not hungry yet, we could go see her."

Goosebumps shivered up all over Landon's body. He nodded.

Niko bungee-corded Landon's wrists together behind his back and guided him out of the cell, keeping one hand around Landon's upper arm. Now that Landon's own un-washed stench didn't fill his nostrils, he was able to notice that Niko smelled nice. Sort of natural and spicy. Landon glanced sideways at his captor, who was his own height and maybe his own age. With his beautiful classic-statue profile and unusual but urbane accent, Niko was totally the kind of guy Landon would have hit on in one of the clubs he had, on rare occasion, slipped into for some adventure.

Right. If he weren't an enemy, holding Landon prisoner. Oh hi, Stockholm Syndrome. Landon snorted humorlessly to himself, and shoved those fancies out of his head.

Diverting his attention was easy enough to do, since where they were going was getting eerier by the second. After skirting the edge of the fields full of ghosts, Niko led him into a crevice in the wall, hidden behind an outcropping of rock. Niko switched on a flashlight. The tunnel sloped downward. Its sides got so close together Landon could have touched both at once if his arms had been free. The air got stuffier and hotter, as if some furnace waited at the bottom. Or some hell.

Then, scaring him enough he actually yelped, a flame whooshed out of the wall. Niko didn't seem perturbed. He only switched off his flashlight and kept walking. The flames kept up with them: one after another flared into life just ahead of their footsteps, and winked out again a few yards behind them, as if a motion sensor was being activated.

But it didn't feel like a mechanical trick. It felt real. Uncanny. And dreadfully identical to what he'd already seen in his darkest memories.

Before he'd had time to absorb the horror and wonder of the familiar honeycomb of cells they entered, containing one sad-looking ghost apiece, Niko had parked him in front of a cell. Landon beheld his grandmother.

He lurched toward her. She regarded him with unhappy blue eyes, her form translucent. Unlike Landon, she wasn't confined by bars or handcuffs; just one of those vine ropes, wrapped around her waist and fastened to the wall. Her space was tiny, a closet of rock with a flame burning in the floor at her feet.

"Landon," she answered. "They caught you too. Oh, I'm sorry, dear." Her voice sounded like it always had, but deadened. Thinner, defeated.

"Grandma." Panic thumped within his chest. "Are you all right? I mean—you're not, I know, but…"

"This is the natural order. It's where we have to be, when we've made the wrong choices too often." She sounded unhappy, not tranquil like the other souls he'd met.

"But—Thanatos is still right, aren't they? This—this is all wrong, this is what we have to stop—"

"We can't stop this. No more than we can stop the sun rising. No, dear, it's been like this long before our group existed, and will be for as long as humans live. Thanatos was misinformed. I see it now." Her gaze dropped to the flame in her cell.

"But what do I do? I was trying to carry on your work, and—and they've captured me. They killed you! They're not right either. They can't be."

"Too much killing," his grandmother said. "Too much harm. On both sides, yes. But far more on ours." She looked at him. "I was one of them once. An immortal. In the ancient times."

He felt dizzy. "No."

"Perhaps it's why I strived to know more about them, in this life and others. But I went about it wrong. Don't be a part of it anymore, Landon. Don't end up here."

He looked about the stuffy, hellish cave in desperation, then back at her. "Are you always alone? Does anyone ever come talk to you?"

"They've come to ask me about Thanatos," she said. "Adrian a couple of times, and him a couple of times too." She nodded toward Niko. "He also asked me if I forgave him. I said I did. I think that helped us both, according to the laws down here. But only a little."

Landon turned to stare at Niko in bewilderment. Niko's light eyes held Landon's for a second or two, then his gaze drifted aside as if the topic mattered not at all. Landon didn't have to ask if it was true. Souls couldn't lie. He knew that much now.

Landon and Betty Quentin spoke a few minutes more, but most of what she said was along the same lines as before: Thanatos had been wrong. The last thread of what he used to know was getting pulled out of the fabric of his life. Was there one single thing left of his former identity that he could still cling to and trust? No. Not really.

Still, as he trooped back up the tunnel with Niko, he tried to rationalize it. "They get warped down there. Right? Their minds—it's supposed to make them feel guilty all the time, or something."

"Tartaros does suppress happiness," Niko said. "Makes you focus on what you've done wrong. But 'warped,' not really. If anything, it gives you clarity. Shows you what your actions caused."

"Were you ever down there, between lives?" Landon asked.

"Oh, who could ever find fault with me?" But his irony sounded brittle, which piled another suspicion onto Landon's confused mind.

Stepping out into the open cave fields again was a relief in comparison with the stuffy tunnels. His legs felt weak; he looked forward to lying down a while on his blankets, and to having his hands untied. Small pleasures.

On the way back to the cell, Niko picked up one of the souls to be Landon's next guard. It was the dark-skinned woman in the long red dress—Rhea. She had been killed by Thanatos a few months ago, caught in India. She had a way of scrutinizing him that gave him the shivers. Didn't help that she said occasional things out of the blue like, "The Goddess surely does not like the path you are on, Landon Osborne."

At least right now she was being quiet.

Landon ran his tongue around his teeth, which felt thickly coated and disgusting. After Niko propelled him into the cell and removed the bungee cord from his wrists, Landon asked, "Do you think I could get a toothbrush? Please."

Niko's eyes traveled around Landon's face, carrying a glimmer of something like pity. "Sure. Why not. Razor too, maybe." He pointed at Landon in warning. "Safety razor. No cutting your wrists."

Landon shivered, and nodded in acceptance. Insane and

unpleasant though this experience had been so far, Thanatos rarely treated their captives this politely, he had to admit.

"So you're good cop," Landon said. "Who's bad cop? Zoe? Adrian? Sophie?"

"If they want to be, they're free to." Niko stroked Landon's week-old beard with thumb and finger—a surprisingly gentle sensation. "But mostly, dear boy, I think you are your own bad cop."

He left the cell, locked it, and left Landon with Rhea as guard, the knife tied to her hand.

Landon watched until Niko was out of sight. "What does that even mean?" he said aloud.

Rhea gazed after Niko. "With that one, it is not always easy to tell."

CHAPTER THIRTY-SEVEN

Each morning after Hades' and Persephone's souls had departed, Hekate climbed high in the sky on her spirit horse to clear the encircling oaks and seek her parents' signals. She sensed nothing for almost two months. Then one day, during a rain that was swelling all the rivers and soaking her in mid-air, she gasped. They were out there, across the stormy sea.

She wheeled her horse that direction and shot off at top speed. Even if it meant crossing the great ocean, she would brave it. Their signals, like a pair of lighthouse flames, would guide her.

But they weren't far at all.

"Sicily," she said to Hermes later that day, when she arrived in his borrowed room in Athena's palace, where he was staying a few days. Sopping wet with rain, she gripped his tunic, and laughed when he winced at how she dripped upon him. "They're in Sicily! My parents. Can't you sense them?"

His face changed as he focused. Then he closed his warm hands around hers. "I do! That's fabulous. Then you've gone to them?"

"Yes, but of course they're still in the womb. All I could tell was they were in neighboring towns, and her family seems to be a large one with lots of children already, and his might be an unmarried younger mother. I couldn't be sure, not without asking nosy questions that would be odd from a traveling stranger."

"And you are indeed the strangest of travelers." He peeled off her wet wool cloak. His naughty smile unfurled. "Let's get you out of these chilly things. All of them."

In the next few months, Hekate paid frequent visits to the Great Goddess' temple near the Sicilian villages where her parents' souls had been reborn. It was another site of intense energy, which no longer surprised her. She familiarized herself with the temple, showing up often enough that she became known among the worshippers.

One day while mingling in the crowd there, she sensed the approach of her father's soul. She whirled around. Among the others stood a young woman holding a baby.

Hekate strode forward. The young woman looked up in alarm, for Hekate was tall, dressed in midnight blue robes and Underworld jewels, and known to be an immortal with powerful magic. Hekate smiled to calm her, and said, "Welcome. I don't believe we've met. Who's your little one?"

"I'm Symaethis. This is Akis." The color deepened in the girl's face. "My family was disgraced when I became pregnant. I—I'm not married. But the temple here took me in, and their midwives were so kind. They've cared for us and allowed us to stay. This is our home now."

Hekate couldn't stop smiling at the three-month-old infant with his sweet, plump face. "Yes, around here we're much more interested in being kind to each other than in silly notions of marriage and disgrace." She touched Akis' palm with one finger, and he gripped it and beamed a toothless grin at her.

If she'd had any doubts this was her father, they would have been dispelled at the touch. Finally making physical contact with him again was like breathing the air after swimming a long time underwater. Hekate basked in the warmth, even as her eyes filled with tears. "Stay here as long as you like," she said, still gazing at him. "We'll make sure they take good care of you."

PERSEPHONE'S SOUL, MEANWHILE, HAD BEEN BORN INTO A family who lived not far from the temple. She was the only girl (other than her mother) in a house full of boys, and from a distance Hekate judged the home to be a stable enough place to grow up, though the family didn't seem to smile much as far as she saw.

As the years passed, Hekate kept checking up on her reincarnated parents, with varying degrees of worry or happiness about their progress. She worked on the establishment of new temples and the business of murdered souls. Then she sought relaxation in Hermes' bed, wherever it happened to be that day.

Although she still possessed greater affinity for magic than anyone, she slowly discovered, as her own awareness deepened, that her immortal companions all used magic to some degree too, though most didn't realize it. She already knew they must, since they had been able to learn how to switch realms. But as she got better at reading fine variations in energies, she found the immortals each had at least one skill for which they channeled enough power that she would say they were performing magic.

Hermes' talents in sleight of hand and influence over others involved magic. Aphrodite's erotic thrall over people did too. Apollo, Artemis, and Ares used it to make arrows strike exactly where they wanted. Athena and Rhea used it to calm others and discern truth versus lies, which made them excellent diplomats.

When Hekate brought up this revelation at one of the meetings, most of her friends shrugged it off as unimportant. If they didn't know they were doing it, what did it matter? Some were intrigued, but none of them seemed able to stretch their powers any further than they already extended, so they eventually dismissed the issue too.

As to Poseidon and Amphitrite, she had credited them with at least some water magic, as everyone knew of their uncanny luck around the sea. But they approached Hekate after the meeting to speak to her alone, and surprised her with their confession.

"We've known of our water magic for decades," Amphitrite admitted. "We've always been able to control it consciously. I even had it as a mortal, but it got much stronger when I ate the fruit. As strong as his." She tilted her head toward Poseidon.

"Even as a mortal?" Hekate marveled.

"When Zeus and Hera were alive," Poseidon added, "we didn't want it known, because we didn't want to be pressured into fighting sea wars. But we doubt you'd make us do that."

"Oh, no, I've no such inclination. But you must show me! I want to see."

A covert investigation, just the three of them down at the shore, proved their magic utilized the same water energies Hekate sometimes used, but Poseidon and Amphitrite outshone Hekate in sheer strength for this particular element.

"I'm glad of it," she laughed. "More magic in the hands of more good people."

Of course, she later found herself brooding over the possibility that powerful magic could find its way into the hands of evildoers. Her only consoling thought was that the power would likely rebound or be revoked if it was used for cruelty, as had happened in her own case. But that didn't undo the evil deed itself.

Sometimes when she explored the world's energies, she sensed there might even be ways to combine or twist spells so a magic-worker could put off natural punishment for years—not that she herself would ever try such a thing. But surely the wrong type of person would, if they thought of it. Unfortunately she couldn't say with confidence that the Earth's forces would prevent such a thing. After all, they allowed a great deal of violence among the world's creatures, and though the caves of Tartaros performed their role admirably, it often seemed punishment that came too late to do any good. Hekate should have understood better than anyone why the world worked the way it did, but she still could not explain it. All she could do was keep trying to serve love and justice through her own actions.

Hekate took the strawberry tree Hermes had brought her at the start of their affair and planted it near a tributary of the Underworld's main river. The tree grew vigorously, and over the years its leaves turned a moonlight white, and its berries a wine purple. The berries tasted as bland as ever, but did have the effect, she found with amusement, of acting as an aphrodisiac. Hermes laughed too when she told him, and gobbled up several to test it.

"But," he admitted later, lounging naked next to her, "it's not as if you and I need those."

It was true. Even without magic in berries or spells, they enjoyed a fiery passion for one another. She had expected him to grow tired of her after a few months, but he kept coming back to see her year after year, steady as ever.

She knew he sometimes saw other lovers. He encouraged her to branch out as well, and once in a while she did: priests at the temples, usually; men she had gotten to know and felt an affinity for. However, once a woman had become accustomed to the ingenious mind and seductive talents of the trickster god, mortals rarely satisfied her for long.

She put no claims on Hermes despite her longing for him, and her lack of insistence on a commitment was, she supposed, why he didn't abandon her. On days when jealousy or loneliness darkened her skies, she reminded herself he surely had been seeing her longer now than any other except Aphrodite, and his demeanor toward Hekate was more romantic than she ever saw him act toward Aphrodite, so she should be grateful. Besides, if Hermes and Aphrodite could enjoy an intimate-friends arrangement for all these decades (as had other pairs of immortals), Hekate could surely manage it too.

She did miss him on the days when he was away, which were frequent. Much as he loved being with her, he also had a never-ending number of adventures and tasks to pursue in the world, as did she. They fell into the habit of meeting at least every few days, though, and on the days they were apart she often detoured into the fields of souls to pluck a handful of the strawberry tree's leaves, and take them with her on her errands. Touching the cool leaves in the pocket of her robes served as a reminder of her love.

One day, at a temple on a spot of high-intensity magic, she paused in her discussion with the priestess to take out the leaves and stare at them. She had absently slipped her hand into her pocket, and felt them nearly vibrating, like a bronze goblet ringing in response to a note from a flute.

She said, "Just a moment," to the priestess, and strode around outside the temple, investigating other plants and materials. There was a mortal-world strawberry tree not far off, and its leaves responded the same way. Other than that, nothing else resonated except a carved disc of Underworld gold on a necklace she wore.

Hekate approached the confused priestess, who wore a twist of gold in the shape of a snake around her upper arm. Hekate's touch upon that gold found no magical ringing. "Was this gold mined in the living world?" she asked.

The woman nodded in perplexity.

"Strawberry tree leaves from either realm, and gold from the Underworld." On an impulse, Hekate seized the priestess' hand. "Let's try something."

By that evening, the seemingly impossible had been achieved: a mortal switched realms, without being escorted by an immortal.

"It scared her more than it delighted her, I think," Hekate mused to the rest of the immortals at their hastily-called meeting the next day. "She was happy to let me keep this piece of gold for now and not try to use it again herself. Still, I wonder, did it only work because she's a priestess, and therefore trained to sense the other realm?"

"This raises a lot of questions," Athena said. "That's just the beginning of them."

The others looked unsettled on the whole. Tired. It was how they often looked lately. Being around them felt like the chill in the evening air that signaled the end of summer. Only about half of them came to the regular meetings anymore, and the debates over new candidates for immortality had grown jaded. Thanatos was murdering new immortals almost as fast as they were made—old ones too, but new ones seemed easier to trap. The killer cult was wearing everyone down. More and more immortals retreated to the spirit realm for more of the time, and kept their identities secret in the mortal world. They just wanted to live. They no longer had a stomach for big decisions like voting on candidates. Similarly unwelcome was this news of a portal between realms—possibly lots of portals—through which anyone could stumble with the right tools.

"But it could help our allies, our temples," Hekate pointed out. "Say they're attacked, and could slip into the other realm to wait it out. Or they could leave messages for us there, somewhere the enemy wouldn't be able to intercept them."

At least Athena, Rhea, and Hermes were interested in the news, and eager to explore the possibilities. Over the next few years they approached temple leaders in more places, evaluating them for trustworthiness. Eventually, at twelve different sites, they taught select initiates how to enter the spirit realm. Hekate brought them specially made tokens of Underworld gold for the purpose, hammered out by Hephaestus in the shape of strawberry tree leaves and etched with lettering or symbols to mark which site the token belonged to.

The tokens were entrusted only to the top priest or priestess of each site and guarded with the utmost care.

"Is this such a good idea?" Hekate asked Hermes, one evening after they had handed out their fifth token on the island of Lemnos. "Won't the wrong people get in eventually?"

It had been discussed often enough in the meetings, so it was by now a rhetorical question. She was seeking reassurance, not new information. He slipped his arm around her. "Likely they will, at some point. But the wild beasts will eat them if they try to get anywhere. There's a faint chance it'll give someone the advantage if they're looking to find and kill an immortal, but not *much* of an advantage. And what it does do is give our allies a chance to protect themselves or leave a message for us, unmolested. Or to see off their departed."

He spoke the last bit softly. In most places, the mortal temple worshippers had thought of a use for the sacred spots that Hekate hadn't foreseen. If you took a dying person there and brought them into the other realm to breathe their last, you could watch their soul pull free before your eyes, and exchange clearer goodbyes than you might have gotten otherwise. It gave people such comfort that the immortals let them do it. By performing this ritual, the mortals fully understood and believed in the true afterlife, and returned afterward to their daily lives with more tranquility.

"Giving them this knowledge isn't a perfect solution," Hermes conceded. "But it's better than withholding it from them."

Dionysos brought Ariadne from Crete to meet the other immortals. When he escorted her to the Underworld for her first visit, Hekate took an instant liking to the woman. Ariadne was small in frame, with paler skin and redder hair than most Greeks, and she was older than Hekate expected, likely around forty. Her face was lovely, full of feistiness and intelligence. Hekate sensed it even before taking Ariadne's hand in greeting and confirming her generous strength of spirit. She also sensed (and saw) Ariadne's trepidation at being among the souls of the dead, so Hekate smiled to put her at ease, and encouraged her to talk of her journey.

It turned out Crete was becoming less enlightened than it had been in Hades' and Rhea's day. As high priestess in Knossos, Ariadne had held out against Thanatos as long as she could, but even the king had fallen sway to the cult. Many in the Goddess' temple had been killed, and the resistance against Thanatos was falling apart as people fled for their lives, or turned meekly silent to stay safe. The Knossos palace was finally overtaken by the king's guards. Ariadne had been thrown into the labyrinthine prison within the palace complex, where captured wild animals also prowled. She would certainly have been eaten by them, or at least would have starved to death, if Dionysos hadn't tracked her, appeared inside the labyrinth, and rescued her.

The fact that he could track her meant, of course, that they had already slept together, which was no surprise to Hekate. He had been going to visit Ariadne for months by this point.

Soon, at the assembled meeting of immortals, Dionysos formally proposed Ariadne's name to the group as a candidate for immortality.

"I intend to marry her," he said, "whether or not she's voted in. I know some of you will understand." He cast a smile toward Poseidon, who had married Amphitrite when she was mortal; and another toward Hekate, who was of course the offspring of Hades and the once-mortal Persephone. Hekate smiled back in encouragement.

The group voted Ariadne in, with just two black stones against her. Dionysos married her not long after.

CHAPTER THIRTY-EIGHT

WHAT MADE SOPHIE'S HEART FEEL DIFFERENT LATELY, WHAT made the darkness seem to be lifting—aside perhaps just from time passing—was her memories of Galateia and Akis. She rarely texted anything to Adrian about them, and he rarely asked how they were unfolding. But discovering them in her mind, and knowing he shared them, felt almost as sweet as the discovery of her Persephone memories had last fall.

On a morning in early February, as she made breakfast in the Airstream and waited for Tab to finish her shower, she replayed the sweet memory she had dreamed last night.

Galateia at age fourteen, dragged along through the village one day by her father and older brothers, snagged gazes with a boy her own age going the opposite direction. He had dark, smooth hair falling to his shoulders, a wreath of fresh bay leaves on his head, and a crooked nose but the loveliest brown eyes. They gazed at each other and the world seemed to slow. She looked over her shoulder as they passed. He was looking back at her too.

Galateia thought herself ugly. The standard of beauty for Sicilians at the time included lovely skin as the top priority, which decidedly meant no freckles. And Galateia was all freckles. It wasn't fair—her brothers hardly had any, but she was speckled in brown from toes to forehead. Plus she was short, undeveloped for a fourteen-year-old, and no good at arranging her hair, which had a way of slipping out of every pin or string she tried to confine it with. Studying Galateia, her mother often shook her head and said things like, "Well, at least you have good teeth," or "Your eyes are nice enough, anyhow."

But the way this boy was looking at her, she almost believed he saw something better than "nice enough."

Unfortunately, his brown cloak and bay leaves proclaimed him an attendant at the Goddess' temple, as did the company he walked with: priests and priestesses. Galateia's parents were not worshippers of the temple. They'd heard disturbing stories about unnatural beings, favorites of the temple folk, who were looking to overthrow humankind. Street preachers had told them all about it, they said. Galateia had no reason to doubt her parents, and hadn't given the matter much thought since she didn't have any close friends who belonged to the temple. But now she found herself thinking that no boy so lovely, so clearly gentle, could possibly be a dangerous enemy of humankind.

Sophie poured boiling water through the ground coffee, and puffed out her cheeks in an exhalation. Galateia's own parents, members of Thanatos? Yikes. That was a star-crossed set-up for sure. But Adrian and Zoe had said Galateia's lifetime turned out all right, so she'd do her best not to worry.

Anyway, they were all here now, alive again. Somehow, after weeks of feeling lost in a fog, she was finally coming into a clearer patch where she caught sight of that thought once more and managed to hang onto it more often than not.

When Tab had showered and breakfasted, they put on their coats and went outside.

"Groundhog Day," Tab noted.

"Yep." Sophie glanced up at the sky. "Cloudy. Guess that means early spring instead of six more weeks of winter."

"At least if the same weird-ass rodent rules apply in Greece, in the spirit realm."

"I hope they do. Spring sounds good."

Tab looked around. "Where you want to go?"

Sophie turned to the rocky hill. "Up."

They began hiking to the top.

Tab glanced back at where they had left Liam, with Zoe in his trailer and Terry and Isabel outside it. "Where's Liam in his memories?" Tab asked.

"He's gotten a lot farther. Poseidon and Amphitrite had their daughters. Amphitrite and the girls became immortal. The youngest got killed by Thanatos—he didn't like that."

"Oh, is that when he was being a grump a few days ago and wouldn't talk to anyone?"

Sophie nodded. "Now it sounds like he's getting to maybe the decline of the Greek gods. 'Everyone's getting bummed out' is how he put it. So he's slowing down on the memories and focusing on real life. Which is probably healthy."

"Yeah, we do have plenty of shit to take care of in the here and now. Like an actual prisoner, for one."

Sophie grimaced. The thought of Landon, and how close he now resided to all of them, still sent unease writhing through her. She knew her parents acted as his prison guards sometimes, but she personally hadn't been to see Landon again, nor had Liam. "Sounds like Niko and Zoe wrung some info out of him, at least."

"Not as much as they'd like, but yeah, they're working on it."

"Even gave him the pomegranate. I'm still not sure about that."

"Me neither," Tab said. "But then again, I don't know. Charming him over to our side might be our best hope. He does seem easier to sway than some people."

"I suppose I don't want to execute him. Or let him go, all full of hatred for us. So, fine, converting him's the only other option. Still sounds crazy." They reached the top of the cliff. Sophie gazed out at the sea as she caught her breath from the climb, then she looked over at Tab.

Tab waggled her eyebrows. "Ready?"

Sophie took out a lighter and held it up. "Ready as I'll ever be."

From the pocket of her leather coat, Tab pulled out a string of firecrackers, broke one free, and handed it to Sophie.

Sophie turned her back to the wind to shield the fuse, and after a deep breath, flicked on her lighter. She'd been practicing fire exposure for the past week, starting with the candles and moving up to building a fire in a circle of rocks they'd arranged outside the trailers as a fire pit. Though proximity to flame still raised her heart rate, the effect was receding a bit every time. Now, faced with starting an explosion, even just a dinky one, her panic kicked up strong again. But she motored past: she lit the firecracker's fuse, then flung it several feet away, more of a flail than a graceful toss. When it exploded with a bang, she jolted, but then laughed afterward at her own reaction—and laughed because Tab had jolted too.

"Right on, dude." Tab handed her another firecracker. "Try again. I brought this whole string up here; I'm not carrying 'em back down. You've got to light them all."

Sophie lit off every firecracker, one by one. By the last one, she was flinging them with flair, and cheering rather than jumping when they exploded.

"I think *someone* is getting her comfort levels back," Tab said after the last bang. She seized Sophie in a big hug that lifted Sophie off the ground, then put her down. "You feel like going out? Buy yourself some cute new jeans, maybe?"

"Yeah, maybe. Just a sec." Sophie got out her phone, called up the list, and sent a strikethrough across the word "explosions." She tucked the phone away. "Let's shop. Clothes sound good, but I also need a new computer, since the old one got melted in the fire. There's only so much online stuff I can do from my phone."

"Excellent. We can make that happen."

"Plus I want to restock the Airstream's pantry. I miss making real dinners."

"Girl, I've been missing your cooking." Tab danced ahead, leading the way back down the hill.

Chapter Thirty-Nine

OH, YEAH." ZOE TOUCHED THE SNOWDROP'S FLOWER BUDS. "Something promising there. Health energy of some kind. That's the usual for plants down here, isn't it. Getting turned into medicines."

"That or food." Sophie watched, itching to know what Zoe felt when she touched the plants. She had brought Zoe down here to check on the magical development of her spring bulbs now that they'd had a few weeks to stretch their roots into the Underworld soil. "What about the bluebell?" She swung the flashlight beam onto the next bud over.

Zoe set her fingertips on that one. "Hmm, similar. Health of some kind, not sure what yet. As for the crocus..." She touched the pale orange tip of flower that was starting to open. "Whoa."

"What?" Sophie said in alarm.

"Oh, it's all right, just not what I expected." She kept touching the tiny plant at different angles, upon leaf and stem and bud. "We had crocus down here before, mostly for medicine. You probably remember."

"Yeah," Sophie said. "But this one's different?"

"Quite. Must be a different variety. There's some of that health energy in it, but also something much stronger. Something about...time. Strength. Permanence? Or at least, near-permanence. Maybe that's it."

"Permanence? What would that do?"

Zoe sat back on her heels, gazing at the sprouts. "Well, it feels kind of like the spell I cast to protect something—to make something last. Like the one I put on the clay jar with the owls way back when. We got lucky; that jar was well hidden, but usually the spells do wear off, you know. I'm not sure, but feels like maybe if I used this plant in combination with a spell like that, it might help it stick longer."

"That sounds handy. A permanent protection spell, or at least a longer-lasting one?"

"Yeah." Zoe patted the dirt next to the crocus. "But we have to let these guys grow a bit more first. They're not full strength yet, and we don't have many of them." She stood and dusted off her knees, then grasped the titoki tree's leaves. "Now how about this pretty lady? Ah. Interesting." She stroked its branch. "Huh."

"What?" Sophie prodded.

"I'm not sure how to describe it. It's...in touch with the Fates, or Tartaros, or just all the criss-crossing energies, but especially the ones down here."

Sophie blinked at the modest little tree. "Aren't all the magic plants down here in touch with that stuff?"

"Yeah, it's just, this one's, like, channeling those forces, the ones that judge the souls and put them in Tartaros or not."

Sophie shivered. "Yikes. So it's a scary tree."

"Oh, no, not at all. It's only kinda...picking up that station and rebroadcasting it. It's a signal-booster tree." She gave Sophie a grin.

"So what good is that?"

Zoe straightened up, chewing her lip as she gazed at the titoki. "What good indeed. I'll have to ponder that." She flicked her bangs out of her eye. "Let's check on our chrysomelia."

They tromped through the wilderness that had once been Persephone's tidy gardens. Some of the original garden plants were still here, but gone wild: nettles and mints and berry bushes all battling in a tangle. It needed work. Project for this year, perhaps. After Thanatos was dealt with.

They passed through the pomegranate orchard and reached the orange tree. Sophie knelt and slid her thumb across the fruits. The two oranges were now bigger than golf balls, and their green skin was yellowing toward orange. You'd never know they had blue flesh inside.

Zoe crouched next to her and touched the fruits too. "Almost there. I'm starting to feel the power in them. I'd say they're not full strength, though. Give 'em a couple weeks."

"If we have a couple weeks. Thanatos is sure to be getting all up in our business any day now."

"Ah, well, that's what this is for." Zoe untied the strip of sage-green cloth knotted around the trunk and opened it to show Sophie the tiny coil of hairs inside: black, brown, and blonde. Sophie remembered pulling out a few of her hairs to give to Zoe, the day Zoe was running around setting up wards. She'd been collecting them from everyone. "Special-access spell," Zoe said. "Only the people whose hairs are in here—that is, our group—can see the thing this is attached to; namely, this tree." She wrapped the hairs up and tied it back onto the trunk.

"Awesome. So, what, for everyone else it's invisible? Would they just walk into the tree because they couldn't see it?"

"Invisible, yeah, but they should walk round it. Should sort of repel them without their noticing."

"But, brute force…" Sophie had to ask.

Zoe's features seemed to fall into shadow. "Well. Yeah. Someone sets off a grenade round here, this little spell isn't going to protect the tree." She forced a brighter look onto her face. "But that's what the other wards are for, the ones I reinforce every day so they're fresh. One outside the cave, one in the entrance tunnel, one at the river, one at the edge of the gardens…same deal, you guys can all walk through them because I've buried hair-bundles like that at each wall, but others would be stopped."

"But the wards weaken every day?"

"Gradually, yeah." Zoe sighed, standing back up to full height and raking her hand through her hair. "Magic's never as perfect as you'd like. There's always some counter-spell or shakedown someone else can do to mess up yours. Which is why I hope we put together a murderous ghost army who just stabs invaders as soon as they get in here."

"I'm liking that idea," Sophie said.

They started hiking back toward the fields.

"Hey, I almost forgot," Zoe said. "I've not been giving you two the anti-nightmare magic for a few days now. Got lost in the shuffle. Should I start up again?"

"Oh." Sophie lifted her eyebrows. "I hadn't realized. No, it's fine, actually. I'm letting in the memory dreams again, and they're keeping me happy. Liam seems fine too, but you can ask him."

"All right then. Brilliant."

"Hey," Sophie added shyly. "Thanks for not asking me if I planned to eat one of the chrysomelia."

Zoe tapped Sophie's arm with her flashlight. "Took great restraint. But I still *hope* you eat one."

"We should vote people in properly, like in the old days. So first the group has to approve me."

Zoe snorted. "Yeah, 'cause we might chuck you out. But I suppose you're right. Best get ourselves some black and white voting stones."

CHAPTER FORTY

HEKATE FOLLOWED THE SENSE OF HER PARENTS' SOULS ONE day when they were fourteen, intrigued to note they seemed to be near each other. In fact, as she tracked them down on foot, along a forest path between their villages, she soon realized they were together. Her heart pounded in delight. She had been seeking some way to introduce them, to give the Fates a nudge, but apparently these two souls were already pulling toward one another.

She edged up to a large tree trunk and peeked around it.

The slender river flowed through the forest. Galateia and Akis sat mostly concealed on the downward slope of the bank between path and stream, the riverside trees and shrubs screening them all around. Hekate just barely glimpsed Galateia, a smudge of red gown and pale leg among the leaves. Akis was invisible in his brown cloak until he moved, then Hekate spotted his hand for a moment, rising as if to caress Galateia's face, and heard his voice in a low chuckle and words she couldn't make out.

Hekate knew Akis well by now. He was a temple acolyte, gentle and intelligent, and loyal to the anti-Thanatos cause. He and his mother had grown up in the cluster of houses belonging to the temple. He made Hekate proud every time she visited and spoke to him. But she had never told him who his soul had been in a past life. He was young yet, and such information was too weighty for his shoulders.

Hekate didn't know Galateia nearly as well. The girl's parents kept her close to the house most of the time, and they weren't temple worshippers. In fact, Hekate had seen Galateia's father at Thanatos gatherings, shouting support for hate-spewing street preachers. Perhaps Galateia disagreed with her parents—or, Hekate thought with a chill, maybe she agreed with them, and was working to entrap a supporter of the immortals. Was that possible? Could Persephone's soul be capable of such despicable loyalties, under the right—or rather, the wrong—influences?

She tiptoed back to the path and waited there, leaning against a tree and twisting a ring around her finger in consternation. Eventually she sensed the two souls stirring and parting. Galateia moved upstream and away. Not long after, Akis walked toward Hekate, his feet snapping twigs unconcernedly.

He came out onto the path a few paces away, a dreamy smile on his face, his shoulder-length hair mussed up, bay wreath in his hand. He ran his fingers through his hair, dislodging a dead leaf or two, and fitted the wreath back onto his head.

He finally noticed Hekate, with a start. "My Lady." He bobbed, then stopped. She had asked the temple folk over and over not to bow to her as if she were the Great Goddess, and merely to address her as a friend.

"Hello, Akis." She smiled.

He approached. His face glowed with a distinctive lover's flush. He was an ordinary-looking boy most days, but with that glow he became beautiful. "Are you going to the temple?" he asked. "I'm headed back that way now."

"Yes, soon." She looked up the path. "Do you know Galateia, then?"

The question sucked the flush out of his cheeks. He glanced

all around, then appealed to her with scared dark eyes. "You saw her? Please don't tell anyone. It's dangerous. For her."

"I haven't, don't worry. What's the trouble? Her family's in Thanatos?"

Akis nodded. He bowed his head, eyebrows furrowing, trouble chasing love across his mobile young face like alternating clouds and sunshine. "That and they've planned for her to marry at the end of summer."

"Oh dear. To whom?"

"The son of someone else in the cult. He's younger than her by a couple of years, and he's horrible, one of those violent and stupid boys, but she's supposed to be grateful because he's 'willing to have her.'" He nearly spat the last words, with the concentrated bitterness only a youth could manage.

"So we have a few months. But is she involved in the cult herself?"

"She doesn't agree with them, but she pretends to, around her parents. I've talked with her about the other realm. Told her I've learned about it—seen you perform magic—and that it's all good, or at least nothing like those idiots say. She believes me. But what can she do? Even if she fled to the temple, that's too close. They'd find out where she was and use it as an excuse to attack us. Everyone at the temple could get killed, and it would all be because of me!"

Hekate set her hand on his bare arm, backing up the soothing gesture with a subtle dose of magic. "Calm down. Nothing's happened yet. Listen, if she does want to be free of them, I'll help her. But you must bring her to me so we can talk. I doubt I can just walk up to her parents' door and ask for a chat." Hekate was easily the best known immortal in the area, recognized throughout this village and all the neighboring ones.

A meek smile crept onto his face. "No, you probably shouldn't."

"Then arrange for her to meet me. All right?"

IT STARTED WHEN GALATEIA WAS GATHERING WOOD IN THE forest on a spring day. She stayed near the path, and people and pack animals passed sometimes, going between villages. She paid them no mind, lost in thought. As usual, she was thinking about her dreadful future husband, whom she had once seen torturing a cat with his vicious friends. She was hoping for some miracle of deliverance from that match. In addition, her thoughts were threaded through with the poignantly appealing image of that boy from the temple, the one who had gazed at her in passing a few days ago. If only she could have been matched up with a boy like that instead.

"Is it firewood you're after?" someone asked.

She turned, arms full of sticks, and found the very same brown-cloaked boy standing there. Her tongue seemed stuck. She nodded.

He held out a handful of dried reeds, the sort that grew beside the river. "Take some of these too. They catch fast. Excellent kindling." His voice was as gentle as his demeanor, already deepened into adult tones.

"Thank you." She took the reeds.

No one else was around. It probably wasn't proper to talk to him unchaperoned. But he seemed harmless, and his eyes were even lovelier than she remembered from that glimpse a few days ago. Tree-filtered sunlight lit up specks of gold in the dark brown. "You're from the temple?" she asked before he could turn away. Nothing wrong with a few pleasantries, she reasoned.

He nodded. "I was born there, have always lived there."

"What's that like?"

"Can be strange. But good. Not as bad as you've probably heard."

She piled the sticks and reeds into the small cart she'd

wheeled along. "I've heard crazy things. They couldn't all be true."

"Some are and some aren't." He glanced down the path, then smiled at her. "Can I help you with the firewood? I'm supposed to scrub pots when I get back. My least favorite job. I'd rather put it off a while."

She consented with more pleasure than she should have felt.

By the end of that day's wood-gathering and conversation, she was dazzled. She mentioned her regular task of gathering water each morning and evening at a certain spot along the river. When he "happened" to be walking by that spot the next morning, she began sensing he was dazzled too.

They were in love before the moon had completed a full cycle. They contrived to meet every day somewhere in the concealment of the forest. Mostly they held each other and talked, conjuring dreams of a future where they could spend all their time like this, where Thanatos wouldn't try to keep them apart or destroy Akis' noble immortal patrons.

But they shared kisses too, and playful tangles and increasingly breathless touches. He told her she was beautiful; he even loved her freckles. His hair smelled like bay leaves. His body fitted so perfectly against hers. Every day it was harder to tear herself away. They both knew better than to get her with child, but they began to understand how so many couples had fallen into that situation. Galateia loved him for his wisdom, kindness, and grace; and lusted for his body in the basest fashion. And Akis professed in a thousand ways that he felt the same for her.

Although she believed everything he said about the temple and the immortals—or because she believed it—the prospect of meeting the goddess Hekate in person frightened her. She agreed to it because Akis assured her she'd be safe, and indeed this might be their only way to get Galateia out of her arranged marriage. Still, she trembled as he led her to the tall, black-haired woman at their meeting spot in the forest.

She had seen Hekate from a distance before, and always thought she looked otherworldly. This was the first time Galateia had gotten up close to her, and now the woman seemed even more so. The dark blue of Hekate's ankle-length robe was a deeper and more vibrant hue than Galateia had ever seen an indigo dye achieve, and the garment's folds fell slim and long, different from the shorter, fuller style everyone in Sicily wore. Gold, bronze, and jewels shimmered on her body: a ring, a bracelet, a line of stones on her belt, a cuff high up on her ear, a bauble dangling from one of the small braids in her hair. Other than the few braids, that black hair was a careless mass that looked windblown. She was paler than average, as if she seldom spent any time in the sun, and her skin, face, and posture were perfection, unnerving beauty.

But when Hekate took Galateia's hand, spoke her name in greeting, and smiled, Galateia felt relaxation flow through her. Was it the calm intelligence of those dark gray eyes?

"So tell me about your family's involvement in Thanatos, and what you think of it all," Hekate said, with both hands folded around Galateia's.

Galateia spoke truthfully, relating how her parents had become more spiteful lately in their invective against the "foul" immortals and their worshippers. How she frequently heard hints of violent plans that might become reality if some incident ever tipped the conflict too far. How they told her she was ugly and therefore should be grateful to be betrothed to a despicable twelve-year-old boy, and how the nuptials would take place at the autumn equinox. "I can't see any way out of it," Galateia finished, her voice catching in despair.

Hekate's eyes now looked more human than before, full of sympathy. She released Galateia's hand, and her lips thinned as she thought for a moment. "What if," Hekate said, "I came and claimed you for the temple? Insisted divine inspiration had led me to you, and that—no, that would only anger them."

Akis was already shaking his head in dissent before she reached the conclusion herself. "Stealing people's daughters, that's how they'd put it. It'd be an act of war in their eyes, even if she told them she wanted to come."

"And—not to treat you as a commodity, my dear," Hekate said to Galateia, "but could we buy her, do you think? Riches are easy for me to come by."

"Oh, I don't think so." Galateia shivered at the thought. "They'd be terribly offended. Just offering could make things so much worse."

"Well." Hekate regarded Akis, and then Galateia. "We have other temples. In other lands. If you're both willing to…" Hekate sighed, as if giving up the idea. "Leave the only island you've ever known. I suppose that's not a wondrous plan either."

But Galateia glanced in hope at Akis, and he returned the glance. "Still," he said, "if we ran away, wouldn't they come after us?"

Hekate's tight smile became a touch otherworldly again. "Not if they thought you were both dead."

Galateia stepped back. "No. That's too much. We can't… I can't grieve everyone like that." She looked helplessly at Akis. "Nor can you."

"We'd tell my mother the truth." Akis looked at Hekate. "Wouldn't we?"

Hekate shrugged, seeming to allow that, but Galateia pulled back another step. "I'm sorry. I don't see how…just, can't we wait a little, see if we can think of something else?"

"Of course," Hekate said. "I'll keep thinking on it."

Akis looked downcast, but he walked Galateia back through the forest after they said goodbye to Hekate. The lovers held each other for several long breaths before parting. "We'll find a way," he said, and kissed her.

"Galateia!" a furious voice shouted.

She whirled around. Her father stood on the path, just visible through the trees. He was glaring at them—at Akis, in his brown cloak and bay wreath. Her father began stomping forward through the underbrush.

Galateia looked at Akis in terror. "Run."

"But I won't leave you to—"

"He won't kill me—he'll kill you! Run!"

Akis' chest rose and fell fast. "I'll get Hekate," he said, and took off at a sprint.

Galateia's father lurched after him, but he was middle-aged and stiff-muscled, and couldn't catch a swift fourteen-year-old boy. Besides, Galateia clutched his arm and hung onto it, weighing him down, as she pleaded, "Don't, Father! We're innocent. Please."

He swung around and struck Galateia in the side of the head so hard she staggered and almost fell. Through the ringing in her ears she heard him shout after Akis, "We'll be coming to the temple in revenge, you scum!"

Then he hauled Galateia around, her skin pinching under his grip. "And you, slut. Home. Now."

CHAPTER FORTY-ONE

A KIS BOLTED DOWN THE FOREST PATH, HIS HEART GALLOPING to keep up. "Hekate!" he shouted over and over with the few shreds of breath left to him. But she was gone—likely slipped back into the other realm.

He reached the temple, still didn't find her there, and in desperation seized the sleeves of his mother and one of the priests instead. "There's a girl, I'm friends with her, her father saw me embracing her, they're in Thanatos, I'm worried they're going to beat her or kill her, or—"

"Show us where," the priest said. Righteous anger lit up his eyes.

Akis ended up leading a group of five temple folk to the gate of Galateia's house, some armed with thick staffs but no other weapons. The priest rapped upon the gate.

Galateia's father stalked out. "What could you filth want?" His gaze fell upon Akis. "You dare show your face here?"

"Don't hurt Galateia," Akis said, trembling—more in fury than in fear, though in fear too.

"We were told your daughter was in danger," the priest said.

"I know what kind of danger *he* poses for her. You're not the law around here. Get out."

"It isn't like that!" Akis protested. "We've never—I wouldn't—"

"We're trying to keep an innocent girl safe," Akis' mother told the man. "We're her friends. We assure you he's done nothing wrong, nor has she, so if you could just let us see she's all right—"

Just then Galateia peeked out from a window in the front of the house, and Akis drew in a sharp breath. Her eye and cheekbone were puffy with bruises, her hand shaking as she clasped the shutter.

"What have you done to her?" Akis demanded.

"She isn't yours," her father said. "And you'll never see her again." He glared at each of the temple delegation. "You can all be sure the insult you've paid my family is going to be avenged many times over. Now get out before I start taking that revenge now."

Akis lunged forward, ready to tear the hinges off the gate and pummel the man until he could get past and rescue Galateia. But her father grabbed a pitchfork, and Akis' mother and friends hauled Akis out of the way and back onto the safety of the road. He fought them the whole way back to the temple, a white heat of heartbreak ripping him in half.

"The Lady Hekate will help you when she returns," his mother reminded him. "You know she will. Calm yourself, son." An ironic note of humor entered her voice. "And tell me what in the world you've been up to with this girl."

At their house in the temple grounds, he did tell her, including Hekate's idea of spiriting them out of the country altogether. "But I don't want to leave you if I don't have to," he added wretchedly.

"I don't want you to get killed," she returned. "Much better to have you happily married in another country, if that's our only option."

They had just begun to cook dinner, a miserable semblance of a normal evening, when the cries started up.

"Fire!"

Akis and his mother raced out. The temple's stables were

going up in a billow of smoke. As Akis watched, three more flaming arrows arched overhead and landed among the gardens, roofs, and fields of the community. New screams arose.

His mother ran with others to free the trapped livestock in the stables, and to fetch water. Akis sprinted to the road dividing the temple houses from the rest of the village, and skidded to a stop. A small army milled there, some twenty men and women in sackcloth masks, armed with bows, spears, and torches.

Akis stood rooted to the ground in horror. Exactly as he'd feared, it was happening: the temple was being attacked, because of him.

Before he could decide whether to fight back, to rush to the aid of his friends, or to run to Galateia's house, a hand clutched his arm. He looked up to find Hekate, holding onto him but glaring at the enemy.

"Don't go anywhere," she told him.

Then she let go of him and twisted one hand upward. The clouds thickened overhead, darkening the sky. Rain began pouring down. Another gesture from her, and the sound of splintering wood crackled from the army—spears and bows breaking in half in the hands of the startled attackers.

"What do you folk think you're doing?" a man's voice called.

Akis and Hekate turned to see the prince approaching with a score of armed men. He was one of the sons of the island's king, and was appointed to keep the peace in this region. Even if he wasn't a temple worshipper exactly, Akis had seen him at some of the year's larger festivals, and knew him to be fair to everyone, temple folk included.

"We can leave this in his hands," Hekate said, sounding relieved. "Come, let's get Galateia before her father returns home."

She wrapped her arms around Akis and yanked him into the spirit realm—or at least that's what it must have been.

He had only a moment to gawk around at the wilderness in amazement, then she tugged him again and they ran, through the growing darkness, across meadows and through a forest. Akis followed Hekate, who seemed to know her way. At some seemingly arbitrary spot, she stopped and pulled him back into the living world.

They were right outside Galateia's house, in the back garden, near the stone fence.

"I'll fetch her," Hekate said. "Wait here." She walked toward the house. Her dark blue robes vanished in the shadows.

Akis waited motionless beneath an old olive tree that grew beside the stone fence, though he longed to run to the house and throw his arms around his love. He'd die beside her if he had to, but they couldn't keep them apart, he couldn't take it…

In a puff of wind, Hekate reappeared out of nowhere next to him, her arms sheltering Galateia. Startled, Akis almost fell over. Then he murmured a wordless sound of gratitude, and Galateia leaped from Hekate's arms to his. He held her, both of them shaking. He touched the bruises on her face. Tears stung his eyes, and he spat curses against her parents, then held her tight again.

Hekate's arms slid around them both. They glimmered into the spirit realm. "All right, children," Hekate said. "How is that fake death looking now?"

THAT NIGHT, AT THE SHORE, THE TWO LOVERS CLIMBED INTO A rowboat and launched off to sea. A pair of reliably planted witnesses saw them go, and took note of the red paint on the boat's sides, and the single round lantern they took aboard. So the next morning, when the overturned red boat washed back up on shore, along with a drenched round lantern, Akis' cloak, and one of Galateia's sandals, the whole community bemoaned the tragic drowning of the two lovers.

Hekate, of course, had transferred them into a larger ship bound for Greece, manned by expert sailors, before capsizing the red boat. Then she returned alone to Sicily to help weave a temporary peace.

The prince held stern councils in the village, with the temple and Thanatos representatives in attendance. With both sides aggrieved at the loss of young life, everyone had become more subdued. Hekate's mood-altering spells did have something to do with that. They all agreed to keep their disputes free of violence, and to consult the prince or other lawmen over any conflict rather than taking matters into their own hands.

The truce wouldn't last, she suspected, but it was better than some towns ever achieved. And the important task had been accomplished: Akis and Galateia were together and safe. They were also, she confirmed when she later went to see them, married.

Wow, were we ever star-crossed. Galateia and Akis, Sophie texted Adrian that night, as she got ready for bed.

Weren't we just, he responded. *Maybe it isn't the best thing to be remembering right now. Kind of violent...Thanatos and stuff... sorry...*

No, it helps. It honestly does. B/c it turned out ok. Great even. :)
Good then. Whatever helps. I'm glad.

Sitting on the Airstream's bed, she smiled, gazing at the messages. *It's late here, I should go to sleep*, she thumbed in. *But stay safe for me, ok? Knowing you're out there also helps.*

His answer flickered in a minute later. *Knowing you're out there has kept me going so many times. Not just this life. Sweet dreams.*

She bit her lip to catch the flattered grin that wanted to spread there. *Sweet dreams*, she typed back. *Wherever they take you. ;)*

Sentiment in text message didn't translate into a full relationship recovery, and didn't mean she'd be able to snog him without anxiety. But hey. Baby steps.

Before going to bed, she opened her shiny new notebook computer and called up the files Zoe had finally sent her: Adrian's random writings from his teen years. Sophie read them for at least an hour, lulled by their ordinariness and charm, drawn into the mundane details of yet another life.

CHAPTER FORTY-TWO

AKIS' MOTHER KNEW THE TRUTH, AND PLANNED TO JOURNEY over the sea to visit them someday soon. Galateia's parents—well, maybe they could be told she was alive in some future year. But Hekate planned to keep their location a secret even then.

She established the couple at the temple nearest the Underworld, a seaside village that considered the local deep cave a sacred site. Hermes came to meet them as well. Akis remembered him from a couple of visits to Sicily in earlier years. Together Hermes and Hekate brought Akis and Galateia to the Underworld for a tour.

There Hekate told them who they had been: the king and queen of this magical realm, the first living people to discover its secrets. Their eyes grew round, and both youths looked around at the cave with new scrutiny.

Hekate offered them the pomegranate while Hermes stood quietly at her side. Her heart raced.

But the lovers looked at each other, then at her, and Akis shook his head. "I think not yet. We've...been through enough lately."

"We just want to get settled first," Galateia added. "As normal people. We want a calm life."

Hekate stared, astounded. Never had she expected them to turn it down. They were Hades and Persephone! "But then surely, when you're older—and the immortality fruit—you *must* join us. I'm sure the others will vote you in at once."

"Of course we would," Hermes assured.

"Goodness, no." Akis laughed, sounding shocked.

Galateia did too. "That would require even more thought. I can't say I'm ready for that."

"Well—I'll ask again when you're older." Hekate tried to recover her smile. "You can be sure I will."

"To think, you were our daughter." Akis studied her in amazement.

"No wonder you've been so good to us," Galateia said. "I feel honored just to have this knowledge. Just to be brought here."

They had a new home to get back to, furnishings to acquire, neighbors to meet. A life on the Earth's surface to live. Hekate returned them to it. She assured them she'd see them often, and fetch them down here anytime they liked.

"But what if they actually do decline?" she fretted to Hermes that night, lying on her front on the hearth rug in the Underworld's sitting room.

"We can't force them." The firelight bathed his figure as he relaxed beside her. "They're adults. In charge of their own lives."

"Adults." She snorted.

"Fourteen does begin looking dreadfully young after a point, to some of us." He grinned at her. "How old are you now, darling? Forty?"

"How skilled you are at counting."

He crawled over, rolled her onto her back, and straddled her. "I'm bedding such an *old* woman. My my."

"Ha. How old was Aphrodite by the time you found her? Eighty?"

He laughed. "Probably not quite, but she won't say exactly."

"Neither will you." Since their skin was already touching

in a few places, she surrendered to impulse and sent a shot of truth-telling through him. "How old are you, really?"

But he sensed the magic, or guessed what she was doing, and leaped off her. He pressed his mouth shut just long enough for the spell to wear off, then gave her a dirty look. "Play fair, love."

Ashamed, she sat up and wrapped her skirts over her knees. "I'm sorry. I've never done that to you before, I promise."

He leaned back on his hands and stretched out his legs toward Kerberos, who snoozed in front of the hearth. "Yes, I would know if you had. But it's nice that the magic's rebounding on you and making you say so."

It wasn't done rebounding. She kept talking, against her better judgment. "I love you, but I feel like you don't tell me enough. Like this relationship, if that's what it is, doesn't really count to you. Sometimes I think of it like a marriage, but now that I've seen my parents' souls together again, in a true marriage, I see how ours isn't one. And I sometimes want what they have. With you."

The words were out. A sort of horror washed over Hekate in their wake.

Hermes drew up his knees too, and gazed at the fire. The flames crackled. Kerberos sighed in his sleep. "What a dangerous force, that spell of yours," Hermes finally said.

The rebound wore off at last, having done its damage. She stared at the fire as well. "Forget I said anything. It doesn't matter."

"A marriage with me? No one would want that."

"I only said I *sometimes* want it."

"And I don't tell you everything because you wouldn't like to hear it. As I'm sure you already suspect."

She closed her eyes a moment, and opened them again. "Yes."

"But..." His voice altered from defensiveness to what

sounded like sincerity. "You still know me better than anyone else does, despite not having every little fact at your disposal. If you do want one relevant fact…" He held out his arm toward her, without looking at her. "Go ahead, give me the truth spell. Then ask this one question. Ask me who I love most in the entire world."

Her hurt melted into tenderness. Tears rose in her eyes, making the flames glimmer. "Yourself?" she teased.

"Go on."

She set her fingers gingerly on his arm. "Who?" she whispered, and sent the shimmer of magic into him.

"You," he said.

She let her fingers drop, weak with relief.

He set his hand on her knee. "To have you love me still, after all these years…it's more than I deserve. It's made me happy." He smiled at her in his usual mischievous fashion. "Like I've stolen something no one else was able to steal."

"Well, *that's* a feeling you're familiar with."

"One I like very much." He jumped onto her, flipped her skirts up, and wriggled his shoulders and head between her legs. While she laughed in surprise, he began kissing the dark curls there. "When Apollo shot that arrow through me," he said, "I was one year older than Galateia and Akis are now. There. Let's see how skilled you are at counting while I'm doing this."

THERE WASN'T MUCH TO SAY ABOUT THE SAD LIFE OF KROKOS in long-ago Crete. Well, you *could* say a lot about it, Landon supposed. You could write a whole novel about any life if you went into enough details. But he'd been over the whole of Krokos' lifespan now, and could have summed it up in a minute. In fact, it was best done that way. The long version was too depressing.

Krokos was gay, which was tolerated in Knossos and

vicinity as a leisure activity, but not regarded as a marital option. In his teens, he met the sexiest man he'd ever seen, a guy with green eyes, an unbelievable body, and, it turned out, a false name and a habit of lying. After a few amorous visits to Krokos, the guy left the island and didn't return.

Krokos, heartsick, eventually bowed to familial pressure and married a girl. He hated being married, and she hated him before long. She bore him one kid, then the rest of the kids had to be some other guy's, because Krokos sure wasn't sleeping with her anymore. Not his thing, sex with women.

He went on farming and being miserable until the wondrous happened: the gorgeous man returned. He didn't look a day older, though it'd been fifteen years since Krokos had seen him. No wonder; turned out he was an immortal, the famous Hermes. This time he was a tad more honest with Krokos. And somehow Krokos felt better about the lies from before. After all, being lied to by the divine trickster was far better than being lied to by some ordinary jerk. It was practically an honor.

He got the impression Hermes pitied him rather than loved him, and that pity was probably the reason he was being more honest now. But the trickster paid him frequent visits for another month, and caressed and cajoled Krokos into a happier frame of mind.

Maybe the affair would have gone on even longer if Krokos hadn't been killed.

Thanatos, original edition, had been spreading like a weed in Crete. People recognized Hermes as one of the hated unnaturals. Soon they also figured out who his local lover was. One day at dusk, while Krokos walked back to his house from the fields—bam. Blow to the head from an unseen assailant. Here lies Krokos, sad mortal lover of a Greek god.

For Landon, there were several upsetting take-aways from that lifetime. For one thing, he had loved an immortal and Thanatos had killed him for it. And yes, it was confirmed

Thanatos was responsible. In the Underworld afterward, a downcast Hermes showed up and told Krokos' soul that Thanatos was claiming credit for it in their latest hate speeches in Knossos. He'd tried to find out the exact culprit who wielded the stone so he could drag them to local justices, but had no luck identifying them so far. Besides, Thanatos too often *was* the local justices in Knossos lately.

For another thing, this wasn't the only life where Landon was gay and closeted and miserable. In fact, it was a constant in pretty much every life he'd recalled so far. That was beyond sad; it was outrageous and pathetic. No wonder Niko and probably lots of other people had seen right through his denial, because shit, gayness was apparently a fundamental aspect of his soul.

As for the third-most disturbing thing, it was more a strong suspicion or gut instinct, and was also actually more strangely comforting than disturbing.

He waited until Niko reappeared as his guard, then Landon walked up to the bars, as close as he could get, and looked straight into those green eyes.

"Yes, that's you, isn't it," Landon said in the ancient language Krokos had spoken on Crete. "Hermes."

"Poor Krokos," Niko answered in the same language. "You didn't deserve that fate."

Landon's heart, so long shielded by a wall of fear, broke open then—at the eyes, the voice, the reconnection of souls, some mix of tragedy and hope. A miserable laugh tumbled from his lips. He leaned his forehead on the bars, still gazing at Niko. "Why did you give me that pomegranate? I didn't need to know what a loser I was in every single goddamn life. I want to drink from the spring of forgetfulness instead."

"So far we haven't found such a thing." Niko drew close to the bars too, and took hold of one. "Maybe Sophie knows of a plant that does that. Some days, or at least some hours, I'd eat it too."

Landon wrapped his hand around Niko's. Niko stayed still and allowed it. "Krokos and Hermes," Landon said. "Is that why you kept tracking me down?"

"It's *how* I kept tracking you down. Convenient that way."

"Great. Another million things I don't understand."

"Such is life, Petal."

Krokos was the name of a flower, the crocus. Thus the nickname Petal?

Their hands still touched. Niko's hands, these hands here, had killed Betty Quentin, because she was the head of Thanatos. But in another life Thanatos had killed Landon, because he had loved an immortal. Who to trust anymore? Who to care about?

"One thing's for sure," Landon said, staring at their overlapping fingers. "If I ever get out of here, I'm *coming* out. I'm gay, I always was, everyone can tell, I might as well own it."

"Finally, a decision of yours I can applaud." Niko caressed Landon's fingers with a stroke of his knuckles, and pulled his hand away.

CHAPTER FORTY-THREE

At the Blue Caves on the island of Zakynthos, Erick Tracy drew out the ancient gold leaf from his pocket, along with his latest batch of strawberry tree leaves. It was sunset, and the other tourists had left. Now only he and Tenebra stood on the narrow rock ledge, sea caves arching over their heads, blue water slapping the rocks at their feet.

Since joining their team, Tenebra had been bewitching the gold artifact to conceal it from everyone except herself and Tracy, and even then, Tracy never let it out of his possession. She'd also frequently been throwing glamours onto the members of the central team when they went out—Yuliya and Krystal as well as Tenebra and Tracy—so they'd go mostly unnoticed if anyone was looking for them. The way it worked, Tenebra said, was that it caused a sort of reflection: instead of seeing you, the rest of the world saw someone or something they believed belonged there, and which therefore escaped their notice. He and his teammates couldn't see the glamour on themselves, but could see it on each other. It turned his companions into blandly uninteresting folk whom his eyes wanted to drift away from. And he had oddly blank interactions with cashiers and taxi drivers and such when he wore the spell. They treated him like he was someone boring they saw every day, unworthy of paying much attention to. A bit off-putting, actually.

But Tracy had no doubt they were indeed being followed. A couple of times, both in Bulgaria and Greece, he suspected he glimpsed Adrian Watts, though if it was Adrian, he was in some sort of disguise himself. These glimpses were always in public, where Tracy couldn't very well attack him, and in any case he didn't have the heavy weaponry on him that an attack on an immortal would require. But so far the immortals hadn't molested them, nor sent the authorities after them, nor even left any new ominous lipstick messages. Most importantly, they hadn't got hold of the gold leaf, which surely they would have stolen if they could. So Tenebra's magic was working.

Tracy thus remained content to continue amassing his small army and preparing to take over the Underworld. That powerful kingdom might be right here on the other side of the wall between realms, within these shadowy blue caves echoing with surf.

"Ready?" Tracy asked Tenebra.

She nodded. She looked more attractive lately—a gleam to her eyes, her generous breasts and hips bulging under her long black dress. All part of a glamour to charm him? He didn't mind if so. He'd help her feel young again if that's what she wanted, and he did like the idea of what that magic might be able to do to him in bed.

But for now, he had to focus on breaching the other realm with her.

He slipped his arm around her waist, and gave her a smile when she arched an eyebrow at him. "This is how it works," he told her. "You know that. Now, let's see…"

He had switched realms a few more times alone, at other sacred sites, but this was the first attempt at one of the Greek seaside caves, and also the first time transporting another person with him. But the switching got easier each time, and now it only took a few seconds before the world did its jiggle and he swooped into the spirit realm, pulling Tenebra along.

Out in the stretch of sea visible beneath the cave arch, all the boats vanished. The cries of strange creatures filled the air, and several red-winged birds, startled by Tracy and Tenebra's sudden appearance, burst into flight from their cave roost and flew out over the water.

"Ha," he said in triumph.

"Ahhh," she exhaled—her creaky-door sound of satisfied wonder. She touched the rock walls, and knelt to squint at the water, where fish of all sizes darted and rippled. "So much power here. Different and untapped. Marvelous."

"Yes." Tracy frowned around at the sea caves, still full of echoing water and shadows, looking about as they did in the regular world. "But this isn't the Underworld, is it."

Tenebra stood again and examined their surroundings. "No souls. Likely not."

"I thought so." He sighed. "None of our sources say it's on an island, so I imagined Diros was the likelier set of caves, not Zakynthos. Still, this is useful to know."

"We will try Diros soon, then. It is just across the water, yes?"

"On the mainland and further south. Ah, there, see?" He pointed. In the deepening twilight over the water, a glowing human soul streaked southward. As they watched, other faint streaks dashed across the sky, all going the same direction. "If I had to triangulate from them, I'd say Diros was exactly where they're headed. We'll know soon."

"Yes." She grasped his hand. "Now take me back and forth some more. I must sense this magical wall better, learn how to hold it open for our soldiers."

Tracy took her over the boundary and back several times. They were fortunate in having the section of cave to themselves, but it wasn't a large spot. There was only this narrow ledge to stand on. You couldn't even get down here by land; they'd arrived by a small motorboat they'd rented. It was that or swim, which wasn't appealing in the biting February wind and choppy waves.

"I think I begin to see," Tenebra said after a few minutes. "But it will take some study, some practice. Perhaps—"

Her sentence was interrupted by a giant creature who surged up out of the water at their feet. Its honking roar reverberated in the sea caves. Tracy caught a glimpse of meter-long tusks and other huge teeth in an open mouth big enough to swallow both their heads at once, all attached to a several-ton brown body throwing itself onto the ledge.

He barely had time to scrabble for the gun in his pocket when Tenebra pronounced, *"Sormajhaturm!"*

The animal grunted and fell limp. Even dead, it was tremendously imposing: lying in a heap, it rose as high as Tracy's chest, and reeked of marine life.

He grimaced, and prodded its leathery hide with his now-soaked shoe. "God in heaven. What is it? Part walrus, part hippo, but twice as big as either?"

"There are dangers here." Tenebra regarded the beast grimly. "As we have been told. However..." She tilted her head as she studied it, then pulled out a utility knife from a pocket. "This may be of use, magically. Help me take some blood while it is still warm."

SOPHIE HELD A DINNER PARTY IN THE AIRSTREAM A COUPLE OF nights after Groundhog Day. Just family, or close enough: Liam, Tab, and Zoe got treated to her cooking, Rosie got to nose around on the floor for scraps, and the souls of Terry and Isabel hung out during dinner and joined in the conversation. Sophie made vegetarian chili from scratch, along with corn-bread—also from scratch, naturally.

"Those boxed mixes will not do," she informed her guests.

"When you get to know her longer," Tab told Zoe, pouring her another glass of red wine, "you'll learn she says that every time she makes or serves cornbread."

"Because it's true," Sophie defended, while everyone laughed.

"That's my girl," Terry said.

There'd been a lot of laughing, actually. On her part too. Tonight was the first time she'd felt anything like the domestic warmth and happiness she'd been missing with such agony. It was inspiring that she could manage this even in the spirit realm, with her parents in ghost form, in a crowded trailer borrowed from her on-hold boyfriend who was out there making sure a cult wasn't going to attack anyone tonight.

Must be the scents and nourishment of a proper home-cooked meal at last. And the wine. And the chocolate cake—from scratch. Couldn't discount those.

The comfortable glow stayed with her after everyone had departed for the night. Zoe and Tab had done the dishes and put away the leftovers, so Sophie was at leisure to lean against the counter with a mug of chamomile tea and gaze at the candles that still burned on the table. A Greek radio station played Euro-pop at low volume.

She had to decide what life was going to look like for the better part of her future, and she couldn't decide that until the latest imminent Thanatos threat had been smacked down. But if her future included occasional evenings like this, in a home that felt like this—but a little bigger—she could be content with that. Maybe it could be managed after all, a life that balanced the spirit realm and the living realm. Tonight it felt more plausible than usual, though she had a lot of logistics to sort out yet.

Her gaze strayed to the bathroom. She ought to change the towels tonight, and wash them tomorrow along with the sodden dish towels hanging over the sink. Small tasks now. Big life decisions later. She set her mug down and got on her knees to dig into the lower cabinet where Adrian had stashed towels, toilet paper, soap, and other supplies.

Including condoms. She found the box of them, still unopened, under a folded washcloth, and pulled it out to stare at it in surprise. Adrian had never mentioned owning these. But then, he and she hadn't quite worked up to doing *that* yet. Just other things. Really lovely other things.

Her mind danced down those steamy stepping stones: insatiable immortals Persephone and Hades, newlyweds Akis and Galateia, and seventy-some other lives in between until getting to Sophie and Adrian unable to keep their hands off each other in the twenty-first century.

A bolt of lust shimmered through her—easily the first time she'd felt that in almost two months.

It dissolved away, but left her contemplating many interesting questions as she changed the towels and finished her tea.

In Freya's latest life, up until becoming immortal, she had been a women's health practitioner and sex therapist. Pretty much inevitable for that soul, Sophie figured. What with that consideration and others, Freya stood as pretty much the only person who could now answer Sophie's question.

So after drying out her mug, she picked up her phone and texted Freya.

Hey! Random question, just curious. What's the best method of birth control w/ immortals these days?

Goodness, Sophie, Freya responded a minute later. *Who do you have in there with you?? ;)*

Haha. No one. I found condoms though, not sure why they're here, and it made me wonder.

Oh yes, I told Adrian to get those, months ago when he was talking about finding you. They're one half of the best method. Other half is cloudhair seeds, as before.

But condoms... Sophie texted. *Wouldn't things...break through?*

No. Our men don't do *everything* at super strength. ;)

Ohhh-kay, now came the blushing.

Ha. Guess not, she responded. *So then, cloudhair seeds too?*

Yes. I made capsule form. No more chewing the nasty things. I'll bring u some tomorrow!

No rush, but thx. So that all works, really?

Has worked for me so far, Freya answered. *I'll of course keep researching other methods. Let me know if you think of any with your plants too.*

I will, thanks, Sophie texted back.

Well, okay. There was one possibility for the future. Go in with Freya on spirit-world-sourced birth-control botanicals. Always a market for that.

Sophie snorted a laugh, and stashed the condoms back in the cupboard.

CHAPTER FORTY-FOUR

ADRIAN WAS ALARMED AT FIRST WHEN FREYA SHOWED UP TO find him. It was night, and he was wandering the streets in the village on Zakynthos where the Thanatos team was staying. He was wearing pieces of the inane disguises Niko had brought him, and supposed his current look was meant to be "uni student on holiday," as it was a tan wool blazer made forty years ago, his blond-streaked wig and thick-rimmed glasses, and a beige Cambridge University cap.

Freya had no trouble recognizing him, of course. She strolled up to him in her blue ski parka, tight jeans, and beret. "Hello, dear. Have a moment?"

"Sure." He beckoned her into a cobblestoned alley, empty of life except for a couple of cats. "What's wrong?"

"Nothing. Just a friendly visit." She swung a leather bag off her shoulder and unzipped it. "How is it going, tracking our dickhead friends?"

"The usual." He sighed. "Krystal's staying in a house at the end of this street. Tracy too, I think. They go in, they go out, they talk to people, but sometimes I lose track of them, like I don't know, maybe they've got secret ways to sneak in and out or something. I see other people, but I rarely see the ones I'd recognize. I can't find this golden leaf thing anywhere in their rooms, nor anything like weapons that could get them arrested, but I don't dare get close very often. They've come to Greece, so they're closing in on us. They'll work out which sacred cave is the Underworld any day now. They might be making colossally important plans right this minute and I wouldn't bloody know because I can't just pop into the room and listen, nor read their phones over their shoulders, nor track any of them except Krystal...argh." He shut up, and returned the glare one of the cats was giving him from a window ledge.

"Relax," Freya said. "Take a break and do something nice for yourself. Here, humor me. Come into the other realm a minute."

"Fine. What." They switched realms, and wound up on one of the scrubby hillsides facing the sea, of which Greece seemingly had a million. The sea at the moment, though, was a softly thundering expanse of black, invisible under the moonless sky.

Freya turned on a couple of camping lanterns and set them on rocks nearby. She took the hat and wig off Adrian's head. Then she pulled items out of the bag: comb, scissors, and electric clippers with various attachments. "Look at me," she said. "Hold still."

He obeyed.

The clippers began buzzing. "You could rock this bearded Hades look," she said. "But it needs a little grooming." The clippers zapped his upper lip in one spot, then another.

"Ow!"

"I said hold still."

She kept buzzing and trimming a few minutes, then let him rub his mouth and cheeks with his sleeve. He spat out the stray bits of hair that had fallen on his lips.

"There." She held up a compact mirror for him. "Much better, yes?"

His lips were visible again, with a few centimeters cleared around them, and the thin beard on his chin and jawline had gone from chaotic scruff to a defined shape. He looked a good deal more like some bloke in an ad for man-scented body wash. "I guess that's…a good thing?" he said, in response both to his own thought and to what he saw in the mirror.

"Uber-hot. She'll like it." Freya tucked away the mirror.

She. Right. Tenderness bruised him inside again.

Adrian bowed his head, running finger and thumb around his admittedly more kissable mouth. "I don't know. If you were her, wouldn't you just walk away from the person who unleashed all that horror into your life?"

"If you two were any other souls, maybe. But when have you ever walked away from each other without regretting it, in any life? She knows that."

"I'm not so sure."

"Goddess of love. Trust me." Freya turned off the lanterns and stashed them in the bag.

Adrian exhaled a puff of air. "Anyway, thanks. I look better."

"You do, and she'll notice. I think she already has. Otherwise why would she ask me about birth control for immortals?"

He snapped up his head. "What?"

Grinning, Freya swung her bag back onto her shoulder. "Nothing, dear." Then she frowned, and turned abruptly, as if listening.

Adrian listened too. "What are you…"

"Zeus. I sense him. He's near."

"That's odd."

They switched back into the living realm together, reappearing in the shadowed alley.

On the nearest street, a silver sedan with a taxi sign on top rumbled past. "I think he's in that car," Freya said.

They crept to the end of the alley to look after it.

"You said he was someone we didn't know, right?" Adrian said.

"Yes, but I only looked him up once, over a year ago. I

never found out his name or anything. He was in England at the time, in a pub, with a bunch of younger women."

"Sounds like Zeus all right."

The taxi stopped at the last building in the street's dead end. Its tail lights glowed as it idled. The passengers got out and ambled into the house.

"That's Erick Tracy and the Russian woman," Adrian whispered.

Freya stared. "He's Zeus."

SOPHIE GAZED AT THE RED VIOLETS GROWING IN FRONT OF HER as she sat in the circle they'd formed for the latest group meeting. While the others settled into their places, she snuck another glance at Adrian, across from her. He'd trimmed up the scruff into a proper beard, not unlike Hades' in some phases. And damn. He looked hot.

It was good to feel that a guy looked hot. Especially her guy, if she could still call him that. But when he glanced at her, she dropped her gaze back down to the flowers. They had issues on the agenda today rather more important than relationship questions. No point distracting herself until those were dealt with.

"Okay, everyone," Adrian said. "Well, a few things to discuss. As you've heard, Freya has just learned Erick Tracy and Zeus are one and the same."

"Would've been nice to know that earlier." Tab wiggled her boot against Freya's blue ballet flat as if to show she was only teasing.

"I would have said something if I could tell he was in Thanatos before," Freya defended. "I couldn't. I checked on him out of curiosity last year, but he seemed like a prick, so I left him alone. I never came near him again until last night. I've been helping out down here."

"It's all right," Adrian said. "No harm done. In fact, this

is great. One more window into the cult. But Freya, it does mean you're going to be the one responsible for watching him, since you're the only one who can track him."

Freya sighed. "Yes. All right."

"Thanks, Freya," Sophie said, and smiled when Freya glanced at her. Sophie remembered Freya doing surveillance on Quentin for her a few months ago, and finding it dreadfully tedious then too. Not the goddess of love's ideal pastime.

"I will have to sleep sometimes," Freya pointed out.

"Luckily they do too," Adrian said. "But let's have you get full time on following him, please, until we can close in and take them down."

Freya nodded, though she twisted her lips into a pout.

"So," Adrian said, "Zoe tells us the chrysomelia will be ripe soon, maybe in a couple more weeks. In that case, the question of who else to initiate. I know we've all been considering it. Zoe and Sophie, you were saying we should take up the group vote again?"

"Yes." Sophie sat taller. "Like in the old days." She looked at her mother, father, and grandfather, as well as Rhea, Sanjay, and Adrian's mum—the representatives of the dead in this circle. "We should include you, the souls, this time too, though we'd have to think of a way for you to cast your vote since you can't touch the stones."

But most of them shook their heads with grateful smiles.

"This is a matter for living immortals," Rhea said. "You are the ones it concerns most."

"Besides," Sophie's grandpop said, "we dead don't make good voters. We're too forgiving. We'd say yes to everybody."

"Not the bad guys," Liam warned. "Don't be too forgiving to them. You still have to stab them for us."

"Oh sure," Grandpop said. "To defend you guys, *that* we'll do."

"You say 'living immortals,'" Sophie said to Rhea. "I agree.

Liam and I shouldn't vote yet. In fact, the rest of you have to vote on whether or not to let us in."

Nearly everyone snorted or rolled their eyes. Sophie overrode the murmurs. "I know. You probably will. But it's the proper procedure and you should observe it."

Adrian said, "I think it's a good precedent to set, given how *some* fruits were handed out without group discussion."

Tab and Zoe sent guilty grins at Niko, who smiled angelically.

Adrian looked around the circle. "Re-establish the group vote, then? All in favor?"

"Aye," everyone chorused.

"Then I officially propose the names of Sophie and Liam." Zoe smiled.

"Woohoo!" Liam pumped his fists in the air.

"I—" Sophie dropped her gaze. Her face heated in a flush. "I should tell you I haven't completely decided yet. Whether to eat it, I mean."

"Still, we can approve you," Niko said, "then you can decide when it's ripe."

"Wait," Liam said. "What about Rosie?" While the group's gaze drifted to the boxer snoozing behind him, Liam continued, "It's just, Adrian has an immortal pet, which is really cool, and Rosie went through a lot with us, so if I'm going to eat it—which I totally will, if I can—then I want her to eat it, too."

"Fair enough," Zoe said. "We can vote on that."

"So who else?" Adrian asked. "There are former immortals we could yet approach. But…"

"But just because someone's a former immortal doesn't make them a brilliant choice," Zoe said.

"Obviously," Freya said. "Look at Thanatos. Quentin was Hera, Tracy was Zeus, and Krystal was Ares. A pack of douchebags."

"Right," Adrian said. "And the others, say—Artemis,

Athena, Hephaestus—they're people with their own lives now, and if we're not particularly drawn to the idea of immortalizing them, then why not only pick the people we are drawn to? Even if they weren't immortal before."

"That's what I was thinking too," Sophie said. "Like Zoe's parents. You know they'd say yes, and we all like them."

The group nodded in encouragement. Zoe smiled and cast her gaze upward. "My mum and dad around for eternity. Oh Goddess, is the world ready for that?"

"But people like that," Sophie said, "the ones we love, the ones we can trust, they're the ones who should be our candidates. Besides, *every* soul knows about the Underworld, if you unlock their memories. Every soul knows about the immortals. We're legends down here. We're part of the common knowledge."

"True," Freya said. "It's not like only former immortals could understand about this realm."

"Well," Adrian said, "there should be plenty of orange to go around if we add a few more names. Anyone for us to think on?"

"Zoe's parents." Niko smiled at her. "I propose them officially."

"And your dad?" Zoe said to Adrian.

He lowered his gaze. "Nah, he won't do it. I've tried."

A pang of sympathy struck Sophie. Adrian's mother was already dead, and if his father wouldn't accept immortality, eventually he would age and die too. Their souls, like her own parents, would someday leave the Underworld to be reborn, and would be temporarily lost to their children. She and he would have that grief in common, some year in the future. All of that flashed through her mind within a few seconds, and complex though it was, she could have sworn he thought the same thing. Because he glanced up at her after a moment, and the solemnity in his eyes seemed to carry all those notions.

"Anyone else, then?" Niko looked around the circle.

No one spoke up. Surely they'd already pondered this. Sophie had too. Tab was already immortal, Liam and Rosie already on the list, her parents out of reach. She had no one else to add. She wasn't even sure she'd accept for herself; how could she throw anyone else onto the horns of this gigantic decision?

"So it's those five," Adrian said after the spell of silence. "Sophie, Liam, Rosie, and Zoe's mum and dad. We can propose more in the future as we see fit. Do we adjourn to vote later, like in the old days, or…"

"In this case," Freya said, "we know everyone well enough and have already been thinking about it. We could vote today."

So after a brief break, Sophie returned with some of her empty plastic plant pots and a chunk of white chalk. Niko picked each pot up and chalked a candidate's initials on the side. Zoe dumped a pile of beach pebbles into the middle of the circle, some white and some black.

"Those voting, take five of each color," Zoe said.

While the immortals picked up their stones, Sophie beckoned to Liam. "Come on. Let's take a walk."

They walked together toward the river, letting Rosie stay asleep near the group.

"So you're going to become immortal if they let you?" Sophie asked her brother.

"Duh. What, you're not?"

"There's something to be said for a normal life."

"Like what?"

Sophie folded her arms and studied the river. "For starters, not having people get all suspicious of you because you're not aging."

"Versus *not aging*. Hello."

"Not being a target of Thanatos."

"Being strong enough to destroy Thanatos."

"Being…you know, normal."

"Never getting diseases," Liam countered.

"Okay, I admit that one is really tempting."

"All right, guys!" Zoe called from across the field.

They abandoned the debate and walked back to the group.

The smiles wreathing every face told them the answer even before Sophie's gaze fell upon the scattering of all-white stones next to each pot.

"Congrats," Zoe said. "All of you are in."

"Huh." Liam shoved Sophie lightly. "That's a pretty wide smile for someone who 'isn't sure.'"

"I'm just happy for you and Rosie and Zoe's folks." But Sophie met Adrian's gaze again, and read the speculation in it. Her mind was doing some heavy speculating of its own.

She'd been willing and prepared to eat the fruit a couple of months ago. Her circumstances were different now, and so would be some of her reasons for eating or not eating it. She loved Adrian, and still intended to become his lover again eventually. Judging from his teenage writings, she would have loved him even if they'd both been mortals, clueless about this realm, and had happened to meet somehow in real life. Zoe's old files had laid Sophie's doubts about their compatibility to rest.

But Adrian *was* immortal now, and they did have this other realm and all their memories to deal with, and she did have to consider all of that as well. Besides, to become a worthy immortal herself, she had to stand strong on her own as a human with something valuable to contribute to the world, not just as someone who loved another immortal. She needed to be completely sure before popping a wedge of blue orange into her mouth.

Adrian broke eye contact with her and looked around at everyone else. "Okay then. I'd say meeting adjourned, so we can get back to the task of stopping this attempted invasion. Suppose it's time to try our hand at forming a ghost army."

Freya caught her breath. "He's here."

Everyone's gaze shot to her. Sophie's heart tightened in fear.

"Zeus," Freya said. "Tracy. I just began to sense him. He's somewhere close by."

CHAPTER FORTY-FIVE

RACY AND TENEBRA STOOD OUTSIDE THE ENTRANCE TO Diros Caves and examined the hillside that encased the cave system. The glamours they wore ensured that no one gave them a second glance. For all Tracy knew, they looked like employees or bus drivers or extra rocks. Tourists paid their admission and disappeared inside for their subterranean boat tour, but that wouldn't be Tracy's way in today.

"We can't very well switch realms from within a boat full of people, I suppose, even with glamours on," Tracy remarked.

"Well, we'd fall in the water. And returning would then be trickier."

"So shall we try from outside?"

"Might as well." Tenebra cast him a sultry look from under her eyelashes.

Yes, he could bed her soon if he wanted. Oh, there was Yuliya to be cast aside first, but she had to know the hook-up had about run through its appeal. He'd taken her to dinner the other night and behaved nicely enough; it was as good a way to end an affair as any. But that could be dealt with later. The Underworld awaited.

He leaned his back against the rocks and encased Tenebra beneath his arm. In his hand he held the gold leaf and the fresh strawberry tree leaves. He reached for the other realm.

And got thrown back. It felt like bumping straight into a wall. He blinked and tried again, and got rebuffed again.

"Stop." Tenebra sounded satisfied, of all strange things.

He frowned down at her.

"It's magically protected," she said. "I can feel it. A ward, a good strong one. That tells us all we need to know, don't you think? This is the site."

"Ah." He looked up the rocky hillside. "How I'd love to see it, though."

"We will. I must bring extra supplies next time, is all. Then I can dismantle the ward and let us through."

"You're sure?"

"Of course. You doubt me?" But she said that with a sultry glance too.

He smiled. "Never. But shouldn't we at least try to get through today?"

She shook her head. "If they are in there, which they probably are, whoever set up this ward will know when it is broken, and would likely attack us. Our invasion would be over before it has begun."

"Very well. I regret not getting a look in, but you're right. Best to bring our army when we do enter."

She nodded. "Do we move everyone closer to here?"

Tracy slipped his various leaves back into his coat pockets. "I rather think not. We're likely being watched, at least whenever they manage to catch a glimpse when our glamours wear off. So let's stay over on Zakynthos—most of us, anyway. Let them think we're entirely on the wrong track. Maybe they'll relax their guard a bit too much."

"And now he's leaving," Freya said. She peeked out from behind the boulder in the living world, where she, Zoe, Niko, and Adrian were hiding. They hadn't dared let Tracy and the unknown woman see them—no good letting them know they'd hit the right site. "He's getting into the taxi," Freya added.

"That's them, the couple getting into the taxi?" Adrian was confused. "But he looks nothing like Tracy. And I don't know who the woman is."

"The sense. I'm telling you, it's him."

"Could be a good disguise." Niko sounded reluctant to believe his own suggestion. "A really good disguise."

"Or magic." Zoe squinted at them. "But Thanatos has never used magic before. Have they? I'd have to get closer to tell, and I don't dare."

"Well, they're researching how to switch realms, so anything's possible," Adrian said.

"But they didn't switch realms today," Zoe said. "I mean, I can't tell from here if they tried and the wards made them fail, but..."

"We don't know that they ever have switched realms, in fact," Niko pointed out. "And even if they are hiring magical practitioners, none of them could compare to you, love."

"I wouldn't be so sure." Zoe sounded wretched with worry. "There've always been people born with a talent for it. If they study and work at it, they can become quite strong."

Concerned, Adrian looked at her. "Do you know of anyone who can use magic the way you can?"

"Not in this life, but only because I haven't properly been looking. They could be out there. In past lives, there've been some who've come close. I studied with them, when I was practicing witchcraft in one life or another."

"Ah, but," Freya said, "they cannot use it for evil without it bouncing back upon them threefold. Right?"

"Hm, well." Zoe wrung one hand inside the other. "You always hear about ways to get round that. To twist the powers to do what you like. I mean, it might rebound on you unexpectedly someday, and in any case you'd serve serious time in Tartaros after you died. But if you didn't care about that, or didn't believe in it…"

They stared grimly after the departing taxi.

"Still," Niko said. "We don't know for sure."

"But they came here." Adrian set his teeth together. "I do not like it."

"We have wards," Freya said. "And soon we'll have a ghost army." But she sounded worried too.

"You found the Underworld?" Krystal's eyes gleamed with malice. Or maybe bloodlust. With her, bloodlust was always likelier. "Let's do it! I'm *so* ready."

"You aren't." Tracy cast a stern look at her legs, though nowadays she stood on them without crutches. "You're coming along brilliantly with your physical therapy, but I'd feel much better if you gave it another week."

"God damn it, Tracy—"

"You're one of my best soldiers." He used his most soothing and syrupy tone. Might as well turn up the charm, even though she'd never want to sleep with him, and the feeling was mutual. "I want you in tip-top shape so you can charge in there, guns blazing, just like you want to. All right?"

She pouted, her lips painted with that absurd fuchsia lipstick. "Fine."

"And," Tracy added, "tonight you and I will go over the layout of the cave. I've found geologic maps for Diros. They may be useful, since landscape forms tend to be similar in the other realm, as far as I've seen. I want your thoughts on what equipment we'll need."

He already had plenty of thoughts, but might as well flatter her. It worked; her pout smoothed into a calculating smile.

Tracy turned to Yuliya. He smiled and laid his hands on her shoulders. "For you, dear, I've a very important job.

I need someone on the mainland to put together the army. Someone discreet, someone I can trust. It can only be you."

She pouted too. "For how long? A week?"

"A week, perhaps ten days. Let's see how it goes. Then we'll all be together again."

Her reluctance to leave him sang in her sad, round eyes, and she shot a distrustful glance at Tenebra. But finally she nodded. "Yes, of course."

"Lovely." He kissed her on the forehead. "Let's slip you out tonight, under a glamour. Hopefully our enemies won't even notice you've gone for a couple of days, and by then they'll find it hard to locate you."

After all, it seemed to be Krystal and possibly even himself who suffered from this uncanny tracking issue. Tenebra had done her best to scan them for any magical trace, but had shrugged and said she detected nothing. The immortals' abilities were truly mysterious, and dangerous. Good thing Tracy and his team were about to kill them all.

Also a good thing Yuliya would be off to the mainland, leaving him free to seduce Tenebra. He beamed at his team, and managed not to rub his hands together in glee.

CHAPTER FORTY-SIX

NIKO UPENDED A RUCKSACK AND SPILLED A PILE OF LETHAL-looking combat knives on the pale grass at Adrian's and Zoe's feet. "Fifty for now," he said. "Can acquire more as needed."

"Do I want to know if you paid for these?" Zoe asked.

"Better still, I stole them from a group who shouldn't have them. I'll say no more."

Adrian ran his eyes over the weapons and nodded. They'd agreed guns would be too risky to strap to souls, since accidentally-fired bullets could do a lot of damage to any innocent mortals who happened to be around—such as Sophie and Liam. Knives would suffice for the time being.

"Well, then." Adrian looked up at the souls of Terry and Louis, Terry's father, who had both drawn closer to examine the knives. Adrian switched to the Underworld tongue and raised his voice to address all the nearest souls. "Your attention a minute, please. I—we—need your help. We're looking for souls willing to defend the Underworld, and us. We'd attach these knives to you, the way we've done for some of the guards already. We're expecting an attack soon from Thanatos, the group who thinks no one should be immortal. But we'll probably need guards even after that, so the post would be for as long as you can spare the time." His voice faltered. "It might mean killing someone. I...I don't know what that translates to in the judging system, killing someone after you're already dead; if that calls for punishment or…"

"Not in self defense," Zoe protested. "Nor defense of someone else. Stopping a would-be lethal attack."

"I hope not." Adrian looked in desperation across the vast fields of souls. "But I understand if you don't want to do it, so…just, whoever's willing. If we don't have more guards, the cult might get in here and destroy us, along with the tree of immortality and everything they can lay their hands on. So, please. Anyone. And…thank you."

The message rippled outward in a murmur.

"Well, you've got us two." Terry nodded toward his father's soul. "But you knew that."

"And me." Isabel's soul wandered over.

"Thank you," Adrian said with sincerity.

"And obviously us." The voice was behind him, and he turned to find Sanjay, Rhea, and his mother.

"Thanks," Adrian repeated. "Though I hope it's not *just* you lot."

"It won't be." Zoe was watching the crowd. "See. Here they come."

Individual souls threaded their way through the masses and came forward. Adrian noted five or six at first, then more came into view from farther out. And more, and more. They formed a loose ring all around, young and old and in between. Most were grown men and women, but some were boys and girls as young as ten or eleven.

"The children—no, we can't," Adrian said to his friends.

"Why not?" Niko studied the accumulating volunteers. "They can't get hurt. And how creepy would it be to have the ghost of a child coming at you with a knife? That'd shake the resolve of even the nastiest thug, I bet you."

"He's right, you know," Zoe said.

"Well. Then perhaps."

"Hey, is that Freddie Mercury?" she said with fascination. "I think it is."

"Indeed." Niko gave Freddie a thumbs-up. "Tabitha made friends with him, I gather."

"And Ciaran! Hi, Ciaran." Zoe exchanged waves with the soul of the Irishman killed by Erick Tracy.

As Adrian turned and scanned all the faces, another realization struck him. His breath caught, and tears filled his eyes.

Zoe noticed his reaction. "What?"

"They're..." He cleared his throat. "Most of these are people I helped. The murder victims. The ones I placed anonymous tips for, to get their murderers caught."

"Someone needs to be down here doing that," a man in his forties said—a shopkeeper in Texas, killed in a late-night hold-up, Adrian remembered. "We want to keep you around."

"You helped us. We want to help you," a young woman said. Australian, kidnapped and murdered by a neighbor.

"I—I didn't know if anyone would be willing," Adrian said.

An older woman smiled. From India, killed by a niece no one had suspected. "All you had to do was ask," she said.

"Thank you." This time Adrian's voice vibrated with gratitude.

Zoe swung her arm around him.

Among the milling souls Adrian spotted two solid figures: Sophie and Liam, just outside the ring of volunteer soldiers. Sophie must have witnessed the gathering, seen the loyalty of these souls to Adrian. Now she met his gaze across the crowd, her sweet, proud smile shining brighter than any soul.

He smiled back.

"Well, this is far more than fifty," Niko remarked. "I am going to have to get more knives."

Landon's terror had diminished, which was perhaps strange, in his situation. Then again, the immortals and their cohorts were still not torturing him, and seemed unlikely ever to do so. So it did seem he could ease up on the fear. Instead new emotions had taken its place. Longing, for one.

Lately his heart rate picked up whenever Niko appeared for a guard shift. And he then missed Niko when others guarded him, even though Niko didn't talk to him much, and usually only teased him or said something annoyingly enigmatic if Landon did try to strike up a conversation. Still, he caught glances from those green eyes that carried at least pity, maybe even the echo of past-life fondness. Landon didn't delude himself into thinking there was much in the way of current fondness. But he was also pretty sure Niko didn't actively hate him. Like, maybe if they were strangers who met in a club, Niko might even welcome his advances. Probably just for one night, but still, that was more pleasant to think about than a lot of the other topics on Landon's mind these days.

Such as guilt. That was another nasty emotion that had mushroomed up in his brain. Having rearranged his thoughts about the world—about Thanatos, the immortals, what human decency looked like and what evil looked like—Landon now viewed his own life quite differently.

Finally one day when Terry was guarding him, Landon walked up to the bars and said to him, "I'm so sorry. For what we did to you. I should have said it a long time ago. I—I wish I had stopped it. I've wished it every day since it happened."

Terry inclined his head gravely toward Landon. "Thank you for saying so. I wouldn't have been keen on forgiving you when I was a living man, but it's easier now. I forgive you, and Isabel will too, if you say the same to her."

"I will," Landon promised.

"Sophie and Liam, now…" Terry winced. "They're going to find it harder."

"Can I see them? I want to apologize even if they hate me anyway. I want them to know."

"I'll get them here," Terry said. "It'll do them good to hear it."

So a short while later, Terry and Isabel brought Liam and Sophie. Zoe accompanied them, hanging back in silence but glowering at Landon as if ready to eviscerate him if he did anything offensive.

Sophie stopped outside the cell and regarded Landon with cold poise. Liam kept his unruly head bowed next to her and his gaze averted, aside from occasionally flashing Landon a glance of homicidal loathing.

"I just wanted to tell you that I'm sorry." Even though it sounded lame and insufficient, Landon kept on. "I was deluded. I believed I was acting for a good cause, but I can see now I wasn't." He stood still too, hands at his sides, in front of the locked door. "I know there's nothing I can say that will help now. But I wanted you both to know that I never liked it, the violence, the…the killing. I'm never going back to Thanatos. Even if I was free, I wouldn't. You never have to worry about me hurting you again. Or hurting anyone—I never want to again." He dropped his gaze. "Anyway, I just wanted to tell you that. In case it helps at all."

They stayed silent and still. "It does help," Sophie said at last. "A little. I'd be lying if I said I forgive you. But Mom and Dad told me they do, so maybe someday I will. I guess saying you're sorry is all you can do at this point, though, so I appreciate it." She glanced over at Liam, who returned her glance but remained mute. "Come on," she told him softly.

They walked away without a goodbye.

Landon mulled over the notion of forgiveness for the rest of the day. And when Niko showed up to take over as guard,

Landon looked up from his seat upon the ground and said quietly, "I forgive you for killing my grandmother."

Niko turned his pocket knife over and over in his hand, gazing at it. "As she said, there's been too much killing on both sides. But thank you, I suppose."

"Why didn't you kill me too? I was head of Thanatos. Same as her."

Niko kept tilting the knife. Its blade flashed in the light of the two bare bulbs strung up outside the cell. "I killed her because of what she'd done to my friends. And because it seemed she would never change, no matter what we said. Only Tartaros would shake her conviction. You're different, though."

"You knew you could charm me, convince me."

Niko shrugged.

"I'm glad you didn't kill me," Landon added. "I'm glad you did charm me."

Niko sent a wry glance around the confines of the cage. "This inspires gladness in you?"

"In some ways it's better than how I was living. I'm not lying to myself anymore. That counts for something."

"True. I recommend only lying to others."

Landon smiled, remembering the tricks and lies of the ancient Hermes. "I could fall in love with you again if I let myself."

Niko met his gaze, wearily sympathetic. "Fall in love with the bloke who killed your grandmother? That's twisted, mate."

"Yeah, well. Twisted is nothing new for me."

Niko smirked.

"I don't suppose," Landon added, "you could ever love me?"

Niko traced his finger along the edge of the knife, his eyes following its path. "My heart, such as it is, belongs to another. Still, Petal, you've given me something valuable."

"What's that?"

"Oh…" Niko folded the knife shut and caused it to vanish somewhere inside his jacket in one of those nimble-fingered tricks of his. "'Redemption' and 'salvation' are words too grand for the likes of me. But something along those lines."

Landon pondered that. "Because I forgave you for killing my grandma? And because you've saved me from the dark side instead of becoming darker yourself by killing me too?"

Niko neither nodded nor shook his head. But the sage little smile he gave Landon suggested he was proud of Landon for getting the right answer.

Chapter Forty-Seven

THE TREE OF IMMORTALITY WAS NOT ITSELF IMMORTAL. When Hekate began to understand that, the disquieting discovery rumbled deep beneath her world like the earthquakes that sometimes shook Greece.

The orange tree had been growing steadily, and Hekate had been plucking its fruits over the years to give to the select folk who were voted in for immortality. The tree had always produced a modest but constant supply, enough for their needs.

But lately, in Hekate's fortieth year, she found prematurely dropped oranges beneath the tree more often than she used to—tiny, hard, and green. She could tell by a mere touch that they had no power in them. Fewer flowers bloomed now too, which meant the crop of fruits was dwindling.

Hades and Persephone had talked about planting other immortality trees from the seeds of this one, but ultimately had decided against it. The fruit's power was too momentous. It felt unwise to proliferate it without a good deal more thought, they had said. And in any case, they always had more than enough oranges for the small number of immortality candidates each year.

Now Hekate counted five oranges growing, none mature yet, and twelve blossoms forming. Any of the fruit or flowers could wither and drop before maturity.

In alarm, she infused the tree with as strong a health spell as she knew. And she cut out the seeds from one of the fallen oranges and planted them, all in the vicinity of the first tree. Within a month, three of them sent up shoots: they were growing. She relaxed a little.

But it would be at least a couple of years before the tiny new trees could produce fruit, and in the meantime the original tree still wasn't truly healthy. Her daily spells seemed to give it especially glossy foliage, but the fruits hadn't ripened yet, and four of the flowers had already fallen off without setting fruit.

In a panic, she brought Hermes to the garden. Most of the immortals still didn't know which tree was the chrysomelia, but over the years he had it figured out, somehow or other. As far as she knew he had kept its identity a secret, and had never taken one of the fruits. She kept a close count on those and would have known.

"I need you to go to Asia and find me another tree like this one," she told him.

"It's still not doing well?" He leaned close to frown at one of the small green fruits.

"No, it isn't. Don't touch it! I touched one this morning and it—it fell off." She wrung her hands. That moment of the lifeless fruit plummeting into her palm had felt unnervingly awful, almost like delivering a stillborn child.

"And *you* can't fix it?" He sounded baffled.

"I'm trying! I'm not my mother. I don't have the same touch with plants. Or maybe orange trees just don't live very long, and if so, I can't do much about the natural cycle of life. So I need a new one, and fast."

"Then to the East I go." Carefully he cut a twig with several leaves on it, and picked up one of the shriveled fallen fruits. "To get as close a match as possible," he said. He tucked them under his cloak, kissed her, and dashed out.

He was away almost a month. When he returned he

brought four little trees in pots. "Each a different variety," he told her. "Unfortunately there are lots of varieties over there—dozens that I saw, and probably more in the areas I didn't get to. Goddess, you can't even begin to imagine how big Asia is. But these are my best guesses."

So it came down to more anxious waiting as the seven small trees grew in the Underworld's soil. Hekate placed more daily spells on them, and considered trying again to make Galateia eat the pomegranate, just so she could gain access to Persephone's plant-rich knowledge. But Galateia was pregnant now, and Hekate had no wish to add to her stress, so she left the young couple alone and fretted over the tree by herself, consulting only Hermes, Rhea, and Athena.

Two of the new trees from Asia died within the first month. By winter solstice, two of the seedlings from the original tree had died too. And on the original tree, every piece of fruit had dropped.

It was time to tell the others.

Hekate did so at the solstice meeting of the immortals, in Athena's palace in the spirit realm, near Athens.

They listened in stricken silence.

"We don't have *any* immortality fruits?" Artemis said.

"None." Hekate sat with shoulders drooped.

"Does the tree have flowers?" Aphrodite asked.

"A few, so there's hope. But I've never seen it this sick. Or at least this unproductive."

"But you're still growing three new trees," Apollo said. "Right?"

"Yes. Two that Hermes found in Asia, and one from the original tree. But it could be years before they can bear fruit, and I don't even know yet if the Asian ones are the right type. No one knew where exactly the first one came from. It was something my mother got from a trader long ago."

Most of the others looked only unhappy. But Ares glared at Hekate. "How do we know you're telling the truth? What if you've decided to take control of all the fruits, and are hiding them?"

She glared back. "You're welcome to come down anytime and check."

"How could I? You've always kept it a secret, which tree it is. I'm tempted to come down there, indeed, and find out the truth."

She curled her hands into fists in her lap. "I repeat, you are welcome to. And I *will* show you the tree now—any of you—since we're having such difficulties with it, and its fate concerns us all. But anyone who tries to steal or damage what rightfully belongs to the Underworld may find themselves staying down there a very long time indeed."

Ares' dark eyebrows lifted in disdain. "You're threatening me?"

"You did threaten her first," Hermes put in.

"Leave the Underworld alone, Ares," Aphrodite said. "She knows what she's doing."

"It doesn't sound like it," Ares retorted.

Rage thundered inside Hekate's chest—because he was right; she didn't know what she was doing, too much of the time. "I suppose you always know what you're doing." She let the sarcasm drip off her words. "You know every future repercussion of every one of your actions. You act with complete knowledge and self-control, every time. Yes, that's exactly what I've heard about you."

"Go back to hell where you belong, little girl," Ares said.

Hekate rose, and with a burst of focused magic, sent Ares' weapons and battle gear flying backward into the roaring fire in the hearth: the daggers, helmet, breastplate, and spear he had lain on the ground at his feet. Then she turned and strode out of the meeting, while his snarls—and Hermes' laughter— echoed in the hall behind her.

SOPHIE WASHED THE LUNCH DISHES IN THE AIRSTREAM WHILE Tab lounged on the front steps, texting and scrolling through social networks. Sophie had made a spring-greens salad with a fresh vinaigrette and they'd eaten it with slices of crusty rustic Greek bread slathered with butter, washed down with chocolate milk. It felt seriously good to be cooking and eating for real again.

But, she thought as she heard Tab chuckle about something from outside the door, it felt silly to be babysat by an immortal friend everywhere you went. That right there was another argument for becoming immortal herself. Sure, the need for babysitting would diminish after they dealt with this imminent Thanatos attack, and she would eventually settle into a more independent life, even if she stayed mortal. Galateia and Akis, not to mention every other lifetime except Persephone's, had shown her how plenty of glory and love could be had in a mortal life too.

But…

Adrian. Immortal Adrian. The last item on her trigger list.

After hearing Landon's apology a few days ago, seeing the humility in his eyes, and glancing around at his miserable jail cell, she had lost her fear of him, and had finally crossed "the people who took me" off her list. Yes, Krystal was still out there, and facing her would still freak Sophie out. And Thanatos was nosing around the actual entrance to the Underworld, so trouble surely loomed on their doorstep. But lately, having been digging and moving the plants of the Underworld, turning the Airstream into a temporary home, and discussing surveillance developments every day with her godly friends, she had reached a certain strange peace. She did belong with them, in this realm, equally as much as she belonged to regular old Earth.

Adrian was immortal, which couldn't be changed, as far as she knew. He had thrown in his lot with this realm. Liam was raring to do so as well, despite all the dangers. Who was she to turn it down, and require the rest of them to protect her when she wanted to hang out in the spirit world?

Sophie shut off the tap, carried the damp dish towel to the table, and wiped the crumbs off its surface. Then she sat and gazed out the window, absently twisting the towel on the tabletop.

Once, not so long ago, she and Adrian had sat here at this table, and he had asked, "What would you have done? If we'd been the other way round?" If she had become immortal first, with her head full of Greek-god memories, and he'd been the mortal boy, her oblivious soul-mate.

"I'd totally have kidnapped you, too," she had admitted.

She smiled, relaxing her grip on the towel.

The crocuses, snowdrops, and bluebells were all blooming now. She'd seen them this morning in her daily visit to the Underworld. And Valentine's Day was coming up.

She took out her phone and sent a text to Adrian.

I know you're busy lately, but would you like to have lunch on the 14th?

She waited, almost enjoying the frenetic drumming of her heart, that age-old rhythm produced by asking out someone you love.

Her phone buzzed.

Sure, he responded. *Airstream, or where?*

Airstream, yeah. Cool, see you at noon on the 14th. :)

ADRIAN PACED ALONG A MEDITERRANEAN BEACH IN THE spirit world, clutching his phone. Niko leaned against a boulder nearby with arms folded. "I mean, she used a smiley face," Adrian said. "So that's good. But on the other hand, she said 'the fourteenth.' She didn't call it Valentine's Day. So that means the intention is *not* romantic, right?"

"You are the god of overthinking," Niko said. "Go to lunch on the fourteenth and find out."

"But do I bring flowers? Chocolate? Argh, I hate Valentine's Day. I've no idea how to interpret these things."

"Yes, Day of the Dead is much more your thing, I know."

Adrian narrowed his eyes at him. Niko smirked. Adrian wheeled back and kept pacing over the same stretch of wave-worn rocks. "Flowers. She likes flowers. I can't go wrong with flowers, right? Even if she's about to break up with me for good."

"Did you call me here just to deliver this monologue? Did I need to be here?"

"Do you think the flowers are a good idea?" Adrian shouted at him.

Niko lifted his hands in the international "don't shoot" gesture. "Yes, my Lord Hades, give her flowers. I'm going to go now, all right?"

Chapter Forty-Eight

HEKATE BEGAN RECOGNIZING A STRANGE EMPTY PORTION IN her life. It seemed connected with Galateia and Akis growing up, marrying, and starting a family. When they'd been children on Sicily, Hekate had watched their development with the fondness of a loving relative. Although she couldn't get as close to them as she liked, it had almost been as though they were linked to her—which their souls were, of course, though they didn't know it.

But these days Galateia and Akis still politely declined the pomegranate, so although they knew of their past lives from her telling them the story, they didn't feel the connection as strongly as she did. Hekate had to let them make that choice. She wouldn't trick anyone into eating the pomegranate, least of all those two people. So she began drawing back and letting them live their lives, and stepped in only from time to time to see if they needed anything.

A child who truly belonged to her, then: that seemed to be what she desired. She longed to extend her bloodline, even if the ailing of the chrysomelia tree meant the child couldn't be made immortal.

Easy enough to get pregnant. And in terms of appealing traits to pass along, she could think of no better father than Hermes: cleverer than anyone, beautiful, and good-natured to boot. The trouble was, he was also one of the people least likely to want children. His freedom outranked everything in life for him; he gloried in how he enjoyed love without ever marrying. He'd fathered Pan, and two other children she barely knew anything about, for the other two hadn't become immortal. But in all three cases, the pregnancies had been a surprise, and he'd put in minimal assistance in the raising of the children. The way she heard it, he dropped off astounding amounts of riches and foods every so often once he heard about the existence of the offspring, but didn't get to know them until they were grown. An irritating pattern, but even so, Hekate found she chafed with envy for those mothers—all of whom were now long dead—because by bearing his children they had accomplished what she never had.

So far she had been using her magic to ward off pregnancy, or cloudhair seeds during those few years her magic had left her. The spell was easy enough; after sex, she focused on all the substance within her that came from his body rather than her own, and swept it back out. It was painless, and had worked every time.

One midwinter night, nestled in the Underworld bed with Hermes after another amorous tangle, she asked, "What would you think of having a child together?"

He was still and silent too long. She watched the red light cast by the hearth's embers throb and wane on the walls, and her hopes waned with it. "Haven't you seen what raising a baby is like?" he said. "I'd think even you would find it exhausting."

"As if you would know?"

"I do listen when others talk, and I do observe. And I think you know I'm right."

"Then you wouldn't help, is what you're saying."

"Love," he said, "our world is falling apart. Surely you see it."

"No," she said, though she did see it. She just didn't want to.

"Invaders are attacking more of Greece, more often, and they're starting to win. Thanatos is gaining in numbers, and killing more of us."

She closed her eyes, remembering last month's dreadful arrivals among the souls: two more of the Muses killed.

"We're fighting among ourselves," Hermes went on. "Ares and sometimes others keep backing the wrong armies, allying with horrid people. And until we fix the tree, which we might never, we can't keep our own numbers up. Why would you want to bring a child into a world like this?"

"All of those things can be dealt with, and prevailed over. The tree isn't dead yet. Even in the worst case, if we can never make new immortals, we and our allies can still get into this realm. We know now how to do it, at the sacred sites."

"Yes, but if the future's that dismal, why—"

"Because how better to keep our world going?" she said.

"How about by caring for what we already have? It's more than we can take on, as it is."

She dropped into silence. Much as it depressed her to review their current list of woes, what hurt most was the simple knowledge that he didn't wish to have a child with her.

"I worry about you already," he added. "I'd worry twice as much if there was a baby too." His tone became more teasing. "So you're still doing that spell to prevent it, right?"

"Yes, don't worry about that," she snapped.

But his disapproval didn't quash her longing. She brooded over it for days, and kept coming around to the same wish. If he wouldn't take on the role of a father, so be it. She was determined anyway to create life to counter all this death. All she needed from him was one blissful moment of the type he had already given her a thousand times.

After their next several liaisons, she didn't perform the magic; she only pretended to, cleaning herself off as usual.

By the next month, Hekate was pregnant.

WITH HER STOMACH DOING BACKFLIPS, SOPHIE OPENED THE Airstream door at noon on Valentine's Day and beckoned Adrian in with a smile. "Hey."

"Hey." He climbed the steps cautiously, as if they were a swaying rope bridge over an abyss. Poor guy was probably as nervous as she was. At the door, he presented her a handful of flowers, white and star-shaped. "To brighten the place up."

"Pretty. Thank you." She sniffed their sweet scent. "I've seen these in the Underworld."

"Yeah, I'm not sure what they're called. One of the things that only grows there, possibly." As he stepped into the trailer and glanced around, she caught the familiar whiffs of his deodorant and shampoo. His black hair was in its tightest curls, the way it got when newly washed. He'd spruced up for her.

She turned to the sink. "Have a seat. I'll just get a glass for these."

She had spruced up too, though not to full "we're on a date" levels. She didn't even have date-quality clothes right now; they'd been burned along with the farmhouse. But her favorite purple sweater and the secondhand black jeans she'd bought in Greece the other week made a flattering enough combination, and she had bobby-pinned back her hair in a couple of twists and applied a subtle smudge of shimmery green eyeliner. From the lingering glance he gave her, he noticed the effort.

"Food smells good," he said.

"Calzone. It's almost done." She brought the flowers in their water glass to the table, and sat opposite him. She folded her hands on the table, which felt ridiculously formal, so she unfolded them and scratched one thumbnail against the other. "How's Freya liking the surveillance?"

"Hates it. But she occasionally sees something suspicious,

like shady-looking blokes coming to talk to them, so, safe to say they're hiring thugs. Again. But as far as we can tell, Tracy and Krystal still haven't left Zakynthos since that one scouting mission to our cave last week."

Sophie nodded. They'd covered this in yesterday's group meeting, where she had tried not to engage in too much eye contact with Adrian. She finally gave him a second of it now. "You saw Tab outside there?"

"Yeah."

"I told her to let us talk a while and not disturb us." Sophie's gaze slipped to the flowers. "She was dying to know why, I could tell. You probably are too."

"It…" His voice was a bit creaky. "It has occurred to me to wonder."

She moistened her lips with her tongue. "When the chrysomelia fruits are ripe, I plan to eat a slice." She kept her eyes on the flowers, but heard him draw in his breath. "I haven't told anyone else yet. It felt right somehow to tell you first."

"Good," he said softly. "Excellent. I'm…I'm so happy to hear you say that."

But hesitation was laced around his words. After all, it was completely possible she could become immortal *and* still never want to touch him again. Probably what he was thinking.

So she took a breath and went on. "Also, I've been picturing what my life would have been like if you'd never approached me, and…"

He turned his face downward, features immobile as stone. He awaited his fate.

"And it would have been pretty dull," she finished. "Compared to this, anyway."

He blinked. He lifted his gaze to her, still wary.

"I will forever wish we had done things differently," she went on. "To protect my family and everyone else. But now, at least, no one can hurt my parents anymore. We're all getting smarter. And now I know I'm stronger than I ever realized. I've learned I can go on even when I thought I couldn't."

The shell of restraint around him began to break, torment showing through the cracks. "I'll never forgive myself." He almost whispered the words. "For wanting you with me so much that I'd risk everyone else, rip your life apart. I'm so sorry. I'm worse than a stalker, I'm—"

"If we'd been the other way around," she cut in, "I totally would have kidnapped you, too."

He hesitated, then his face softened as he recognized the declaration. "Are you sure? You're not just saying that?"

Now she turned one of his own declarations back upon him: "I've never lived a life without you. I don't want to start now."

He tried a smile. His poor mouth looked like it hadn't formed that shape in the longest time and couldn't quite remember how it went.

She slid the flower glass aside and turned her palms up on the table in invitation. Adrian drew his hands up from his lap and set them on hers. Sophie laced their fingers together, and smiled to realize she found the contact comforting, not scary.

She looked into his dark brown eyes again, which now scintillated with longing. "I'm so sorry I pushed you away. I didn't want to, but I was...hurt, shell-shocked..."

"No, I know. It's not your fault. Don't apologize."

"But it wasn't yours either. It seemed like I was blaming you, and I know you blamed yourself, but I never wanted you to feel that way."

"You can blame me a little." He sounded aggrieved.

"What good would that do?"

They held each other's gazes. Their fingers shifted against each other.

"Here." Sophie got up, reclaiming her hands. She came around the table and wedged herself onto the bench next to him. "I want to try something." She cupped the sides of his bristly face, smiled as her thumbs swiped his beard, then took a moment to admire his lips. Shapely as ever. She leaned in and kissed them.

For a dark second or two, fire bloomed in the December sky over the farmhouse again, blood ran from bullet holes, painful electric shocks rocketed through her. But she clung to the here and now: the texture of rough facial hair and warm lips, the smell of spruced-up Adrian, the comfort of the arms slipping around her. He still responded delicately, the gentlest of kisses, no plunging tongues or ravishing clutches. And as she waited it out and focused on him, the embrace began to feel lovely again, the way it had almost every time, every lifetime. The exquisite moments far outnumbered the horrific ones, if you tallied them up.

Blood, smoke, and screams faded and blew away, making room again for passion and love.

They pulled apart a few inches and examined one another. Adrian's eyebrows lifted in subtle query.

Sophie beamed. "All good." She leaned in again, then paused. "That is—if you still want me, after how I pushed you away—"

He huffed out a laugh, tugged her closer, and commenced the ravishing variety of kissing. Wrapped in his arms, she shifted up onto his lap. He slid a hand around her leg to secure her there, with a rakish squeeze. Then he buried his face against her neck and just held her, breathing. "I've. Missed. You." He separated the words, making each resound.

In picturing this reunion in past weeks, she had thought she'd be weeping by now. Instead a smile split her face. She felt like she was made of spring sunshine. She cradled him, swaying back and forth. "I've missed you too. Tons."

He lifted his face again. She allowed a moment to drink in the beauty of his dark eyes, then sank both hands into his hair and plunged back into a kiss.

The oven timer interrupted them with its beep a few minutes later.

Sophie broke her mouth away and caught her breath. "Ah. Calzone's done."

"Oh. Right." He looked flushed and dazed. Just how she liked him.

She slid her hand over his hip, where shirt gave way to jeans. "How about I turn it off and let it stay warm a little longer?"

He nodded. "Good plan."

She hopped up and switched off the oven. She cracked it open to peek inside, and was met with a blast of hot dough-and-sausage-scented air. "Nice and golden." She shut the door. "It'll be fine."

A hand sliding down her rear told her Adrian had gotten up and followed her. She grinned, turned, and let him pin her against the counter for another long bout of pashing.

"Hang on." She slipped aside. She opened the trailer's door, poked her head out, and spotted Tab sitting on the ground, reading her phone. "Hey, Tab."

Tab looked up. "Hey."

"You can go if you want. Adrian's here, so he's…got me covered." She glanced back. Adrian was peeking over her shoulder, and waved at Tab.

Tab's smile turned sly. "Well, sweet. Rock on." She jumped up. "'Kay, then I'm out. Text me later, homies." She saluted with her phone and sauntered off to her spirit horse.

Sophie closed the door and turned back into Adrian's waiting embrace. "Guess what gossip's going to be all over the Underworld in ten minutes," she said.

"Hmm." His hands, flexing against her hips, sent a long-missed liquid heat through her. "I expect we'll have to endure some innuendoes and waggly eyebrows when we next see everyone."

"I can deal. Speaking of which, check out what Freya gave

me." Sophie drew Adrian to the bed, took a small plastic bag from the shelf, and held it up.

He squinted at the brownish-green capsules. "Um. Drugs? But since you say it was Freya…"

She flapped the bag against his shoulder. "Not drugs, you dork. Cloudhair seeds. She says using them in combination with these, which you already had, we'll be all taken care of." Sophie pulled down the box of condoms too, and gave him a level gaze.

He winced, and took the box. "Right. Forgot I had those. Look, I got them for you, no one else—"

"I know."

"And it was before I even properly met you, which is horrible and presumptuous, I know, but I suppose I wanted to be prepared, in case things—in case you wanted—well, I didn't know what you'd want, but—"

"Shush." She wrapped her fingers around his wrist. "I do want. Let's do this."

Amazement danced all over his face, temptation looking likely to topple that last flicker of caution in his eyes. "Today, now? Really?"

"I love you. I've loved doing this with you every lifetime I can remember. Besides, come on, it's Valentine's Day. We have to."

He grinned and stepped forward, leaning on her so she fell back on the bed. He climbed on top of her. "You didn't say 'Valentine's Day' in your text. You said 'the fourteenth.' I bloody agonized over that."

"Aw." She slid her hands down his body. "Let me make it up to you."

SOPHIE WAS WILLING—ADRIAN COULD SEE THAT IN THE DE-termination with which she unbuttoned his shirt and jeans—

but from countless numbers of past experiences with her, he knew she could be more passionate.

He'd rather work her up to that first.

"No rush, slow down," he said, his lips against her jaw. He gently caught her hands and stopped her from pulling his shirt off. He left it hanging open, and kept his jeans on, just their top button undone. He settled down on top of her. "You're beautiful." He caressed her hips. "And I've missed this. I want us to enjoy it."

She smiled. Her body relaxed beneath him, and she tucked her arms inside his open shirt to slide her hands up the skin of his back. "I always do enjoy it with you. Every lifetime I can remember."

"So many lives. So many trysts." He shifted to kiss her throat, enjoying the softness of her sweater against his bare chest. "So many...positions."

Her laughter was soon swallowed up in his mouth as he kissed her again. He spun out several luscious minutes that way, the contact warming him through and through as she caressed his back. Adrian's hands crept up inside her sweater too, to savor the soft skin of her belly, the curve out into her hips.

She was breathing faster now, more responsive to every squeeze of his hand or swirl of his tongue. He peeled the sweater up until uncovering her lace-edged pink bra. Behind her back his fingers found the bra's hook and unfastened it with a pinch. He pushed the bra up out of the way, gathered her breasts in both hands, and drew a gasp from Sophie when sealed his mouth around one nipple. Feeling it harden against his tongue, he grew harder too, and let himself press more firmly against her.

"My sweet lover," she murmured, and he realized after a moment that she'd said it in German. An echo of what she had called him in the lifetime before this one.

"Sometimes, all I can think about is touching you." He

said it in German too. Another echo of something he had said decades ago, under another name, in another country. Adrian stripped the sweater off her. She unstrung the bra from her arms and dropped it on the floor. He wriggled out of his shirt and wrapped his arms around her, his face to her neck, their bare flesh pressed together from waist to shoulders. They melted against one another; he felt safe and complete, even as his body ached for more.

"I love your skin against me." Now she said it in Hindi— from the life before the German one.

"You feel like silk." He answered in Chinese, from the lifetime before that. "Like fire made flesh."

They were writhing slowly against each other, and soon she rolled him over so she was on top. Her hair was coming unpinned, getting gorgeously disarrayed in its curls. "I'm going to get my languages mixed up soon here," she said in the Underworld tongue. "You're being very distracting."

"That's my intention," he said in the same language. Then he bit his lower lip as he watched her sit up and, with her eyes upon him, slowly unfasten her jeans and ease out of them. That heat in her eyes now—there, that was more like it.

She traced a finger down the front of his jeans, making him twitch in response. "Zippers are so uncomfortable sometimes, don't you think?" she said, in English again.

"Mm," he agreed. Or rather, half agreed, half groaned.

She unzipped them. A moment later, Adrian shoved his jeans into the pile of clothes on the floor. With only her white bikini underwear and his boxers between them, they tangled into an embrace, kissing with tongues, wrapping their legs around one another. He rolled her again to pin her beneath him, moving against her the way he wanted. That occupied them for several delicious minutes; then she shifted down beside him so she could haul the boxers off him and dip her hand between his legs.

With a moan, he did the same to her, tugging the bikini

to her mid-thighs and slipping his fingers between the slick folds of her flesh. "How is it," he breathed, "that I never get tired of this, after thousands of years?"

She suckled his lower lip, synchronizing the movement with the strokes of her hand. "Wanting each other is part of being alive. And I'm not tired of being alive. Are you?"

"Never."

She helped roll a condom onto him. He lay on his back, letting her take the lead. But she lay down next to him and pulled at his arm to draw him onto her. "Let's be traditional about this." She smiled and took hold of his hips, her hands hot against him. "Besides, I like how you feel on top of me."

"Oh, Goddess," he managed. And he had a few seconds in which to congratulate himself on getting her to the wanton state he had desired, a few more seconds to feel ecstatically in love with her. Then her hand and body were guiding him in, and he was encased in her, and the world became whole again for the first time in so, so long.

She was tense and tight in his arms, and he held still a moment. "Is that all right?" he asked, worried.

She took a few breaths, and he felt her ease up again. She nodded, hooking a leg around his. "Very. Keep going." She lifted her hips. "Please."

He kept to a slow pace. As slow as he could, which increasingly was not so slow, because she was encouraging him with the sounds she was making, the way she was stroking his back, sucking his tongue. She shattered into quivers before long, and Adrian tumbled after her. A pillow fell off the bed, along with a bobby pin or two from Sophie's hair.

When they finally eased to a halt, he slid off her and cradled her against him.

Joy washed through every bit of his flesh. Like a raft reaching shore, he found himself delivered with happy humility back to the present. This lifetime was just as epic as any of the others and deserved some kudos too. It might even turn out to be the best yet.

"Hey," he said. "I'm Kiwi Ade. I comment on your blog sometimes. I'm going to be in your area, do you want to get together for coffee or something?"

She hugged him closer. "Sure. Sounds fun. I'm looking forward to meeting you."

He nuzzled one of her stray curls. "I love you. Have I said that?"

"Technically no. But it goes without saying." She kissed his shoulder. "I love you, too. That was…" She sighed blissfully. "So good."

"Beyond good. I'll have to dig into those other languages for another way to say 'fabulous.'"

"Sweet as?" she suggested.

"Definitely sweet as."

"We've done this in so many lives, it almost didn't feel like it was the 'first time,' you know?"

"Hmm. So is someone not a virgin if they've eaten the pomegranate and have had sex in previous lives? Interesting question."

"That would mean Niko's shagged, like, half the souls in the world," Sophie said. "If we're counting everyone, ever."

"Uh-huh. Including Zoe."

Sophie propped herself up on her elbow. "Yes! Hekate and Hermes. Zoe said something, but I didn't know if it was just like one time, or…?"

Adrian shook his head, grinning. "I asked Freya, since Aphrodite was around at the time for that kind of gossip. She said—" He lapsed into an imitation of Freya's Swedish accent. "'Oh my God, so much sex. For years and years.'"

Sophie gasped in scandalized delight. "No wonder Zoe and Niko have been so weird around each other! Have you noticed?"

"Oh, for sure. The awkwardness, it burns."

"How can we use this to tease them? I mean, we have to."

"I'm sure the right moment will present itself."

Sophie settled down on his chest. "Unless," she said, "Thanatos gets us first."

"Don't even say that."

"That's partly why I wanted to do this, though. Because if anything happens to either of us, I would regret not having done it."

He stroked her bare back. "I'm telling you, this time we won't, we can't, let it happen. You said it yourself: we're all so much smarter now. Hey, we have a ghost army. We're going to end this cult. The whole bloody thing."

"I hope so." She sounded grave, but not scared. It gave him strength.

But it didn't quell the fear that had taken up residence in his own heart, and burned there every day like a cinder he couldn't reach. He could never control everything. Possibly no one controlled everything, not even the Fates or the Goddess or whoever. And when you lived in the Underworld, wielding slightly-limited immortality, someone was always going to want to kill you. Always. You could hide and cower, or you could push back.

He intended to push back. But it didn't mean he wasn't afraid.

CHAPTER FORTY-NINE

HEKATE WAS ABLE TO KEEP THE WORST OF THE PREGNANCY nausea at bay with magic, but it took constant vigilance. The effort taxed her, and she walked about feeling as if she were doing everything at one-fifth the usual speed.

Hermes noticed, of course. He dropped in for a visit a few days after the symptoms had set in, and frowned at her. "Are you all right?"

"Oh, it's just—this war. I'm exhausted, running about trying to decide what's to be done. Worrying."

He nodded solemnly. Anatolia had been raiding Greek cities and settlements again around the Aegean coast with larger forces than ever. Thanatos appeared to be mixed up in it somehow, influencing the might of the invading armies to target and destroy immortals who were helping defend Greece. No immortals had died yet in the latest month of fighting, but there'd been a couple of near misses. Artemis and Poseidon had both barely escaped from armed mobs in time. It was enough to put dark smudges of worry under the eyes of any immortal, so Hermes accepted Hekate's story for now.

But during the next few visits, each six or seven days apart, he studied her more shrewdly and his questions retreated into what she recognized as his place of silent calculation. Only a matter of time, she thought with weary acceptance.

Finally one day, he embraced her as usual upon arriving in the Underworld, then held her at arm's length, and swept a look from her swelling belly and hips to her breasts, now twice as large as they'd ever been, and finally up to her face. "You're pregnant." No teasing now. Through his touch she felt alarm, grimness, maybe anger.

She nodded, letting her gaze slip down. "You were right. It's already absurdly exhausting."

He let go of her, pivoted, and stalked over to the cold hearth. She detested the smell of smoke lately, and hadn't lit a fire in days. He stared at the hearth with arms folded. "Well. On purpose, then, I assume? You were always so careful before. And you lately did state your interest."

His aloofness made her want to weep, but then lots of stupid things did lately. She turned the emotion to anger, to match his, if he wanted to be this way. "And you stated your lack of interest. That's fine. I still plan to go it alone, as I do with most of life."

He kept his back to her. "Indeed. You got what you needed from me. Or was it even me?"

Her fury boiled over. Without lifting a finger, she made a sandal rise from the floor and fly across the room to smack against his back.

He jumped and spun around, outrage on his face.

"Yes, it's yours," she said. "Another month or so, and you'd be able to sense that yourself. But I forgot, you have no patience whatsoever."

Hermes kept his arms folded, and furrowed his brow as he looked her up and down again. "You're mad. I mean, you're actually acting completely unlike yourself."

"It isn't fair! You say you love me, but women you've barely loved at all have borne your children, and I haven't. Why shouldn't I?"

He blinked and gave his head a rapid shake. "You see,

mad. There's no connection between one of your statements and the next."

She stamped her foot. "Yes there is! I do this out of love. For you and for this child. All I ask is that you treat me with kindness, not this—this contempt."

He walked back to her, his hands shifting to settle on his hips. "And you say you love *me*, but you disregard my wishes and outright lie to me."

"Oh, I'm sorry. Only you were allowed to lie in this world, Lord Divine Trickster?"

His eyes grew colder, though she thought she detected hurt and fear in their centers. A touch on his skin would tell her. But she wouldn't stoop to stealing a glimpse in that manner, not now. "I wish you well, love," he said. "I always have. I wish you *both* well." His gaze touched her belly for a moment. "But don't come find me again until you've decided you're done being insane."

He turned, cloak flaring, and stalked out.

Zoe stormed up to Niko, who was sitting outside Landon's cell, playing some bloody game on his phone while Landon behind the bars was playing one on some other phone. Niko looked up at her with a calm smile. She kicked his leg.

"Ow!"

"I was pregnant with your child, and you left me?" she shouted.

Landon looked up, round-eyed.

"Not this life," she snapped at him. "Ancient times. Mind your own business."

Landon obediently turned his attention back to the phone.

"Well, you could at least keep going with the memories." Niko rubbed his bruised leg. "See how it turns out."

"That doesn't change that you called me insane and walked out. Of course I was insane! Hormones, you idiot!"

Niko got to his feet, and slipped his phone into his pocket. "We didn't know about hormones back then. Science was not exactly a thing yet."

"Assholery was apparently fully a thing."

"Steady on." He laid his hands on her shoulders. "You did get pregnant intentionally, using me as a sperm donor after I'd specifically said I didn't think we should. If some woman other than you did that to me, what would you think?"

She shook his hands off her. "I'd think—well yeah, I'd think she was mental, but I'd also tell you to go over there and massage her bloody feet!"

Niko exchanged a glance with Landon, who was wisely staying silent, then lifted his eyebrows at Zoe. "Would you like me to massage your feet?"

"No! I'm not pregnant!"

Niko glanced again at Landon. "Excuse us a minute." He slipped his arm around Zoe and led her down the path between stalagmites and columns, far enough to be out of earshot of Landon but still able to see him.

"What's this, we're giving video games to the prisoners now?" Zoe said.

"Well, it's that or listen to him angst about things."

"Ugh. You're just—you're—"

"Okay." He stopped and leaned against a column, hugging her against his side. "By modern standards, I acted like an asshole. In fact, by modern standards I often still do."

"Too right."

"But you know what? I'm flattered you care this much."

"Bite me." But the touch of his body told her he really was flattered. The affection coming off him took the edge off her fury. So she stayed, sulking, under his arm.

"Here," he said. "Right here and now, go skimming those memories further ahead."

"Why? So I can see some amazing moment in which you're not a douchebag?"

"That, and because I want to be here when you meet our son."

Zoe's knees wobbled as the full force of that idea finally hit her. She clutched the side of his coat for balance. "Oh," she said. "Golly."

HEKATE SENSED THE DIRECTION IN WHICH HERMES LAY, of course, if she left the Underworld and cleared the oak forest. But she refused to go see him. There was no point until this poisonous mix of anger, hurt, and guilt sorted itself out and pointed her to the right thing to say. Which, of course, would depend on what *he* had to say.

One day in the fourth month of her pregnancy, after working down a decent lunch of fruit and fish, she flopped onto the bed and let her weariness knock her into a nap. Wading out of sleep some time later, she assumed she was dreaming the sweetly strong sense of Hermes beside her. She opened her heavy eyelids, tried to roll from her side to her back, and met resistance to her movement. He was lying behind her, his arm latched over her.

She turned to gaze at him. He blinked slowly, as if he'd been napping too.

"You're back," she said, her voice husky with sleep.

"Yes." He settled his hand low on her belly. "I sense the little one now." Solemn love streamed from his touch and his voice.

Hekate's heart released its bitter constraints; tenderness washed over her and soothed her. "Me too. I've been able to feel him, or her, moving for a few days now."

Hermes resettled onto his back, drawing Hekate up against him with one arm. "I went to see Pan. Hadn't seen him in a while."

"Oh. How is he?"

"He's well. He reminds me of you, you know. The reason we rarely see him is he's always out in the wilderness investigating the forces of nature. He can't manipulate them quite like you can, but he senses them better than most."

"Yes. I've noticed that about him." She decided to humor him, see where he was headed with this discussion, before cornering him into exchanging proper words of reconciliation.

"Lately he's concerned about the volcano on Thera," Hermes continued. "The citizens of the island are concerned too. It's been rumbling and belching."

"Those earthquakes we've been feeling. I think they come from that direction."

"I wouldn't doubt it. Pan's studying the volcano, as close as he can get without the lava incinerating him." Hermes chuckled. "Crazy man."

"Well, *that* he gets from his father."

Hermes caressed her arm, gazing up at the dark ceiling. "I'm proud of him. I'm proud of all my children. I know I'll be proud of this one too. Especially because it's yours."

She wrapped her arm across his chest and burrowed in closer. "Thank you for coming back. I know I handled it wrong, underhandedly. Not telling you."

"That's no more than I would have done. The trouble was…" He sighed. "I liked what we had, and you changed it." He turned his face so his lips rested against her hair. "But what's done is done. I can adapt. It's just, now I have more to worry about. I hate worrying."

"I understand. I do."

"How is the tree?" he asked.

"Still not producing. And I still can't tell if the smaller trees will be of any use."

"More worries."

They reclined in their embrace a while, until an earthquake jolted through the cave. Hermes clutched her close, and Hekate cast a protective spell around them—including Kerberos within it, who had jumped onto the bed to stand and bark. Bits of rock clattered to the floor; bronze goblets clinked against one another and fell over. In a few breaths the shaking died away, and the Earth lay still again.

"Whew. Speaking of those," Hermes said.

"More and more frequent. I don't like it."

"They're in both realms at once?"

"Yes. Earthquakes always are. They're connected to some deep part of the Earth that both realms have in common, is how it feels to me."

"Don't suppose you can settle them down with your powers," Hermes said.

"No, that's far beyond me. And don't tell Rhea or Ariadne, but I don't think sacrificing people on Crete stops them either."

He chuckled, sounding relaxed. Even through his skin, she felt the brief spike of tension over the earthquake slipping away, far faster than it did for her or most people. He did indeed adapt well.

"Will you keep coming every so often to see me, just as you did before?" she asked. "That's all I wish, really. I liked what we had, too."

"Of course." He slipped a hand under her tunic and played with her breasts, which had grown stupendously heavy lately. "Maybe even a tiny bit more often than usual."

True to his word, he kept visiting her over the months, despite the rest of her becoming heavier and less agile too. His good humor made her laugh, which kept her spirits above water when the rest of life—the pregnancy, the ailing chrysomelia tree, the battles, the earthquakes—threatened to drown her. It was Hermes who dashed out to fetch her appointed midwives, Rhea, Amphitrite, and Galateia, when her labor pains began after the ninth moon.

And it was Hermes who lay beside her afterward in the middle of the night, there on that same bed, and watched in pleased interest as she coaxed their newborn son to catch her nipple in his mouth and suck down some milk.

"I've never actually stayed through that whole process, you know," he remarked.

"You didn't faint. Congratulations."

"You forget how much blood I've endured on other occasions. This wasn't *quite* so much in comparison."

She thought of the night she'd been kidnapped by Thanatos, and remembered with a shudder the sight of Hermes and Dionysos fighting the intruders while blades hacked at them and blood soaked their clothes. "Sorry. No, of course."

"But Ares would have fainted." Hermes sounded fully unoffended and confident. "I'm certain of that."

Hekate laughed. "Agreed." She stroked her knuckle against the fine brown fuzz on the baby's head. "I've decided on his name. Eleusis."

"Ah, after the town?"

"The temple, yes. Where my magic came back to me."

"And where a few other things happened after that." He managed to sound ribald even at such a moment, which made her laugh again. "Eleusis," he said. "Perfect."

CHAPTER FIFTY

H, GOLLY," ZOE SAID AGAIN. SHE AND NIKO HAD SLID DOWN to sit against the bumpy stone column. His arm was still around her, and now she leaned her head on his chest and laughed in giddiness. "He was beautiful."

"And I'll tell you now, we had every reason to be proud of him. But…"

Dread clutched Zoe's heart. She looked up. "What? What happened to him?" She could have torn through her own memories to find it, but that would take longer, and suddenly she cared too much to bear any delay. Strange—technically she'd heard about Hekate having a child, secondhand from Adrian a long time ago, and it hadn't occupied her mind much at all until now. She'd assumed it was farther ahead in Hekate's future, some distant event. But here it was, all at once vitally important.

"Nothing happened to *him*, really," Niko said. "He was all right. But since we're here…keep going in the memories. It's just a little further now."

He sounded quiet and grim, almost the way he'd sounded a few weeks ago when the topic of his killing Quentin came up. Zoe went so cold with fear that she felt nauseated. But it was all long ago and done, she reminded herself. It was best to know.

She curled up tighter beside Niko, and remembered.

ANOTHER EARTHQUAKE THUNDERED THROUGH THE UNDER-world one day when Eleusis was just shy of a year old. He'd been crawling through the pale grass after some spirit cats, but the jolting ground dropped him onto his chin and set him wailing. Hekate scooped him up and knelt with him in her arms, keeping her balance as best she could while the earth rumbled and shook. This quake lasted longer than any of the others lately, and by the time it settled down she was trembling with alarm.

She turned toward the river, knowing there'd be casualties streaming in after such a tremor, and her heart already ached for all the mourning families around the region.

A fresh cluster of souls did soon arrive, and she walked to them and began collecting accounts of the earthquake. But some, from Thera or within sight of it, also reported the volcano was erupting.

Before long Hermes dashed in. He stayed down here more often than not lately, to help with Eleusis, but still spent a fair amount of time dashing about in the upper world to collect news. Their year together hadn't been perfect, of course—like any couple with a new baby (who, as expected, was mortal), they were stressed and tired, and argued often. But on the whole he'd been a more present father than Hekate had ever imagined he'd be, and he had retained his sanity-saving ability to make her and the baby laugh.

"You've heard about the volcano?" he said as he jogged up to her.

She nodded, and surrendered Eleusis to him as the baby reached out for his father.

Hermes took him. "Yes, little man. Giant clouds of gray smoke, and lightning, billowing up into the whole sky." He gave the words a happy tilt, as if telling a pleasant story, but

357

he looked at Hekate with serious eyes. "Everyone's trying to get off the island. I'm not sure they'll be fast enough."

She swallowed. "I've told you, against a volcano there isn't anything I can do. I can cast safety spells, but among so many people it won't do much good."

"I know." He kissed Eleusis on the hand as the baby grabbed for his nose. "This isn't a case for magic, most likely. But it is a case for as many of us herding people into boats as we can, and rowing as fast as super-humanly possible."

"Let me come. I can leave Eleusis with Galateia and Akis, and do some good up close if I can. Make the winds push our boats out of the way, or—"

"Don't you dare." He kissed the baby and handed him back to Hekate. "You two stay right here, where you're safest. Promise me. I mean it."

Though she shook with fear, and what she hoped fervently was not premonition, she nodded, holding their son close. "Be careful," she entreated. "So careful. Please."

"Better yet, I'll be fast." He kissed her on the lips. "See you soon."

Out he dashed.

Hekate paced the fields, trying to play with Eleusis or sing songs to him. But the next earthquake, more violent than the last, dropped her to her hands and knees. After it settled, she wrapped Eleusis against her back, stalked out of the fields, and mounted her spirit horse.

A short flight up brought them to the top of the seaside hill, and she gasped. The sky was filling with black clouds, as Hermes had reported, with evil-looking lightning flashing within their folds. Thera was out east in the middle of the Mediterranean, almost as far away as Crete, but the size and force of the rising ash clouds made it look like it was just a valley or two away.

She watched a long while, heart in her throat. The sky darkened—from ash, not sunset. Beneath her, in the forces of the Earth, she felt a terrible deep tension, a power quivering and about to burst.

Please keep them safe, she begged, sending the spell out through every thread of energy she could touch. But that Earth power gathering below: that, she knew, she could not harness or shift, any more than she could have cleared the ash from the sky by flapping a fan at it.

The tension suddenly mounted, becoming an unbearable shriek in her eardrums. Cringing, she leaped back onto the spirit horse with Eleusis, and let him carry them at full speed back into the cave.

Her feet had just touched the ground in the entrance chamber when the explosion rocked the world. The bang throbbed through her head, knocked her to the floor, and set Eleusis howling. She curled up with him beneath her body, covering his ears and shushing him, wrapping a protective shield of magic around the two of them, while the ground heaved and thundered. Stalactites snapped off and smashed onto the floor. Through her ringing ears, she heard Kerberos barking frantically, and soon he skidded across the jolting ground and huddled against Hekate and Eleusis, inside their protective bubble.

The roar rolled past after a long, long reign, and she finally dared lift her head. Total darkness loomed in the bit of sky visible through the cave mouth, and a rain of ash sifted down through the opening.

The souls streamed in thick—so many new dead, oh, too many.

The earth was still rumbling, but Hekate sank back on her knees and gazed up at the end of the world. The aftershocks gradually died away, her hopes dying with them. The influx of souls came and came, and soon brought the ones she had dreaded.

Hermes settled his luminescent, immaterial feet on the

rock-scattered floor, and knelt before her. Behind him, like birds folding their wings, arrived others she knew.

Aphrodite. Dionysos. Ariadne. Pan. Apollo. Artemis. Athena. And more. Oh, Goddess, almost everyone.

She looked into Hermes' sad, sympathetic eyes. "How?" she whispered.

"We weren't fast enough." His mouth formed a small smile. "Would you believe, we actually got everyone off the island and into the boats. But when the volcano blew, it took out everything and everyone for a wide swath all around. Obviously." He looked back at the thick flow of arriving souls.

"Even immortals." Hekate's mouth was dry and gritty with dust. She couldn't even weep yet; she was too shocked. Her gaze lifted to travel across all her freshly dead friends, who regarded her with tenderness.

"Now I'll be staying with you every day, not just occasionally," Hermes said, sounding almost lighthearted. Almost. "And I will stay, at least until he's grown." He ran his intangible hand through Eleusis' arm. The baby had stopped wailing and was gazing at his father's soul with a confused frown. "I know it's cold comfort, but I do want to be near you both a while longer."

"Lots of us will stay and help," Dionysos said. "As much as we can."

"Our company is surely worth something, at least," Aphrodite said, with the same beguiling smile that had dazzled thousands when she'd been alive.

Hekate nodded. Then with one arm around her dog and the other holding her child, she bowed her head and let her tears fall.

ZOE KEPT HER EYES SQUEEZED SHUT, AND SNIFFLED. HEY, SHE wasn't actually sobbing, so that was a victory. Just, you know, some mistiness here, bit of a lump in the throat.

"Goddess," she squeaked. "That fucking blows."

Niko chuckled. "Nice choice of words."

"You can laugh about it?"

He gave her a squeeze. "Like I said, I'm thrilled you care this much. And look. Look, look." He gently shook her.

She dabbed her jacket sleeve against her eyes. "What."

"Life," he announced. "The twenty-first century. Us, alive again, and better yet, immortal. So chin up."

"Suppose." She sniffled again, and straightened her back so she wasn't slumped against him like a weakling. "Thera, that's what, Santorini now?"

"Yep. Now crescent-shaped because of the volcano blasting out the middle of it."

She considered that sweet brown-haired baby, and let her memories unspool further: he became a talking three-year-old, a cleverly rhyming five-year-old, a gawky but patient eight-year-old. Probably more, if she had the energy to think about it, which she did not right now.

"Who's Eleusis today?" she asked.

He took out his phone, tapped a few things, and handed it to her with a photo on the screen: a young man, maybe thirty-ish, his kind features looking at least part Asian, one shoulder swathed in the orange robes of a Buddhist monk.

"Wow," she said. "I'm guessing he's doing something good with his life."

"Quite. He's one of the youngest Buddhist leaders in Thailand. He's also…" Niko scratched his ear, avoiding Zoe's gaze. "My son."

"In *this* life? You have kids in this life?"

"I know, right? How could a child of mine have ended up choosing celibacy?"

"How many? How many children do you have?"

He let his hand drop, and met her eyes. "Three. With three different mothers, in three different countries. All are grown up now, and I've had very little to do with any of their lives.

But I do check up on them regularly, and though I'm sure they despise me for being such a deadbeat dad, I'm deeply proud of each of them."

Zoe swallowed, and regarded the photo of the monk, whose eyes did indeed carry some of the slyness of Niko's. "Okay. I've officially hit overload. Too many emotions for one day." She handed him back his phone, then scowled at him. "You made me remember your death just to turn me as soft on you as possible, didn't you?"

"Can you blame me? How often will I get to play that card?"

She smiled, and bowed her head so her temple brushed his shoulder again. "Ah, mate. My soul loves yours. It does. But this lifetime, my body won't get on board. I've tried, and it refuses. I don't suppose we can just be platonic together?"

"I've had platonic relationships. I'm capable of it, believe it or not. But with you…" He caressed her knee. "I do tend to want more, I admit. Besides, would that arrangement really make *you* happy?"

She considered a biromantic, unsexual future, and her heart admitted defeat. She looked at him with her lips twisted in a grimace in answer.

"That's what I thought," he said. He touched his nose to her cheek. "Don't fret. Sexuality can be fluid, as they say these days. Maybe your body will change its mind someday."

"You wish."

"I do wish."

At that moment both their phones buzzed with a new message. Part of the extra wiring lately added to the Underworld included signal repeaters so they could stay online inside the cave—important for security these days. She grabbed hers out of her pocket and looked at it, fearing some all-points-bulletin of disaster.

But it was from Adrian, sent to her and Niko. *Could one*

of you please track Mars tonight? I want to stay with Sophie. P.S. Turns out she did mean "Valentine's Day." :)

Niko chuckled, reading the same message on his own phone. "I knew it."

"Yep, that cinches that. Tab texted me about it earlier. See?" She navigated to Tab's text, and showed Niko.

Soph and Ade just sent me away so they could have private time. Aw yeah, the good ship Hades/Persephone sails again!

Niko laughed. "You didn't tell me that."

"I was a bit wrapped up in the memories. That seemed more important at the time. Besides, who's surprised they got back together, honestly?"

"Well, no one." Niko tapped at his text messages. "Shall we stake out Thanatos together tonight?"

"Weirdest and least fun date ever. Let's do it."

CHAPTER FIFTY-ONE

THE VOLCANO'S ERUPTION THREW ALL THE LANDS AROUND the Mediterranean into disaster. Ash fell from the skies for days, suffocating crops and polluting the water in streams and wells until most of it was undrinkable. The explosion had not only killed everyone in the boats around Thera; it had also caused a giant wave to rush ashore on Crete, where it had toppled buildings and drowned hundreds.

"Does the Goddess despise us?" Hekate asked her friends as she huddled under an Underworld tree, nursing Eleusis.

Rhea had survived, having been farther north when the eruption took place, and she had come to see Hekate today. The souls of Ariadne, Dionysos, and Hermes sat around her too, in a disconsolate circle. Several other immortals still lived, at least, Poseidon and Amphitrite among them. Also apparently Ares, who at least wasn't down here right now.

Hekate had rushed up to check on Galateia and Akis the first day, but they and their baby were all right; just frightened, like everyone, and busy putting their disarrayed village back in order.

"Volcanoes have always existed, as far as we know," Rhea said. "Does the Goddess use them to punish us? Or are they just natural forces that act out sometimes? I've never been sure, but I feel it's the latter. At least, I hope so."

"It's interesting that Crete suffered in this event," Ariadne said, "not long after Thanatos took over. Perhaps the Goddess was trying to do some good that way."

"But at the cost of all this?" Hekate waved her hand at her dead friends, and widened the gesture to include the fields of souls, where the volcano had sent so many innocent folk. "And why must the chrysomelia trees be ailing at the same time? I must be doing something terribly wrong to be punished like this."

"It isn't only you who's being punished," Hermes pointed out. "Nor are you responsible for everything that happens in the world. That said, love, there's much you could do to help up there. You know they need it."

She looked at his ethereal face, though tears still filled her eyes every time she did so. She nodded. "You're right. I'll go up today."

Rhea squeezed her knee. "I'll come with you."

Hekate strapped Eleusis to her back with a length of cloth, and went out with Rhea into the devastated world. They visited villages and performed grim but helpful work: setting broken bones and treating injuries, dragging collapsed walls and roofs out of the way, and, in Hekate's case, using magic to separate grit from clean water and to blow away the fallen ash from vegetable gardens. But the latter didn't do much good, as most of the plants had been crushed and killed. Food was going to be an issue for the coming year or more. Widespread famine, with disease surely on its heels—what next?

One man was too badly injured to save. His house had collapsed and crushed his body from the navel down. He was growing old and lived alone, and his neighbors had pulled him out of the rubble, but Hekate could tell at a glance—and confirmed by a touch—that he wouldn't last long. She began taking out some of the dried red violets from the Underworld for him, but he clutched her cloak.

"Please," he said. "Finish me off quickly. I beg you."

"I—I can numb your pain with these," she said.

But he shook his head. "I want it to be over. You can do it fast, I know you can."

He must have heard of her magic, though she wasn't in the habit of using it to kill anyone, even out of mercy. Hoping for guidance, she looked at the neighbors who stood nearby, a man and woman. The woman shrugged in helplessness, and the man gave her a grave nod. Rhea, standing near, added a nod too. Easy for her to endorse. She'd sacrificed healthy people back in her priestess days.

Hekate laid her trembling hand on the patient's chest, not even sure how to do what he asked. Stop his heart? His breath? Wouldn't both of those cause at least some suffering? She probed his ebbing life energy, then sensed something she'd rarely dared look for in anyone: the winding line, like a long seam, where his soul connected to his body. Perhaps in him it was easier to detect because he was so close to death already, and the seam was starting to come apart, like stitches pulling loose.

"Please," the man echoed.

She looked at him. "Are you ready, good sir?" she asked, her voice almost a whisper.

He nodded, gaze fixed on her in fearful gratitude.

Hekate closed her eyes, found the seam, and wrapped her will around the man's soul like she was embracing it. She pulled.

A gasp wracked her lungs. The man shuddered and went limp. His soul streamed away to the other realm; she felt his energy flow past. She withdrew her hand, shaking all over, and looked at the others. Rhea looked composed, but the man and woman stepped back and were making every warding-off-evil gesture they could think of.

"It—it's all right," she told them. "He's...at peace. I wouldn't—I've never—this is the first..."

Rhea gathered them out of the way, gently offering to help with the man's funeral preparations. Hekate shut her mouth and sat stunned. No one would believe she'd never ripped out a person's soul before. She'd done it so efficiently here. It was in theory a useful skill to have—at least against Thanatos or in similar situations—but at the moment it horrified her to know she possessed such an ability.

They returned to the Underworld, Hekate dreading how to tell Hermes and the others about this newfound power. Would they encourage her to use it more? The notion filled her with revulsion.

But when she entered the fields, those ruminations were chased out of her head when she spotted Ares stalking toward her, his usually groomed clothing dusted with ash. Behind him, Aphrodite's soul looked after him in an attitude of concern, hands clasped before her. As Ares approached Hekate and Rhea, she noticed his reddened eyes and nostrils, and realized he'd been weeping. Probably Aphrodite was one of the few people he'd ever loved, and he grieved for her. For a moment Hekate's heart softened toward him.

Then he opened his mouth.

"A lot of good you do us down here," he said. "Where were you when the world could have used your 'powers'? How could you let this happen to so many of our own?"

She tried to sound conciliatory. "Ares, I would have stopped it if I could. My powers are quite limited compared to the Earth itself. I tried, and there was nothing I could do—"

"Bring her back!" He stamped his foot on the grass. "You must have a way!"

"I don't." Despair entered her voice. Yes, she could rip out souls, but reinstalling them was surely a great deal harder. "If I did, don't you think I'd have used it by now? For my parents? For Hermes, for my friends?"

He shook his head, his gaze cutting her up and down, as if deciding she was a complete loss. "And you stand as our representative down here. You control our immortality fruits. How are those, by the way? I suppose they're still failing."

Hekate nodded, letting her gaze fall.

"Then that's it." He sounded cool, almost resolute. "I no longer recognize your authority here. It's time to let someone else take over this realm. Someone who can properly use its powers and restore us to what we were. What we should be."

"Give her time, Ares," Rhea said. "She is doing everything she can, as we all are. And she *is* the one who understands the powers best. There is no one else."

"We won't know until someone else tries." He marched out.

"He's only upset," Rhea assured Hekate. "He'll cool down and see he's making no sense."

Fear stayed coiled inside Hekate, tangled with grief and rage. "Ares isn't known for cooling down and making sense."

"He doesn't even like the Underworld. He won't bother to make good on his threats."

"I think he views us as an enemy country. And what does he do to enemy countries? He attacks and conquers them."

Rhea looked troubled. "Shall I bring down some of the others who could help you, just in case? You can consult with them, if nothing else."

Hekate hesitated, then nodded. "Please. If anyone's willing."

Rhea ended up bringing down Amphitrite and Poseidon that evening, and resolved to go out again the next day to talk to others. Amphitrite and Poseidon had planned to come to the Underworld soon anyway to see their many departed friends. So rather than discussing Ares and his hotheaded words, they spent the evening talking with the souls of Aphrodite, Dionysos, Hermes, and others, including their youngest daughter, whom Thanatos had killed years ago. Their other two girls still lived.

They all shared a meal in the Underworld, then Hekate arranged beds for Amphitrite and Poseidon so they could stay overnight. The next day they had only begun to discuss Ares when all of them paused, in their wander through the cave, and looked toward the entrance. They sensed him. He was returning.

"Shall we go see what he wants?" Rhea asked.

"No, let him find us," Hekate said. But his presence troubled her, especially since he seemed to be lingering out there near the entrance, staying still for some reason. She exchanged another glance with Rhea, Poseidon, Amphitrite, and Hermes' soul. Then she adjusted the cloth that strapped Eleusis to her back, and turned toward the entrance. "On second thought, I don't trust him."

They had been walking far from the river, out into the back reaches of the cave. When they finally crested a hill and got within sight of the river again, all of them sucked in a breath of alarm. Ares, in full gleaming battle armor and with spear in hand, was striding up the slope, having just crossed the river on some makeshift rope bridge he'd thrown across. And with him came soldiers: Hekate estimated twenty of them, all brawny and armored and swinging weapons. A few of them, carrying burning torches, turned and set off down the path toward the orchards. Hekate saw the immediate danger to the trees—especially the chrysomelia. She sent a quick arrow of wind magic at them. It hit its target, and blew out all the flames. The soldiers cursed, stopped on the path, and set about pulling items from pouches—probably flint and pyrite to relight the torches. She'd have to keep an eye on them to see if they succeeded, but in the meantime, Ares and the rest of the aggressors had to be dealt with.

"They must have dropped down a rope ladder to get in," Hermes said. "That's what he was doing out there. Switching his army into this realm and climbing down."

Rage tingled in Hekate's hands, as if her powers were ready to call lightning down upon Ares. "Well. This will be too easy." She unstrapped Eleusis and handed him to Rhea. "Stay here, and keep him safe."

Rhea took the child, but frowned at her. "Hekate—"

"Do it. Please." Hekate looked to Amphitrite and Poseidon. "Are you two ready to use the river as a weapon, if needed?"

They nodded, and walked forward with her. Hermes came along. There was little he could do if it came to a fight, but his presence fortified her.

"All right, Hekate," Ares called as they neared one another. He spoke with his usual cockiness. "You've been repeatedly warned. I'm ousting you. Cede control of the Underworld to me, or we burn all your trees and do our very best at killing anyone here who can yet be killed." He sneered at Hermes, as if taunting him for being dead already.

"Ares, you haven't thought this through," Hermes said. "I know you're looking around at all these pretty dead girls and lusting after them, but, thing is—*you can't touch them.*" He whispered the last words as if confiding a secret to a friend. Hekate smiled in spite of her fear. Good to know Hermes could still make stinging remarks.

Ares only snorted, and returned his gaze to Hekate, tapping the end of his spear against his armored foot. "Ready to pack your possessions? We'll see you out."

Hekate filled her lungs with air to calm herself. "No, Ares. We will see you out. Turn and leave now."

Ares made a hand signal to the men arrayed behind him. As one, they pointed their spears, blades, and bows at Hekate, Poseidon, Amphitrite, and Rhea. "Last chance, girl," Ares said.

Hekate shot the magic at them without moving. It tore the weapons from the hands of the whole army—but this time they didn't fly backward as she intended. They caught against some restraint, and fell back within the men's reach, and each soldier seized hold of them again and aimed them at her with new determination.

As she stared in bewildered dismay, Ares smirked. "Yes, I remembered your little trick. I had the men tie their weapons to themselves in case you acted so predictably. See, Hermes? I do think things through."

"Oh, I really don't think you did," Hermes answered.

On the heels of his last word, Hekate lashed out with a stronger wallop of magic. A sudden windstorm howled through the cave and knocked down five or six of the men. Ares staggered, but stayed upright and charged forward with his spear. His soldiers began unleashing arrows, and ran toward Hekate and the others.

Shockingly fast, the standoff became a melee. Knives and arrows flew; flesh thudded against flesh; people grunted and yelled. In the center of it, with every scrap of power at her disposal, Hekate wheeled from one side to another, knocking down soldiers or breaking their weapons, but too many got up again and kept fighting, and Ares himself had maneuvered past her. Thinking of her son's safety, she spun and used the Underworld's ready Earth magic to lift a boulder and knock him flat with it. Then a spear entered her back, and she screamed and had to tear it out, turn again, and pin down the nearest soldier with it through his meaty calf. Meanwhile, at her side, Poseidon and Amphitrite fought with their immortal strength and whatever confiscated weapons they could lay hold of. If they could get just a bit closer to the river, Hekate knew, the water magic would be within their grasp.

Though bloodied, they were almost there. The soldiers were edged back toward the river, and a moment later, Poseidon and Amphitrite called up a huge wave from its black depths, which crashed down upon the closest three soldiers, dragging them over the bank and into the stream. They shouted for help, struggling to stay afloat in their heavy armor, and the distraction made their companions pause long enough that Hekate, Amphitrite, and Poseidon were able to shove them farther back and wrap the next tendrils of water around them. That took care of all of them, except for the ones with the torches off by the trees, and of course—

"Hekate!" Hermes shouted. "Ares is going after Eleusis!"

Hekate pivoted, and sprinted toward Ares. He had shoved the boulder off himself, and though streaked with dirt and blood, had reached Rhea and Eleusis. The damage he'd done had been swift. Rhea lay writhing in pain on the ground, with Ares' spear in her belly, and Ares held the wailing Eleusis aloft in one hand. He pointed his sharp bronze dagger at the boy's neck. Hekate's heart plummeted. All her powers sizzled and snapped, ready to shoot forth with damage of her own—but how to do so without endangering her baby?

Ares smiled at her. "Ready to surrender?" He poked the knife closer, and Eleusis wailed harder.

"Ares," Poseidon said, behind Hekate. "He's a baby. And mortal. This is the act of a coward. That's not you."

Hekate would have disputed that, but she stayed mute.

"Surrender," Ares answered.

Hekate didn't know if this magic would even work on an immortal. Nor if the Goddess would strip her of her powers again for doing it. She didn't care. She reached out with her mind anyway, because her child's life was worth it, and this was a mother's wrath.

She found the seam where Ares' soul connected to his body, and ripped it apart.

It hauled a great deal of power out of her, much more than she'd needed for the dying man. Weakened, she swayed and fell to her knees. But even through her temporarily blurred vision, she saw Ares collapse to the ground, leaving his soul standing in place, looking shocked. Eleusis fell from the lifeless hand and landed on Rhea's lap. Hekate crawled to him and picked him up. Though he howled louder than ever at all this rough treatment, he seemed unhurt. She sent waves of calming and healing magic through him just in case, though her reserves were awfully low at the moment.

She pulled the spear from Rhea and helped her sit up. Poseidon and Amphitrite knelt by them. Hermes and the other souls who had witnessed the battle gathered closer, all gazing at Ares' soul.

"What have you done?" Ares stared at his own body, face-down on the ground.

"I've removed your soul from your body." Hekate's voice was weak, her throat parched.

"But then—" He stepped backward, and looked at her in terror. "What's pulling me? Is it—"

"Tartaros. Yes. I'm sorry, Ares."

"Put me back," he begged. "You were able to take me out, now put me back!" He fell back another step, though he visibly fought it.

Hekate considered. She picked up a scrap of willow-and-ivy rope lying on the ground, and tossed one end to him. He caught it, and his hands stuck to it. She pulled him forward, and climbed to her feet weakly, cradling Eleusis to her chest. "I don't know if I can," she said. "I've never tried, nor have I taken the soul from anyone but you, and one dying man."

"Try. Please. I'll do anything. I don't want to go to that place."

"Anything? Including never attacking us again?"

"Yes," he agreed at once.

"And never attacking anyone else again either? No matter the circumstances?"

"Yes, I promise."

"You must spend the rest of your life doing good deeds, the best you possibly can. Then *maybe* Tartaros won't pull you down for so long when you do die. Maybe you'll even get out of it, if you work hard enough."

"I swear. I will."

"I'll hold you to that vow," she warned. "You know now what I can do if you break it."

He nodded at once.

"Then…" She drew in her breath. "I'll try. Here. Lie down into your body again."

He obeyed, lying on his front so his soul's form fitted into his body's. He still glowed around the edges, and when Hekate knelt to touch him, she found soul and body were indeed still two separate entities. It wasn't as simple as placing them near one another, evidently. It would take magic again.

"Hold still." She shut her eyes and concentrated. She rebuilt the seam, stitching it up all the way from his head to his toes. As she did so, she suspected that this would only work in the rare case where the body was still sound. Putting a soul back into a deeply diseased or injured body would surely be a lost cause. But this, perhaps...

His body jolted. He turned his head and sucked in a breath. The glow faded as his soul sank deep into him again.

Everyone watching drew back.

Ares pushed himself up to his knees and sat breathing raggedly. Wincing, hand splayed on his chest, he looked at Hekate. "I feel weak. Different."

"Well, you were just dead."

"But I...am I still immortal?"

She reached forward again and laid her hand on his shoulder to read his vital energies. Sobered by what she found, she let her hand drop and shook her head. "It seems severing the connection makes you mortal if you do come back to life. I'm sorry. I didn't know."

"Then—" With terror in his eyes, he looked toward the orchards.

Everyone else looked too, and Hekate hissed her breath inward. An orange glow of fire came from one side of the gardens—the side where the chrysomelia trees grew.

She found her strength and ran in that direction. Her friends came with her, and Ares followed, though he fell far behind, winded and weak in a way he'd never felt before.

The immortals caught up to the three soldiers who had set fire to the trees, and flung them all into the river, then used all the water magic within reach to douse the roaring flames. But when the fires died, Hekate's whole body drooped in sorrow.

"They're gone, aren't they," Hermes said quietly.

"Yes," she said.

Ares had caught up, and stared in horror from them to the smoking remains of the trees. "They—they got the right trees?"

"Yes." She nodded to the burned pomegranates and willows surrounding them. "Some others too. But all of the immortality fruits are gone."

"How did they know which trees they were?" Poseidon demanded of Ares.

"They didn't." He looked shocked and crestfallen. "They just...happened to burn the right ones, I suppose. Bad luck."

Hekate dropped to her knees, holding Eleusis. She closed her eyes, and buried her nose in his fragrant hair so she wouldn't have to smell the acrid smoke.

"And what was your plan there, Ares?" Hermes asked. "How was that going to help you?"

"I thought I'd...start clean," he said hollowly. "Fetch new trees from Asia. Succeed where you failed."

"Yes, Hekate's been trying to do all that," Rhea snapped.

"Can't you put them back?" Ares must have been addressing Hekate, though she didn't look up. "The way you brought me back to life?"

She shook her head. "Their forms have been destroyed. There's nothing to return life to."

Everyone was silent for a spell. A few dying embers hissed and crackled.

"Well, get out," Amphitrite said—surely to Ares. "Start your life clean, while we mop up here."

Hekate lifted her face just enough to see Ares shuffle away without another word, escorted by the bristling, silent Poseidon.

Chapter Fifty-Two

RACY LET THE WEEK OF PREPARATION DRAG OUT AN EXTRA couple of days, because he was so right about the wondrous things Tenebra could do in bed. The sensations she could send into his flesh, the appearances she could take on—he honestly felt that in the space of a few nights, he'd had sex with every type of woman he'd ever been attracted to, all in technically just one woman. She seemed to enjoy it too, or at least found it empowering to hold him in such thrall. He let her indulge her smugness. He knew he'd get tired of even her before long. It would start to feel distasteful or fake, and he'd want actual innocent nubile flesh again, one of these weeks. But he liked to enjoy each partner as long as the pleasure lasted for him, so he made good use of their vacation-rental bed on Zakynthos.

Krystal worked hard at her physical therapy in the meantime, as promised. She had fought her way up to running on the beach, short jogs at first, but longer each day. She was young, strong, and determined, and like any good weapon, if aimed and used correctly, she'd unleash considerable damage.

So then, the plan for using his weapons. The sullen Yuliya was doing her part too, over on the mainland. This mission required special soldiers, not just street thugs. You had to pick people who wouldn't fall apart in a panic when finding themselves in a cave full of glowing ghosts. At least the ghosts were no threat: according to what Sanjay had reported all too trustingly to his guru, and according to snippets of their Decrees too, the apparitions were passive and intangible, if unnerving. So all you needed do was select soldiers with iron nerves.

Today, the fifteenth of February, Yuliya texted him to say she had collected the requested fifty personnel. They were all in the region, inconspicuously staying in various places. They had collected the necessary firearms and explosives, and stood ready to converge upon the cave.

Does she have the means to open the door for them? Yuliya asked. The chilliness toward Tenebra came through even in text message.

Well done, he texted back. *And yes she does.*

He and Tenebra had again visited the Blue Caves here on the island recently, and tested her hand-crafted magical artifact: a knife-like object of stone and driftwood, the materials collected from both realms and wrapped up together with a bloody sinew from that walrus-hippo beast. That plus a few incantations and invisible forces on her part, and she was able to hold open the boundary between the realms when Tracy accessed it, at least for a minute or two. Her spell caused a shimmering door, like a sheet of water suspended in the air, which you could walk back and forth through, from one realm to the other.

Magnificent, that woman. And incredibly dangerous. He'd have to be bloody careful not to get on her bad side when he did tire of her, especially if she got her way and became immortal.

Then it's time, he added to Yuliya in text. *We'll see you tonight.*

He exchanged a nod with Tenebra, who read the texts over his elbow as they reclined together in bed in the morning light. He set down the phone, and they both got up and began to pack.

It would feel good to get this quest done: to accomplish at last what nearly every head of Thanatos had been unable to do. Imagine it, the Underworld and spirit realm at his command and Tenebra's. They could begin reshaping the world the way they wanted, starting tomorrow if all went well. They would be unstoppable.

AFTER THEIR BLISSFUL VALENTINE LUNCH IN THE AIRSTREAM, Adrian and Sophie returned to the Underworld for a wander through the fields and orchards. They allowed their friends to rib them about being all lovey-dovey together again. Sophie talked about the plants as they walked, in the animated way he'd missed so much—which trees or herbs had which powers, and which ones she'd managed to dig up specimens of and move to hiding places just in case. She broke off leaves and fruits and flowers to show him how they looked or smelled up close, reviving dozens of memories in his mind. She sounded like a woman with an avid interest in life again, which was the greatest of all the gifts that had fallen into his hands lately.

They flew back to the Airstream for a long romantic evening, and even got to sleep in the next morning. But on the fifteenth, while freshly showered and eating lunch with Sophie on his lap, his phone buzzed with a message from Niko.

Mars on the move, w/ group going to mainland. OK there must be something happening w/ disguises or spells here b/c Freya says Jupiter is one of them too, but we don't recognize them by sight.

Adrian and Sophie exchanged frowns. Jupiter was their code name for Tracy.

"So Krystal and Tracy and some others are coming this way, but in awesome disguises?" Sophie said.

"I guess." Adrian had lost his appetite. He thumbed in a response: *OK. Standing by. Keep us posted.*

He sighed and indulged in a lingering kiss before shifting Sophie off his lap. "Suppose I better make sure the ghost army's ready."

Worry clouded her green-brown eyes. "But you'll come back here for the night. Promise?"

"Promise. Let's send for Tab to stay with you in the meantime."

He did so, and took off for the Underworld as soon as Tab arrived. He left Kiri with her too, for extra protection. Rather than diving straight into the cave, he reined in his spirit horse and landed just outside the cave mouth. He unhooked the carabiners that held up the rope ladder, and let the whole thing drop down into the entrance. Might as well not give Thanatos an easy way in, if they did manage to switch realms outside the cave. If they switched inside—well, that was what the ghost army was for.

He swung back onto his horse, then paused. Some movement out among the oak trees had caught his eye. The sun was bright, making the shadows darker, so it was hard to see, but for a second he made out its shape. A small panther? No, a jackal or some other dog-like animal, mostly dark colored but with lighter touches here and there. Then it dissolved away into the shadows, the way wild creatures were so good at doing. Oh well. Likely nothing to bother about right now. He had more imminent problems.

The ghost army was already on high alert. Tab had received the message and told their spirit generals, Rhea and Sanjay, to assemble the volunteers. Adrian spent a couple of hours walking round the Underworld, consulting the armed souls and stationing groups of them in various parts of the cave, since, trouble was, they didn't know where exactly Thanatos would pop in, assuming they could switch realms at all. And if they couldn't, he was wasting his time here, which was bloody annoying when he could be back in the Airstream getting deliciously naked with Sophie. He had a lot of lost time to make up for on that front.

Texts flew back and forth among the group as the day ticked by. Niko, Freya, and Zoe followed Krystal and Tracy, and reported they were getting closer to Diros. So far they couldn't see any armed people forming up to attack in a group, but such people were probably hiding so as to keep the local police from noticing. Tab stayed at the trailers with Sophie and Liam, where all of them were going mad with the need to know what was happening and the desire to help.

Late in the evening, Niko reported: *They seem settled for now. 2 different rooms in Areopoli. Maybe to sleep and do nothing tonight? But can't count on that.*

Areopoli was just a short drive north of Diros Caves. This did not bode well.

Any of you able to stay on them all night? Adrian texted to Niko, Freya, and Zoe—whom, he well knew, already had been out pretty much all of last night keeping tabs on the enemy. *I want to stay near the Underworld*, he added. Guarding that was, after all, the top priority. And his ghost army, though unnerving, wasn't undefeatable. Knock the knives off their hands and you could zip right past them—or through them.

Freya and I will stay here, Niko answered a few minutes later. *Zoe's coming back to help you. That's where our best magic should go.*

Cheers, mates, Adrian responded. *I'll go back to the trailers for now, but get me the second anything happens.*

Will do, Zoe answered.

He returned to Sophie's grateful arms, and took shelter in them, and in her delicious cooking—because evidently when she was stressed and had a kitchen at her disposal, she tended to cook. "That or I garden," she explained, setting enchiladas, tossed salad, and freshly blended fruit juice on the table for Liam, Adrian, Tab, and herself.

Since Niko and Freya continued to report quiet on the Thanatos front, Adrian gave in to Sophie's entreaty to get some rest that night. He had just dozed off in the quiet Airstream when his phone buzzed him awake again. He grabbed it and squinted at the bright screen.

It was 1:00 a.m. and Niko's message said, *They're mobilizing. F & I will try to stop them before they get anywhere.*

"Bloody hell." Adrian scrambled out of bed.

Sophie, already awake, scrambled out after him. They stood shaking with alarm, staring at each other.

"Time for me to go," he said.

"Oh, Goddess," she whispered.

"Listen." He cupped her face in both hands. "Tab will come with me, but I'll leave Kiri here to guard you and Liam. *Do not move* from here."

"You can't tell me that! There has to be something we can do."

He shook his head, trying to look stoic, though fear was shooting through him and numbing every part of his body. "After everything you've been through because of us, please, no. Sit this one out." He forced his mouth into a smile. "Once you're immortal, then you can fight alongside us."

"The Underworld is mine too. You said so. I want to protect it."

"It is yours, as much as it's mine or anyone's, but it is not the safe place for you tonight. Please. Do as I'm asking."

She had a mutinous set to her jaw, but nodded. They dressed and went outside, just as Liam and Tab were leaping down the steps from the neighboring trailer, flashlight apps on their phones lighting their way.

Terry and Isabel's souls were hanging out here too, as they often did lately, tied by the waist on long ropes even though they said they'd probably be able to stay here by will alone.

"What about calling the local police and having them come to the caves?" Sophie said. "We can at least do that without getting hurt."

"Yes. Do that." Adrian kissed her again. Gratitude that she was thinking of good rational ideas made a tiny spark of light in the midst of his uneasy darkness. He looked at Tab, then around at the windy night. "Well. Let's be off."

"I love you," Sophie said before letting go of him.

"Love you too." He tried to tell himself this was better than last time, because at least Sophie wasn't in so much danger...but the rest of them might be about to meet a lot more danger, if the worst of their fears were true. He stepped back and looked his dog in the eyes. "Kiri, stay with Sophie. Guard her."

Kiri settled her bum closer to Sophie's feet, but kept her eyes on Adrian, and gave one of her unhappy snorts.

Tab hugged Liam and Sophie, then trotted after Adrian toward the tree where their spirit horses were tied up. "Let's ride."

Just after he mounted his horse, he looked back once more at Sophie, who gazed after him with sorrow and worry in her eyes. He prayed this wouldn't be the last time they saw each other on the same side of the life-death divide. Then he and Tab took off, and within a minute or two were plunging into the Underworld.

Chapter Fifty-Three

OKAY, WE'RE GOING TO OBEY FOR A MINUTE," SOPHIE INformed her brother, as she did a quick search on her phone for the Greek equivalent of 911. Finding it, she dialed, and told the answering operator, in a mishmash of English and her messed-up ancient-flavored modern Greek, essentially: "Hi, my brother and I were out for a late drive, and we saw a bunch of people trying to get into Diros Caves after hours. I'm pretty sure they had guns or explosives or something. I'm not sure what they're going to do, but it didn't look legal."

The operator asked a few follow-up questions about when this happened and how many people there were, to which Sophie made up her best guess at answers, (Just five minutes ago, and maybe twenty people.) They thanked her, told her the police were on their way, and advised her to keep out of the way since she was currently in no danger and they'd like her to stay that way.

She thanked them too, hung up, and looked at Liam. He was practically twitching in excitement. She regarded her glowing parents too, who listened and watched with mild concern.

"But we're going to do more than that, right?" Liam said.

"Oh, hell yeah," Sophie said. "That is my goddamn orchard, my gardens they're trying to blow up down there. We are not letting that happen."

Liam was already nodding in vigorous approval. "But how would we get there?"

Sophie looked at her parents again. "We have two souls who'll get pulled straight to the Underworld. All we've got to do is hold onto the other end of the vine."

"Then you'd walk?" her dad said. "At night?"

"Sure. It's only a couple of miles. You can see the cliff from here, when it's light."

"I'm up for that," Liam said.

"Through the forest, with the animals?" her mother said.

"Why not?" Sophie glanced down at Kiri. "We have an immortal beast to scare them off, or protect us if it comes to that."

"What about weapons?" Liam was bouncing up and down on his big, sneakered feet.

"We've each got a stun gun, right? Let's take those and anything else we can find." She smiled at her parents. "We'll strap knives onto your hands too, so you can start your ghost-army duties right away."

Her mother saluted, eyes twinkling. "At your service."

"Let's get armed up."

Sophie fetched the stun guns and four knives—two from the kitchen, which she tied onto her parents' hands, and one combat knife apiece for herself and Liam, left over from the ghost-army stash. When she tucked her stun gun into her sweatshirt pocket, it crunched against drying leaves and fruits and twigs—the plant bits she had picked while walking in the Underworld with Adrian. She pulled out one of the hard fruits: a purple olive from a massive tree that was likely thousands of years old, too large for her to move, though she'd transferred smaller saplings into pots. When eaten, these olives had the amusing but mostly useless property of making you able to command dogs in their own language of yips and barks. She remembered, as Persephone, laughing riotously with Hades over it when they discovered its powers.

She glanced down at Kiri, who watched her. Maybe this olive wouldn't be so useless tonight after all.

But not for Rosie this time. She was still a mortal dog, and Sophie and Liam had no intention of putting her in danger. They petted her and reassured her, and shut her inside Liam's trailer with some extra food and water.

Sophie tried not to think about the possibility that they might not be able to come back for her.

"GOODNESS, A LITTLE LATE FOR A CAVE TOUR, ISN'T IT?"

The cheerful voice made Tracy turn abruptly, interrupted in the midst of packing one of the cars' trunks full of weapons. It was the middle of the night in the small city of Areopoli and no one should have been wandering the streets, let alone remarking on a cave tour when they weren't even at the caves yet. Besides that, Tracy was under a glamour and shouldn't have been noticeable. This was clearly an enemy, then, and a cheeky one at that.

Even before he got a good look at the stranger under the weak street lamp, three of his half-dozen companions leveled their guns at the man. The bloke gamely stopped and raised both hands. Then he vanished as if he'd been nothing but an illusion.

"Bugger," Tracy said. "He's one of them."

"Yeah, I think I remember that dude," Krystal growled.

"Don't worry," Tenebra said, beside him. "I am ready."

A good thing she was, because a second later someone materialized right up against Tracy's back and latched an astonishingly strong arm around his throat.

"Let's put all the guns and explosives away and go home, friends," the stranger said, "or that's it for your dear leader here."

Tracy made a gesture at them to obey, and they all grudgingly dropped their guns—but only because they knew what would come next.

"*Sormajhaturm*," Tenebra pronounced.

The body holding Tracy spasmed, tightening around his neck for a painful second. Then the bloke went limp and slid to the ground.

Rubbing his throat, Tracy turned round and prodded his toe against the fellow's side. Young, tall, fit, handsome. Dead. How wonderful.

An enraged shriek tore through the air, and some golden-haired woman shot out of nowhere and slammed into Tracy like a wildcat. They crashed to the ground. He tussled with her a mere few seconds, amazed at her strength and intoxicated by her sultry perfume, before Tenebra repeated the death curse.

"*Sormajhaturm*."

The woman's body jerked, and she choked in one last breath. Then she wilted on top of Tracy in an armful of warm curvy flesh. A shame to have killed this one, he thought, when he rolled her over and found her face as stunning as her body. But...

"Thank you," he told Tenebra, while still gazing down at the mysterious blonde. "She was likely one of them too."

"So the curse does work on them." Krystal grinned, resting her gun's barrel on her shoulder. "Fuckin' A!" She kicked the dead man. "Yep, that's the bastard who did Quentin in and screwed everything up that night. Got you now, you fucker."

"What should we do with them?" one of their hired guns asked.

Tracy regarded the two beautiful dead immortals. "Let's bring them along. If we meet their friends, I expect the sight of these bodies could prove quite demoralizing."

"I SUPPOSE, NOW THAT YOU CAN'T LIE," HEKATE SAID TO Hermes' soul, "I should take advantage of it and ask you a few things."

It had been three days since Ares' attack on the Underworld and the destruction of the chrysomelia trees. Hekate and the other survivors were settling into a new dismal version of normal as best they could. Finally today a quiet moment presented itself, with Hekate and Hermes walking together on one of the winding paths between pale grassy hills, Eleusis wrapped snug against her back.

"Ask away," Hermes said. "Strange thing about being a soul. I don't hate having to tell the truth the way I would when I'm alive."

She licked her lips, unsure where to begin. "I'm not sure I actually want to ask about other lovers."

"Ah. Those. Of course I had several, even while I was with you. You did too. We agreed we should."

She nodded, keeping her face composed, though a needle of jealousy stabbed at her.

"But," he added gently, "there's no one I ever loved as much as you."

She swallowed against the lump in her throat, grief and happiness rising there in an odd mix. "Then why all the resistance to being my husband? Or the father of my child?"

"Mainly because I felt I didn't deserve you. You're worlds too good for me, Lady Hekate. I knew someday you'd realize it and get tired of me, and that would hurt too much. So I played the games I knew how to play, to keep you interested."

"The hard-to-get games? The I'm-so-mysterious games?"

"Yes, essentially. It wasn't always kind, and I regret that. But it worked, so I kept at it."

"Not good enough for me?" she said. "That's ridiculous.

I'm a mess. I'm strange and difficult in a hundred ways. It would take the best person in the world to put up with me for as long as you did."

"Nonsense. You're the treasure of the Earth. I only wish I had treated you better, loved you more—or no, since I couldn't possibly have loved you more, I wish I had let you know it more, that's all."

Hekate wiped a tear off each cheek with the knuckle of her thumb. "Well. That's all right. The way you did it, the mystery and games, did make it alluring, just as you intended. Maybe neither of us is cut out for a sedate, reliable marriage."

"I don't think we are. But love as wild and powerful as—as that infernal volcano? That we can manage."

CHAPTER FIFTY-FOUR

ZOE HAD PUT ON A BULLETPROOF VEST FROM THEIR NEW ARmory of equipment, as had Tab and Adrian, and they had tucked helmets under their arms. That would help, but it wasn't foolproof. Nor were her wards, but she was pacing around shoring them up anyway.

She stopped near the river, and frowned toward the entrance tunnel when the spirit essence of two of her friends intruded on her senses. Why in the Goddess' name were Niko and Freya returning? They were supposed to be staying on top of Thanatos!

Two souls detached themselves from the perpetual influx of the dead over the river and soared to her. As she recognized them, she reached out a useless hand, and moaned in agony. Grief froze her tongue.

They settled in front of her.

"Be careful, love," Niko's soul said. "They've got magic, all right."

"A very powerful sorcerer," Freya's soul added. "Some woman. I don't know what else she's capable of, but she was able to do this."

"Zoe?" Adrian called from somewhere behind her. "Are Niko and Freya here? What are…" He stopped as he spotted their souls. Then he roared toward somewhere farther off in the cave, "Tab! Tab, get here now."

Zoe's legs shook. She wanted to drop to her knees and cry, but she willed herself to remain standing. Swallowing hard a few times, she recovered her voice. "How? How'd they do it? Magic? Not explosives, or..."

"Just a spell." Niko sounded intrigued, if anything. "Can't imagine the dreadful deal she made with the afterlife to borrow that kind of power."

Adrian walked up behind Zoe and hugged her with one arm. He was trembling, his breath hitching in a fast cadence. Despair radiated from his touch. A second later, Tab came running, footsteps thumping the earth. She screeched through her panting breaths, "What the fuck? No!"

"Wait, but—" Zoe looked back at the two souls. She wasn't going to panic, she wasn't, she wasn't, she wasn't. "Your bodies then, they're intact? Because—there's a way to put you back, if they're unharmed and if we can get them soon."

"They were intact when we last saw them," Freya said dryly. "But who knows what Thanatos has done since then."

"The thugs are on their way here now," Niko added. "We thought it best to get here fast and warn you."

"Where did it happen?" Tab's voice trembled; her blue eyes were full of tears. "I'll go right now, damn it. I'll go get your bodies." Her voice broke on the last word.

"Areopoli," Niko said. "Latch a vine onto me and take me along and I could show you, I suppose, but I don't know if that's—"

"Yes!" Zoe said. "Do it."

"Is there really a way to bring them back?" Adrian's voice was uneven too, and when Zoe looked aside at him, his face was pale as he gazed at his murdered friends. He still had his arm around Zoe, and she could feel the grief and terror drowning him.

"I did it as Hekate," Zoe answered. "When I...tore out Ares' soul. Which I suppose is what this other sorcerer did. I was able to put it back, but then he was mortal afterward, and anyway I've never done it any other time."

"Try it," Adrian said. "We have to."

Tab nodded. "I need a vine—where's—"

"Here, come with me," Zoe said. She paused to squeeze Adrian's hand in reassurance, or at least support, before slipping away from him and jogging across the field with Tab. She had left a few coils of willow-and-ivy rope next to the path, not far off, and she led Tab there.

As she handed Tab one of the coiled-up vines, their gazes held, and Tab pulled in a shuddering breath. "I'm scared, you know?" she squeaked.

"I know," Zoe said. "So am I."

"In the memories, I got to my death last night. I mean as Dionysos." She grimaced and smeared a tear out of one eye.

"That was a dreadful one. I'm so sorry."

"Hermes and Aphrodite died that same night, same way. And now they show up here dead, so I can't help thinking: am I about to die too?"

"We're not going to let that happen," Zoe promised, though of course she *couldn't* promise it. The other side had someone who could rip out souls in a second, and if Zoe didn't identify her and stop her first—which would probably necessitate murdering her by the same method—then they could all be dead within the hour. The Underworld would fall to the enemy. The season of immortals would be cut short again in the midst of its regenerative spring bloom.

"It would just suck." Tab sniffled. "I mean, to die before I even got to meet her."

"Her? Oh. Ariadne."

Tab allowed a bashful smile. "Well. I kinda meant any 'her' who I could fall head over ass in love with, whoever she is out there. I wanted to meet her, you know? But Ariadne in particular, yeah. Maybe I mean her too."

Zoe smiled back, though she still only wanted to cry. "Let's make a pact. Neither of us is allowed to die today, because we each still need to meet a proper 'her'."

At that moment they both jerked to attention.

Ares' soul was near, seemingly right outside the cave.

"They're on us." Zoe met Tab's gaze. "Stick round a bit before taking off, won't you?"

Wide-eyed, Tab nodded.

IT WAS ABSURDLY EASY TO GET INTO THE UNDERWORLD. TRACY frowned when their car, the second in the group of ten, rounded the bend and saw the flashing lights of two police cars waiting by the cave entrance.

"Don't worry," Tenebra said. "I will get us by."

At her urging, they walked right up to the gates: their entire entourage of fifty people armed with guns, grenades, and other cave-invading necessities, not to mention two dead bodies slung over the shoulders of the burliest men. Tenebra moved as if in a trance; it took effort to cast a glamour over so many people at once.

But it worked. A police officer strolled toward them, and Tracy said, "Geologists. We have prior permission. All of this is our equipment."

The man nodded and waved them past, and recommenced pacing around and looking for the dangerous people with guns whom the pathetic opposition had surely reported by phone. Tracy shook with silent laughter. Too easy by half. He leaned over and kissed Tenebra on the cheek. She didn't react, but when he accidentally caught Yuliya's hurt, silent gaze, he looked away swiftly. He hadn't had much time to talk to her since the whole group got back together tonight. But he promised himself he'd set her up with a lovely villa wherever she liked once their new world order was in place. As long as she agreed not to be a bother to him.

While the inattentive police patrolled behind them, Krystal snapped the gate locks with a pair of bolt cutters, and they all trooped inside and down the steep metal staircase, illuminating their way with flashlights. Moist stalactites pointed down all around like the teeth of a carnivore, some so close that the taller members of the team had to duck on their way past. Entering like this, they had deduced from studying the geologic maps, would be far easier than switching realms outside the cave and then trying to descend into it. They had no idea whether there'd be a staircase in the spirit realm. There probably wasn't, so they would have to rappel in or throw down rope ladders—maneuvers to avoid if you could, when invading somewhere. You could do maximum damage, on the other hand, if you were able to pop up directly in the heart of the place and open fire right off the bat. Which, therefore, was the plan.

Also, they didn't encounter any magical wards blocking their way in the living world. The unnaturals must have known that such a thing would have gotten in the way of all the tourist traffic in and out of the cave, and would have attracted unwanted attention. As for the wards they would encounter when they tried to switch realms, well, Tracy had faith in Tenebra when it came to dealing with those.

Rowboats painted Greek-flag blue floated on the river at the bottom of the stairs, moored by ropes. The team untied five of them, split into groups and climbed in, and used the long poles lying in the bottoms to push them along the river. As they drifted deeper into the tunnels, the darkness, silence, dank smell, and closeness of the cave began to unnerve Tracy, though he would never have admitted it aloud. Yes, you could feel this was an ancient sacred place, and a dangerous one, even from within the living world.

Krystal and one of the hired men were consulting the geologic map by flashlight, and after a bend in the river, they pointed, and the man called, "Here."

They pulled the boats up to the shore. A tall metal fence

wedged between stalagmites blocked access to the cavern beyond. Tracy knew from studying the maps that the official Diros Caves tour only took people into some parts of the caves, and that vast caverns and twisting passages lay in the off-limits areas. They had selected the biggest cavern on the map, and decided it was likeliest to correspond to the giant underground field of souls described by their sources. They couldn't know for certain, of course, and appearing in the wrong place—or even the right place—might result in their being cornered and quickly killed. But such was the risk of any invasion.

Tracy's heart galloped as he climbed out of the boats with the rest of his team. He glanced about at the others, and his courage mounted. They were all risking their lives for his cause too. If he fell today, at least he would not fall alone. And their chances of success were better than ever, really, thanks to the wondrous Tenebra. He smiled in triumph as he caught sight of the two bodies of the immortals, which the men lifted out of the boats and hefted onto their shoulders again.

Everyone picked their way between stalagmites and columns until reaching the metal fence.

Krystal unholstered one of her guns. "This where we switch?"

Tracy closed his hand round the gold leaf and strawberry tree leaves in his pocket. "Yes. We'll try, at any rate."

"There is indeed a ward." Tenebra swished her hand slowly through the air. "A moment, please." They waited while she fished out her blood-soaked knife artifact and muttered some words. Then Tracy felt a strange jolt like a shudder, or a pulse of sound deeper than human hearing. "The ward is down," Tenebra declared.

"Ready, then?" Tracy asked.

Guns, knives, and flamethrowers clicked into position all around. Brisk nods answered him. Krystal looked fierce and indomitable; Tenebra looked tranquil; Yuliya kept her gaze fixed on him, but the hurt in her eyes had been mostly displaced by military determination.

"Please," Tenebra invited Tracy.

He held the leaves tight, and reached his mind toward the other realm. He sensed Tenebra catching the opening spiritual door, as it were, and holding it ajar. The shimmering gateway formed before them, just centimeters in front of the metal fence. But through it, instead of the fence, he could see eerie images of human shapes, glowing and greenish, their numbers so great that they stretched away beyond the reach of vision.

The faces of his team registered awe, along with a healthy amount of fear. But when Tracy waved his hand toward the gateway and said, "Krystal? Charge," she bolted forward without hesitation and dove through the shimmering gate. The others all followed. Last of all, Tracy joined hands with Tenebra and they stepped into the Underworld, and let the gate dissolve behind them.

CHAPTER FIFTY-FIVE

ADRIAN WAS TREMBLING HARDER THAN EVER. HIS BULLET-proof helmet was tucked ready under his arm, an ultra-strong stun gun in his belt. Niko's and Freya's souls stood beside him, knives vine-wrapped onto their wrists.

The enemy was coming. He was letting them come, hoping to trap them in a circle of armed ghosts and crush them by any means possible. But he didn't like this plan at all, not when someone among the invading army could murder anyone, even immortals, at the utterance of a single spell. Still, it was hard to take the ghost army anywhere other than the fields, so, fine. Let the wankers try. At least his dead soldiers couldn't be harmed.

As soon as they had sensed Ares' soul approaching, Tab and Zoe had raced up to spy on the invaders. Adrian instructed them—practically yelled at them—to stay out of sight, to do nothing at this point, just to observe and report back. It was too dangerous to act against them yet.

Zoe soon texted: *Police are outside, but the army walked right in! Ugh. Magic. As we already knew.*

Fine, what are they doing now? Adrian answered.

A couple of minutes passed, then Zoe responded: *Getting into boats, coming down river. With bodies. Niko's and Freya's. Please let me fucking kill these people.*

First you stay safe and come back here, he typed. *It's good they brought the bodies, yeah? Saves us a trip.*

Yeah, she said. *Tab and I are crying but yeah.*

Niko was reading the texts over his shoulder. Adrian tilted the phone to make sure he saw that one.

Niko smiled affectionately. "Maybe she does love me somewhere deep down."

Adrian tried to smile back. He and Sophie had wanted to tease Niko and Zoe for their past-life amorous attachment. Now he couldn't even bear to tease; he only wanted to cry too. Sure, Niko and Freya could be pains in the arse, but they had also been valiant and bright and buoyant. They were his friends. The world was better with them in it, alive, and they'd been snuffed out in seconds like match flames.

Adrian cleared his throat, fighting to restore his brave facial expression. "Hey, we're not counting you as dead yet. She'll use that magic and put you back, or at least try. You'll see."

"Hmm." Niko gazed across the field at Freya's soul, who was helping organize a phalanx of ghost soldiers. "Could be interesting. But let's take care of the army of dickheads first."

"They're getting closer." Adrian lifted his chin in the direction of the river. "I feel her coming. Krystal."

Zoe and Tab sprinted back into the fields a minute later. "They're close," Zoe panted.

"I know," Adrian said. "So their disguises, that was magic all along?"

She nodded. "Glamours, I'd say."

"Why don't we have glamours?" Tab asked. "That sounds awesome."

"They're dishonest," Zoe protested. "They're nearly always used for the wrong reason, therefore the magic would rebound on me. Because unlike some bitches, I don't have a special evil bargain with the Fates. But—" She gasped, and froze.

A weird shudder seemed to scud through the whole field. "What was that?" Adrian asked.

"One of the wards." Zoe stared toward the river. "She knocked it down. Ripped through it like it was tissue paper. Goddess, that's one powerful bargain she made."

Adrian knew they should mobilize now, but his feet felt rooted to the grass. Were these his last few minutes alive? Would he soon be stuck here in soul form, along with Zoe and Tab and everyone? Sophie would be devastated, furious. And he hadn't even told her about Niko and Freya yet; he couldn't bear to…

Shouts and the rattle of automatic gunfire echoed through the cave. He couldn't see the battle from here; it was apparently taking place behind hills and columns, around a bend of the river. But it was undoubtedly beginning.

"Well." With shaky hands, he fitted his helmet onto his head and lowered the clear shield. "Time to go."

"Here," Zoe said. "This once, I think us wearing glamours would be okay with the powers that be."

She closed her eyes for a second, then the air shimmered around Tab and her, and their appearances shifted: they both seemed to turn into ghosts, shimmery greenish versions of themselves. Zoe opened her eyes and blinked at him. "Well, it's working on you. Is ours working?"

"Yeah, you look like souls." Adrian prodded Zoe's arm just to make sure she was still solid, which he was thankful to find she was. He frowned at his own arms and legs. "But I don't look any different."

"Yes you do. You just can't see it on yourself." Another burst of gunfire rattled through the caverns. Zoe made a motion like putting something on her head—the helmet, he supposed, though her glamour warped appearances so that he couldn't actually see it. "All right," she said. "Let's go end this, one way or another."

"For the Underworld," Adrian said as they began to run toward the melee.

"For the pantheon," Zoe added.

"For the good guys!" Tab shouted.

"Ugh," Niko remarked, running alongside them with Freya. "You're all terrible at motivational battle speeches. I should have written one for you beforehand."

TRACY HAD TO ADMIT IT CHILLED HIS BLOOD WHEN HE STEPPED into the Underworld and found himself surrounded by uncountable numbers of glowing ghosts, as expected—and at least twenty of them wielded actual physical knives, which he had not expected. Aside from that, a few were children, which was especially spooky.

"They're armed!" Krystal and several of his other soldiers were shouting to him.

"Indeed. That wasn't supposed to be possible." Tracy whipped out his handgun and pointed it in warning at one of the souls who advanced upon him. "Well, then. Attack them."

Krystal shrieked some sort of war cry, and started firing one shot after another. Though their faces had become sheens of fear-sweat, the other soldiers lashed out too, some with knives and some with guns.

Tenebra gripped Tracy's arm and said in his ear over the noise, "I am keeping the glamours only on the two of us. It will save my powers and let us get past under cover."

"Good plan. Besides, it doesn't look like the glamours were keeping the ghosts from spotting any of us."

"No. I suspect souls see straight through these spells, but until now I would not have known." She sounded academically curious rather than alarmed.

"A-ha, there." Tracy pointed. One of Krystal's shots had hit the knife on a ghost's hand, and sent the knife spinning off into the cave, leaving the ghost defenseless. A great improvement over the other shots, which had gone straight through all the souls with no effect whatsoever except to ricochet dangerously off the cave's columns and walls.

"Go for the knives!" Krystal shouted to her comrades. "Disarm them!"

"They've got it under control," Tracy told Tenebra. "They'll be causing quite a diversion. Shall we slip off and find our treasure?"

Tenebra shimmered into a glamour that resulted in giving her the appearance of a soul, translucent and luminous. She gave him a cagey smile. "I am thinking you might take a bite too before we destroy this tree. If we even wish to destroy it?"

He smiled back. "Let's find it and see."

She took his hand. They left the noisy battle behind and ran alongside the river, heading upstream toward the multitude of black, gray, and white trees visible in the distance. They slipped past countless souls, most of whom were migrating toward the battle in curiosity, but he didn't see Adrian Watts or any other immortals or living folk along the way. Tenebra might not have the chance to yank out their souls, then; Krystal's team might have to manage it with explosives, if she and the other soldiers didn't get killed first. Ah, well. He could become immortal first and dole out the fates of the survivors later.

It hadn't been too harrowing, walking through the spirit-world wilderness in the middle of the night. Sophie and Liam heard lots of rustles or squeaks from forest animals, and caught glimpses of reflective eyes or furry limbs or scaly tails in their inadequate flashlight beams before Kiri snarled and sent the creatures scurrying off. Some they spotted were extremely cool, such as a cluster of moths with bioluminescent blue wings. The worst was when something fell on her shoulder from a tree overhead, and turned out to be a black centipede-like creature almost a foot long. She screamed and knocked it to the ground with a swipe of her arm, and Liam yelled too when he looked down at it. Even her parents' tranquil souls exclaimed in surprise. But it scuttled off on its zillion legs into the underbrush without doing her any harm.

"Probably fell off the branch by accident," she remarked as they continued forward, trying to sound collected after that super-girly shriek. "Clumsy thing."

The stream of souls overhead grew thicker, and they drew within sight of the mouth of the Underworld in just half an hour. They paused at the edge of the oak trees, Sophie and Liam staying behind tree trunks as best they could.

"As soon as we get out past the oak cover," Sophie said, "the others are going to sense us."

"Probably be mad at us," Liam remarked.

"Yeah, well. We're free agents." Sophie rolled the olive between her fingers in her pocket, planning to eat it as soon as they got down there, then direct Kiri to do whatever needed to be done. She didn't want to make the sweet dog kill anyone, but...

Kiri growled again. Sophie looked at her, then peered in the direction the dog was staring. It took her a moment to make out the shape between the dark trees, some twenty feet away. She shone her flashlight at it.

"Jackal?" Liam said, his voice hushed.

The brown and black animal growled, then whined and ducked his head, and paced back and forth as if wanting to approach but unsure of his welcome. Larger dogs—no, spirit-world wolves—lingered behind him, melting in and out of the shadows. Sophie ignored them and stared at the animal who had come forward. Recognition washed over her, astounding her. It couldn't be.

"Not a jackal. A dog." Sophie cleared her throat and called, in the Underworld tongue, "Kerberos. Here, boy!"

The dog's ears perked up. Kiri looked dubiously at Sophie and then back to the other dog.

"No way," Liam said in wonder.

"We thought Kiri was Kerberos reborn," Sophie said, reverting to English. "But we never knew for sure. Come to think of it, I'm not sure I know what did happen to Kerberos in the end."

"Huh." Her dad studied the dog. "I think you may be right." Demeter had known Kerberos too, after all. Had even helped Persephone pull Ares' spear out of the poor dog once.

"Kerberos!" Sophie called again, using the Underworld language. "Kerberos, it's all right. Come here. Good dog."

He padded forward a few steps, and his tail began wagging.

Tears filled her eyes. "Good boy! Good boy, Kerberos. Have you been out here all this time, huh?"

He whined in longing. Now that he was closer, she could see his fur gleamed with health, even with its occasional mats of pitch and mud. She glanced up to see his wolf packmates slip away and vanish into the forest, apparently uninterested in making friends with humans.

"Could that be?" her mother asked in wonder. "Could he have survived this long?"

"Well, Rhea lived all this time, or at least she did up until last fall. And he knows us, look. Sit," she commanded the dog in the Underworld tongue, just to make sure.

He sat, gazing at her, and his ears perked up to full height. Everyone grinned.

Sophie knelt and stretched out her hand. "Do you know me, boy? I'm in a different body, but do you know me still?"

Kerberos walked forward, his tail whipping back and forth. He accelerated as he reached her, and planted his front feet on her knees and licked her face, whimpering like a puppy. Sophie laughed along with everyone else, and squeezed her eyes shut a moment against the warm tongue. Kerberos flipped over on his back, pulling up his paws and baring his belly in complete submission.

She scratched his tummy. "Yes, you did this the first time I met you. You're a sweet little spaz." She had to revert to English for "spaz." The Underworld tongue didn't have that exact word.

"Well, I'll be damned," her dad said.

"Adrian and Zoe are going to be so happy to see you," she told Kerberos, scratching his warm hairy ribs. She smiled mournfully at imagining Adrian's reaction. *Please, Goddess, don't let Thanatos destroy any of us before we can find each other…*

"Two immortal dogs!" Liam was jumping up and down again. "This is freaking awesome!"

Kiri was watching Kerberos' belly-rub with something like patient disdain. "Three, if we get Rosie on board." Sophie scratched Kiri behind the ears too. "We'll have a dog army *and* a ghost army."

Kerberos flipped back to his front, but stayed lower than Kiri, and wriggled over to nudge his nose against her paws. She acknowledged his submissive gesture by nuzzling one of his ears. They sniffed each other's faces, grumbled and snorted, then both looked up at Sophie again.

"Well." She rose and gazed toward the mouth of the Underworld. "Guess we've got one more dog to carry now." She looked at Kerberos and switched back to the language he knew. "You want to go find Hades? Should we go help Hades?"

Kerberos barked in excitement, his dark eyes alert.

"Then let's do it." Liam strode out from beneath the tree cover.

Sophie and her parents followed, with the two dogs trotting along. At the huge yawning hole that formed the cave entrance, full of the flashing gleams of endlessly arriving souls, they leaned over and looked in, then exchanged frowns.

"Rope ladder's gone," Liam said.

"Yeah." Sophie exhaled. "Damn it. They probably took it down so Thanatos couldn't use it. Makes sense. But what do we do now? We can't just jump in. And we don't have spirit horses, even if we wanted to try them."

Liam's gaze flicked up and down their mother's soul, then their father's. "But we've got a spirit mom and dad."

"What does that even…" Sophie got it, and fell quiet in speculation. Then she drew in her breath. "Okay. I'm willing if you are."

Sophie took the excess length of the vine wrapped around their father and tied it around her own waist so she was attached to him. Liam did the same with their mother's vine. Liam picked up Kiri, and Sophie picked up Kerberos.

"Ugh." Sophie wrinkled her nose. "You may be immortal, boy, but it's clear you haven't had a bath in centuries."

Kerberos repaid her by licking her squarely on the nose.

"Okay," her dad said. "We'll take it slow. Ready?"

Sophie and Liam nodded, and gripped the vines as tight as possible, which was challenging with the dogs in their arms.

Terry and Isabel stepped into the blackness. Sophie's feet got pulled off the solid ground; all her weight dragged from the straining coil of the vines, which now seemed desperately thin for such an endeavor. She squealed in terror as gravity and the Underworld's magic pulled them downward into the dank cave.

Liam was yelling too: "Mom, slow down, slow down, slow down!"

"Dad, oh my God!" Sophie shrieked.

Kerberos grunted and lunged, and she almost dropped him.

"Hang on," her dad said. "Almost there."

The soles of her shoes hit the rock floor, and she stumbled and rolled, with Kerberos wriggling against her, to a more or less safe landing. She got up and dusted off, and grinned at

Liam, who was doing the same. The whole drop had probably taken five seconds, in retrospect.

"That was awesome," Liam said. "I'm totally doing that again sometime."

"I'm not sure I approve, as your mother," their mom said.

A rattle of gunfire echoed through the tunnel from somewhere downstream. They all stared that direction in dread.

"It's starting," Sophie said.

Liam pulled out his stun gun. His knuckles whitened around it. "Then let's go help."

Sophie took out the olive, popped it in her mouth, and chewed it up. After wincing at the bitter taste and spitting out the pit, she examined the two dogs. Then she addressed them, in dog language (mostly yips and grumbles), "Protect Liam and me, and our friends. We need to go stop the people who shouldn't be in here."

Both dogs' eyes lit up, and they each woofed in assent—in fact, what Kiri said was, "Finally! You're talking my language." And Kerberos said, "I miss my people! I want to find them and protect them." They loped ahead into the tunnel.

Liam was snickering at Sophie's foray into dog-speak.

"Oh, sure, laugh," she told him, in English. "But if you're not nice, I'm going to tell you what they said about you."

CHAPTER FIFTY-SIX

ADRIAN AND HIS ALLIES RACED AROUND THE RIVER'S BEND, leaping over rocks and whipping through slower-moving souls, toward the increasingly loud gunfire and shouts. Soon they were upon them: Krystal and at least forty other people, mostly men, all in bulletproof vests and bristling with a variety of weapons, which they were now using to knock the knives off the hands of his ghost soldiers. They'd disarmed nearly all the souls already, and several of the enemy were breaking through and running forward into the cave, toward Adrian and the rest.

Zoe extended her hand and must have slammed ahead some kind of spell, because all at once the enemies' weapons went flying up into the air and landed several meters away.

"Ha," Niko said in triumph.

That only paused the assault for a moment. The enemies bolted around, grabbing weapons back where they could. Adrian leaped on one guy and zapped him with the stun gun, rendering him helpless and quivering on the ground, then pivoted and did the same to another. Tab picked up a man, who screeched in alarm to find a "soul" could touch him, and threw him in the river. Niko and Freya slashed their knives at a few other men, forcing them back and keeping them from recovering their guns. Adrian was pretty sure he saw Freddie Mercury stab a guy.

But the enemy still had other weapons: soon most of them began tugging out new knives and guns strapped somewhere upon them, and Adrian was disheartened to note a lot of them wore grenades. Apparently the spell had only knocked away the looser gear.

Zoe, meanwhile, shot off a new spell, which yanked Niko's and Freya's bodies through the air toward them. "Ade, catch!" she yelled.

He reached up just in time to catch Niko's body, and fell over backward with it. Zoe did the same with Freya's, then knelt, panting, and examined them both. It chilled him to see how pale and limp they were, how blue their lips had turned...

"I think it'll be okay," Zoe said. "I think this'll work."

"Look out!" Adrian shouted.

Krystal was racing toward Zoe, raising a knife, her face feral in its menace. Apparently even thinking Zoe was a soul, she was ready to attack.

Zoe looked up and walloped Krystal with a spell that knocked her backward a few meters. She landed on her arse with a grunt.

Adrian stood. "Take the glamour off me. I want her to see."

"Done," Zoe said.

Adrian removed his helmet. He had the pleasure of seeing Krystal's face change as she stared at him: her fury intensified, then disbelief crept in, along with what he hoped was terror.

"I warned you the Underworld would claim you soon," he said. "There's a nice little solitary cell deep down in the flames, just waiting for you. Want to see it?"

Her discomfort seemed to vanish. She smirked. "Right. If you're so powerful, how'd we walk right in here? And what's about to happen to all your precious magic trees? Huh?"

The trees were nowhere near here, so Adrian was disinclined to take her threat seriously—that is, until he glanced at Zoe and found her looking around, perturbed.

"None of these people feel like they've got any magic," she said in the Underworld tongue. "Where's their sorcerer? Where's the actual dangerous one?"

"Let's get to the trees. Now," Niko said, in the same language.

"Go," Adrian told her. "I'll deal with Ares here."

Zoe nodded, and she and Niko sprinted away.

Adrian locked eyes with Krystal again, who still sat on the ground, wincing and taking hissing breaths, as if the hard landing had re-injured her hip. Good. He pondered how exactly to handle her: vengeance in the form of a quick death, or relative mercy in the form of getting her thrown in prison for life?

Angry screams from Tab's direction made him look aside. She was grappling with one of the biggest soldiers, who had managed to sink a knife into her shoulder. Freya's soul darted up behind him and stabbed him in the neck. As he howled, Tab head-butted him, then pitched him into the river. She yanked out the knife in her arm and flung it after him.

Then, most frightening yet, Adrian realized he could sense Sophie. She was near. So was Liam. He looked around wildly, though surely he wouldn't be able to see her yet. Oh, Goddess, no, what had happened? Were they here as souls, dead, like Niko and Freya?

That moment of inattention cost him. Pain speared through his throat. Choking, he crashed to his knees and grasped at his neck. He pulled out the knife that had landed there, which Krystal obviously had flung, but he still could barely breathe. Spots were blooming in his vision, and blood welled up into his mouth.

Before he could recover, her foot shoved against his chest and planted him on the ground. She unhooked and tore aside his bulletproof vest, then picked up a long knife and sank it straight between his ribs, in a slice of white-hot agony, until he felt its point emerge at his back. Now he truly couldn't breathe. He couldn't switch realms either; he tried. If only she'd go away, just for a minute…

"Nuh-uh, you bitch," Tab said, and pounded toward them.

But Krystal produced a grenade and held it out over Adrian's prone body. "You come at me and I drop this."

Tab evidently stopped, but retorted, "You have been a serious asshole in every life, you know that?"

"Whatever. This place—what the hell?" Krystal's last word became a shriek as something dark, four-legged, and growling shot out of nowhere and knocked her to the ground.

The grenade went rolling. Adrian desperately lifted partway up on his elbow to watch. Tab yelped, leaped for the grenade, and flung it far away downriver. Then she plugged her ears with her fingers and cringed.

Nothing exploded, and Freya's soul told her, smiling, "The pin hadn't been pulled yet."

"Well, for fuck's sake," Tab said, and exhaled a long breath.

Meanwhile, the animal's snarls and Krystal's screams were still bouncing off the cave walls, but soon the screams were cut short in a horrible gurgle. Adrian rolled over to see Krystal's soul rise up, stunned, from her bloodied body. The wolf or dog or whatever it was backed off, slinking, blood dripping from its jaws. Adrian barely glanced at it; he locked gazes instead with Krystal.

"What's happening to me?" She was already taking jerky and seemingly unintentional steps toward Tartaros. "Where am I going?"

Adrian couldn't talk, what with the knife wounds. Freya answered for him: "Just where he told you you'd go. We're sorry." She did even sound sorry. Aphrodite had been fond of Ares in some fashion, after all. Maybe not in this life, but once upon a time.

"No. Please. I—I'm sorry! Fix me! Please!"

But of course there was nothing any of them could do. They watched solemnly as the invisible forces drew Krystal's soul, the once god of war, out of their sight and down to a long solitary confinement.

Tab walked into Adrian's line of sight, a stony look on her face as she gazed at Krystal's body. Then she pulled in a shaky breath, stood up straight, and smiled more warmly across him, at someone he couldn't see. "Hey, you. What the heck?"

Adrian tried to look that direction, but his neck still wasn't fully cooperating. In addition, his lack of breath was starting to make the whole world fuzzy.

Someone pulled the knife out of his chest and laid a cool hand on his cheek, helping him turn his head.

Sophie. Alive. Oh, thank the Goddess.

She smiled tenderly. "Hey."

"Wh…" Adrian coughed, spat out blood, and managed a few wheezing breaths. She took his hand, and he held onto it tightly. Finally he got his voice to work. "You shouldn't be here. What are you doing here?"

"Saving your butt, apparently." She nodded to the blood-stained dog, who crept forward, sniffed him, and whined. "With Kerberos' help."

"Kerber…" He blinked, clearing his vision, and examined the dog in bewilderment.

The dog sat and gazed longingly at him. His tail thumped against the ground. Adrian took in the familiar jackal-ish pointed ears, the brown chest and black mask, the spot on one side of his nose. Astounded, he looked at Kiri, who had arrived with Sophie, and was now diligently licking his wounded neck. "What," he finally said.

"Right, well…"

"What happened?" demanded Liam's voice, not far off.

Sophie looked up, then gasped, and apparently forgot the topic of the dogs. "No," she yelped. She and Liam had spotted Freya as a soul, he realized, and likely had also noticed the bodies of Niko and Freya.

"They have magic," Freya said. "Of a powerful sort. Now we need to go make sure it isn't being used against anyone else. Nor against our trees."

CHAPTER FIFTY-SEVEN

As Zoe ran for the orchards, she felt occasional wallops of power through the air: the sorcerer knocking down each of Zoe's wards as she reached it.

"Bugger, I'm so stupid, why'd I even bother?" she said to Niko.

"How was it stupid to set up magic to protect the place? It's slowing her down, at least." Niko kept pace with her easily. Souls didn't usually move fast, but it seemed they could if they wanted to. She still didn't dare think about the likelihood that he'd stay a soul—that she might fail again.

"If she can sense the wards, she'll know exactly the areas we're protecting. They're leading her straight to the bloody chrysomelia tree!"

"Hm. There is that. Ah—I see them." Zoe and Niko had reached the outermost pomegranate trees in the orchard. He pointed ahead to what looked like two souls walking through it. She realized they must be wearing glamours, and that the dead, Niko among them, wouldn't be fooled by glamours.

Zoe slammed a glamour-dissolving spell at the pair. Their appearances rippled and morphed into the ordinary solidity of the living: a middle-aged man and woman, who were now a mere twenty meters or so from the chrysomelia tree. They jolted and looked at one another, then glared back at Zoe and Niko, who kept sprinting forward. Zoe had dropped her glamour when she started running here. Not much point using any power to maintain it.

But she rather wished she had when the man casually lifted a rocket launcher and fired it at her.

She had a split second to fling up a magical shield. The bubble of protection formed around her, fire and deafening explosion searing around its outsides. Trees burst into flame; branches fell.

Niko's soul leaped into the bubble with her—he was unhurt, of course, but apparently worried about her safety. "You all right?" he said.

She had been crouching with her arms over her head. She lowered them and nodded. With another sweep of magic, a special indoor rain moved in to douse the flames, its water pulled from the nearby river. She squinted through the smoke and steam. "What are they doing?" She cloaked herself in a soul-like glamour again, and she and Niko rushed forward.

Another wallop through the air: the woman had knocked down the protective ward around the chrysomelia tree. But she and the man couldn't actually see it yet, Zoe realized— they were looking around everywhere except at the little tree itself. At least her spell of "invisibility except to the right people" was still holding. Zoe didn't count on it lasting much longer, though. This woman was dangerous, and worked fast.

"That one," Niko said to Zoe quietly. "She's the one who killed us. Are you prepared to do the worst?"

Ripping someone's soul out. Two someones, possibly. She had to gulp to make her throat swallow properly, but she nodded. "If they won't stop, yes. May the Fates forgive me."

But before she could prepare the spell, Niko warned, "Look out!"

Zoe flung up another bubble of protection, again just in time. Another explosion crashed in brilliant orange flame around her. A grenade? She couldn't tell, nor did it matter much. But it was setting more of the Underworld's gardens on fire, and it hadn't come from either the man or the woman in front of her.

She threw her glamour back on, swept the flames aside so she could see, and soon spotted the culprit: another woman, curvy and blonde and a bit younger than the sorcerer. Grenades studded the harness across her chest. She raced up to the pair.

"Yuliya," the man said sharply. "Why did you follow us? What's going on?"

"The others are all defeated. We must do this and run. Quick, where is the tree?"

"Here somewhere, we think." He hesitated. "But…"

"It must be right here," the other woman said. "It is cloaked somehow."

Still a couple of paces from them, and hidden under a soul-glamour, Zoe shot a spell at all three of them that should have knocked them unconscious. It had worked fine on Krystal and this Yuliya woman the day they kidnapped Landon. But the sorcerer had apparently put a shield on them, because they only jolted a bit and looked at Zoe, startled and squinting.

"Bugger," she swore. She pulled together the earth energies that would shake apart the shields, but before she could throw them forward, the sorcerer glared at her and began pronouncing a word wrapped with palpable, lethal evil.

"*Sormaja-*"

"Zoe, now!" Niko shouted.

Panicking, Zoe flung her senses toward the woman's soul, seized at its connecting edges, and tore it from its body. The body crumpled, leaving the soul gaping at Zoe, who staggered, weakened by using such a blast of death.

The woman's soul was already being drawn toward Tartaros. Zoe could almost physically see the dark tendrils reaching for her, like shadows of the vines that would soon hold her.

"Wait!" the woman called. "You have powers. There is a way to revive me, I am sure of it. We will call a truce. Anything."

Leaning over with hands splayed on her knees, Zoe gave a weak laugh. "And get in the way of the Fates? I wouldn't dare. They're dying to sink their claws into you, mate."

The woman's mouth opened, but she had the dignity to avoid screaming "No!", or anything at all. She succumbed to the pull of the shadows, and was swept away, out of sight.

Zoe turned her gaze upon the other two, who watched in horror.

The man—surely Erick Tracy—dropped his rocket launcher and raised both hands. "A truce. Or rather, a deal. Anything at all, in exchange for one of those fruits of yours."

Zoe stared incredulously at him. He seemed completely sincere.

"Not what I expected from a member of Thanatos," she said.

"Zeus, though," Niko remarked. "Figures."

"I'm sorry, what?" Tracy cut in.

Niko and Zoe exchanged brief shrugs, and Niko told him, "Your soul, you were Zeus. We should have known earlier. Smug pain in the arse, and all that."

"Wait." Tracy's eyes gleamed. "Then—well, good Lord, all the more reason we should work together, yes? Tell me more. If I can become like you, then truly, anything, any truce—"

"No!" Yuliya screeched. "That was not the plan! She has corrupted you. No one should ever have it!"

And before Zoe could proceed with knocking them out and handing them over to the police outside, Yuliya snapped two grenades off her gear, pulled the pins on both, and flung them at Tracy.

"Shit." Zoe ducked and covered, under yet another protection bubble.

One grenade sailed out among the trees. The other bounced

off the ground mere centimeters from Tracy's feet—right near the chrysomelia tree. Both exploded a second later.

Zoe shut her eyes. More fire, heat, deafening noise, even through her protective bubble. When she opened her eyes a few seconds later, and frantically swept a surge of water over the fire, she caught a glimpse of the souls of Yuliya and Tracy being pulled to Tartaros. As for their bodies, those were all but destroyed.

As was the tree of immortality.

She stumbled forward, not wanting to believe it, and fell to her knees in the ashes. Cinders burned holes in her jeans; she flinched at the scorch, but kept digging desperately in the fallen branches and burned leaves.

She found its little trunk, recognizable by the charred cloth tied around it, containing the coil of hairs from each of them. Her spell, which had made the tree invisible but did nothing to protect it from actual harm. The tree was broken off at the top, reduced to a bare stick, its leaves and immeasurably precious fruits incinerated and blasted away. Everything stank of acrid smoke. Behind her, trees and plants still burned, and she sent more indoor rain toward them with a listless wave of her hand to keep the rest of the gardens from unneeded harm. But so much had already been lost.

She bowed her head over her knees, face in her hands. "Oh, Goddess. How am I going to tell Sophie?"

Niko crouched beside her. "Ah, love, don't despair. Remember how I always have tricks up my sleeve? This time is no exception."

She raised her face to grimace at him. "How are you going to fix this? When even *I* can't?"

"I'll show you. But first, let's go fetch that body of mine, and Freya's, before they get any colder. All right?"

Sniffling, Zoe nodded and dragged herself to her feet.

ZOE AND NIKO MET THE OTHERS ON THE PATH BESIDE THE river. Adrian carried Freya's body in his arms, and Tab held Niko's over her shoulder in a fireman's carry. Zoe blinked in confusion at the sight of Sophie and Liam hurrying along with them, their faces a mixture of triumph and worry.

"What are you—is everyone—" Zoe began.

"Krystal's dead, and the rest are knocked out and tied up, ready for the police." Adrian laid Freya's body down on the ground. "Sophie and Liam defied orders and jumped down here to help. Did you find the sorcerer, and Tracy?"

"Both dead." Zoe sighed. "But they set off grenades, and the...the chrysomelia tree..." Her throat closed up as she fought sobs, as if the tree had been a close relative of hers. In some ways it was, or even more important than that.

"Oh no," Sophie said in a tiny, despairing voice.

"I'm sorry," Zoe whispered.

"And," Niko put in, "I've instructed you not to give up hope, because of things I'll explain in a moment, but first, darling, do you mind trying to bring us back to life?"

"Right. Sorry." Zoe wiped her nose and sent an apologetic glance toward Freya's soul too.

Freya smiled, then focused her attention on the blonde lifeless body lying on the ground. Tab set Niko's body down next to her.

"So then." Zoe crouched by them. "You two come over here, and lie back down into yourselves, to start."

"Or," Niko proposed, "here's a thought. What say I take Freya's body, and she takes mine?" He looked at Freya's soul. "If you're up for it, that is."

Freya lifted her eyebrows and turned to Zoe. "Would it even work?"

"Er. I have no idea. But why would you...? Oh." Blood

rushed to her cheeks again, in that everlasting blush that always came with thoughts of Hekate's relationship with Hermes. "Hang on. Just for me, you'd get a complete body switch and sex change?"

"Well, not *just* for you." Niko regarded Freya's body with interest. "I'd quite enjoy driving that around, I think."

"I would like it too." Freya considered Niko's body. "I would finally get to have sex with all the beautiful gay men who would not touch me before."

Zoe laughed in shock, as did Adrian, Sophie, Tab, Liam, and all the souls clustering around to watch this bizarre event.

"Dude, you'd get periods," Tab reminded Niko. "Are you sure? Really, really sure?"

Niko waved the concern away. "I've been a woman in some lives. I know the drill."

Zoe found herself trembling—out of excitement, not fear. The soul of the maddening but beloved Hermes/Niko, in the perfect-ten body of Freya? That was too awesome a solution to be real.

"It wouldn't fix everything," she argued, more for her own benefit than Niko's. "I mean, we'd still not be the ideal couple. We'd have issues, we'd need counseling…"

Niko shrugged. "Who's ideal? Other than them, I mean." He gestured at Adrian and Sophie.

Sophie smiled and sidled over to take Adrian's hand. He pulled her closer and kissed her on the cheek.

"Okay. In that case." Zoe drew in her breath, and opened her palm toward the two bodies. "Get situated in whichever one you want."

They settled in, everyone smiling at the oddity of it: Niko's soul overstretching the shorter confines of Freya's body, Freya's translucent curves spilling out the sides of Niko's slim frame.

Zoe closed her eyes and found the edges of both souls at once, and felt the fading energies of the unhurt but cooling bodies. "This may take a lot of power," she said. "Fitting them into spots they didn't belong to before."

Please Goddess, please Fates, help me do this, she prayed. *Take all my energy if that's what it requires, but let them live again; and if it's not asking too much, help me pull off this switch...*

And though the response didn't come in actual words, more of a feeling in the available energies, she would have said the answer was something like: *Asking too much? All of you have wandered as mortals for thousands of years before finally finding your immortality again, and you've come here to serve this realm once more at last. Daughter, ask whatever you wish. The powers are here to help you.*

But it did indeed take an immense amount of power. As she worked at the strange and complicated spell, sweat broke out all over her. Nausea crawled in her belly. She kept at the endless effort, eyes shut in the familiar darkness she had lived in before her sight had been given to her, finding soul-edges and stitching them to resistant bodies, while her friends waited in a hush.

Right before she passed out, she sensed a burst of energy like a match being struck and a flame coming to life.

Two flames, in fact.

CHAPTER FIFTY-EIGHT

I s SHE GOING TO BE OKAY?" LIAM SOUNDED AFRAID. HE AND everyone else crouched near the unconscious Zoe, who had collapsed on her side on the white grass.

Sophie rested her fingers on Zoe's neck and felt the regular tapping of a pulse. "Heart's still beating."

"Yeah, she's still in there," Adrian said. "Probably just knocked out from all that magic."

"I'd expect so. That was quite the blast of power."

Sophie turned with everyone else to peer at the person who had spoken: the resurrected Freya, or at least her voice emerging from her mouth, in her body that was now sitting up and flexing her fingers.

But the accent, the cadence—those hadn't been Freya's.

"Niko?" Adrian said in amazement. "Yeah. You're in there, aren't you."

The blonde woman winked at him in a way much more reminiscent of Niko's sly winks than Freya's sultry ones.

Sophie—and everyone else—moved their gaze to the male sitting nearby, running his fingertips delicately through his short hair and frowning. "Oof," he said, and shifted his sitting position, then groped himself between his legs. "Living with these takes some adjustment. I had forgotten."

Freya's Swedish accent, through Niko's windpipe.

"Meanwhile I get these." Newly-female Niko hefted one of her own boobs and lifted an eyebrow at it in approval.

Tab cracked up, and threw herself upon each of them with a huge hug. "Dudes. What do we even call you now?"

Niko shrugged. "I can still be Niko. I'll just say it's short for Nikoleta from now on."

"And I can be Frey," the newly-male Freya said. He smiled. "Still a god."

"Except," Niko said, "we're mortal again. I must be. I can't sense any of you."

Freya—or rather, Frey—furrowed his brow. "You're right. Nor can I."

Desolation swept in once more upon Sophie. "And now we can't fix you, and Liam and I can't be immortal either. They killed the tree!"

"Ah. As to that, all may not be lost." Niko crawled toward Zoe on hands and knees, and grunted. "Oof. Stiff joints from being dead. I hate mortality."

"What do you mean, all may not be lost?" Sophie demanded. "Can she bring the tree back too?"

"No, it's not that." Niko spoke gently, as if his mind weren't really on it. Rather, *her* mind. Damn, those pronouns were going to be confusing for a while. Niko sat next to Zoe and drew her head and shoulders up onto her lap.

"Then what?" Adrian said. "How are we supposed to fix this? We won, but we also kind of lost, right?"

"Patience, darlings." Niko gazed down at Zoe, and stroked a wayward strand of hair off her ear. "It can wait. Trust me."

Sophie sighed in frustration, and Adrian growled. But they sat down too, and waited, all worried eyes on Zoe.

THE WORLD WAS ALL DARKNESS. PERHAPS SHE WAS BLIND again. But she didn't mind, for she was at peace, and love was wrapped around her. It poured in from someone's touch, flooding her head, her arms, her back.

As Zoe's consciousness filtered back in, she recognized whose.

"Niko?" Her lips felt thick; her energy was still at lowest ebb.

A hand stroked her shoulder blades. "In the flesh. Well. Not the original flesh, but even better."

She finally hauled her eyelids open. Faces illuminated with flashlights formed in her vision. Her sight did still work, then. She was on her side, her head on Niko's lap. She flopped onto her back to look at him.

Her whole face blossomed into a grin when she put together what she was seeing. Freya, physically: bobbed golden-blonde hair with a fetching degree of bedhead tousle, lips like Eros' bow, flawless skin, mesmerizing long-lashed eyes, and the swell of generous breasts under her blue knit top. But in the glint of those eyes, and the impish curl upward at the edge of those lips, Zoe saw and sensed the soul of the trickster beaming out.

As if to make it even more certain, the woman's lips parted and her tongue touched her upper lip as she gazed down at Zoe in the calculating expression Zoe knew well, from Hermes and Niko and others in between.

Zoe dragged herself upright, not taking her eyes off the new Niko. She set her dirt-smeared palm against the woman's cheek. "Wow."

Niko tipped her face forward just enough that their noses grazed one another. "Well done, sweet Hekate." His accent and words in a sultry female voice. Yeah, Zoe had likely died and gone to some delusional heaven.

But all their friends were crowding round, so it wasn't the time to try snogging her, she supposed. Adrian and Sophie and Tab needed reassuring hugs, and she had to turn and laugh in delighted astonishment at Freya flexing Niko's lanky limbs and infusing his smile with coyness and his voice with a Swedish accent.

And then she noticed there were more than the usual two dogs, Kiri and Rosie, hanging around and whipping her with their tails. Some third dog, black and brown and smelling pungently canine, was whining and practically crawling into her lap.

"Who—Kerberos??" She seized him by the furry sides of his head and looked into his panting, grinning face.

"Yep." Sophie stood nearby, arms folded with pride. "I found him outside. Thought I'd let him in."

"But how—what—"

"He's been alive for like *three thousand years*," Liam said. "How freaking cool is that?"

"No," Zoe said. "How does that even…what…"

"You tell us," Adrian said. "You were the last one to own him. Did you set him free, or did he run away, or…?"

Zoe rubbed at her temple. "Uh. I've not got that far. Bloody hell, there's still a lot I don't know."

"I can tell you that," Rhea said. "Eleusis adopted him after Hekate's death. Kerberos became the official pet of the Eleusinian Mysteries. They agreed to take care of him and keep his immortality a secret. He might have lived centuries with them; I've no idea."

"But he was in the spirit world," Sophie said. "With wolves."

"Then someone must have taken him through to this realm at some point," Rhea said. "One of the priestesses, at their sacred portal. They set him free, perhaps. Or else he escaped, in order to look for the Underworld again."

"Then why hadn't we seen him until now?" Adrian asked.

"Wolves roam around," Sophie pointed out. "Maybe his pack wasn't in the area very often. Besides, we're usually down here, and he wouldn't have had any way to get into the cave without a big scary fall."

Everyone absorbed that a moment. Zoe was a bit stuck on the casual phrase "Hekate's death," for her part. But then, she'd known it happened eventually. She scratched the ecstatic Kerberos under his chin. "You poor doggie. You've been lonely, yeah? Don't worry, boy, we're back now."

Then she remembered the chrysomelia tree. Her smile died, and she looked at Sophie and Adrian and Niko. "But the tree."

"Ah yes," Niko said. "It's time now, I suppose." She helped Zoe up, dusted off her tight, curve-packed jeans and gave the group a chipper smile. "Come with me, loves. Sophie, you in particular should come, I think."

Sophie almost felt a glimmer of hope. "Where are we going?" she asked.

"I'll show you." Niko glanced around. "Nearest horse we can use?"

"We're both mortal," Sophie pointed out. "Should we be riding one of those?"

"We're not going far. And didn't I hear that you hitched a ride down by dangling from a human soul?"

"Well. Yeah, but just for a few seconds."

"Which is all we need. Come." She tugged Sophie down the path. Everyone else followed too.

They picked up Niko's usual spirit horse, tied to a tree partway down the path, and led it along. Sophie wondered where they were going, and why they were taking a spirit horse deeper into the cave rather than outside, but soon she forgot her questions and gasped in horror.

"They burned so much! Oh my God, the orchard, oh no…" She twisted every which way as they walked, taking in the wrecked trees and shrubs, the piles of burned leaves. The stench of smoke stung her nostrils, recalling too strongly the trauma of her house burning down. And for a second the trapdoor began to creak open under her again, ready to plunge her into that place of eternal terror...

Niko squeezed her hand, and Adrian took hold of her other.

"The pots you moved," Adrian said. "Remember? Things will be all right."

Sophie pulled in a breath. The trapdoor solidified into ground again. She pictured all the various hideaways where she'd stashed potted Underworld plants. She'd been keeping them watered and healthy, and they were well out of this area. They'd be all right. That was something.

"Keep coming," Niko said.

In the sweeping beam of her flashlight a moment later, the titoki tree and the spring bulbs from Carnation met her eye in a healthy burst of colors. They were set apart from the other trees, and they, at least, had escaped damage. That also loosened some of the pain in her chest.

But Niko still didn't pause. She led them onward, past the trees, and into the tangle of columns near Landon's cell.

Oh yeah, Landon. Sophie glanced down the path and glimpsed him at the far end, gripping the bars and looking toward them in a pose of fearful desperation. Adrian's mother's soul stood by, guarding him. Sophie looked away again. Dealing with him was another task that would have to wait till later.

"Mate, exactly where the hell are you taking us?" Adrian asked.

"Right here." Niko stopped and tilted her head back, looking up into the dark, high, stalactite-studded ceiling.

Sophie and the rest looked up too, saw nothing, and turned their stares back to Niko.

"Honestly," Niko said, "did the rest of you never wonder what was up there?"

"Bats?" Adrian said.

"And slimy wet rocks," Sophie contributed.

"Also hiding places." Niko climbed onto the saddled spirit horse and held out her hand to Sophie.

Sophie hesitated. "Why me?"

Niko's eyes beamed benevolence, barely any mischief in them for now. "Because this is for you, Persephone."

"Be careful," Adrian said as Sophie climbed on behind her.

"I will." She latched her arms around Niko's newly soft and curvy waist.

Niko glanced over her shoulder and tipped her a wink. "Hold on tight." She clicked her tongue and told the horse, "Slow. Up."

They rose into the air like an untethered helium balloon. Niko swung the reins to dodge them expertly around stalactites as they ascended, and bounced them off one large one with a push of her hiking boot. Sophie ducked below Niko's shoulders to avoid whacking her head against rocks, and shone her flashlight around in curiosity. Dripping rock in all sizes, yes; the occasional startled bat swooping and taking off too.

But also things she had never known about: more gems in all colors, puffy faintly-glowing mushrooms and lacy lichens, and small nooks and ledges tucked among the jumble of glistening rock. Niko steered the horse to one of the roomiest ledges, which was still less than a foot square.

Sophie gasped in wonder when the flashlight beam fell upon the little plant sitting on it. "Is that...?"

Niko brought the horse to a hovering stop beside the ledge, so they were within reach. Nearly forgetting how high up they were, Sophie stretched out her hand and touched the glossy leaves.

"When Rhea gave me the immortality fruit," Niko said, "I saved the seeds. I planted this one; the other seeds are still safely hidden. I'm rather surprised the rest of our companions didn't show such foresight, really."

Sophie could have wept with gratitude. She drank in the

sight of the little chrysomelia. It was only about a foot tall and was growing in a battered and dented old saucepan. "And you hid it here, because it has to grow in the Underworld to work."

"With Underworld soil and everything." Niko sounded proud. "Even an automated drip system." She pointed to the thin soda-straw stalactites directly above, from which water droplets occasionally plunked into the pot.

"What is it?" Adrian's voice shouted up from below, echoing. "What's up there?"

"We'll show you!" Sophie shouted back, then looked at Niko. "Can we bring it down now?" She arched her eyebrow. "Or were you saving it for some nefarious purpose?"

Smiling as shamelessly as ever, Niko picked up the pot and tucked it into the crook of Sophie's arm. "I was saving it to give to whomever I wanted to make immortal, of course. And it turns out that's you and me and Liam and Frey, for starters."

"And Zoe's parents, and Rosie."

"Quite. And any other allies we find worthy along the way."

Cradling the tree like an infant, she looked down at it. "But it doesn't have fruit yet. Or even flowers."

"No. This tree's only a bit over a year old, and it took the first tree two years to make fruit. We'll just have to make sure we keep it safe for another year, yes?" Niko twitched the reins, and told the horse, "Down."

ELEUSIS WAS GROWN UP AND HAD BECOME A GREAT TEMPLE leader, working alongside the aging Akis and Galateia, who loved him like family. In Greece the world was changing, and not for the better. Destruction had become commonplace. Refugees from one invasion fled to new cities, only to be caught in another invasion the following year. Chaos sprawled, and

Thanatos triumphed, because it was easy in such an environment to convince people that the gods were evil and cruel. But Eleusis, Akis, Galateia, and the other temple folk who had personally known the immortals kept the truth alive, and their temples provided havens of calm in the devastation.

"I promise you," Eleusis told Hekate, every time she visited him and despaired about the latest events, "the people haven't forgotten. We're making sure of it. We have sacred sites to take refuge in, and we're keeping those secret except to the initiated; but the stories of all of you, those we're spreading far and wide." He gave her the merry grin he had inherited straight from his father. "You know we Greeks will always tell stories, no matter how many armies invade us."

Hekate never found a new immortality tree. She thought of the sealed jar, assembled by her parents, that contained an old chrysomelia fruit, but she rejected the thought. The seeds were surely too old to sprout. Anyway, Eleusis, in his implacable and peaceful way, told his mother that he would refuse to eat the fruit even if it were available.

The other immortals were all dead now, except for Rhea and Hekate. Over the years the remaining immortals showed up in the Underworld as souls—killed by enemies, or driven to quiet suicide when they wanted to forget and be reborn at last. As to method, for those who couldn't face leaping into a fire, it apparently worked to give yourself up to a carnivorous animal. Poseidon and Amphitrite had done it together, summoning one of those sea monsters and letting it devour them quickly.

Hermes, along with most of the others, had left to be reborn. It had been almost a year ago now, and he was somewhere far away across the great ocean to the west. So far she had not found the courage to follow, but she wanted to. One way or another.

Hekate sat long in meditation these days, the way her father had once done. Through reaching out to the Fates that way, she came one day to an understanding, or at least constructed a story that soothed her. She would tell it to Rhea and Eleusis when she returned to the Underworld, she decided.

She ate the red violets that made a person comfortably numb all over. Then she rode her spirit horse to the surface, let him go back to the Underworld without her, and walked to the seashore. She waded into the waves, and reached out in search of the sea monsters who had once helped her return to land. One sensed her, and swam closer.

It rose up in the sea in front of her. She sent it the message: *Yes, I'm ready. Please help.*

Through her numbness, she only knew the tentacle had seized her by realizing she couldn't breathe anymore. Then she was seeing the darkness as the creature's mouth engulfed her, and she struggled only a short time in suffocation before blacking out. And then, soon enough, she was free and full of light, and flying to the Underworld.

"It's all right," she assured the weeping Rhea and Eleusis that night, when they found out. "It's just winter time. Time for the gods to rest under the earth, like roots. The Fates, or the Goddess, or whoever they are, didn't have a grand plan for immortals when they created us, any more than we have grand plans for the flowers and crops whose seeds we sow. We just want them to grow and live and enrich us. Some of us have different strengths or powers, and it's the same as plants having different colors and flavors. Maybe the Goddess loves variety just as we do and has a use for all different kinds. And the worshippers, or the powers above, or all of it together, will bring immortals back for a springtime someday. I'm certain of it. They made us come alive before, and they brought my father and mother to the Underworld as living humans, so surely it will happen again. You needn't worry."

"I agree with your vision, Mother." Eleusis wiped his eyes. "I'll try not to be sad long. I tell everyone not to be, because we know what the Underworld is. But I'm finding it's human nature to be sad anyway, isn't it?"

Hekate smiled at him, full of love for her wise son.

"I'm not ready for death." Rhea sniffled. "I've lived too long to let go of life. But…yes, I just want to sleep like the roots too."

"There is another option," Hekate said. "I want to be reborn, but if you just wish for a long sleep, there are some berries here you can eat. Potent and dangerous, but I think they would work. I can show you which, when you're ready."

"But you have to say goodbye to me first," Eleusis scolded Rhea. "No surprising me like she did."

Rhea nodded in grave agreement. Hekate let her gaze drift placidly across the fields, reveling in tranquility and the promise of rejuvenation. It was easy to be patient now.

Epilogue

THEY KEPT THE LITTLE CHRYSOMELIA TREE SAFE FOR AN-other year. They kept each other safe, too.

After the battle for the Underworld, their first order of business was to turn over the surviving invaders to the police. Under glamours so they looked like police officers themselves, they also transferred the remains of the dead — Krystal, Tracy, Tenebra, Yuliya, and two of their hired men — out to the living realm, to be found and accounted for. They provided no explanation as to what the invaders were doing in the cave. Let the survivors try to explain themselves, they decided.

Thanatos would have a hard time regrouping. Sophie's next order of business was to go to Landon and tell him he was going to turn state's evidence. She informed him he would describe his involvement in the cult to the police who were trying to solve her parents' murder. He was to tell them exactly what the cult had done, but he would frame their beliefs as delusional, rather than trying to tell the authorities about the spirit realm. For now. He would lead them to arrests of members involved in other Thanatos murders. And with any luck he would be pardoned and would only get probation.

Landon agreed at once. In fact, he seemed profoundly relieved, if anything, to hear that his former team had been destroyed and that he would be forced to give up the cult affiliation. Sophie and Liam's parents' murder was finally declared a closed case, with all participating criminals now either dead or, in Landon's case, pardoned. Sophie and Liam used the considerable insurance money to start construction of a new house on the site of the old farmhouse in Carnation.

In case the global crackdown on other Thanatos operatives wasn't enough, Zoe investigated the magical properties of the remaining plants in the Underworld, and came up with a new safeguard. She held a piece of Underworld gold and a clump of leaves from their underground titoki tree, and used the titoki's signal-boost properties to seek out all the other bits of Underworld gold in the living realm. Traveling the world with Niko and Kerberos (whom she had adopted), she tracked each piece down. There weren't many Underworld gold artifacts left—five in museums, two in private collections, and the rest buried deep and forgotten. They stole some (leaving valuable jewels in their place), dug up the ones they could, and let the last two lie since they were deep in the earth beneath buildings by now and were almost impossible to get to.

Then, just to be sure, Zoe visited as many sacred sites as she could, and brought special charms of wrapped-up titoki leaves and petals from the new crocus Sophie had planted. The crocus added permanence to her protective wards, and the titoki channeled the Fates' judgment so that, in theory, anyone bad enough to get put in Tartaros would also be barred from entering the spirit realm as a living person.

It wasn't foolproof, she fretted. There were always loopholes; someone would always find a new way to cause trouble. Nevertheless, as Niko assured her, things were now much, much better.

When they ventured down to Tartaros to check on their deceased attackers, they found thick vines securing them to their gloomy cells, ensuring a long stay. In Tenebra's case, in fact, her cell was darker than usual, she was caught in a deeper state of fear than most punished souls, and the twisted vine was wrapped around her not just once but three times. A threefold rebound of magic, as Zoe had expected.

Sophie and Liam returned to school in September. In her summers and other vacations, Sophie used Underworld fortunes to anonymously fund a program that sent students out to remove invasive plants from the landscape, start up community gardens for vegetables, and plant wildflowers among and between croplands, and in any available space really, to help bees and other pollinators—and just to make the world prettier. She spent days here and there going out to help with the planting and digging herself.

Landon went to work for the organization full time. Under the watchful eye of his parole officer, he spent his days pouring compost, measuring out seeds, and talking to West Coast communities about establishing gardens. On weekend nights, he went out with Frey to nightclubs. Sophie thought there was still a wistful look in his eye when he looked at the changed person he had once been fond of, but she figured he'd likely meet someone soon in one of those clubs and finally be happy.

Tab disappeared to travel the world rather than return to school, but she kept Sophie updated with texts. One day she sent a photo from Ireland, of herself and a lovely, petite redheaded woman. She copied Zoe on the text too.

I'm head over ass in love. She was in Ciaran's coven. And yeah, she's Ariadne reborn. But I'd adore the crap out of her even if she wasn't.

The following spring equinox, Sophie's twentieth birthday, the first two fruits were ripe. Sophie, Liam, Rosie, Niko, Freya, and Zoe's parents divided up the slices and ate them, and became immortal.

They saved all the seeds, too.

THE COOL MORNING BREEZE IN ATHENS CURLED THE WHITE

curtains inward, carrying the scents of sea, traffic, cigarettes, lemon, and oregano. On the bed in their rented room, Niko rolled over and lifted Zoe above her so that Zoe's arms and legs dangled down. "Ha," Niko crowed. "I've missed being this strong."

Niko had let her blonde hair grow long over the past year, and seemed to enjoy wearing it loose and flicking it around like a supermodel. She also enjoyed lounging on beds in nearly-transparent stretchy white tank tops and boy-short underwear, the way she was doing now. Probably because she knew she looked amazing like that.

So bloody vain, Zoe thought with affection. She humored her, letting Niko hold her up in airplane-ride mode. "Big deal," Zoe said. "I could still throw you across the room any-time I want."

Niko swung her down and leaped on top of her, strad-dling her. "Ah, you want to play rough? You know I'm up for it."

Zoe was stripped to her T-shirt and skivvies too, so the contact was especially erotic. They'd already devoted most of the night to erotic activities, but insatiability was one of those problems about being immortal. Zoe grinned, grabbed Niko's tank top between the breasts, and pulled her down for a long snog. "It's morning and you're still here. I'm surprised. Why aren't you jumping on a spirit horse and traveling the world, now that you're free to?"

"I will eventually." Niko's voice dropped to a purr. "There are things involving stamina I'm determined to do more of today."

"Mm. So you'll leave me later, is what you're saying."

"But I always come back. You know that."

They were in the middle of a deeper snog when their phones buzzed in unison.

Niko stretched out to grab hers from the bedside table. Still draped on top of Zoe, Niko read the message aloud. "It's

Adrian. He says: 'Hey guys, meet for brunch? By the way, you two seem really close together. You're not getting each other off, are you?'"

Zoe snorted. "Cheeky sod."

"I know how to answer this." Niko's thumbs tapped against the screen. "'Do. Not. Disturb.'"

"Indeed." Zoe slid her hands under the waistband of Niko's shorts, down onto the warm curves of her rear. "But be nice. Add a smiley face."

"Done." Niko finished the text, tossed aside the phone, and got back to the important business of pouncing Zoe.

LIAM LET A FEW WEEKS PASS AFTER BECOMING IMMORTAL, so he could adjust his way of walking and talking and everything to that of a guy around eighteen, rather than his actual fourteen. The fruit had made him grow all the way up in the space of a night, the same way it had done to Hekate once, they told him. He was bigger now for sure, and more handsome, and at least all these memories and crazy experiences had helped him become much smarter. He'd been putting those smarts to use by studying Japanese when the rest of his homework was done.

Finally, on a May day, he jumped a spirit horse and hopped the Pacific, and followed his sense of Amphitrite to a beach on Tokyo Bay.

Five or six girls were there in a group, in their navy and white school uniforms, talking and darting around on the sand. But one sat apart, on a rock, her knees pulled up, showing a flash of skin between dark socks and plaid skirt. Her face was turned down, her sleek dark hair flapping in the wind, and she was poking at a tide pool as if fascinated by it.

Liam took off his shoes and socks, and padded up barefoot on the sand. She lifted her face to him. Their eyes met, and his heart wobbled.

"*Konnichiwa*," he said.

Curled around Sophie, half-asleep, Adrian let his mind drift to one of his absolute favorite memories. It would never get tiresome, not even if he re-lived it a thousand times.

On the spring equinox, Hades lay with Persephone upon their spread cloaks beneath a canopy of oak trees. Euphoria streamed through him endlessly, like the waterfalls from the mountains, because now he knew Persephone loved him. Demeter's protective lies had kept them apart, but today the truth had shone out and its light could never be smothered again. Persephone beamed and laughed as if she had just received everything she ever wanted in the world, and to think, it was his words, his caresses, that had bestowed that radiant smile upon her.

Her crown of flowers was falling to pieces. Petals lay scattered on the ground around her head. Hades paused between kisses to gaze at the breathtaking picture she made. "You look like a goddess of spring." He touched one of the torn narcissus blossoms that still clung to her braids. "Strange match for the king of the dead, people will say."

"I'm more than some girl playing in the flowers, and you're more than the Underworld's king." Her eyes dancing with happiness, she stroked his cheek with her knuckle. "Besides, neither of us cares what others think."

"Mm. True." He kissed the soft underside of her wrist. "We're better together than apart."

"We *can't* stay apart. See? We tried. Look what happened."

Hades curled his arm beneath her, cradling her warm, slim body against his. "I won't make that mistake again. Don't ever let me go another day without telling you I love you."

"I won't. And don't let me, either."

Adrian's drowsy eyes opened, meeting the comfortable dark of the Underworld's bedchamber. As Sophie slept, he ran his hand down her bare arm, stroking the new muscle that had formed there, savoring the texture of her supple skin, now burnished to perfection by the magic of the immortality fruit.

This same soul, in his arms again. With him in Underworld darkness or Mediterranean sunshine, in New Zealand or the Pacific Northwest.

They were better together, by far.

She stirred, pulling in a deep breath as she awoke.

"I love you, Persephone," Adrian whispered. "Good morning."

THE END

AFTERWORD

Well, I did it: not only did I wrap up the trilogy, but I went ahead and told you exactly where the geographic location of the Underworld is. Diros Caves is a real place, as maps and websites can tell you—not one I've been to, alas, but one I examined online as closely as I could. It does indeed have historic (and prehistoric) sacred significance, and some folk in the past did reputedly view it as an entrance to the realm of Hades. It even comes complete with an underground river, on which you can take boat tours. That said, I changed up the geology to suit my story, giving it bigger interior caverns and a dramatically vertical and deep entrance that, as far as I can tell, it doesn't have in real life. I'm sure it doesn't need to be said for a fantasy series, but settings in this novel are used quite fictitiously indeed, and, in the case of the caves, are also highly altered from their real state.

The volcanic eruption on Thera (present-day Santorini) was also a real occurrence, and I stuck somewhat closer to scientific fact for that. Geology places the eruption at somewhere around 1600 B.C.E., which lines up with where I put it in my story. You can run a web search on it to learn more, if you're into catastrophic natural disasters.

The story of the young lovers Akis (or Acis) and Galateia (or Galatea) is not properly a Greek myth. It's from Ovid's *Metamorphoses*, and is therefore a Roman myth from many centuries later than Homer and company. It ends tragically, as most love stories in mythology do: a jealous giant (Polyphemus) kills Akis. Twisting the myth as I always like to, I had Thanatos be the mean giant trying to wreck things, and let Akis and Galateia get away to live happily ever after. Incidentally, some may note that Galatea is also the name commonly given to the statue-turned-flesh whom Pygmalion falls in love with. But in ancient texts, Pygmalion's statue is not given a name. In the 1700s Jean-Jacques Rousseau decided to call it Galatea in his adaptation, and the name stuck.

Eleusis being the son of Hekate and Hermes is actually backed up in at least in some shady corners of Greek mythology. In some sources Eleusis is female, a minor goddess of Eleusinian Mysteries, and in other sources is male, a king of the town of Eleusis. He, or she, is generally called the child of Hermes, with the mother's name most commonly given as Daeira, an Oceanid nymph. However, awesome sites like Theoi.com tell us that Daeira, whom we don't know much about, may have been another name for Hekate (or even Persephone). In any case, Hekate and Hermes are paired as "divine consorts" in several mythological analyses, so that part's not nearly as much of a stretch as some of my inventions in this series. As Hermes says, they make a good match, in their strange way.

- M.J.R.

Acknowledgments

Finishing a trilogy turned out to be backbreaking, or at least sanity-breaking, work, and because of that I must thank my family first and foremost. My husband and kids, my parents and siblings and in-laws: you all had to live with me while I struggled with this story, and yet you're still here and you still love me. I love you too, and thank goodness we can all be happier now that this achievement is done!

My beta readers are also standing deservedly upon the winners' podium of awesomeness, so here are the medals I drape around their necks:

Abbie Williams, literally a gold-medal-winning author, and such a sweet and hilarious woman: thank you for your enthused support on this series, and for being there throughout the year to buoy me up in grumpy hours with your happy nature (and photos of hot people for our casting dreams).

Ray Warner, super-smart fan and thoughtful soul, for helping see this trilogy through to the end, and pinpointing what worked and what needed tweaking. As ever, I owe many fabulous "Aha!" moments to your insights.

Dean Mayes, for fitting this into your life between your own writing and other jobs, making sure I was square with Joseph Campbell, and being lovely and patient in every interaction. People like you help defy the myth of the arrogant writer.

Jennifer Pennington, for taking on the manuscript in the same month as your own gosh-darn wedding: I'm amazed and humbled you could turn in such logical thoughts in the midst of that madness. Thank you for catching several errors and unanswered questions for me, and felicitations to you newlyweds!

Melanie Carey, for congenially stepping in and accepting this daunting job, and hitting it out of the park: thank you for not only all the thoughts on scenes and characters, which helped me gauge whether I wrote them right, but for all the in-person gab sessions too, which always make me feel grounded and validated. Even we sensitive-hermit-writer types need that from time to time.

Beth Willis, for loving this crazy series for years and years now: thank you for giving honest gut reactions to these various characters and scenarios, and amusing the hell out of me while doing so. Rock on! (Which I mean literally, since you're a rock musician and all.)

This series wouldn't be what it is without Michelle Halket, my editor: you go so far above and beyond for your authors that you're currently somewhere in the stratosphere. I don't know how you find time in the day to take care of it all, but thank you for making that magic happen, and for being so cheerful and encouraging throughout this arduous process. I know you'll keep taking us farther yet!

I also must thank my friend Tracy Erickson, who one day piped up to say he'd like to have his name used for a character. Good guy or bad guy?, I asked. He chose the path of evil, and thus was christened Erick Tracy. Our actual real-world Tracy, of course, is not evil or slimy; he is cool and delightful and a great supporter of fantasy authors, and I'm glad to know him.

Thanks as well to Felicia Simion, amazingly talented young photographer, whose photo of the couple in the grass seized my heart and Michelle's when we saw it. Getting to use the shot for this book's cover made me downright blissful.

Bibliographically speaking, I continue to owe thanks to the fabulously compiled Theoi.com website, to Walter Burkert's *Greek Religion*, and to the beautifully illustrated D'Aulaires' *Book of Greek Mythology*, where the inspiration for this series all started back when I was a kid.

And even though I've pulled back from Facebook this year, I do keep the author page running and have been delighted at the growing number of fans and interactions there, as well as on other sites. So if you've ever reviewed my work, emailed me, Tweeted me, left a comment for me, or otherwise gotten in touch, this bouquet of Underworld flowers is for you! Keep the correspondence going. It makes the world a better place.

Other Books by Molly Ringle

The Ghost Downstairs
Summer Term
What Scotland Taught Me
Relatively Honest

Persephone's Orchard
Underworld's Daughter